Clarence E. Blake

A Lexicon of the First Three Books of Homer's Iliad

Clarence E. Blake

A Lexicon of the First Three Books of Homer's Iliad

ISBN/EAN: 9783337223199

Printed in Europe, USA, Canada, Australia, Japan

Cover: Foto ©Andreas Hilbeck / pixelio.de

More available books at **www.hansebooks.com**

A LEXICON

OF

THE FIRST THREE BOOKS

OF

HOMER'S ILIAD,

TOGETHER WITH

Lines 1-219 of Book IV.	Lines 119-236 of Book VI.
Lines 457-544 of Book IV.	Lines 369-529 of Book VI.
Lines 1-165 of Book V.	Lines 468-617 of Book XVIII.
Lines 590-710 of Book V.	Book XXII. entire.

Lines 468-804 of Book XXIV.

PREPARED BY

CLARENCE E. BLAKE, A.M.,

PRINCIPAL OF SPRINGFIELD (MASS.) COLLEGIATE INSTITUTE.

NEW YORK:

D. APPLETON AND COMPANY.

1886.

WHATEVER OF GOOD MAY BE FOUND IN
THESE PAGES

Is Affectionately Inscribed

TO MY WIFE.

PREFACE.

———◆———

For many years it had been my wish to prepare a Lexicon to that part of the Il'-i-ad commonly read in our preparatory schools. For a long time I was deterred from so doing by the fear that teachers would not allow their classes to read Homer with a partial Lexicon as usually compiled. But, being convinced that there was a growing demand for such a work, in 1878 I determined to make a beginning.

It has been the author's aim to give the student a *full knowledge of each word found in the work*, not confining the explanation wholly to the Homeric usage; so that not only the definitions, but the derivations, compositions, etc., may be learned as well as from a complete Lexicon. If this has been accomplished, the author has avoided the chief objections against the use of a partial Lexicon.

C. E. B.

Springfield, Mass., 1885.

LIST OF ABBREVIATIONS.

acc.	signifies	accusative.	encl.	signifies	enclitic.
acco.	"	according.	Eng.	"	English.
act.	"	active.	Ep.	"	Epic.
adj.	"	adjective.	epith.	"	epithet.
adv.	"	adverb, adverbial.	esp.	"	especially.
Æol.	"	Æolic.	eu.		
aor.	"	aorist.	euph.	"	euphonic,
apo.	"	apodosis.	euphon.	"	euphonicum.
Att.	"	Attic.	f.	"	future.
augm.	"	augment.	foll.	"	following, followed.
com.	"	common, commonly.	foreg.	"	foregoing.
compar.	"	comparative, comparison.	freq.	"	frequent, frequently, frequentative.
compd.	"	compound.			
compo.	"	composition.	f.pf.	"	future perfect.
conj.	"	conjunction, conjunctive.	gen.	"	genitive, general.
			Hom.	"	Homer, Homeric.
contd.	"	contracted.	Il.	"	Iliad.
contr.	"	contract.	imperat.	"	imperative.
copul.	"	copulativum.	impf.	"	imperfect.
dat.	"	dative.	indecl.	"	indeclinable.
defect.	"	defective.	indicat.	"	indicative.
demon.	"	demonstrative.	inf.	"	infinitive.
dep.	"	deponent.	intens.	"	intensive, intensivum.
deriv.	"	derivative, derived, derivation.	interj.	"	interjection.
			interrog.	"	interrogative, interrogatively.
disjunc.	"	disjunctive.			
Dor.	"	Doric.	intrans.	"	intransitive.
doub.	"	double.	Ion.	"	Ionic.
du.	"	dual.	irreg.	"	irregular, irregularly.

Iter.	signifies	iterative.	prep.	signifies	preposition.
Lat.	"	Latin.	pres.	"	present.
leng.	"	lengthened.	prin.	"	principal.
lit.	"	literally.	priv.	"	privativum.
mas.	"	masculine.	pro.	"	protasis.
metaph.	"	metaphorically.	procl.	"	proclitic.
mid.	"	middle.	pron.	"	pronoun.
n.	"	noun.	proparox.	"	proparoxytone.
neg.	"	negative.	rare.	"	rarely.
neu.	"	neuter.	redupl.	"	reduplicated.
nom.	"	nominative.	reg.	"	regular, regularly.
obsol.	"	obsolete.	short.	"	shortened.
opp.	"	opposition, opposed.	signif.	"	signification.
opt.	"	optative.	sing.	"	singular.
orig.	"	original, originally.			strengthen,
par.	"	parallel.	streng.	"	strengthened,
parox.	"	paroxytone.			strengthening.
part.	"	participle.	stric.	"	strictly.
pass.	"	passive.	subj.	"	subjunctive.
pers.	"	person, personal.	subst.	"	substantive.
pf.	"	perfect.	sup.	"	superlative.
pl.	"	plural.	sync.	"	syncopated.
plup.	"	pluperfect.	syno.	"	synonymous.
poet.	"	poetic, poetry.	trans.	"	transitive.
poss.	"	possessive.	usu.	"	usual, usually.
pr.	"	proper, properly.	voc.	"	vocative.

NOTE 1. "Also," following a comma and followed by a comma, indicates that the definitions following it to the next semicolon correspond to the Latin word already given ; see ὕλη.

NOTE 2. The expressions "see Lat., etc.," and "compare Lat., etc.," indicate that the Latin words are to be compared with the given definitions to see if they are synonymous in meaning.

NOTE 3. In syllabicating and accentuating proper names, the author has endeavored to follow the rules of Webster.

NOTE 4. To understand well the following pages, the use of a book on Latin Synonymes is required.

LEXICON.

A.

a-, a prefix. 1. *alpha copul.*, expressing an idea of *union, equality, like-
ness*. 2. *alpha priv.*, expressing an idea of *want, absence*. 3. *alpha
euphon.*, for *eu. effect*. 4. *alpha intens.*, giving *strength* to compds.

ἄαπτος, ον, (a priv., ἅπτω,) Lat. *inaccessus, unapproachable, not to be
touched ; unconquerable*, A 567.

ἀάσχετος, poet. form for ἄσχετος, ον, which see.

Ἄβαντες, ων, οἱ, *the A-ban'-tes*, inhabitants of Eu-bœ'-a.

Ἄβας, αντος, ὁ, *A'-bas*.

ἀβλής, ῆτος, adj., (a priv., βάλλω,) *not hurled, not shot ; not used, new*.

ἄβλητος, ον, (a priv., βάλλω,) *not struck* or *touched, unhurt*.

Ἄβυδος, ον, ἡ, *A-by̆'-dus*, a town of Tro'-as.

ἄγαγον, Ep. for ἤγαγον, 2 aor. of ἄγω ; inf. ἀγαγεῖν.

ἀγάζομαι, Hom. for ἄγαμαι, Lat. *mirari*.

ἀγαθός, ή, όν, compar. very irreg., see Grammar, Lat. *bonus, good ; able,
efficient, capable, brave, bold, noble ; excellent*, Lat. *praestans ; profitable*,
B 204 ; *good, upright, virtuous*: τὰ ἀγαθά, *wealth* ; τὸ ἀγαθόν, *the
highest good*.

ἀγαλομαι, par. form to ἄγαμαι, ἀγάομαι, Ep. 2 pl. ἀγάασθε, (deriv.
uncertain, ἄγαν, ἄγη,) *to wonder, behold with wonder, admire*, Γ 181,
Lat. *mirari, admirari* ; Lat. *indignari, to be angry* or *indignant at*,
see ἄγαμαι ; *to envy*, Lat. *invidēre*.

ἀγακλειτός, ή, όν, Lat. *inclitus, praeclarus, illustrious, famous*, B 564.

ἀγάλλω, f. αλῶ ; aor. ἤγηλα : *to glorify, honor ; adorn* : mid. and pass., *to
glory, take delight in, exult*, Lat. *gloriari, exultare ; make display ;
of ships, exult in the breeze*.

ἄγαλμα, ατος, τό, *that which gives pleasure, a delight ; a present*.

ἄγαμαι, impf. ἠγάμην, f. ἀγάσομαι, aor. mid. ἠγασάμην, aor. pass. ἠγάσθην :
Ep. forms, pres. 2 pl. ἀγάασθε, inf. ἀγάασθαι, f. ἀγάσσομαι, aor. mid.
ἠγασσάμην Γ 181 and ἀγ- : *to wonder* : also trans., *to wonder at* in the
sense of *admire* ; *to envy* ; *be angry* or *indignant at*, ἀγαλομαι com.
used in this sense.

Ἀγαμέμνων, ονος, ὁ, *Ag-a-mem'-non*, king of My-ce'-næ and leader of the Greeks against Troy.

ἄγαμος, ον, (a priv., γαμέω, γάμος,) Lat. *coelebs, unmarried.*

ἀγάννιφος, ον, (ἄγαν, νίφω,) Lat. *nivosus, snow-capped, covered with much snow,* A 420.

ἀγανός, ή, όν, (a copul., γάνος,) Lat. *lenis, mild, gentle, kind; friendly,* B 164, Lat. *blandus.*

ἀγανοφροσύνη, ης, ἡ, (ἀγανόφρων (ἀγανός, φρήν),) *kindness of heart.*

ἀγάομαι, see ἀγαίομαι.

Ἀγαπήνωρ, ορος, ὁ, *Ag-a-pe'nor,* leader of the Ar-ca'-di-ans before Troy.

ἀγαπητός, η, ον, (adj. from ἀγαπάω,) *loved.*

ἀγάρροος contr. -ους, ουν, (ἄγαν, ῥέω,) Lat. *celeriter fluens, strong flowing, swift flowing,* B 845.

Ἀγασθένης, εος, ὁ, *A-gas'-the-nes,* king of E'-lis.

ἀγαυός, ή, όν, (ἄγαμαι,) Lat. *praeclarus, admirabilis, illustrious, noble;* mostly of kings, heroes, etc., *high-born,* Lat. *illustris;* with κήρυκες, Γ 268.

ἀγγελία, ας, ἡ, Hom. — λίη, ης, (ἀγγέλλω,) *a message, tidings, report; order;* in Γ 206 as a casual gen., *he came because of a message,* etc.

ἀγγελίης, ου, ὁ, (ἀγγέλλω,) *messenger,* this nom. mas. is allowed by some and rejected by others : see foreg.

ἄγγελος, ου, ὁ and ἡ, (ἀγγέλλω,) Lat. *nuntius, a messenger,* A 333 ; *an angel,* Lat. *angelus.*

ἄγγος, εος, τό, *vase, vessel, bowl; box; any thing* to hold milk, wine, and travelling stores.

ἄγε, ἄγετε, (stric. imperat. of ἄγω,) Lat. *age, quick! come! well!* see εἰ δ'ἄγε.

ἀγείρω ; f. ερῶ; aor. ἤγειρα ; pf. ἀγήγερκα ; aor. pass. ἠγέρθην, Ep. 3 pl. ἤγερθεν : (ἄγω,) Lat. *congregare, colligere, to collect, assemble;* mid. *to assemble, come together,* B 52.

ἀγέλη, ης, ἡ, (ἄγω,) Lat. *armentum, grex* (what is the difference between *armentum* and *grex?*), *a herd of cattle,* ἀγέληφι, *with the herd.*

ἀγέμεν, Ion. for ἄγειν.

ἀγέραστος, ον, (a priv., γέρας,) Lat. *inhonoratus, without a gift of honor, not honored with reward.*

ἀγέρωχος, ον, *impetuous; high-minded; brave,* Ῥωδίων ἀγερώχων, B 654 ; Τρώων ἀγερώχων, Γ 36.

ἀγηνορία, ἡ. Lat. *virtus, manliness, bravery, prowess.*

ἀγήνωρ, ορος, adj., (ἄγαν, ἀνήρ,) *manly, heroic, brave, bold; haughty, arrogant, headstrong, insolent,* B 276 ; *generous, noble; splendid.*

ἀγήραος, ον, contr. ἀγήρως, ων, (a priv., γῆρας,) *ageless, undecaying, not waxing old.*

ἀγητός, ή, όν, (ἀγά(ο)μαι,) *exciting surprise* or *wonder*.

ἀγινέω, Ion. form for ἄγω, *to convey, bear, lead.*

Ἀγκαῖος, ου, ὁ, *An-cæ'-us,* son of Ly-cur'-gus.

ἀγκαλίς, ίδος, ἡ, *arm.*

ἄγκος, εος, τό, *a curve; a hollow; a curve in a mountain, a valley, vale,* or *glen; a gorge, defile;* compare Lat. *uncus, vallis.*

ἀγκυλομήτης, ου, Ep. εω, ὁ, ἡ, (ἀγκύλος, μῆτις,) Lat. *versatus, wily, crooked in counsel;* epith. of Cro'-nus, Lat. Sa-tur'-nus.

ἀγκύλος, η, ον, (deriv. uncertain,) *bent.*

ἀγκυλότοξος, ον, (ἀγκύλος, τόξον,) *with* or *having a curved bow.*

ἀγλαΐα, ας, ἡ, (ἀγλαός,) *beauty, grace, grandeur, splendor.*

Ἀγλαΐη, ης, ἡ, *Ag-la'-i-a.*

ἀγλαός, ή, όν, and ός, όν, Lat. *splendidus, fulgens, limpidus,* splendid, shining, clear, bright, brilliant, illustrious, as epith. of beautiful objects, B 307 ; of men, *stately, noble, illustrious, famous,* Lat. *clarus, illustris, nobilis.*

ἀγνοέω, ῶ, Ep. ἀγνοιέω; f. ἡσομαι and ἡσω; aor. ἠγνόησα and Ep. ἀγνοίησα, 3 sing. ἀγνώσασκε for ἀγνοήσασκε ; pf. ἠγνόηκα : Lat. *ignorare, to fail to recognize, be ignorant, not to know; to mistake, be in error.*

ἄγνυμι, f. ἄξω; aor. ἔαξα, Ep. ἦξα, part. ἄξας and ἔαξας, inf. ἆξαι; pf. ἔαγα; 2 aor. pass. ἐάγην, ἄγη Γ 367 : Lat. *frangere, to break, shiver, shatter.*

ἀγνώσασκε, see ἀγνοέω.

ἄγονος, ον, (α priv., γόνος,) Lat. *non natus, unborn; unfruitful, barren,* with gen. *barren* or *destitute of,* Lat. *sterilis.*

ἀγοράομαι; f. ἡσομαι; Ep. impf. 3 pl. ἠγορόωντο; we find pres. ἀγοράασθε B 337, impf. ἠγοράασθε : (ἀγορά,) *to meet* or *sit in the assembly;* Lat. *concionari, to speak publicly, harangue in the assembly,* A 73 ; *hold an assembly.*

ἀγορεύω; f. εύσω; Att. f. ἐρῶ, 2 aor. εἶπον, pf. εἴρηκα : (ἀγορά,) Lat. *concionari, to harangue,* A 109 ; *to speak, say as in an assembly* or *in public;* A 571, B 788, 796, Γ 155 ; *to proclaim, declare; to counsel :* mid., *to cause a thing to be declared.*

ἀγορή, ῆς, Ep. and Ion. for ἀγορά, ᾶς, ἡ, (ἀγείρω, ἄγω,) Lat. *concio, a convoked assembly, an assembly of all the people* or *army* as opposed to the council; *a speech in public,* B 275, Lat. *concio; a discussion,* B 788, 370 ; *a place of meeting, market,* Lat. *forum.*

ἀγορῆθεν, adv. *from the assembly.*

ἀγορήνδε, adv. Lat. *ad concionem, to the assembly.*

ἀγορήτης, ου, ὁ, (ἀγοράομαι, ἀγορή,) Lat. *concionator, haranguer, speaker,* esp. of Nestor, A 248.

ἀγός, οῦ, ὁ, (ἄγω,) Lat. *dux, chief.*

ἄγριος, ια, ιον, and ος, ον, (ἀγρός,) (is Lat. *agrestis* the equivalent of this?) *living wild* or *in the fields; wild, savage, fierce,* of beasts, Lat. *ferus, ferox;* of men, *ferocious, wild, furious, boorish,* also, of combatants, *savage, dreadful, cruel,* of the tumult of battle.

ἀγρόμενος, ένη, ενον, aor. mid. part. of ἀγείρω; *assembled.*

ἀγρός, οῦ, ὁ, compare Lat. *rus, ager, rusticus, field.*

ἀγρότερος, Hom. for ἄγριος, α, ον, (ἀγρός, ἄγρα,) Lat. *agrestis, rusticus, wild; rustic; loving the chase.*

ἄγυια, ἡ, (ἄγω, γυῖα,) *a road, place for travel, street, public place;* in pl. *a city* from no. of streets.

ἄγχι, adv. Lat. *prope, near, hard by.*

ἀγχίαλος, ον, and η, ον, (ἄγχι, ἅλς,) Lat. *maritimus, near the sea.*

ἀγχιμαχητής, οῦ, ὁ, (ἄγχι, μάχομαι,) *fighting at close quarters.*

ἀγχίμολον, (ἄγχι, μολεῖν, see βλώσκω,) *near.*

Ἀγχίσης, ου, ὁ, *An-chī´-ses,* father of Æ-ne´-as, mentioned in Vir´-gil.

ἄγχιστα, superl. of ἄγχι, Lat. *proxima* or *-mum, very near.*

ἀγχιστῖνος, η, ον, leng. for ἄγχιστος sup., adj. form, of ἄγχι, *very close together.*

ἄγχιστος, ον, superl. adj., no positive in use, (ἄγχι) Lat. *proximus, nearest, very near;* Hom. has only neu. -στον, or pl. -στα with μάλιστα, B 58, *very nearly.*

ἀγχοῦ, (ἄγχι,) adv. Lat. *prope, near.*

ἄγχω, f. ἄγξω, aor. ἦγξα, *to press tight; to strangle, choke, hang,* Lat. *angere;* Γ 371, Ep. impf. 3 sing.

ἄγω; iter. impf. ἄγεσκον; f. ἄξω; aor. ἦξα, Ep. inf. ἀξέμεν(αι); more com. 2 aor. ἤγαγον; 2 pf. ἦχα; aor. pass. ἤχθην; pf. pass. ἦγμαι: Lat. *agere, to lead, lead away* A 338; *to lead* or *conduct* A 390, Γ 401, *lead along,* or *carry with one;* usu. of persons and cattle, φέρειν of things, ἄγειν καὶ φέρειν, *to carry off both cattle and things as plunder,* like Lat. *agere et ferre, plunder, carry off; to lead on* or *towards; to bring up, educate;* Lat. *educere, to draw out; to celebrate, observe; to consider; to conduct, guide; to bring to* or *in, import:* mid., *to carry* or *lead away for one's self, take to one's self;* Γ 72, *let him lead;* ἄγετ', B 659, *marry.*

ἀγών, ῶνος, ὁ, (ἄγω,) Lat. *certamen, an assembly; place of assembly; a struggle, contest; place where the contest takes place.*

ἀδαήμων, ον, (a priv., δαήμ-, see δάω,) see Lat. *ignarus, not knowing.*

ἀδάκρυτος, ον, (a priv., δάκρυ,) Lat. *sine lacrimis, without tears, tearless, not weeping, happy,* A 415; also, *unwept.*

ἀδελφειός, Ep. for ἀδελφεός, and this is Ep. and Ion. for ἀδελφός, οῦ, ὁ, (a for ἅμα, δελφύς,) Lat. *frater, brother;* in pl. *brothers and sisters; near kinsman.*

ἀδινός, ή, όν, (ἄδην,) Lat. *densus, dense, close, crowded, numerous, thronged,* B 87 ; *loud, incessant, strong, vehement ;* ἀδινὰ δάκρυα, *plentiful tears :* adv. ἀδινῶς, ἀδινόν, ἀδινά, *vehemently.*

Ἄδμητος, ου, ὁ, *Ad-me'-tus,* lit. *untamed,* king of Phe'-ræ, husband of Al-ces'-tis ; see Classical Dictionary.

ἄδον, Ep. for ἔαδον, see ἀνδάνω.

Ἀδράστεια, Ion. Ἀδρήστεια, ας, ἡ, A-dras'-ti-a, a town on the Pro-pon'-tis.

Ἄδρηστος, Ion. for Ἄδραστος, ου, ὁ, *A-dras'-tus,* king of Ar'-gos and Sic'-y-on ; lit. *not fleeing,* (a priv., διδράσκω).

ἀδροτής, τῆτος, ἡ, (ἀδρός,) *thickness, full development.*

ἀεθλεύω, Ep. for ἀθλεύω, (ἄθλος,) *to strive in contest for a prize ; to endure hardship.*

ἄεθλον, Ion. for ἄθλον, ου, τό, *the prize of the victor in a prize contest, a prize, a reward ; a gift ; also, a prize contest.*

ἄεθλος, Ep. for ἄθλος, ου, ὁ, *a contest ;* Lat. *certamen, a prize contest ; a combat in war ; trouble, hardship :* this form is com. used by Hom.

ἀεθλοφόρος, ον, Ep. for ἀθλοφόρος, (ἄθλον, φέρω,) *prize-bearing.*

ἀεί, Ion. and poet. αἰεί, or αἰέν, Lat. *semper, always, ever ;* τὸν ἀεὶ χρόνον, *for ever.*

ἀείδω, Att. ᾄδω ; f. ἀείσομαι, ἀείσω and ᾄσω, Att. ᾄσομαι ; aor. ἤεισα, Ep. ἄεισα ; pf. ᾖσμαι ; aor. pass. ᾔσθην : Lat. *cantare, to sing,* A 604 applies to *any song,* of man, bird, insect, etc. ; *to sound, whistle, twang :* trans., *to chant, sing,* or *relate* anything *in song,* A 1.

ἀεικείη, -ίη, ης, ἡ, *disgraceful treatment, insult, abuse.*

ἀεικής, ές, (a priv., εἰκός, part. of εἴκω,) *detestable, disgraceful, pitiful,* A 456 ; *unseemly, shameful, mean, insulting;* does either Lat. *indignus* or *turpis* correspond to any of these definitions ? ᴀ

ἀεικίζω, Ep. aor. ἀείκισσα, (ἀεικής,) *to maltreat, abuse, insult, treat with indignity.*

ἀείρω ; f. ἀερῶ, contr. ἀρῶ ; aor. ἤειρα ; pf. ἤερμαι ; aor. pass. ἠέρθην ; plup. Ep. 3 sing. ἄωρτο : Lat. *tollere, to take up, raise up, lift ; bear, take away, carry ; to offer, give, produce ; to plunder, rob ; to capture* or *carry off as plunder :* mid., *to take up for one's self* or *one's own use ; carry off, win, take :* pass. *to raise one's self, arise.*

ἀεκαζόμενος, η, ον, (part. of ἀεκάζω (a priv., ἑκών),) *not willing, loath.*

ἀέκων, ουσα, ον, (a priv., ἑκών,) Lat. *invitus,* A 301, *reluctant, unwilling, against the will ; without intent.*

ἄελλα, Ep. ἀέλλη, ης, ἡ, (deriv. uncertain ; some suggest ἄω, others εἴλω,) Lat. *turbo, a tempest, a stormy wind,* when winds meet, *whirlwind :* ἀέλλης κονίσαλος, *a cloud of dust,* Γ 13.

ἀελπέα, see foll.

ἀελπτής, ές, (a priv., ἐλπίς,) *not expected.*

ἀερσίπους, πουν, adj., gen. ποδος, (ἀείρω, πούς,) *lifting the feet, fleet, quick-trotting,* Γ 327.

'Αζείδης, ου, Ep. αο, ὁ, *son of A'-zeus.*

ἄζομαι, (what is the difference between Lat. *vereri* and *venerari ?*) used in pres. system, *to fear and reverence, stand in awe of,* Α 21 ; *fear to do, shrink from.*

ἄζω, *to become dry, to be parched :* pass., of the heart, *to waste away through sorrow.*

ἀήρ, ἀέρος, ἡ, Ep. and Ion. cases, ἠέρος, dat. ἠέρι, Γ 381, acc. ἠέρα, from these a nom. ἠήρ was afterwards formed ; Lat. *aër, the atmosphere* or *lower and denser air,* as opp. to αἰθήρ, the pure unclouded upper air or firmament ; *mist, darkness, cloudiness ; air.*

ἀθάνατος, ον and η, ον, (a priv., θάνατος,) Lat. *immortalis, immortal, undying ; everlasting, eternal ;* used as subst.

ἄθαπτος, ον, (a priv., θάπτω,) *without burial.*

ἀθερίζω, f. ίσω, Ep. aor. ἀθέριξα or -ισσα, (a priv., θέρ(απεύ)ω,) *to make nothing of, despise, make light of.*

ἀθέσφατος, ον, (a priv., θέσφατος (θεός, φημί),) *impossible for a god to express, inexpressible,* Γ 4 ; *vast, enormous.*

'Αθῆναι, ων, αἱ, *Ath'-ens.*

'Αθηναίη, ης, or 'Αθήνη, ης, ἡ, *A-the'-na,* the Min-er'-va of the Ro'-mans.

'Αθηναῖος, α, ον, *A-the'-ni-an,* used also as noun.

ἀθρόος, α ον, (a for ἅμα, θρόος,) *crowded together,* Β 439; *all at once ; numerous, frequent, abundant ; collective ; immense ; continuous ;* only pl. is found in Hom.: adv., *suddenly :* is Lat. *universus* the equivalent of this ?

αἰ, Ep. for εἰ, Lat. *si, if;* αἴ κε or αἴ κεν, *if only, so that,* Lat. *dummodo.*

αἴ, αἴθε, interj. expressing strong desire, Lat. *utinam ; O that ! would that !* Hom. always has αἴ γάρ or αἴ γὰρ δή, except αἴθε, Dor. and Ep. for εἴθε.

αἴ ; αἴ, αἴ or αἰαῖ, Lat. *vae,* interj. expressing grief and astonishment : *ah ! alas ! woe !*

αἶα, αἴης, ἡ, Hom. form for γαῖα, Lat. *terra, earth ;* φυσίζοος αἶα, Γ 243, Β 162.

Αἰακίδης, ου, ὁ, *son of Æ-a-cus.*

Αἴας, αντος, Ep. voc. Αἶαν, ὁ, *A'-jax,* the name of two heroes, one the son of Tel'-a-mon, the other the son of O-il'-e-us ; see A'-jax in Classical Dictionary.

Αἰγαίων, ωνος, ὁ, *Æ-gæ'-on,* Α 404, the name of one of the hundred-armed giants (the sea-giant acco. to many writers), called by the gods Bri-a'-re-us ; these giants are regarded as personifications of the unusual powers of nature ; see Classical Dictionary.

αἰγανέη, ης, ἡ, (ἀκή,) Lat. *jaculum, a javelin, spear ; hunting-spear.*

Αἰγείδης, ου, ὁ, *descendant of Ae-ge'-us, The'-seus,* A 265.

αἴγειος, εια or είη, ειον, leng. for αἴγεος, (αἴξ,) Lat. *caprinus, of a goat, goat ;* ἀσκῷ ἐν αἰγείῳ, Γ 247, *in a goatskin bottle.*

αἴγειρος, ου, ἡ, *black poplar tree.*

αἴγεος, έα, εον, = αἴγειος.

αἰγιαλός, οῦ, ὁ, (ἄγνυμι, ἅλς,) Lat. *litus, the sea-shore, strand; beach,* B 210.

Αἰγιαλός, οῦ, ὁ, *Æ-gi'-a-lus,* name of A-cha'-i-a ; a town in Paph-la-go'-ni-a ; see foreg.

Αἰγίλιψ, ιπος, ἡ, (αἴξ, λείπω,) *Æg'-i-lips,* name of a district of Ithaca ; acco. to some, a city or an island ; lit. *deserted even by goats,* and so, *steep.*

Αἴγινα, ης, ἡ, *Æ-gi'-na,* an island.

Αἴγιον, ου, τό, *Æ'-gi-um,* a city.

αἰγίοχος, ον, (αἰγίς, ἔχω,) *Ægis-bearing,* epith. of Ju'-pi-ter.

Αἰγίς, ίδος, ἡ, (αἴξ,) *the Æ'-gis, the shield of Jove,* by the shaking of which storms and tempests were created, hence *a rushing storm :* see Zeus in Classical Dictionary.

αἴγλη, ης, ἡ, (do Lat. *fulgor, splendor* correspond to this ?) *day-light, radiance, brightness ; brilliancy, glitter, lustre,* of weapons, B 458 ; *a bright light, glory.*

αἰγλήεις, εσσα, εν, Lat. *fulgens, radiant, beaming, resplendent :* of Olympus, A 532.

αἰδέομαι, f. έσομαι, aor. ᾐδεσάμην ; Ep. forms, pres. αἴδομαι, f. αἰδέσσομαι, aor. imperat. -εσσαι, aor. pass. 3 pl. αἴδεσθεν : *to feel shame, fear ; reverence, stand in awe of,* A 23 ; Lat. *verēri.*

ἀΐδηλος, ον, (a priv., δῆλος, or ἰδεῖν, see ὁράω,) *making unseen ; destroying,* B 445 ; *unseen, invisible.*

'Αΐδης, αο, Ion. εω, Ep. gen. "Αιδος, (from old nom. "Αις,) Γ 322 and dat. "Αιδι, ὁ (ἀιδής, *unseen*); Att. "Αιδης, ου ; Lat. *Plu'-to, Ha'-des, the god of the nether world ;* "Αιδόσδε or εἰς "Αιδόσδε, *to the dwelling of Ha'-des,* Γ 322, *within the dwelling of Ha'-des ; the word came to mean Ha'-des, the nether world.*

αἰδοῖος, οία, οῖον (αἰδέομαι), Lat. *venerandus, revered, august, held in honor, venerated ; deserving respect, tender, modest,* B 514 ; *modest, bashful ; excellent :* compar. both reg. and irreg. ; irreg. compar. in -έστ-.

αἴδομαι, Ep. for αἰδέομαι, which see.

"Αιδος, "Αιδόσδε, see 'Αΐδης.

ἄιδρις, ι, ιος and εος, (a priv., ἴδρις,) *ignorant, not knowing*, Γ 219; does Lat. *ignarus* correspond in meaning to this ?

αἰδώς, όος or οῦς, ἡ, Lat. *pudor, shame, virtuous shame, modesty, diffidence; a sense of honor; respect for others, reverence; that which causes shame; dignity, honor, respect;* B 262, *cover thy shame* or *nakedness.*

αἰεί, αἰέν, see ἀεί.

αἰειγενέτης, ου, ὁ, B 400, Hom. for ἀειγενέτης, (ἀεί, γενέτης, γενητός, γενέσθαι,) Lat. *sempiternus, everlasting, eternal, immortal.*

αἰετός, short. ἀετός, οῦ, ὁ, *an eagle,* the bird of Ζεύς.

αἰζήιος, ου, ὁ, leng. form for αἰζηός, *an active, young* and *vigorous person;* does Lat. *juvenis* correspond in meaning to this ?

ἄιζηλος, ον, see ἀρίζηλος, *conspicuous.*

αἰζηός, αἰζηός, see αἰζήιος.

αἰθαλόεις, εσσα, εν, contr. οῦς, οῦσσα, οῦν, (αἴθαλος, αἰθαλόω,) *smoky, covered with smoke, black with smoke, sooty; burning,* B 415; does Lat. *fumosus* or *fuliginosus* correspond to any of these definitions ?

αἴθε, Ep. for εἴθε, *O that !* Lat. *utinam.*

αἰθήρ, έρος, (in Hom.) ἡ, (αἴθω,) Lat. *aether, ether, upper unclouded air, purer air,* as belonging to the heavens and opp. to ἀήρ, *the lower, thicker air surrounding the earth; space filled by light of day, clear sky,* as dwelling-place of the gods, B 412.

Αἴθικες, ων, οἱ, *Æ-thi'-ces,* B 744, a Thes-sa'-li-an tribe.

Αἰθιοπῆας, A 423, irreg. acc. pl. of foll.

Αἰθίοψ, οπος, ὁ, (αἴθω, ὤψ,) lit. *burnt face,* Lat. *Ae'-thi-ops, an Æ-thi-o'-pi-an,* A 423.

αἴθουσα, ης, ἡ, (αἴθω,) *a porch, sunny porch,* usu. on the east side of the house to receive the sun's rays.

αἴθοψ, οπος, (αἴθω, αἶθος, ὤψ,) *fiery-looking; flashing,* as epith. of metals; *red,* of wine, A 462; compare Lat. *fulgidus, coruscus,* and *radians* with these different definitions: metaph., *fiery, keen.*

Αἴθρη, ης, ἡ, *Æ'-thra,* mother of The'-seus, goes with Hel'-en to Troy; stric., *a clear sky.*

αἴθω, found only in pres. system, *to light, kindle, set in a blaze, keep burning;* intr. *burn.*

αἴθων, ωνος, ὁ, (part. of αἴθω,) *blazing, burning, fiery; shining.*

ἀικῶς, see ἀικής, *disgracefully.*

αἷμα, ατος, τό, Lat. *sanguis, blood; carnage, murder,* Lat. *caedes; blood-relation,* kin.

αἱματόεις, εσσα, εν, (αἷμα,) Lat. *cruentus, bloody,* B 267, *blood-sprinkled; made* or *consisting of blood,* Lat. *sanguineus,* also, *murderous, bloody;* ψιάδες, *bloody drops.*

αἵμων, ονος, ὁ, *having understanding.*

Αἰνείας, ου, Ep. gen. -αο or -ω, ὁ, *Æ-ne'-as;* see Classical Dictionary.

Αἰνόθεν, from *Æ'-nus.*

αἰνόμορος, ον, (αἰνός, μόρος,) *of sad destiny.*

αἰνός, ή, όν, Ep. Lat. *terribilis, horribilis, horrendus, frightful, dire, dreadful, horrible:* neu. as adv. freq. in Hom., *extremely, very much; terribly:* the adv. αἰνῶς is also used.

αἴξ, αἰγός, ἡ, ὁ, (ἀίσσω,) Lat. *caper, a goat,* dat. pl. αἴγεσ(σ)ιν.

ἀίξασκον, Ep. iter. 2 aor. from ἀίσσω, which see.

αἰολοθώρηξ, ηκος, ὁ, (αἰόλος, θώρηξ,) *with shining breastplate,* Γ 83.

αἰολομίτρης, ου, ὁ, (αἰόλος, μίτρα,) *of gleaming* or *shining girdle.*

αἰολόπωλος, ον, (αἰόλος, πῶλος,) *with swift-moving steeds,* Γ 185.

αἰόλος, η, ον, *quickly changing; light; gleaming; changing, constantly moving, quick-moving.*

Αἴολος, ου, ὁ, *Æ'-o-lus,* god of winds ; see foreg.; see Classical Dictionary.

αἰπεινός, ή, όν, (αἰπύς,) *high,* of places ; Lat. *arduus, steep, precipitous, hard to climb; lofty,* of bearing.

αἰπήεις, εσσα, εν, poet. for foreg.

αἰπόλιον, ου, τό, (αἰπόλος,) Lat. *grex caprarum, a herd of goats; a goat-pasture,* Β 474 αἰπόλια πλατέ' αἰγῶν, *far-wandering herds of goats.* ⏐

αἰπόλος, ου, ὁ, short. form for αἰγοπόλος, (αἴξ, πολέω,) Lat. *pastor caprarum, one who pastures goats, a goat-herd.*

αἰπός, ή, ον, *high and steep, precipitous, high-lying, high, lofty;* αἰπὰ ῥέεθρα, *streams plunging sheer down; sheer, utter;* metaph., *difficult:* see αἰπύς.

Αἶπυ, εος, τό, *Æ'-py,* a city of E'-lis subject to Nes'-tor, Β 592 ; prob. so named from its situation, see foll.

αἰπύς, εῖα, ύ, Ep. αἰπός, which see.

Αἰπύτιος, η, ον, *of Æp'-y-tus,* Β 604 ; an Ar-ca'-dian chief.

αἱρέω ; f. ἥσω ; aor. ᾑρησάμην ; 2 aor. εἷλον or ἕλον, iter. ἕλεσκον ; pf. ᾕρηκα, Ion. ἀραίρηκα ; aor. pass. ᾑρέθην ; does Lat. *sumere, prehendere* or *tollere* correspond in meaning to any definitions here given ? *to take hold of, take, take up, grasp; seize, take away; take* or *get into one's power; win, obtain; seduce; to capture, rob, plunder; to overpower, conquer, catch, take, kill; to grasp with the mind, comprehend:* mid., *to take one's own* or *what is his, take for* or *to one's self, choose, prefer;* with ἀπό, *lay off, strip off; take with one, enjoy.*

αἴρω, (Att. for ἀείρω, which see,) f. ἀρῶ ; aor. ἦρα ; pf. ἦρκα ; impf. mid. ἠρόμην ; f. mid. ἀροῦμαι ; 3 sing. aor. mid. ἤρατο.

Ἄις, see Ἀίδης.

Αἶσα, ης, ἡ, *the goddess of destiny,* Lat. *Par'-ca,* like Μοῖρα ; *allotted share, part, appointed lot, fate, destiny; length of life; fatal decree* of a god ;

propriety, κατά and ὑπὲρ αἶσαν, *according to* and *beyond propriety*, Γ 59.

Αἴσηπος, ου, ὁ, *Æ-se'-pus*, son of Bu-co'-li-on ; a river of Mys'-i-a, B 825.

αἴσιμος, ον, (αἶσα,) *decreed by fate ; according to fate* and therefore *right*.

αἴσσω ; impf. ἤσσον, iter. ἀίσσεσκον ; f. αἴξω, ; aor. ἤιξα, iter. ἀίξασκον ; aor. pass. ἠίχθην : Lat. *impetu ferri ; to move rapidly, move with a quick motion, shoot, rush swiftly, dart, fly ; charge, spring forward quickly, rush upon.*

Αἰσυήτης, ου, Ep. ao, ὁ, *Æ-sy-e'-tes*, a Tro'-jan leader, father of Au-te'-nor, B 793.

αἶσχος, εος, τό, Lat. *dedecus, infamia, probrum,* (what is the difference between these Lat. words ?) *shame, infamy ; deformity.*

αἰσχρός, ά, όν, and ός, όν, (αἶσχος,) Lat. *turpis, causing shame, disgraceful,* B 298 ; B 216 *ugly,* as opp. to καλός ; *shameful, base, disgracing ; insulting,* αἰσχρὰ ἔπεα *abusive words:* irreg. compar. αἰσχίων, αἴσχιστος.

αἰσχύνω, f. νῶ, aor. ἤσχυνα, pf. ἤσχυγκα, ἠσχύνθην, (αἶσχος,) *to deface, mangle ; to bring disgrace and dishonor.*

αἰτέω, *to plead, entreat, beg, ask.*

αἴτιος, α,ον, *causing ;* in a bad sense, *causing ill, blamable, responsible.*

Αἰτώλιος for **Αἰτωλός**, οῦ, ὁ, an *Æ-to'-li-an.*

αἰχμή, ῆς, ἡ, (ἀίσσω,) *the metallic point of a spear ; spear ; staff ; war.*

αἰχμητά, Ep. for **αἰχμητής**, οῦ, ὁ, (αἰχμή,) Lat. *bellator, spearman, warrior,* A 152, Γ 179.

αἶψα, adv. compare Lat. *extemplo, repente, subito, statim, quickly, forthwith, suddenly ;* αἶψα δ' ἔπειτα *immediately after ;* with μάλα, *very quickly.*

αἰών, ῶνος, ὁ and ἡ, *time, a period of time, a space of time ; a lifetime,* also *time of life* or *age ; endless time.*

ἀκάμας, αντος, ὁ, (a priv., καμεῖν,) *without resting, not tiring, unwearying.*

'Ακάμας, αντος, ὁ, (a priv., καμεῖν, 2 aor. inf. of κάμνω,) lit. *untiring ; Ac'-a-mas,* son of An-te'-nor ; a Thra'-ci-an leader.

ἀκάματος, ον, (a priv., κάματος, κάμνω,) *without weariness, not wearied.*

ἀκαχίζω, from ἀχέω, *to afflict, annoy.*

ἀκαχμένος, η, ον, (part. of obsol. verb,) *sharp, sharp-pointed.*

ἀκέομαι, *to apply a relief* or *cure, heal ;* and so, *to assuage, make good.*

ἀκέων, έουσα, (ἀκήν,) used adverbially, Lat. *tacite, silently, softly, quietly,* A 33.

ἀκήδεστος, ον, (a priv., κηδέω,) *not cared for ; without burial.*

ἀκηδέω, *to disregard.*

ἀκηδής, ές, (a priv., κῆδος,) act., *heedless ; free from care* or *sorrow,* Lat. *securus ; neglected, not buried.*

ἀκήν, adv., Lat. *placide, softly, silently, stilly, quietly, noiselessly;* in phrase, Γ 95, ἀκὴν ἐγένοντο σιωπῇ, *became mute in silence;* stric. acc. of ἀκή.

ἄκλαυ(σ)τος, ον, (a priv., κλαίω,) *not weeping, without tears;* also, *not wept for, not mourned.*

ἀκλεής, ές, (a priv., κλέος,) *without fame* or *glory.*

ἀκμόθετον, ου, τό, (ἄκμων, τίθημι,) *the block for an anvil.*

ἄκμων, ονος, ὁ, *an anvil.*

ἀκοίτης, ου, ὁ, (a copul., κοίτη,) Lat. *conjux, one who occupies the same bed, a husband:* ἄκοιτις, ιος, ἡ, *wife,* Lat. *uxor, conjux.*

ἀκοντίζω, (ἄκων,) *to throw the dart; to strike and wound with the dart; to throw.*

ἄκοσμος, ον, (a priv. κόσμος,) *wanting order, disorderly, in confusion;* in a moral sense, *unseemly, unbecoming, indecorous,* B 213; *unruly:* Hom. uses in a moral sense.

ἀκοστήσας, aor. part. of ἀκοστάω, *well-fed.*

ἀκούω, f. σομαι, aor. ἤκουσα; Att. 2 pf. ἀκήκοα; aor. pass. ἠκούσθην, Lat. *audire, to hear, hear of, find out;* without case foll., *to hear, give attention, listen;* with gen., *to listen to, give ear to,* and with dat., *to listen to* in the sense of *to obey.*

ἀκράαντος, ον, (a priv., κραιαίνω,) Lat. *irritus, without result, unfulfilled, fruitless, vain,* B 138.

ἄκρατος, ον, Ion. **ἄκρητος**, (a priv., κεράννυμι; or a intens., κράτος,) Lat. *merus,* (why not *purus?*) *unmixed, pure, excessive, intemperate, violent.*

ἄκρη, Ion. for ἄκρα, ας, ἡ, *the end,* hence *the top, the summit.*

ἀκριτόμυθος, ον, (ἄκριτος, μῦθος,) Lat. *loquens inconsiderate et sine judicio, recklessly babbling,* B 246; *hard to understand.*

ἄκριτος, ον, (a priv., κριτός, κρίνω,) Lat. *indiscretus, undistinguishable, unarranged, disorderly; endless, lasting; doubtful; untried; without judgment.*

ἀκριτόφυλλος, ον, (ἄκριτος, φύλλον,) *thickly overgrown.*

ἀκρόκομος, ον, (ἄκρος, κόμη,) *having hair on the top* or *head.*

ἄκρος, α, ον, (ἀκή, or κάρα by transposition,) *pointed, outermost, at the end, extreme,* Lat. *extremus, topmost, highest,* Lat. *summus; first, most excellent.*

ἀκτή, ῆς, ἡ, (ἄγνυμι,) Lat. *litus,* B 395, *sea-beach, strand; coast,* Lat. *ora.*

᾽Ακτορίδης, ου, ὁ, *son* or *descendant of Ac'-tor.*

᾽Ακτορίων, ωνος, ὁ, = foreg.

῎Ακτωρ, ορος, ὁ, *Ac'-tor.*

ἀκωκή, ῆς, ἡ, (ἀκή,) compare Lat. *acumen, acies, the sharp edge* or *point.*

ἄκων, οντος, ὁ, (ἀκή,) *a small dart, javelin.*

ἄλαδε, (ἅλς, -δε,) adv., Lat. *ad mare, sea-ward, to the sea*, A 308 ; Hom. also
    has εἰς ἄλαδε.

ἀλαλητός, οῦ, ὁ, (ἀλαλή,) *a war-cry ; a tumultuous shout*, Lat. *vociferatio
    militaris, clamor*, B 149 ; *a cry of fear or woe.*

ἄλαλκε, see ἀλέξω.

ἀλαλκομενηΐς, ίδος, ἡ, (ἀλαλκεῖν, μένος,) *the guardian*, epithet of Mi-
    ner'-va.

ἀλάομαι, part. ἀλώμενος, impf. ἠλώμην, f. ἥσομαι ; pf. ἀλάλημαι ; aor.
    pass. ἠλήθην, Hom. ἀλήθην : (ἄλη:) Lat. *vagari, wander about, rove,
    stray ;* with acc. *wander in or over ;* metaph. *wander in mind.*

ἀλαπαδνός ή, όν, (ἀλαπάζω,) *easily overcome, feeble*, B 675.

ἀλαπάζω, f. άξω, (a euphon., λαπάζω,) Lat. *exinanire, to empty, drain ;
    drain of strength, weaken ; slay ; overcome ; destroy.*

'Αλάστωρ, ορος, ὁ, *A-las'-tor.*

ἄλαστος, ον, (a priv., λανθάνω,) *never to be forgotten, terrible, awful.*

ἀλεγεινός, ή, όν, (ἄλγος,) Lat. *curae plenus, tristis, grievous, sad*, B 787,
    troublesome ; hard, difficult ; act., *causing pain or trouble.*

ἀλγέω, f. ήσω, (ἄλγος,) Lat. *dolere, to feel pain*, in Hom.; *be sick ; feel
    pain of mind.*

ἄλγος, εος, τό, (ἀλέγω,) Lat. *dolor, any pain ; suffering, trouble, grief, woe,*
    A 2 ; *that which causes pain.*

ἀλεγίζω, f. ίσω, used only in pres. system, (ἀλέγω,) with the neg., A 160,
    to have no care, not to concern one's self, etc.; elsewhere, *to care for,
    mind*, with gen. ; does Lat. *curare* correspond to this ?

ἀλεείνω, (ἀλέα,) *to shun*, Γ 32.

ἀλέη, ἡ, Ion. for ἀλέα, (ἀλεύω,) *an escaping, getting away.*

ἀλείς, 2 aor. pass. part. of εἰλέω or more com. εἴλω ; Ep. parts are formed
    in ἐελ-, ἐειλ-, ἀλ-, ἐολ-, see Hadley and Allen's Grammar 518 D, 23 ; *to
    roll up, use force ; to confine ; to press and force together.*

'Αλείσιον, ου, τό, *A-li'-si-um*, a city of E'-lis, B 617.

ἀλείτης, ου, ὁ, (ἀλιταίνω, ἄλη,) Lat. *peccator, one who leads others astray,
    one who goes astray, a sinner or wicked person, scoundrel ;* of Par'-is
    (Γ 28) and the suitors.

ἄλεν or ἀλέν, 2 aor. pass. Ep. 3 pl. of εἴλω, see ἀλείς.

'Αλέξανδρος, ου, ὁ, (ἀλέξω, ἀνήρ,) *Alex-an'-der, man-defender*, the usu. name
    of Par'-is, represented as having a sensual character.

ἀλέξω ; f. ἀλεξήσω, ἀλέξω ; aor. ἤλεξα, opt. 3 sing. ἀλεξήσειε : Ep. forms,
    pres. inf. ἀλεξέμεν(αι) Γ 9, Α 590, 2 aor. ἄλαλκον : *to ward off, avert,
    repel, turn away ;* hence, *to defend*, Lat. *defendere :* mid., *to keep off
    from one's self, keep off, defend one's self ; repay.*

ἀλέομαι, -εύομαι, and -εῦμαι, dep., (there is an act. form ἀλεύω, *to with-*

draw, keep away,) hence the forms of the word from ἀλε- and ἀλευ- : *to avoid ; flee ; to omit to do anything.*

Ἀλήϊον πεδίον, *A-le'-i-an plain.*

Ἅλιαρτος, ου, ὁ, and **ἡ,** *Ha-li-ar'-tus,* a city of Bœ-o'-ti-a, B 503.

ἄλιαστος, ον, (α priv., λιάζομαι,) *unyielding, unceasing, not giving way.*

ἀλίγκιος, α, ον, *similar.*

Ἀλιζῶνες, Ἀλίζωνοι, ων, οἱ, *the Hal-i-zo'-nes,* a tribe of *Bi-thyn'-i-a.*

ἅλιος, α, ον, Lat. *vanus,* Δ 26, *vain, useless ; erring.*

ἅλιος, adj., (ἅλς,) Lat. *marinus, of the sea ;* A 556 ἁλίοιο γέροντος, *the old god of the sea.*

Ἅλιος, ου, ὁ, *Ha'-li-us.*

ἅλις, adv., Lat. *satis, abunde, in masses, in swarms,* B 90, *in crowds,* Γ 384 ; *in throngs ; enough.*

ἁλίσκομαι, f. ἁλώσομαι ; 2 aor. ἥλων, Ep. forms of 2 aor. subj. ἁλώω, opt. ἁλῴην ; pf. ἥλωκα, Att. ἑάλωκα, (is Lat. *capi* the equivalent of this ?): *to be taken, be conquered* or *overcome, to be taken captive* or *taken by the enemy :* with θανάτῳ, *to be overtaken by death, to die ; to be seized.*

ἀλιταίνω, f. ἀλιτήσω, 2 aor. ἥλιτον, 2 aor. mid. Ep. 3 pl. ἀλίτοντο, (deriv. uncertain, perhaps from ἄλη,) *to sin against, commit a fault, err, do wrong.*

Ἀλκανδρος, ου, ὁ, *Al-can'-der.*

ἄλκαρ, αρος, τό, (ἀλκή,) *a protection.*

ἀλκή, ῆς, ἡ, *bodily strength, force ;* in gen., *force, power, might ; strength,* both bodily and mental, *valor, bravery, endurance, steadfastness ; defence, succor ; fight ;* see ῥώμη, (Lat. *robur,*) mere *strength,* whereas ἀλκή is *active strength.*

Ἀλκηστις, -ιδος and **-ιος, ἡ,** *Al-ces'-tis,* wife of Ad-me'-tus ; see Ad-me'-tus in Classical Dictionary.

Ἄλκιμος, ου, ὁ, *Al'-ci-mus,* (ἀλκή,) stric., *strong.*

ἄλκιμος, (ἀλκή,) (do Lat. *validus, fortis* correspond in sense to this ?), *strong, stout,* Γ 338 ; *brave, warlike.*

ἀλλά, (from ἄλλα the neu. pl. of ἄλλος,) conj., *in another way ;* in contrasting, *but, however,* Lat. *autem ; nay, but, rather,* Lat. *immo ;* changing the subject, *but, yet, still, then,* Lat. *at ;* Lat. *tandem, at length, well, now ;* ἀλλὰ γάρ, *but truly, of a truth, certainly ;* ἀλλ' οὖν, *but then ;* ἀλλά τε, *but yet ;* com. both ἀλλά and the other particle retain their force.

ἄλλῃ, dat. fem. of ἄλλος used as adv.: of place, *elsewhere,* Lat. *alibi,* ἄλλος ἄλλῃ, *one in one quarter, another in another, in different parts ;* A 120 the honor goes *elsewhere* (comes to naught), Lat. *aliorsum :* of manner, *otherwise,* Lat. *alias.*

ἄλληκτος, ον, Ep. for ἄληκτος, (a priv., λήγω,) *unceasing.*

ἀλλήλων, (ἄλλος,) gen. pl., the word has no nom. (are Lat. *alius alium, alter alterum, mutuo, invicem* the equivalents of this!), *of one another, mutually;* Hom. has ἀλλήλοιιν for ἀλλήλοιν in the dat. du.

ἀλλοδαπός, ή, όν, (see Lat. *externus, extraneus, peregrinus,*) *strange, foreign, of another land,* as a noun, *stranger,* Γ 48.

ἀλλοθεν, (ἄλλος, -θεν,) adv. Lat. *aliunde, from another place, from else-where;* ἄλλοθεν ἄλλος, Β 75, *one from one place, another from another.*

ἄλλομαι; f. ἀλοῦμαι; aor. ἡλάμην; aor. 2 ἡλόμην, Ep. forms in 2 aor., sync. 2 and 3 sing. ἆλσο, ἆλτο, part. ἄλμενος; notice that these parts of the verb take a smooth breathing, and Ep. subj. ἄλεται: Lat. *salire, to spring, bound,* εἰς ἅλα, Α 532.

ἄλλος, η, ο, Lat. *alius, other;* τἄλλα, τἆλλα, crasis for τὰ ἄλλα; when joined with a subst., ἄλλος agrees with it, or subst. is in the gen.; *any other,* Γ 223; ἄλλο, *besides;* ὁ ἄλλος, *the other;* οἱ ἄλλοι, Lat. *ceteri, the rest;* ἄλλος, Β 75, see ἄλλοθεν; *stranger, intruder; yet, still, besides, moreover, further,* as *for the rest;* ἄλλος μέν . . . ἄλλος δέ, *one . . . another;* the μέν . . . δέ are sometimes omitted; ἄλλος τις or τὶς ἄλλος, *any other, some other;* οὐδεὶς ἄλλος, *no other;* two of its own cases are often used together, as ἄλλος ἄλλῳ, *one . . . to one, another . . . to another,* Β 400; ἄλλη δ' ἄλλων γλῶσσα, *but different is the language of the various peoples,* Β 804.

ἄλλοτε, (ἄλλος, ὅτε,) adv., *another time;* ἄλλοτε . . . ἄλλοτε, *at one time . . . at another;* is Lat. *alias* the equivalent of this word?

Ἀλόπη, ης, ἡ, *Al'-o-pe,* a city in Phthi-o'-tis, Β 682.

Ἀλος, ου, ὁ and ἡ, *A'-lus,* a city in Phthi-o'-tis, Β 682.

ἄλοχος, ου, ἡ, (a copul., λέχος,) (compare Lat. *conjux, uxor,*) *she who shares the bed, wife.*

ἀλόω, see ἀλάομαι.

ἅλς, ἁλός, ὁ, Lat. *sal, a grain* or *lump of salt,* in pl. *salt; the briny deep, sea:* ἅλαδε, *seaward,* Α 308.

ἄλσος, εος, τό, (compare Lat. *lucus, nemus, saltus,*) *grove; a sacred grove,* Β 506.

Ἄλτης, ου, ὁ, *Al'-tes.*

ἆλτο, Ep. sync. 3 sing. aor. 2 of ἄλλομαι.

Ἀλύβη, ης, ἡ, *Al'-y-ba,* a town of Bi-thyn'-i-a.

ἀλυσκάζω, another form of the foll.

ἀλύσκω, f. ύξω, (ἀλέομαι,) *to avoid, flee from; quit, desert, abandon.*

ἀλύω, (ἄλη,) *to wander in mind; be anxious; hesitate, be in doubt.*

Ἀλφειός, οῦ, ὁ, *Al-phe'-us,* a river of E'-lis.

ἀλφεσίβοιος, α, ον, (ἀλφεῖν, 2 aor. inf. of ἀλφάνω *to yield,* βοῦς,) *bringing in cattle, having many suitors;* it was the custom for suitors to make presents of cattle to the parents of maidens.

ἄλφιτον, ου, τό, *barley.*

ἀλωή, ῆς, ἡ, *threshing-floor; a smooth piece of ground; a piece of ground carefully levelled.*

ἀλώμενος, η, ον, part. from ἀλάομαι.

ἀλώω, Ep. for ἀλῶ, 2 aor. subj. of ἁλίσκομαι.

ἀμ-, Ion. and Ep. for ἀνα-.

ἅμα, adv., Lat. *simul, at once, at same time,* A 343 : also a prep. with dat., *together with,* A 348.

Ἀμαζών, όνος, ἡ, usu. in pl., *the A'-ma-zons,* a nation of warlike women in Scyth'-i-a.

ἀμαιμάκετος, η, ον, Hom. for ἄμαχος, *not to be resisted; of huge proportions, immense.*

ἀμαλλοδετήρ, ῆρος, (ἄμαλλα, δέω,) *a sheaf-binder, one who binds sheaves.*

ἀμαλός, ή, ον, *tender, feeble.*

ἄμαξα, ης, ἡ, (ἅμα, ἄξων or more prob. ἄγω,) *a wagon or cart, heavy freight wagon; a road for wagons to pass upon.*

ἀμαξιτός, ον, (ἄμαξα, ἰτός,) *traversed-by-wagons, for wagons to pass;* also a *wagon-road,* as subst.

ἁμαρτάνω, parts formed from ἁμαρτα-, *to miss* or *come short of, fail* of accomplishing; *to do evil.*

Ἀμαρυγκείδης, ου, ὁ, *son of Am-a-ryn'-ceus.*

ἀμάω, *to gather, collect; to reap.*

ἀμβ-, Ep. for ἀναβ-, at the beginning of words.

ἀμβατός, Ep. and Ion. for ἀναβατός, ον, (ἀναβαίνω,) *may be mounted, easily mounted, can be scaled, accessible.*

ἀμβλήδην, Ep. for ἀναβλήδην, (ἀναβάλλομαι,) adv. *starting up; with starts; sudden, fitful.*

ἀμβροσία, ας, ἡ, Ep., ἀμβροσίη, *ambrosia, food of the gods;* stric. fem. of foll.

ἀμβρόσιος, ια, ιον, *immortal, divine :* this is a leng. form of ἄμβροτος : *night* and *sleep* are *ambrosial* or *divine,* as being sent by the gods.

ἄμβροτος, ον, (a priv., βροτός,) *immortal, godlike.*

ἀμέγαρτος, ον, (a priv., μεγαίρω,) *unenviable, unfortunate, unhappy; sad, miserable,* B 420.

ἀμείβω, f. ψω, aor. ἤμειψα, Lat. *mutare, to change, alternate; to exchange anything for something else;* mid. *to change with each other;* A 604, *give in exchange* or *answer; repay, avenge.*

ἀμείλιχος, ον, *unrelenting, hard.*

ἀμείνων, ον, gen. ονος, Lat. *melior,* compar. of ἀγαθός; *abler, stouter,* stronger, braver; better, better fit, more excellent, superior; more advantageous.

ἀμέρδω, f. σω, take away one's portion.

ἀμετροεπής, ές, (ἄμετρος, ἔπος,) Lat. immoderate loquax, incessant or immoderate in words, B 212, sharp or harsh of tongue.

ἀμιχθαλόεις, εσσα, εν, leng. Hom. for ἄμικτος, not mixed; not to be approached, unfriendly.

ἄμμε, ἄμμες, ἄμμι, see ἡμεῖς.

ἄμμορος, Ep. for ἄμορος, (a priv., μόρος,) not having share, destitute of; unlucky, unfortunate.

ἀμοιβηδίς, (ἀμοιβή,) adv., in turn.

ἀμολγός, οῦ, ὁ, (ἀμέλγω,) time of milking, twilight, darkness.

ἀμός, Ep. for ἡμέτερος, which see.

ἄμοτος, ον, not to be sated, insatiable: neu. as adv., unceasingly.

ἀμπ-, poet. for ἀναπ- at the beginning of words.

ἀμπελόεις, εσσα, εν, or εις, εν, (ἄμπελος,) Lat. vitibus abundans, full of vines.

ἀμπεπαλών, Ep. for ἀναπεπαλών redupl. part. 2 aor. from ἀναπάλλω.

ἀμπνέω, see ἀναπνέω.

ἄμπυξ, υκος, ὁ and ἡ, (ἀμφί, ἔχω,) a band for binding up the hair on the forehead of a woman, head-band; head-band for a horse, bridle.

'Αμυδών, ῶνος, ἡ, Am'-y-don, a town.

'Αμύκλαι, ῶν, αἱ, A-my'-clæ, a city of La-co'-ni-a.

ἀμύμων, ον, gen. ονος, (a priv., μῶμος,) Lat. inculpatus, blameless, faultless, A 423; of men and women in respect to their outward appearance and condition; not applied to the gods.

ἀμύνω, f. νῶ, Ion. ἀμυνέω, aor. 1 ἤμυνα, 2 aor. Hom. ἠμύναθον; (a euph., μύνη;) Lat. propulsare, to ward off; to defend, Lat. defendere; help: mid., to defend or avenge one's self; requite.

ἀμύσσω, f. ξω, Lat. lacerare, to lacerate; gnaw, θυμόν, A 243, thou shalt gnaw thy soul with rage.

ἀμφαΐσσομαι, (ἀμφί, ἀΐσσω,) to come quickly on from all round; sail about, move around.

ἀμφηρεφής, ές, (ἀμφί, ἐρέφω,) Lat. undique tectus, covered on all sides, roofed, A 45.

ἀμφαφάω, (ἀμφί, ἀφάω,) to feel all round or all over, handle.

ἀμφέπω, see ἀμφιέπω.

ἀμφί, Lat. utrimque, ex utraque parte, on both or all sides, around, all around: adv., ἀμφί περί, round about; about, round about, on every side: prep., with gen., Lat. de or pro, (with abl.,) about, concerning, also for, rare. of place; with dat., Lat. circa, among, around, about, also Lat. *apud, at, by, with,* ἀμφὶ ὀβελοῖς ἔπειραν, *they fixed on spits,* so that it was *around* them, *about, for the sake of, concerning;* with acc., Lat. *circa, about, around, at, by:* in compo., *around* or *on all sides.*

ἀμφί . . . ἀλείφω, *to anoint all round.*

ἀμφιάχω, (ἀμφί, ἰάχω,) *to make a sound on all sides, to fly about with a loud noise;* pf. part., ἀμφιαχυῖα, B 316.

ἀμφιβαίνω, for prin. parts see βαίνω, (ἀμφί, βαίνω,) Lat. *circumire, to go around; surround, protect,* A 37; *encompass.*

ἀμφίβασις, εως, ἡ, (ἀμφιβαίνω,) *a going round* anything, *a surrounding,* Lat. *circumventio.*

ἀμφίβροτος, adj., (ἀμφί, βροτός,) *around* or *covering the whole man,* as epith. of ἀσπίς, B 389.

Ἀμφιγένεια, as, ἡ, *Am'-phi-ge-ni'-a,* a town, B 593.

Ἀμφιγνήεις, ὁ, (ἀμφί, γυιός, γυῖον,) epith. of Vulcan, *lame in both feet, the lame one.*

ἀμφιδρυφής, ές, (ἀμφί, δρυφῆναι, 2 aor. pass. of δρύπτω,) *torn all round; rending both her cheeks from grief,* B 700.

ἀμφιέλισσα, (ἀμφί, ἐλίσσω,) Ep. fem. adj.; of ships *round on both sides;* or better perhaps (from the meaning of ἐλίσσω,) *twisting* or *rocking both ways, rocking; the rocking ship.*

ἀμφιέπω and Hom. ἀμφέπω, 2 aor. ἀμφίεπον and ἄμφεπον, (ἀμφί, ἔπω,) *to go around, be all round; to be busy about* or *care for,* hence *to do honor to:* mid. *to surround.*

ἀμφιθαλής, ές, (ἀμφί, θαλέω,) *flourishing all round; rich; prosperous.*

ἀμφικαλύπτω, f. ψω, (ἀμφί, καλύπτω,) see Lat. *circumtegere, obvolvere, to cover all over* or *round, enfold, wrap,* as with garments, *envelop, veil,* B 262; *love has enveloped,* Γ 442; *to shelter, cover; to put around another.*

ἀμφικύπελλος, ον, (ἀμφί, κύπελλον,) *double cupped;* with δέπας, *a double-cupped goblet,* one having a cup-shaped base.

ἀμφιμάχομαι, (ἀμφί, μάχομαι,) *to fight around.*

Ἀμφίμαχος, ον, ὁ, (ἀμφί, μάχη,) *Am-phim'-a-chus,* the name of two chiefs mentioned in the Il'-i-ad.

ἀμφιμέλας, ἀμφιμέλαινα, ἀμφιμέλαν, (ἀμφί, μέλας,) *black all round;* in Hom. φρένες ἀμφιμέλαιναι, lit. *diaphragm darkened all round,* metaph. of soul, *darkened, stern, severe.*

ἀμφινέμομαι, (ἀμφί, νέμομαι,) *to dwell round about; inhabit,* Lat. *habitare; encompass.*

Ἄμφιος, ον, ὁ, *Am-phi'-us.*

ἀμφι–περί, see ἀμφί.
2

ἀμφίπολος, ον, (ἀμφί, πέλω,) *being busied about :* in Hom. freq. as fem. subst., *a confidential attendant*, not a slave. Lat. *comes.*

ἀμφιποτάομαι, (ἀμφί, ποτάομαι,) Lat. *circumvolare, to flutter about.*

ἀμφίς, Hom. form for ἀμφί, *about ;* as adv., *on both sides ; apart*, or *in opposition*, ἀμφὶς φράζεσθαι, *to be of different minds*, B 13 ; *round about*, Γ 115 : as prep., with gen., *far away from, apart from ;* with dat., *round about ;* with acc., *about.*

ἀμφιχέω, f. χεύσω and -έω, aor. ἀμφέχεα, aor. pass. -εχύθην, (ἀμφί, χέω, Lat. *circumfundere, to pour around, shed about :* mid., *to shed* or *diffuse itself around*, B 41 ; *to embrace ;* Lat. *circumfundi.*

ἀμφότερος, -έρα, -ον, (ἄμφω,) Lat. *uterque, both;* neu. as adv., as ἀμφότερον βασιλεύς τ' ἀγαθός, κρατερός τ' αἰχμητής, *both a good king and a mighty warrior*, Γ 179 ; κατ' ἀμφότερα, Lat. *utrinque, on both sides.*

ἄμφω, both du. and pl., gen. and dat. ἀμφοῖν, *both*, Lat. *ambo.*

ἄν, a particle which cannot be exactly rendered into Eng.; but in some cases it can be rendered, *probably, perhaps ;* it marks *uncertainty.*

With the indicat. ἄν makes an assertion *conditional*, and is not used with the pres.: ἄν with the f. expresses that which *will probably happen :* with a past tense, ἄν indicates supposition *contrary to reality*, but *assumed as real, would ;* with impf. ἄν expresses *repetition* or *habitual action under certain circumstances that would favor such actions ;* with aor. it implies that something *would have taken place at one particular time if conditions had been suitable :* ἄν is not used with pf. indicat.

With subj. ἄν conveys *the idea of futurity.* A 205, *he will at some time, probably quickly, lose his life through his insolence.*

With opt. ἄν implies a *general uncertainty ; prayers* and *commands* are rendered *less strong* by ἄν with opt.; used in the conclusion, *would.* Ἀν is used with the opt. in the *conclusion* of a *conditional* sentence when the condition is *assumed as possible.* The opt. thus used is called the *Potential Opt.*, and is used in *assertions* and *questions.* In poet., the *Potential Opt.* without ἄν is also found. The opt. with ἄν expresses a wish *conditionally.*

With the inf. ἄν is used where a finite verb, standing independently, would take it.

The part. takes ἄν where a finite verb, standing independently, would take it. Ep. κέ(ν), which see.

ἄν for ἀνά, Γ 261, 268.

ἀν- for a priv. before a vowel : ἄν, conj., = ἐάν with the subj.

ἀνά, prep. with gen., dat., and acc., *up, upon*, opp. to κατά : with gen., *on board :* with the dat. *on, upon*, denoting location without motion,

A 15 : with the acc., has the general meaning of *motion upwards*, opp.
to κατά ; *through, throughout*, B 575 ; *up along, over ;* ἀνὰ στόμα ἔχειν,
to have constantly on the tongue, B 250 ; ἀνὰ θυμὸν φρονέειν, *to revolve
up and down, or continually, in the mind*, B 36 ; ἀνὰ χρόνον, *in course
of time :* as adv., *thereon, thereupon ; throughout ;* ἀλλ' ἄνα, *but up !
be quick !* in compo. *upwards ; towards, up to ; backwards ; has a
strengthening sense.*

ἄνα, as voc. sing. of ἄναξ.

ἀναβαίνω, f. -βήσω, -βήσομαι, aor. -έβησα, 2 aor. -έβην, aor. mid. Ep. 3 sing.
-εβήσετω, pf. -βέβηκα, (ἀνά, βαίνω,) *go up*, Lat. *ascendere* ; with acc.,
to go up to, ascend, A 497 ; with gen. νηός, *embark upon :* causal in
aor., ἀνέβησα, *to cause or make to go up or embark.*

ἀναβάλλω, f. -βαλῶ, (ἀνά, βάλλω,) *to throw up ; to put off or back,* see
second definition under mid. : mid., *to lift up the voice or begin to sing ;
to put off or delay,* B 436, see Lat. *procrastinare, differre, proferre, proro-
gare ; to throw a garment around one's self.*

ἀνάβλησις, εως, ἡ, (ἀναβάλλω,) Lat. *dilatio, postponement, delay.*

ἀναγκαίη, Ep. for ἀνάγκη, ης, ἡ, (ἀνάγω,) *pressure of necessity ; the tie or
necessity of relationship ; need, want ; force, violence,* Lat. *vis.*

ἀναγνάμπτω, f. ψω, (ἀνά, γνάμπτω,) Lat. *reflectere, to bend back, crook,*
Γ 348 ; *to undo,* Lat. *dissolvere.*

ἀνάγω, 2 aor. ἀνήγαγον, (ἀνά, ἄγω,) *to lead up ; to lead up into a
country ; to lead up, raise up ; to lead away,* Lat. *reducere,* Γ 48 ; of
ships, *to put out to sea ; to carry, bear, lead, conduct* = ἄγω ; *to bring
back ; to bring up or educate,* see Lat. *educere, educare :* intrans., *to
withdraw.*

ἀναδέσμη, ης, ἡ, (ἀναδέω,) *a band for the hair.*

ἀναδέχομαι, Ep. 2 aor. pass. ἀνεδέγμην, (ἀνά, δέχομαι,) *to take up ; to take
or receive back ; to suffer, endure ; to take responsibility of, promise.*

ἀναδύομαι, f. -δύσομαι, 2 aor. ἀνέδυν, pf. ἀναδέδυκα, (ἀνά, δύω, δύομαι,) forms
occur from ἀνδύ- ; *come up, rise, emerge,* as from the sea, A 359 ; with
acc. *arose to the surface,* A 496, lit. *to the wave of the sea,* Lat. *emergere,*
but some read *rose up from a wave,* and the word also means with acc.
to plunge back or withdraw ; draw back, Lat. *recedere.*

ἀναείρω, (ἀνά, ἀείρω,) *to take up, lift, raise.*

ἀναθηλέω, ῶ, f. ήσω, (ἀνά, θάλλω,) Lat. *revirescere, to grow verdant again,
bloom again.*

ἀναίδεια, ας, ἡ, Ep. ἀναιδείη, ης, (ἀναιδής,) Lat. *impudentia, impudence,
effrontery ;* ἀν. ἐπιειμένος, *clad with impudence,* A 149.

ἀναιδής, ές, (a priv., αἰδέομαι,) Lat. *impudens, impudent, shameless,* A 158.

ἀναίνομαι, (a priv., αἰνέομαι,) *to discard ; disclaim ; to decline to do ; repent.*

ἀναιρέω, f. ήσω, 2 aor. ἀνεῖλον, pf. ἀνήρηκα, 2 aor. part. ἀελών, A 301, (ἀνά, αἱρέω,) Lat. *tollere, to take up, lift from the ground, raise up, take up,* A 449, 301 ; *to take up and bear away, carry off, to take away ; to make way with, destroy, kill ; to ordain; answer :* mid., *to take up for one's own benefit, take to one's self ; acquire, gain ; require, exact ; to take* or *lift up ; to undertake ; to take back.*

ἀναΐσσω, f. ξω, aor. ἀνήιξα, (ἀνά, ἀίσσω,) *spring up quickly, start up, spring forth.*

ἀνακλίνω, (ἀνά, κλίνω,) *to cause to lean back* or *against; to push back* and *open.*

ἀνακοντίζω, f. ίσω, (ἀνά, ἀκοντίζω,) trans., *to cast up, throw up ;* intr., *to spurt* or *shoot up.*

ἄναλκις, ιδος, adj., acc. -ιδα or -ιν, Lat. *impotens,* (a priv., ἀλκή,) *having no strength ; unwarlike.*

ἀναμίσγω, Hom. for **ἀναμίγνυμι**, (ἀνά, μίγνυμι,) *to mix, cause to mingle ;* mid., *to mix* or *join one's self in company with, associate with.*

ἀνανεύω, (ἀνά, νεύω,) *to throw up* or *shake the head as a sign of denial, refuse by shake of the head.*

ἄναξ, κτος, Ep. dat. pl. ἀνάκτεσι, ὁ, Lat. *dominus, lord, master ; ruler, king,* Lat. *rex ; kindred of kings ;* applied to gods and any *earthly king* or *lord,* but esp. to Ag-a-mem'-non the chief : irreg. voc. ἄνα.

ἀναπάλλω, Hom. ἀμπάλλω, f. αλῶ, Ep. 2 aor. part. ἀμπεπαλών, Γ 355, (ἀνά, πάλλω,) *to swing back and forth ;* ἔγχος ἀμπεπαλών, *having poised for the throw.*

ἀναπείρω, f. περῶ, aor. ἀνέπειρα, Ep. part. ἀμπείρας, 2 aor. pass. ἀνεπάρην, (ἀνά, πείρω,) Lat. *transfigere, to transfix.*

ἀναπετάννυμι, and -ννύω, f. πετάσω ; poet. forms from ἀμπετ., (ἀνά, πετάννυμι,) Lat. *expandere, to unfold, open, unroll,* A 480.

ἀναπίμπλημι, f. ήσω, (ἀνά, πίμπλημι,) *to completely fill :* hence, *to accomplish, perform ; to satisfy,* Lat. *satisfacere.*

ἀναπνέω, (ἀνά, πνέω,) *to breathe again, take* or *recover breath ; to have a rest ; to breathe out.*

ἀνάποινος, ον, (a priv., ἄποινα,) *unransomed,* as adv., A 99.

ἀναρπάζω, f. άξω, (ἀνά, ἀρπάζω,) *to take up violently ; to carry off ; urge hurriedly along ; to take violently.*

ἀναρρήγνυμι, (ἀνά, ῥήγνυμι,) *to tear* or *break up, burst asunder* or *into, burst open ; to cause anything to burst forth.*

ἄναρχος, ον, (a priv., ἀρχή,) *without leader* or *head ; without beginning.*

ἀνάσσω, f. ξω, (ἄναξ,) *to be king, rule,* A 252; with the gen. and dat.; are Lat. *dominari, regnare,* the equivalents ?

ἀναστρωφάω, Hom. for -στρέφω, (ἀνά, στρέφω,) *to turn all ways* or *over and over.*

ἀνάσχεο, see ἀνέχω.

ἀνασχόμενος, 2 aor. part. ἀνασχών, see ἀνέχω.

ἀνατίθημι, (ἀνά, τίθημι,) for parts see τίθημι, to place upon, put on, heap on; to attribute; to give over; to set up; place back.

ἀναφαίνω, poet. ἀμφαίνω, f. φανῶ, aor. ἔφηνα, (ἀνά, φαίνω,) to cause to shine brightly; to make evident, disclose, A 87; make known; manifest; show the difference between Lat. monstrare, ostendere, declarare: mid., to be shown or appear.

ἀνάχαζω, f. ἄσω, (ἀνά, χάζω,) to cause to give way, press back; to draw back.

ἀναχωρέω, ῶ, f. ἤσω, (ἀνά, χωρέω,) Lat. recedere, to withdraw, Γ 35, go back, give away, retire; to come back or revert to the owner, Lat. revertere.

ἀνδάνω, Ep. impf. ἐήνδανον, Ion. ἐάνδανον, f. ἀδήσω, 2 aor. ἐάδον, Ep. εὔαδον, ἄδον, Γ 173; pf. ἄδηκα, 2 pf. ἔαδα; with dat.; Lat. placēre, to please, gratify, Γ 173; with two datives, as in A 24 and 378, please the mind (was not pleasing in mind to) Ag-a-mem'-non, etc.

ἄνδιχα, (ἀνά, δίχα,) adv., in two, asunder.

Ἀνδραίμων, ονος, ὁ, An-dræ'-mon, king of Cal'-y-don, B 638.

ἀνδρειφόντης, ου, ὁ, (ἀνήρ, φένω,) man-killing, see Lat. homicida.

ἀνδροκτασία, ας, ἡ, (ἀνήρ, κτείνω,) the slaying of man, carnage.

Ἀνδρομάχη, ης, ἡ, An-drom'-a-che.

ἀνδροφόνος, ον, (ἀνήρ, φένω,) killing men.

ἀνέεργω, impf. ἀνέεργον, -έργω, -είργω, Lat. cohibēre, hold back, Γ 77.

ἄνειμι; (ἀνά, εἶμι;) for parts see εἶμι, to go up or upwards; to ascend; to approach or go up to; to go out.

ἀνείρομαι, Ep. ἀνέρομαι, (ἀνά, εἴρομαι,) to ask, question, with acc. of pers.; Hom. also has acc. of pers. and thing, ὅ με ἀνείρεαι, what thou askest of me, Γ 177: compare Lat. interrogare, rogare, quaerere.

ἀνεκτός, όν, (ἀνέχω,) tolerable, bearable.

ἀνέλκω, aor. -είλκυσα, pf. pass. -είλκυσμαι, (ἀνά, ἕλκω,) to drag up, support, to draw out to fullest extent; to draw back.

ἀνελών, 2 aor. part. of ἀναιρέω.

ἄνεμος, ου, ὁ, (ἄημι,) Lat. ventus, wind, breath of air: with ἴς, a hurricane; with θύελλα, a whirlwind: Hom. mentions only four, Bo'-re-as, Eu'-rus, No'-tus, Zeph'-y-rus.

Ἀνεμώρεια, ας, ἡ, An'-e-mo-ri'-a, a high town in Pho'-cis; lit. 'windy, prob. from its location, B 521.

ἀνέρχομαι, for parts see ἔρχομαι, (ἀνά, ἔρχομαι,) to go upwards, go up, mount; to come back, return.

ἄνευθε(ν), (ἄνευ,) adv., far away, B 27, 64: prep. with gen., Lat. sine, (with abl.,) without; apart, far away from.

ἀνέχω and ἀνίσχω, f. ἀνέξω, ἀνασχήσω, 2 aor. ἀνέσχον, leng. Hom. ἀνέσχεθον, and Ep. inf. ἀνσχεθέειν, aor. pass. ἀνεσχέθην, (ἀνά, ἔχω,) Lat. *sustinere, hold up, sustain; lift up;* with χεῖρας, *lift the hands in combat* or *in prayer,* A 450; *extol, exalt; to uphold; to continue; to hold* or *keep in*: intrans., *to rise up;* with gen., *to rise up from; to happen; to project* or *come forth; to hold* or *continue*: mid., *to hold one's self up, bear up, endure,* Lat. *perferre,* A 586; *lift up what is one's own; raising himself,* (to strike better,) Γ 362.

ἄνεως, gen. ω, Att. adj., (α priv., αὔω,) Lat. *mutus, mute, speechless,* B 323.

ἀνήγαγον, 2 aor. from ἀνάγω.

ἀνήῃ, Ep. 3 sing. subj. 2 aor. of ἀνίημι, B 34.

ἀνήρ, ἀνδρός, Ep. ἀνέρος, dat. -δρί, acc. -δρα, voc. ἄνερ, pl. gen. -δρῶν, dat. -δράσι, and poet. ἀνδρεσσι: *man,* Lat. *vir,* opp. to γυνή, ἄνθρωπος, Lat. *homo* is *man* opp. to beast; *one of the people,* B 198; *man,* as a term of respect, one possessing the nobler faculties, *hero, a man indeed;* as opp. to the gods, A 544; when πόσις and ἀνήρ are opp. to each other πόσις means a lawful *husband,* ἀνήρ, a *paramour;* see φώς.

'Ανθεμίδης, son of *An-the'-mi-on.*

'Ανθεμίων, ωνος, ὁ, *An-the'-mi-on.*

ἀνθεμόεις, εσσα, εν, or εις, εν, (ἄνθεμον,) Lat. *floridus, flowery, full of flowers,* B 467.

ἀνθερεών, ῶνος, ὁ, (deriv. uncertain) Lat. *mentum, the chin.*

'Ανθηδών, όνος, ἡ, *An-the'-don,* a city of Bœ-o'-ti-a, B 508.

ἄνθος, εος, τό, *young bud; that which blooms, shoot; blossom; grace; honor.*

ἄνθρωπος, ου, ὁ, *man,* Lat. *homo,* opp. to gods and animals; in pl. *mankind, the world; any one;* ἄνθρωπος, ἡ, *woman;* the same difference exists between ἄνθρωπος and ἀνήρ that exists between *homo* and *vir,* as opp. to ἀνήρ it expresses contempt; see ἀνήρ.

ἀνιάω, f. ἀσω and ήσω, aor. ἠνίασα, (ἀνία,) *to distress, grieve, annoy.*

ἀνιηθείς, Ion. aor. pass. part. of foreg., used by Hom. as adj., *joyless, melancholy.*

ἀνίημι; impf. ἀνίην, Hom. 3 sing. impf. ἀνίεσκε; f. ἥσω Hom. ἀνέσω, ἀνέσει Ep. 3 sing.; aor. ἀνῆκα, Ep. and Ion. ἄνεσα, ἀνέηκα, (what verbs form the aor. in κ?) Hom. ἀνέσαιμι from ἀνῆσα; 2 aor. Ep. subj. 3 sing. ἀνήῃ, opt. ἀνείην, ἀνείς and pl. -έντες; pf. ἀνεῖκα; aor. pass. ἀνέθην: (ἀνά, ἵημι,) *to send forth* (Lat. *emittere*) or *up; to produce* or *cause to spring up; to send back; to let go, let loose;* with dat., *to let loose against,* Lat. *immittere; to let alone; to relax, neglect, forsake,* B 34; intrans., *to be careless* or *negligent.*

ἀνίστημι, f. ἀναστήσω, aor. ἀνέστησα, (ἀνά, ἵστημι,) trans., *to cause to stand, set up ; rouse up, stir up, incite,* A 191 ; *to make to rise,* Lat. *excĭtare :* mid., *rise up* for different purposes, *to speak,* A 58 ; *rise up,* B 694 : the pres., impf., f., and 1 aor. are trans.; 2 aor., pf., and f.pf. are intrans., *to stand up, rise, set out.*

ἀνιχνεύω, (ἀνά, ἰχνεύω,) *to trace back by the tracks, track back.*

ἄνομαι, see ἄνω.

ἀνόρνυμι, (ἀνά, ὄρνυμι,) *to disturb, stir up.*

ἀνορούω, f. ούσω, (ἀνά, ὀρούω,) Lat. *exsilire, to spring up, start up.*

ἀνούτατος, ον, (α priv., οὐτάω,) *not wounded, unhurt.*

ἀνουτητί, adv., *without wound.*

ἀνσχεθέειν, see ἀνέχω.

ἄντα, (ἀντί,) adv., Lat. *adversum, coram, opposite, ·over against ;* ἄντα μάχεσθαι, *to fight hand to hand* or *at close quarters :* prep. with gen., *before, in presence of ;* B 626, *over against ; face to face with.*

ἀντάξιος, ία, ιον, (ἀντί, ἄξιος,) *worth, equal to,* with gen., A 136.

ἀντάω, Ion. -έω, (ἄντα,) *to come face to face, meet ; partakc.*

Ἄντεια, ας, ἡ, *An-te´-a,* wife of Prœ´-tus.

ἄντην, (ἀντί,) adv., never as prep., Lat. *coram, against, before, before the face ; openly,* A 187, Lat. *palam.*

Ἀντηνορίδης, ου, ὁ, *a descendant of An-te´-nor,* Γ 123.

Ἀντήνωρ, ορος, ὁ, *An-te´-nor,* a Tro´-jan chief, Γ 262.

ἀντία, strictly neu. pl. of ἀντίος, used only as adv. = ἄντην, which see.

ἀντιάνειρα, ἡ, (ἀντί, ἀνήρ,) epith. of Amazons, *against men,* Γ 189.

ἀντιάω, Ep. ἀντιόω, f. άσω, -όω ; Hom. inf. ἀντιάαν, -άασθαι, etc., (ἀντί,) Lat. *occurrere, to go to* or *against, to meet ;* with gen. *accept of it,* A 67, *go in search of ; prepare, share,* A 31 ; dat. *encounter, meet with.*

ἀντίβιος, adj., (ἀντί, βία,) *opposing with force, hostile,* A 304 ; more freq. as adverbs, -τίβιον and -βίην.

ἀντίθεος, έη, εον, (ἀντί, θεός,) *equal to the gods ;* Hom. uses it of heroes, A 264.

ἀντ.κρύς, ἀντικρύ, adv., (ἀντί, κρούω,) *opposite, face to face, right opposite ; straight, straightforward, right on,* Γ 359, *outright, utterly.*

Ἀντίλοχος, ου, ο, *An-til´-o-chus.*

ἀντίον, see ἀντίος.

ἀντίος, ία, ιον, (ἀντί,) *set against, against, opposite,* A 535, Γ 425, *towards ;* with gen., *before one,* B 185 : Lat. *coram,* advs. ἀντίον, ἀντία, *against, in opposition,* A 230 ; *in turn, in reply,* Γ 203.

ἀντιόω, see ἀντιάω.

ἀντιπέραιος, αία, αιον, Lat. *adversus, lying opposite,* B 635.

ἀντιφέρω, f. ἀντοίσω; for prin. parts see φέρω, (ἀντί, φέρω,) *to carry against, set against :* mid. and pass., *set one's self against, measure one's self with ; difficult to oppose,* A 589.

Ἄντιφος, ου, ὁ, *An'-ti-phus;* an ally of the Tro'-jans, B 864 ; a son of Pri'-am ; a Grecian leader, B 678 ; son of Æ-gyp'-ti-us.

ἄντομαι, (ἀντί,) a defect. verb, only used in the pres. system ; *to meet, fall in with.*

Ἀντρών, ῶνος, ὁ and ἡ, *An'-tron,* a city of Thes'-sa-ly, B 697.

ἄντυξ, υγος, ἡ, *a circumference, the margin of a shield; the rim* or *rail round the chariot front.*

ἄνυσις, εως, ἡ, (ἀνύω,) Lat. *perfectio, an achievement, accomplishment,* B 347.

ἄνω, *to perform, do, finish.*

ἄνω, (ἀνά,) adv., *upwards; above: formerly:* as prep., *above.*

ἄνωγα, old Ep. 2 pf. with signif. of pres. *I command,* Lat. *jubere;* plupf. Ion. ἠνώγεα, 3 sing. ἠνώγει ; ἀνώγει, 3 sing. pres.

Ἀξιός, οῦ, and Ἄξιος, ὁ, *Ax'-i-us,* a river of Ma-ce-do'-ni-a.

ἀοιδή, ῆς, ἡ, (ἀείδω,) contr. ᾠδή, *singing, power to sing,* B 595 ; *song, story, subject of song.*

ἀοιδός, οῦ, ὁ and ἡ, (ἀείδω,) *one who sings, singer.*

ἀολλής, ές, (ἁ copul., εἴλλω,) *crowded together, in crowds.*

ἀοσσητήρ, ῆρος, ὁ, *one that aids, a helper.*

ἄουτος, ον, (a priv., οὐτάω,) *unwounded, not hurt, uninjured.*

Ἀπαισός, οῦ, ἡ, *Ap'æ-sus,* a town of Mys'-i-a.

ἀπάλαλκε, 2 aor. indic. 3 sing. of ἀπαλέξω, f. -αλεξήσω, (ἀπό, ἀλέξω,) *to fend* or *ward off; to defend one from.*

ἀπάλαμνος, ον, (a priv., παλάμη,) *helpless; foolish.*

ἀπαλοιάω, Hom. for -λοάω, (ἀπό, ἀλοάω,) *to thresh out; bruise, mangle, break fine.*

ἀπαλός, ἡ, όν, (deriv. uncertain,) compare Lat. *tener, mollis, delicatus, soft to touch; gentle, delicate, nice.*

ἀπαμείβομαι, f. ψομαι, (ἀπό, ἀμείβω,) Lat. *respondēre, to reply, give answer;* Hom. sometimes adds another word, as ἀπαμειβόμενος προσέφη, A 84, *answering he said.*

ἀπάνευθε(ν), for ἄνευθε, adv., Lat. *procul, far away,* A 35 ; prep. with gen. *away from, without the knowledge of.*

ἅπας, ἅπασα, ἅπαν, (ἅμα, πᾶς,) stronger form for πᾶς, Lat. *cuncti, all, quite all, all together.*

ἀπάτερθε(ν), (ἀπό, ἄτερθε,) adv., *separately,* B 587 ; prep. with gen., *from.*

ἀπάτη, ης, ἡ, Lat. *dolus, cheating, trickishness, dishonesty, deceit;* in a better sense, *craft, shrewdness.*

ἀπατήλος, ἡ, όν, (ἀπάτη,) *deceitful, trickish, wily,* A 526.

ἀπαυράω, not found in the pres., aor. part. ἀπούρας, *to wrest away,* A 356, 430 : Lat. *eripere.*

ἀπειλέω, ῶ, f. ήσω, (ἀπειλή,) ἀπειλήτην for -είτην, 3 du. impf., to menace or threaten, Lat. minari, A 388 ; with the inf., threaten to do anything, A 161 ; to threaten boastingly, boast ; promise.

ἀπεῖπον, a 2 aor., inf. ἀπειπεῖν and Ep. ἀποειπεῖν ; f. -ερῶ ; pf. -είρηκα : (ἀπό, εἶπον :) to speak out, say, tell ; say no, deny, refuse, A 515 ; renounce : for pres. see ἀπόφημι and ἀπαγορεύω.

ἀπειρέσιος, leng. from ἄπειρος, Lat. infinitus, boundless, infinite, vast.

ἀπερείσιος, Hom. for foreg.

ἀπείρων, ον, (a priv., πεῖραρ,) without bounds or number.

ἀπερύκω, (ἀπό, ἐρύκω,) to keep back, drive off.

ἀπέρχομαι, (ἀπό, ἔρχομαι), for parts see ἔρχομαι, to go away ; leave.

ἀπέσσυτο, Ep. 2 aor. from ἀποσεύω.

ἀπεχθαίρω, f. αρῶ, aor. ἀπήθηρα, (ἀπό, ἐχθαίρω,) Lat. odisse, hate intensely, detest, Γ 415 ; to make hateful, render odious.

ἀπεχθάνομαι, f. θήσομαι, 2 aor. ἀπηχθόμην, pf. -ήχθημαι, (ἀπό, ἐχθάνομαι,) to be detested, to be hated ; to be stirred up to hatred and resentment : trans., to cause hatred.

ἀπέχω, f. ἀφέξω, ἀποσχήσω ; 2 aor. ἀπέσχον, (ἀπό, ἔχω,) Lat. prohibēre, to hold off, keep away, avert ; to separate : mid. to absent one's self from, hold one's self aloof from, abstain, Lat. abstinēre ; intrans., to be away from, be absent, be at a distance.

ἀπήμων, ον, ονος, (a priv., πῆμα,) safe, uninjured, A 415 : act., causing no harm, hence propitious, kindly, Lat. prosper.

ἀπήνη, ης, ἡ, a carriage, wagon.

ἀπηνής, ές, harsh, cruel, A 340 ; see Lat. saevus.

ἀπηύρων, impf. and 2 aor. of ἀπαυράω.

ἀπιθέω, ῶ, f. ησω, Hom. for ἀπειθέω, (a priv., πείθω,) disobey.

ἄπιος, ίη, ιον, (ἀπό,) far away, remote, A 270.

ἄπιστος, ον, (a priv., πιστός,) Lat. sine fide, without trustiness, faithless ; incredible : act., distrustful ; disobedient.

ἀπό, Lat. ab and abs, (with the abl.,) prep. with the gen. from ; of place, from, away from ; down from ; ἀφ' ἵππων, on the horses ; far from ; out of ; outside of : origin, from, out of ; cause, because of : of time, from or after : ἀπὸ χειρὸς λογίσασθαι, to reckon off-hand or roughly : in compos., from ; asunder, apart ; away from : adv., far away.

ἀποαιρέομαι, poet. for ἀφαιρέομαι, A 230.

ἀποβαίνω, f. -βήσομαι, for parts see βαίνω, (ἀπό, βαίνω,) Lat. abire, to go away, depart from, A 428 ; step off, dismount, Γ 265, Lat. descendere : to turn out, occur, happen ; issue ; Lat. evenire : also see Lat. evadere : aor. ἀπέβησα is trans., to make to step off or dismount, cause to go out or disembark.

ἀποβάλλω, f. -βαλῶ, 2 aor. ἀπέβαλον, (ἀπό, βάλλω,) Lat. abjicere, to throw off or away, B 183 ; throw away, discard ; reject ; lose, Lat. amittere.

ἀπόβλητος, ον, (ἀποβάλλω,) to be thrown away, rejected, be reckoned as of no account ; despised, B 361, Γ 65.

ἀποδαίω, (ἀπό, δαίω,) to portion out to others, share.

ἀπεδεξάμην, aor. from ἀποδέχομαι.

ἀποδέχομαι, Ion. ἀποδέκομαι, f. -δέξομαι ; for parts see δέχομαι : (ἀπό, δέχομαι:) to accept, be satisfied or content with, A 95 ; admit ; get back.

ἀποδέω, (ἀπό, δέω,) to be deficient, lack.

ἀποδίδωμι, f. -δώσω, aor. ἀπέδωκα, (ἀπό, δίδωμι,) Lat. reddere ; to restore or give back, return, esp. what is one's own or his due, A 98 ; deliver up, Γ 285 ; render ; grant or concede : mid., sell or give away, dispose of.

ἀποδύνω, (ἀπό, δύνω,) to pull, throw, or strip off arms from the slain, B 261 : intrans. in 2 aor. ἀπέδυν : mid., to strip, undress.

ἀποείπον, Ep. for ἀπεῖπον.

ἀποθνήσκω, (ἀπό, θνήσκω,) to die off, diminish, die out.

ἀποθρώσκω, f. -θοροῦμαι, 2 aor. -έθορον, (ἀπό, θρώσκω,) Lat. exsilire, to jump off from ; leap from, B 702 ; leap or rise up from.

ἄποινον, ον, τό, only in pl., recompense, ransom, A 13, 111, B 230 ; price paid for any one, satisfaction, reward.

ἀποκαπύω, (ἀπό, καπύω,) separated by tmesis, to breathe forth.

ἀποκρίνω, (ἀπό, κρίνω,) to put asunder, part ; to select ; to set apart, distinguish.

ἀποκτείνω, (ἀπό, κτείνω,) for parts see κτείνω, to slay, put to death ; cause to be put to death.

ἀπολάμπω, (ἀπό, λάμπω,) to shine ; to reflect, beam, or flash, as from bright metal.

ἀπολήγω, Ep. -λλήγω, (ἀπό, λήγω,) to cease, quit, abandon, desist.

ἀπόλλυμι and ἀπολλύω, f. ἀπολέσ(σ)ω ; aor. ἀπώλεσα, Ep. ἀπόλεσσα ; pf. ἀπώλεκα, (ἀπό, ὄλλυμι,) Lat. perdere, to destroy, kill ; lay waste ; lose : mid. Lat. perire, die ; be lost ; be undone ; disappear ; to be wrecked.

'Απόλλων, ωνος, ὁ, A-pol'-lo, son of Ju'-pi-ter and La-to'-na, brother of Di-a'-na : acco. to Hom., he is the god of soothsaying and of music. He is also the god of prophecy, A 72, and of archery. See Classical Dictionary.

ἀπολυμαίνομαι, f. μανοῦμαι, (ἀπό, λῦμα,) to cleanse one's self in the bath, to bathe, A 313, 314.

ἀπολύω, f. -λυσω, (ἀπό, λύω,) Lat. absolvere, undo, loose one thing from another ; nor released the daughter, A 95 : mid., to redeem for one's self, ransom ; get free ; go away.

ἀπομηνίω, f. ἴσω, (ἀπό, μηνίω,) to be very angry or indignant.

ἀπόμνυμι, *to swear* or *take oath against*.

ἀπομόργνυμι and ἀπομοργνύω, Ep. 3 sing. impf. -μόργνυ, μόρξω, Ep. aor. ἀπομορξάμην, (ἀπό, (ὁ)μόργνυμι,) *to wipe out* or *off, wipe entirely away; wipe clean* : mid. *wipe off from one's self*.

ἀπονάω, (ἀπό, νάω,) aor. ἀπένασ(σ)α, 3 sing. aor. mid. -ενάσ(σ)ατο ; *to send away ; to remove ; to send back* : mid., *withdraw* : pres. obsol.

ἀπονέομαι, (ἀπό, νέομαι,) Ep. word, found only in pres. system, Lat. *redire, to go away, retire ; return, go home*.

ἀπονίνημι, (ἀπό, ὀνίνημι,) f. ἀπονήσω, *to cause one pleasure, give pleasure*.

ἀπονοστέω, f. ήσω, (ἀπό, νοστέω,) *to return home*, A 60, used with ἄψ.

ἀπονόσφι(ν), ἀπὸ νόσφι(ν), ἀπο νόσφι(ν), (ἀπό, νόσφι,) adv., *apart, aloof,* B 233 ; *away:* prep. with gen. *far from, away from,* A 541 : compare Lat. *separatim* and *procul*.

ἀποξέω, (ἀπό, ξέω,) *to cut off*.

ἀποπαύω, f. αύσω, (ἀπό, παύω,) Lat. *reprimere, to check, hinder, to stop :* mid., *restrain thyself,* A 422 ; *desist ;* Lat. *desistere*.

ἀποπέτομαι, f. πτήσομαι, 2 aor. ἀπεπτάμην, (ἀπό, πέτομαι,) Lat. *avolare, to fly off* or *fly away,* B 71.

ἀποπλάζω, (ἀπό, πλάζω,) *to lead* or *keep away from :* pass., *to be kept away from, go away*.

ἀποπνείω, Ep. for -νέω, f. νεύσομαι, (ἀπό, πνέω,) *to breathe out* or *forth, exhale ; to smell*.

ἀποπτάμενος, 2 aor. part. of ἀποπέτομαι.

ἀπὸ ῥῆξε, from ἀπορρήγνυμι.

ἀπόρνυμαι, (ἀπό, ὄρνυμι,) *to set out from*.

ἀπορούω, (ἀπό, ὀρούω,) *to spring away, dart off*.

ἀπορρήγνυμι, (ἀπό, ῥήγνυμι,) *to snap off, break in two parts, break into pieces*.

ἀπορρίπτω, (ἀπό, ῥίπτω,) *to put away ; cast off, put aside*.

ἀπορρώξ, ῶγος, adj., (ἀπορρήγνυμι,) Lat. *praeruptus, abruptus, steep ;* as subst., *a branch,* B 755.

ἀπὸ ἔρριψε, from ἀπορρίπτω.

ἀποσεύω, (ἀπό, σεύω,) *to drive* or *hurry away*.

ἀποστείχω, f. ξω, 2 aor. ἀπέστιχον, (ἀπό, στείχω,) Lat. *abscedere, to go away, depart ; go back, return,* A 522.

ἀποτάμνω, Hom. for ἀποτέμνω, f. τεμῶ, 2 aor. ἀπέταμον, pf. ἀποτέτμηκα, (ἀπό, τέμνω,) Lat. *desecare, to cut from* or *off; cut open,* Γ 292 ; *to separate :* mid., *cut off for one's self* or *for one's own use*.

ἀποτίνω, f. ίσω, (ἀπό, τίνω,) *to pay what is due ; return, pay back,* Γ 286 ; *atone for :* mid., *to avenge one's self,* Lat. *ulcisci*.

ἀποτμήγω, Ep. for ἀποτέμνω, (ἀπό, τέμνω,) to cut off, amputate.

ἀποτρέπω, (ἀπό, τρέπω,) to turn back from, restrain; cause to cease, cease; turn away.

ἀποτρωπάω, Ep. for ἀποτρέπω.

ἀπούρας, Ep. aor. part. from ἀπαυράω.

ἀπουράω = ἀπαυράω, to remove.

ἀπουρίζω, (ἀπό, οὐρίζω,) to lay out bounds.

ἀποφθινύθω, (ἀπό, φθινύθω, poet. φθίνω,) to perish.

ἀποφθίω, Ep. = ἀποφθίνω, (ἀπό, φθίνω,) to perish, die out; trans. inf., to make to perish.

ἀποχέω, (ἀπό, χέω,) to pour out.

ἄπρακτος, ον, Ion. ἄπρηκτος, (a priv., πράσσω,) doing nothing; unprofitable, useless, fruitless, B 121 : also, against which nothing can be done, unavoidable, incurable; impossible.

ἀπριάτην, adv., (a priv., πρίαμαι,) Lat. gratis, for nothing, without ransom, A 99.

ἀπτόλεμος, ον, poet. for ἀπόλεμος, (a priv., πόλεμος,) Lat. imbellis, unwarlike, B 201 ; not to be warred against, unconquerable.

ἅπτω, f. ἅψω ; aor. ἦψα ; pf. ἧμμαι and Ion. ἅμμαι ; aor. pass. ἥφθην and Ep. ἐάφθην : to join or fasten; fasten on to: mid., to fasten one's self to, lay hold of, B 152, cling to; grasp, clasp, A 512 ; attack, touch, Lat. tangere; perceive; reach; gain.

ἀπωθέω, contr. ῶ, f. ἤσω and ώσω ; aor. ἀπέωσα and ἄπωσα, (does Lat. repellere exactly correspond in meaning?) to drive off or away, push back or away, cast off; beat off: mid., drive away from one's self, repel.

ἄρα, Ep. ῥά encl., before a consonant ἄρ, to denote immediate transition, then, immediately, straightway, B 16 ; as explanation; now, now then, next in order; no doubt; the foreg. are Ep. uses, Att. usage = οὖν : joined with causal conj. γάρ ῥα, for indeed, A 113 and 236 ; ὅτι ῥα, because you know, A 56 ; εἴτ' ἄρα, if perhaps, A 65 ; ὡς ἄρα, thus then ; τίς ἄρ, who then? A 8 ; then in due course, A 471.

ἀρά, Hom. ἀρή, ἡ, an invocation, prayer for calamity upon something, imprecation; the answer to this prayer, destruction.

ἀραβέω, (ἄραβος,) to clang, ring.

'Αραιθυρέα, ας, ἡ, A-ræ-thy´-re-a, a city of Ar´-gos, B 571.

ἀράομαι ; f. ἄσομαι, Ion. ἥσομαι, (ἀρά,) pray to a deity, supplicate; implore or vow that a thing may take place; call down upon, hence, curse or call down curses upon, imprecate, Lat. imprecari.

ἀραρίσκω, leng. form of obsol. pres. ἄρω ; f. ἀρῶ, Ion. ἄρσω ; aor. ἦρσα ; 2 aor. ἤραρον, Ep. ἄραρον ; 2 pf. part. ἀραρυίας, Γ 331 ; for forms and trans. and intrans. tenses see Gram.; Lat. aptare, to join together, fit ;

unite; *adapt, fit,* A 136 : intrans. in 2 pf., plup., mid., and pass., 2 pf. part. ἀραρυῖας, *fastened,* Γ 331 ; ἀρήρει, *fit,* Γ 338 ; *to fit,* i. e. *be fitted, fit closely ; to be fitting, proper.*

ἄραρον, see ἀραρίσκω.

ἀργαλέος, α, ον, Lat. *gravis, hard,* A 589 ; *troublesome.*

Ἀργεῖος, α, ον, ("Αργος,) *of Ar'-gos, Ar'-give ;* Ἀργεῖοι, *the Greeks,* A 79.

Ἀργειφόντης, ου, ὁ, ("Αργος, φόντης,) *slayer of Ar'-gos,* see Classical Dictionary ; acco. to some, *swift messenger,* B 103, epith. of Mer'-cu-ry, (ἀργός, φαίνω.)

ἀργεννός, ή, όν, (for ἀργός,) *white,* Γ 198 and 141 ; see difference between Lat. *albus, candidus, albidus.*

ἀργής, ῆτος, adj., poet. dat. and acc. -έτι and -έτα, (ἀργός,) *white, dazzling, bright,* Γ 419 ; of fat, a robe, lightning.

ἀργικέραυνος, ον, (ἀργής, κεραυνός,) *with vivid lightning.*

ἀργινόεις, εσσα, εν, (= ἀργός,) *bright-shining, white,* B 647 and 656 ; applied to cities of Kre'-ta because of the chalk cliffs.

"Αργισσα, ης, ἡ, *Ar-gis'-sa,* a place in Thes'-sa-ly, B 738.

"Αργος, εος, τό, *Ar'-gos,* name of several Gre'-cian towns, prin. one was a town in Ar'-go-lis, B 559 ; also used for the district of Ar'-go-lis and the whole of Pel'-o-pon-ne'-sus ; see Classical Dictionary.

ἀργός, ή, όν, Lat. *candidus, bright, shining ; rapid, fleet,* A 50.

ἀργύρεος, α, ον, (ἄργυρος,) Lat. *argenteus, silver, of silver,* A 219 ; *silver-shining ; silvered.*

ἀργυροδίνης, ου, ὁ, adj., (ἄργυρος, δίνη,) *silver-eddying, silver-rippling,* epith. of streams and running water.

ἀργυρόηλος, ον, (ἄργυρος, ἧλος,) *silver-studded, silver-nailed,* B 45.

ἀργυρόπεζα, ης, ἡ, (ἄργυρος, πέζα,) *silver-footed,* A 538, epith. of The'-tis.

ἄργυρος, ου, ὁ, (ἀργός,) Lat. *argentum, white-metal, silver ; money made from silver.*

ἀργυρότοξος, ον, (ἄργυρος, τόξον,) epith. of A-pol'-lo ; *bearer of the silver bow,* A 37.

ἀργύφεος, ον, (ἄργυρος,) *silver-colored, silver-white.*

ἄργυφος, see ἀργύφεος.

ἀρείων, ον, gen., ονος, irreg. compar. of ἀγαθός, which see ; Lat. *melior, better, braver, more excellent ; stronger.*

ἀρέσθαι, see ἄρνυμι.

ἀρετή, ῆς, ἡ, *goodness, fitness* of anything for its peculiar use ; in Hom. usu. *valor, bravery, courage,* Lat. *virtus.*

ἀρήγω, f. ξω, *to aid, assist,* A 521, 77 ; *to be of service ; to fend off.*

ἀρηγών, όνος, *one that assists.*

ἀρηικτάμενος, ("Αρης, κτείνω,) *killed in battle.*

'Αρήιος, η, ον, Ion. for "Αρειος, ("Αρης,) Lat. *Ma-vor'-ti-us, devoted to Mars, warlike*, B 698.

ἀρηίφιλος, adj., ("Αρης, φίλος,) *dear to Mars, valiant, brave*.

'Αρήνη, ης, ἡ, *A-re'-ne*.

ἀρηρομένος, pf. part. of ἀρόω.

ἄρης, by metonymy *the din of battle*.

"Αρης, gen. "Αρεος or "Αρεως; dat. "Αρεΐ; acc. "Αρη, "Αρην, or "Αρεα; Hom. forms, -ηος, -ηι, "Αρῃ, -ηα: Lat. *Mars, A'-res, god of war, son of Ju'-pi-ter and Ju'-no; war, carnage*.

ἀρητήρ, ἦρος, ὁ, (ἀράομαι,) Lat. *precator, one who prays; a priest*, A 11.

ἀρητός, Ion. for ἀρατός, ή, όν, (ἀράομαι,) *sought in prayer, desired; visited with curses, not blessed, not prospered*.

ἀρι-, streng. prefix.

Αριάδνη, ης, ἡ, *Ari-ad'-ne*.

ἀρίζηλος, adj., Ep. for ἀρίδηλος, (ἀρι-, δῆλος,) Lat. *manifestus, manifest, very manifest, conspicuous*, B 318; see ἄϊζηλος.

ἀριθμέω, ῶ, f. ήσω, (ἀριθμός,) Lat. *numerare, to count*, B 124; *to reckon*.

"Αριμοι, ων, οἱ, *the Ar'-i-mi*, a mythical people of Asia; see Classical Dictionary.

ἀριπρεπής, ές, (ἀρι-, πρέπω,) *very grand, majestic*.

'Αρίσβη, ης, ἡ, *A-ris'-ba*, a town of Tro'-as.

ἀριστερός, ά, όν, Lat. *sinister, left; left-handed, clumsy; ill-fated, inauspicious*, unlucky signs appeared on the left as the augur looked northward.

ἀριστεύς, έως, ὁ, (ἄριστος,) *the best*: Hom. has the pl. ἀριστῆες, *chiefs, heads, principal men, leaders*.

ἀριστεύω, (ἄριστος, irreg. sup. of ἀγαθός,) *to be the best one, be the noblest, be the best in the fight, bravest*.

ἄριστος, η, ον, and ὤριστος, irreg. sup. of ἀγαθός, Lat. *optimus, the best in every way, bravest; most excellent*.

'Αρκαδία, ας, ἡ, *Ar-ca'-di-a*, a district of Pel'-o-pon-ne'-sus.

'Αρκάς, άδος, ὁ, pl. 'Αρκάδες, *Ar-ca'-di-ans*.

'Αρκεσίλαος, ου, ὁ, *Ar-ces'-i-la'-us*, leader of the Bœ-o'-tians.

ἄρκιος, adj., *sure*, B 393; *safe; sufficient*.

ἄρκτος, ου, ὁ and ἡ, *a bear*.

"Αρκτος, the constellation, *Great Bear*.

ἄρμα, ατος, τό, Lat. *currus, a chariot; a chariot and horses or the yoked chariot and horses together; the horses*.

"Αρμα, ατος, τό, *Har'-ma*, a town of Bœ-o'-ti-a, B 499.

ἀρματοπηγός, όν, (ἄρμα, πήγνυμι,) *chariot-building*.

ἄρμενος, aor. part. of ἀραρίσκω.

ἁρμόζω, Dor. ἁρμόσδω; f. ἁρμόσω; aor. ἥρμοσα; pf. ἥρμοκα; aor. pass. ἡρμόσθην: (ἁρμός:) Lat. *adaptare, to fit* or *join together; to bind; to put in order* or *arrange, govern; to* (*fit* or) *give in marriage:* intrans., *to fit, be adapted to, fit well,* Γ 333; *to be fit for:* impersonal, *it is fitting* or *proper,* Lat. *decet:* mid., *to join for one's self, prepare; to join to one's self in marriage, marry.*

ἁρμονία, as, ἡ, (ἁρμόζω,) *a joining together, joint; an agreement, compact; a decree of fate; harmony, agreement.*

Ἁρμονίδης, ου, ὁ, *Har-mon'-i-des.*

ἄρνα, an acc. from obsol. nom.; *a sheep, lamb,* Γ 310, see Lat. *agnus.*

ἀρνειός, οῦ, ὁ, (ἀρνός,) *a young ram,* Γ 197.

Ἄρνη, ης, ἡ, *Ar'-ne,* a town.

ἀροίμην, see ἄρνυμι.

ἀροτήρ, ῆρος, ὁ, (ἀρόω,) *one who ploughs, a tiller of the ground.*

ἄρνυμαι, used only in pres. system, leng. for αἴρομαι; *procure for one's self, obtain; carry off a prize; obtain,* (for another,) Α 159.

ἄρουρα, as, ἡ, (ἀρόω,) Lat. *arvum, seed land, cultivated land; ground,* Γ 115.

Ἄρουρα, as, ἡ, Lat. *Tel'-lus, Earth,* Β 548.

ἀρόω, pf. ἀρήροκα, with Att. redupl., Hom. 3 pl. ἀρόωσι, Lat. *arare, to plough, till, sow; to beget* children.

ἁρπάζω, f. ξω; aor. ἥρπαξα; pf. ἥρπακα; aor. pass. ἡρπάχθην or ἡρπάσθην; 2 aor. pass. ἡρπάγην; pf. ἥρπαγμαι or ἥρπασμαι: Lat. *rapere, to tear, snatch* or *hurry away, carry off; plunder; to seize and overpower; to grasp with the mind, comprehend.*

ἄρρηκτος, ον, (a priv., ῥήγνυμι,) *not to be broken, firm; untiring.*

ἄρσαντες, see ἀραρίσκω.

Ἄρτεμις, ιδος, ἡ, *Ar'-te-mis,* Lat. *Di-a'-na.*

ἀρτιεπής, ες, (ἄρτιος, ἔπος,) *quick at speaking, fluent.*

ἀρτύνω or ἀρτύω; f. ἀρτυνῶ, Ep. ἀρτυνέω, ἀρτύσω; aor. ἤρτυνα, ἤρτυσα; pf. ἤρτυκα; aor. pass. ἠρτύνθην: *to arrange, contrive; put in order, place.*

ἀρχέκακος, ον, (ἄρχω, κακός,) *beginning evil* or *trouble, troublesome.*

Ἀρχέλοχος, ου, ὁ, *Ar-chel'-o-cus.*

ἀρχεύω, f. σω, (ἄρχω,) Lat. *imperare, to rule, command.*

ἀρχή, ῆς, ἡ, Lat. *initium, the first, the origin, beginning;* adv. acc. ἀρχήν *at first,* κατ' ἀρχάς *in the beginning,* οὐκ ἀρχήν *not at first, not at all: the prime principle: power, an empire.*

ἀρχός, οῦ, ὁ, (ἄρχω,) *leader, commander.*

ἄρχω, f. ἄρξω, aor. ἦρξα, 2 pf. ἦρχα, aor. pass. ἤρχθην: the act. is more com. in Hom.; the mid. in Att. prose: Lat. *incipere, to begin* or *be the first*, B 378 ; *to precede, to lead the way*, A 495, Γ 420 : with the gen. *to (make a beginning of) begin ; to lead, command, rule, be leader of*, usu. with gen.: with inf. *begin*, B 84 : with the dat., B 805 : *to commence, begin* : pass., *to be ruled, be under another.*

ἄρω assumed as the obsol. pres. of ἀραρίσκω, which see.

ἀρωγός, όν, (ἀρήγω,) *giving aid, useful : as subst., a protector.*

ἄσαι, aor. from ἄω, which see.

ἄσασθαι, aor. mid. from ἄω, which see.

ἄσβεστος, ον, and η, ον, (a priv., σβεστός,) *unextinguishable*, A 599.

Ἀσίνη, ης, ἡ, *As'-i-ne*, a city of Ar'-go-lis ; also a city of Mes-se'-ni-a.

Ἄσιος, α, ον, *A'-si-a: 'Ασίῳ ἐν λειμῶνι, in the A'-si-an meadow*, B 461 ; from *A'-si-a*, a district in Ly'-di-a ; some say, *the meadow of the hero A'-si-as.*

Ἄσιος, ου, ὁ, *A'-si-us*, an ally of the Tro'-jans.

Ἀσκάλαφος, ου, ὁ, *As-cal'-a-phus.*

Ἀσκανία, ας, ἡ, *As-ca'-ni-a*, a district of Bi-thyn'-i-a.

Ἀσκάνιος, ου, ὁ, *As-ca'-ni-us*, a Tro'-jan ally from As-ca'-ni-a.

ἀσκέω, f. ήσω, pf. ἤσκηκα, *to work out with skill and care, work curiously ; adorn.*

Ἀσκληπιάδης, ου, ὁ, son of *Æs-cu-la'-pi-us.*

Ἀσκληπιός, οῦ, ὁ, *As-cle'-pi-os*, a prince of Thes'-saly, a famous physician.

ἀσκός, ὁ, Lat. *uter*, *a leathern bottle.*

ἀσπαίρω, Ion. impf. ἀσπαίρεσκον, (a euphon., σπαίρω,) Lat. *palpitare, to gasp, struggle for air.*

ἀσπερχές, (a euph., σπέρχω,) adv., *hurriedly, hastily, with hot haste, rapidly.*

ἄσπετος, ον, (a priv., εἰπεῖν,) *unspeakable, indescribable ; enormously great.*

ἀσπιδιώτης, ου, ὁ, (ἀσπίς,) *one having a shield, warrior*, B 554.

ἀσπίς, ίδος, ἡ, Lat. *clipeus*, *a round shield*, it was made of hides covered by plates ; *a body of armed men or soldiers, a troop.*

ἀσπιστής, οῦ, ὁ, (ἀσπίς,) *carrying-shield, soldier, warrior.*

Ἀσπληδών, όνος, ἡ, *As-ple'-don.*

ἀσπουδί, (a priv., σπουδή,) *without zeal* or *eagerness* to fight and defend one's self ; *dishonorably.*

ἄσσα, Ion. for ἄτινα, *whatever.*

ἄσσον, compar. of ἄγχι, *nearer ;* also, ἀσσοτέρω.

ἄσταχυς, υος, ὁ, (leng. for στάχυς,) *ear of corn, ear of wheat.*

ἀστεμφής, ές, (a priv., στέμβω,) see Lat. *immotus, firmus, unmoved, unyielding, immovable, firm*, Γ 219, B 344.

Ἀστέριον, ου, τό, *As-te'-ri-um*, a town of Thes'-sa-ly.

ἀστερόεις, εσσα, εν, (ἀστήρ,) *abounding in stars, starry ; shining, sparkling.*

ἀστεροπητής, οῦ, ὁ, Lat. *fulminator, lightener,* A 580.

ἀστήρ, -έρος, ὁ, Lat. *stella, a star; any heavenly luminous body,* Lat. *astrum.*

ἀστράπτω, f. ψω, (ἀστραπή,) *to gleam, lighten,* B 353 ; both trans. and intrans.

ἄστυ, εος and εως, τό, *city, town.*

'Αστυάναξ, ακτος, ὁ, *As-ty'-a-nax, (lord of the city,)* a son of Hec'-tor.

ἀστυβοώτης, ου, ὁ, (ἄστυ, βοάω,) *shouting throughout the city.*

'Αστύνοος, ου, ὁ, *As-ty'-no-us,* one of the Tro'-jans.

'Αστυόχεια, ας, ἡ, *As'-ty-o-chi'-a.*

'Αστυόχη, ης, ἡ, *As-ty'-oche.*

ἀσύφηλος, ον, *low, mean, bad, not respected* or *honored ; disrespectful, treating with dishonor.*

ἀσφάραγος, ου, ὁ, (a euph., σφάραγος,) *the throat, the œsophagus.*

ἀσχαλάω, a defective verb, Ep. 3 sing. ἀσχαλάᾳ, *to be indignant, grieved, vexed,* B 297 ; in Hom. with gen.

ἄσχετος, ον, (a priv., σχεῖν,) *cannot be stopped* or *held in, not to be repressed, irresistible.*

ἀτάλαντος, ον, (a copul., τάλαντον,) *balancing, equal in weight.*

ἀταλάφρων, ον, (ἀταλός, φρήν,) *tender-hearted, gentle, harmless.*

ἀταλός, ή, όν, *delicate, soft, dainty,* Lat. *tener.*

ἀτάρ, Ep. αὐτάρ, Lat. *at, but, however ;* for δέ after μέν, A 166.

ἀτάρβητος, ον, (a priv., ταρβέω,) Lat. *intrepidus, fearless,* Γ 63.

ἀταρπιτός, οῦ, ἡ, *a way, narrow way, track, path.*

ἀταρτηρός, όν, *baneful, hurtful,* A 223.

ἀτασθαλία, ας, ἡ, (ἀτάσθαλος,) *indiscretion, folly ; wickedness.*

ἀτάσθαλος, ον, *rash, careless.*

ἀτειρής, ές, (a priv., τείρω,) *not to be worn out, firm, hard ; untiring ; stubborn ; durable, unyielding.*

ἀτέλεστος, ον, (a priv., τελέω,) *to no purpose, without result ; fruitless ; unfinished.*

ἀτελεύτητος, ον, (a priv., τελευτάω,) *unfinished, not coming to an end ; endless ; not to be performed,* A 527.

ἄτερ, prep. with gen. *without, besides, except ; apart* or *away from.*

ἄτη, ης, ἡ, (ἀάω,) *delusion, infatuation,* B 111 ; *hurt, mischief, ruin.*

ἀτιμάζω, f. άσω, aor. ἠτίμασα, pf. ἠτίμακα, aor. pass. ἠτιμάσθην, (a priv., τιμάω,) *to treat with dishonor, esteem lightly, slight : spurn, neglect, treat disrespectfully.*

ἀτιμάω, f. ήσω, aor. ἠτίμησα, pf. ἠτίμηκα, aor. pass. ἠτιμήθην, (a priv., τιμάω,) Lat. *inhonorare, to dishonor, maltreat.*

ἄτιμος, ον, (a priv., τιμή,) *unhonored, despised ;* with gen., *deprived of the honor ; without compensation.*

ἄτος, ον, *insatiable.*

'Ατρείδης, ου, ὁ, *son of A'-treus;* Ag-a-mem'-non and Men-e-la'-us were the sons of A'-treus, A 7.

'Ατρείων, ωνος, ὁ, A 387, B 192, see foreg.

ἀτρεκής, ές, (a priv. τρέω,) *real, certain, true; strict, exact; upright;* -εως, adv., *truly.*

ἀτρέμα(s), (a priv., τρέμω,) adv., *without trembling, calmly,* B 200.

'Ατρεύς, έως, ὁ, *A'-treus,* son of Pe'-lops and father of Ag-a-mem'-non and Men-e-la'-us.

ἄτρομος, ον, (a priv., τρέμω,) *without fear, intrepid.*

ἀτρύγετος, adj., (a priv., τρυγάω,) Lat. *infructuosus, sterilis, bringing forth no fruit, unfruitful, barren,* A 316.

'Ατρυτώνη, ης, ἡ, leng. for ἀτρύτη, (a priv., τρύω,) *the Unwearied One,* Min-er'-va.

ἀτύζομαι, *to be blinded* or *bewildered.*

'Ατυμνιάδης, ου, ὁ, *son of A-tym'-ni-us.*

αὖ, adv., Lat. *porro, vicissim, again, on the other hand, now,* B 493, Γ 323, *moreover, besides, in turn; again, anew, once more; back, backwards,* Lat. *retrorsum.*

Αὐγειαί, ῶν, αἱ, *Au-ge'-æ.*

αὐγή, ῆς, ἡ, Lat. *splendor, bright light, radiance;* pl., *beams of the sun.*

Αὐγηιάδης, ου, ὁ, *son of Au-gi'-as, A-gas'-the-nes,* B 624.

αὐδάω, f. ήσω; aor. ηὔδησα, poet. iter. 3 sing. αὐδήσασκε; (αὐδή,) *to speak; say; to tell, order; accost, address.*

αὐδή, ῆς, ἡ, Lat. *vox, the voice, a tone.*

αὐερύω, aor. αὐέρυσα, (αὖ, ἐρύω,) *to draw back; to draw back* the victim's head so as to thrust in the knife, A 459.

αὖθι = αὐτόθι, adv., *on the spot, immediately; there.*

αὐλή, ῆς, ἡ, *the open airy court before a dwelling, court yard; a court* or *hall; the inner court; the dwelling.*

Αὐλίς, ίδος, ἡ, *Au'-lis.*

αὐλός, οῦ, ὁ, *a wind instrument; a jet* or *spirt of blood; a socket.*

αὐτάρ, Ep. for ἀτάρ, conj., *but, yet, still; besides.*

αὖτε, adv., Lat. *autem, again, moreover, but; also, likewise,* B 407, Γ 180; *again, hereafter, at another time,* A 340; *again.*

ἀυτή, ῆς, ἡ, (ἀύω,) *cry, shout,* B 153; *battle-shout;* does Lat. *clamor* correspond to this?

αὐτῆμαρ, (αὐτός, ἦμαρ,) adv., Lat. *eodem die, on the same day.*

αὐτίκα, (αὐτός,) adv., Lat. *mox, forthwith, immediately, instantly.*

αὖτις, a leng. Ion. form for αὖ, adv., *again; back, back again, once more, anew, afresh,* A 518; *hereafter.*

ἀυτμή, ῆς, ἡ, (αὔω,) *the breath, that which is breathed out.*

αὐτόθι = αὐτοῦ, adv., Lat. *istic*, *there, on that very spot.*

αὐτοκασίγνητος, ου, ὁ, (αὐτός, κασίγνητος,) Lat. *frater germanus, an own brother*, Γ 238.

αὐτόματος, adj., Lat. *spontaneus, acting of one's own accord, unbidden, of one's own accord*, B 408 ; *of one's or it's self;* hence *accidental :* see Eng. *automaton.*

Αὐτομέδων, οντος, ὁ, (αὐτός, μέδων,) *Au-tom'-e-don*, stric. *ruling one's self*, charioteer of *A-chil'-les.*

αὐτός, ή, ό, pron. *self;* usu. in oblique cases *him, her, it*, Lat. *ille ;* foll. the article, *the same ; self* or *soul* as opp. to the body ; *self, one's self*, as opp. to others, Lat. *ipse ; alone ; of one's self ;* compar. and sup., *more himself, his very self :* in compo., *of itself, of one's self, native ; just, exactly, the very ; alone ; together with.*

αὐτοῦ, adv., Lat. *illico, place, on the very spot.*

αὔτως, (αὐτός,) adv., Lat. *sic, hoc modo, just so, so in this very way : thus ; just so, no different ; as it was.*

αὐχήν, ενος, ὁ, *the neck ;* also, *narrows* of any kind, whether of land or water, *pass of a mountain.*

αὔω, f. ἀύσω, aor. ἤυσα, Lat. *clamare, to shout, to call out ; sound ; call upon.*

ἀφαιρέω, f. ήσω, 2 aor. ἀφεῖλον, pf. ἀφῄρηκα, aor. pass. ἀφῃρέθην, (ἀπό, αἱρέω,) Lat. *detrahere, to take away from ; to take away :* mid., *to take away for one's own benefit, carry off, to seize and take to one's self ; to rob* or *deprive of.*

ἀφαμαρτάνω, (ἀπό, ἁμαρτάνω,) *to fail to hit, to strike away from the mark, miss, not accomplish.*

ἀφαμαρτοεπής, ές, (ἀφαμαρτάνω, ἔπος,) *missing the subject, speaking at random*, Γ 215.

ἄφαρ, adv., Lat. *statim, continuo, at once, forthwith, instantly ; quickly ; thereupon ; continuously.*

ἄφενος, εος, τό, *wealth, possessions, riches.*

ἄφθιτος, adj., (α priv., φθίω = φθίνω,) Lat. *incorruptibilis, unwasting, imperishable.*

ἀφίημι, impf. ἠφίουν or ἠφίειν, ἠφίει, ἦφιε for Ep. ἀφίει, 3 pl. ἠφίουν or ἠφίεσαν ; f. ἀφήσω ; aor. ἀφῆκα, Ep. ἀφέηκα ; 2 aor. ἀφῆν ; pf. ἀφεῖκα ; aor. pass. ἀφείθην : Lat. *emittere, to send forth, hurl*, as of weapons, Γ 317 ; *to dismiss* or *send away*, A 25, B 263, *let go ; to discharge ; throw away ;* compare with Lat. *dimittere, to set free ; to reject ; leave off ; permit :* apparently intrans., (in reality an object is understood,) *to break up* and *march* or *sail :* mid., *to send forth from one's self ; to loose one's self from.*

ἀφικάνω, (ἀπό, ἱκάνω,) *to come to, reach, arrive at.*

ἀφικνέομαι, f. ἀφίξομαι, αορ. ἀφικόμην, (ἀπό, ἱκνέομαι,) *to come to, reach.*

ἀφίστημι, for parts see ἵστημι, (ἀπό, ἵστημι,) *to put away from, put aside; put on one side* or *weigh out; to remove; to repel* or *drive away:* intrans., (for trans. and. intrans. tenses sec ἵστημι,) *to be away* or *stand off; stand aloof; to withdraw,* Γ 33 *; to stand back.*

ἀφνειός, adj., (ἄφενος,) *wealthy; rich.*

ἀφορμάω, f. ήσω, (ἀπό, ὁρμάω,) compare Lat. *proficisci, to cause to start:* intr. *to rush forth, start from a place;* ναῦφιν ἀφορμηθεῖεν, *set out from the ships,* B 794.

ἀφραδής, ές, (a priv., φραδής,) *thoughtless, inconsiderate; unreflecting:* adv., έως, *foolishly.*

ἀφραδία, as, ἡ, compare Lat. *imprudentia, temeritas, stultitia, thoughtlessness, folly, ignorance.*

ἀφραίνω, (a priv., φρήν,) *to be without mind,* B 258.

'Αφροδίτη, ης, ἡ, (ἀφρός,) *the Ro'-man Ve'-nus, Aph-ro-di'-te,* daughter of Jupiter, the goddess of love and beauty ; she came forth from the sea foam : as com. noun, *love, desire; passion; beauty.*

ἀφρός, οῦ, ὁ, *froth, foam,* as of the sea.

ἄφρων, ον, gen. ονος, (a priv., φρήν,) Lat. *amens,* *mad, senseless, foolish; dull.*

ἄφυλλος, ον, (a priv., φύλλον,) *without leaves,* B 425.

ἀφύσσω, f. ύξω ; αορ. ήφυσα, Ep. ἄφυσσα; *to draw liquids from a vessel; to pour* or *heap up, acquire, get gain,* A 171 : mid., *to draw* or *pour out for one's self.*

'Αχαιίς, ίδος, ἡ, also used as adj., *A-cha'-ia,* A 254, Γ 75 *; an A-cha'-ian woman.*

'Αχαιός, ά, όν, Lat. *A-chi'-vus, A-cha'-ian ;* as subst., 'Αχαιοί, *A-cha'-ians, the Greeks.*

'Αχελώιος, Hom. for 'Αχελῷος, ου, ὁ, *Ach-e-lo'-us,* name of a river.

ἀχέω, (ἄχος,) *to sorrow, mourn.*

'Αχιλλεύς, έως, ὁ, Ep. 'Αχιλεύς, Ep. gen. ῆος ; *A-chil'-les,* son of Pe'-leus and hero of the Il'-i-ad.

ἀχλύς, ύος, ἡ, *a fog* or *mist, dim light, darkness.*

ἄχνυμαι, (ἄχος,) Lat. *dolēre, mourn.*

ἄχος, εος, τό, see Lat. *dolor, pain, grief;* ἄχεος νεφέλη, *a cloud of sorrow.*

ἀχρεῖος, ον, Ion. ἀχρήιος, adj., (a priv., χρεία,) *of no use* or *profit:* neu. = adv., *foolishly,* B 269 *; without motive.*

ἄχρι(s), (ἄρκος,) adv., *utterly:* conj., *until,* Lat. *donec:* prep. with gen., *until, as far as, up to.*

ἄψ, adv., *back; backwards; again;* compare Lat. *retro, retrorsum, rursus, iterum.*

ἄψορρος, ον, contd. for ἀψόρροος, (ἄψ, ῥέω,) *flowing backwards.*

ἄω, *to satiate.*

ἄωρτο, Ep. plup. pass. of ἀείρω.

B.

βαθυλήϊος, ον, (βαθύς, λήϊον,) *having deep* or *tall grain, fruitful, rich in crops.*

βαθύς, εῖα, Ion. έα, ύ, Lat. *altus, profundus, high, deep; deep, thick, abundant, luxuriant.*

βαίνω; f. βήσω, βήσομαι; aor. ἔβησα; more com. 2 aor. ἔβην; pf. βέβηκα; aor. pass. ἐβάθην: Ep. forms, f. βέομαι or βείομαι; 2 aor. 3 sing. βῆ, subj. βείω, 3 sing. βήῃ, inf. βήμεναι; pf. 3 pl. βεβάασι or βεβᾶσι, inf. βεβάμεν, part. βεβαώς, βεβαυῖα, *to go, move; to step, walk;* with inf. *to set out* or *start to do anything;* pf. has the sense of *being permanently settled and established in a place, be settled, stand;* nine years have passed and gone, B 134; the *motion* may be often indicated by a part., B 302, 665, *went bearing, went fleeing;* B 339, *whither shall both covenants and oaths go? (what shall become of?);* Γ 262, *to mount;* with μετά and acc., *to go after anything;* with ἀμφί, *guard:* causal in f. and aor., *cause to go.*

βάλλω; f. βαλῶ, Ion. βαλέω; 2 aor. ἔβαλον; pf. βέβληκα; aor. pass. ἐβλήθην; mid. impf. Ion. 3 sing. βαλλέσκετο; Ep. 2 aor. 3 sing. ἔβλητο, subj. βλήεται, 2 sing. opt. βλεῖο, Ion. imperat. βαλεῦ, βλήμενος; pf. Ion. 3 pl. βεβλήαται: Lat. *jacere, to throw, cast, hurl; hit; strike, to push; to let fall, shed:* intrans., *to fall:* mid. *throw around one's self,* Γ 334; *to cast about* or *weigh with one's self, deliberate.*

βάν and ἔβαν, Ep. for ἔβησαν.

βαρβαρόφωνος, ον, (βάρβαρος, φωνή,) *speaking a foreign language,* B 867.

βαρύνω, (βαρύς,) *to load with a heavy load, burden; to trouble, distress.*

βαρύς, εῖα, ύ, Lat. *gravis, heavy, grievous; troublesome; impressive; strong.*

βαρυστενάχων, ουσα, ον, (βαρύς, στενάχω,) *sorrowing bitterly,* Α 364.

βασιλεύς, έως, Ion. ῆος, ὁ, acc. -λέα, Ion. nom. pl., βασιλῆες, Lat. *rex, king, prince;* it is also used as adj., as in Γ 170, hence can be compared.

βασιλεύω, f. σω, Lat. *regnare, to be king, reign, govern,* B 206; with dat., *to be king over.*

βασιληΐς, ΐδος, fem. adj., *regal, kingly.*

βάσκε, imperat. of βάσκω, βάσκ' ἴθι, *hasten,* B 8.

Βατίεια, ας, ἡ, *Ba-ti-e'-a,* a hill before Troy, B 813.

βεβρωκώς, see βιβρώσκω.

βείω, Ep. 2 aor. subj. for βῶ, see βαίνω.

βέλεμνον, ου, τό, see βέλος.

Βελλεροφόντης, ου, ὁ, *Bel-ler'-o-phon.*

βέλος, εος, τό, Hom. βέλεμνον, (βάλλω,) *that which is hurled, a dart, a missile,* Lat. *jaculum.*

βέλτερος, poet. for βελτίων, compar. of ἀγαθός.

βένθος, εος, τό, Hom. for βάθος, (βαθύς,) *depth;* compare Lat. *fundus, profunditas.*

βηλός, οῦ, ὁ, (βαίνω,) *threshold.*

βῆσσα, ης, ἡ, (βαίνω,) (does Lat. *saltus* have the same meaning?) *a wooded valley, a mountain glade, a glen,* in the *glens* of a mountain, Γ 34.

Βῆσσα, ης, ἡ, *Bes'-sa,* a Lo'-cri-an city, Β 532.

βία, as, ἡ, Ion. βίη, *force, strength,* of body, compare Lat. *vis; by force,* Α 430; *Hercules,* Β 658; *Priam,* Γ 105.

βιάω, Ep. for βιάζω, *to compel, force; overpower; to act with violence towards, maltreat.*

βιβάω, Hom. for βαίνω, *to stride along.*

βιβρώσκω; f. βρώσομαι; aor. ἔβρωσα, 2 aor. ἔβρων; pf. βέβρωκα; aor. pass. ἐβρώθην; pf. part. is often short. to βεβρώς: *to eat, devour, entirely consume; to gnaw with teeth; to partake, eat.*

βιός, οῦ, ὁ, Lat. *arcus, bow.*

βλάβεν, see βλάπτω.

βλάπτω, f. βλάψω, aor. ἔβλαψα, 2 pf. βέβλαφα, aor. pass. ἐβλάφθην, 2 aor. pass. ἐβλάβην; Ep. forms, pres. mid. 3 sing. βλάβεται, aor. βλάψα, 2 aor. pass. 3 pl. βλάβεν: *to obstruct, prevent, hinder, deter, arrest, check; to weaken, harm, injure; to deceive.*

βλή–, aor. mid. from βάλλω, which see.

βλώσκω, for parts, etc., see Hadley and Allen's Grammar: *to go or come.*

Βοάγριος, ου, ὁ, *Bo-a'-gri-us,* a river of Lo'-cris, Β 533.

βοάω; Ep. 3 pl. βοόωσιν, part. βοόων, Β 198; f. βοήσω; ἐβόησα, Ion. ἔβωσα; pf. βεβόηκα; aor. pass. ἐβοήθην, Ion. ἐβώσθην: (βοή:) see Lat. *vociferari, boare, to cry out* from emotion, *shout; to sound, howl; to echo:* trans., *call some one; to proclaim in a loud voice.*

βόεος or βόειος, α, ον, (βοῦς,) *of oxen, ox-,* of *or from an ox.*

βοή, ῆς, ἡ, *a loud shout* or *cry of joy* or *sorrow; war-cry; cry of pain;* βοὴν ἀγαθός, *good at the battle-shout, brave.*

Βοίβη, ης, ἡ, *Bœ'-be,* a town in Thes'-sa-ly; Βοιβηῒς λίμνη, *Bœ-be'-an lake,* Β 711, 712.

Βοιώτιος, and -τός, οῦ, ὁ, *a Bœ-o'-tian.*

βοόω, Ep. for βοάω.

βορέης, contr. -ρῆς, Ion. for βοράς, ου, ὁ, *the north wind;* by metonymy, *the north:* personified, *North Wind.*

βόσκω, Lat. *pascere, to feed; to put out to pasture, supply with fodder* or *grass, nourish.*

βοτόν, οῦ, τό, (βόσκω,) that which must be fed and cared for, a domestic animal, a beast.

βοτρυδόν, (βότρυς,) adv., like a cluster of grapes, in a swarm, B 89.

βότρυς, υος, ὁ, (does Lat. racemus have the same meaning as this word?) a grape-cluster.

βου–, in compds. it expresses the idea of greatness.

βούβρωστις, εως, ἡ, (βου-, βιβρώσκω,) insatiable appetite, unnatural desire for food.

βουβών, ῶνος, ὁ, the depressed part of the body just below the belly and above the leg, Lat. inguen.

βουλεύω, f. σω, (βουλή,) see Lat. consultare, deliberare, to take counsel, deliberate, discuss plans; in past tenses, to determine what had previously been considered; consult, A 531; to be of one counsel, B 379; to be in a council.

βουλή, ῆς, ἡ, Lat. consilium, will, purpose, intent; plan, design, A 5, B 340; advice, counsel, B 55: Lat. concilium, council, assembly.

βουληφόρος, ον, (βουλή, φέρω,) counsel-bearing, A 144; advising.

βούλομαι, f. βουλήσομαι, aor. pass. ἐβουλήθην, Lat. velle, to wish, desire; be willing; to prefer, choose, Lat. malle.

βουπλήξ, ῆγος, (βοῦς, πλήσσω,) a goad for driving oxen.

Βουπράσιον, ου, τό, Bu-pra′-si-um, a city of E′-lis.

βοῦς, ὁ, and **ἡ;** gen. **βόος;** acc. **βοῦν,** Ep. **βῶν, βόα;** Hom. dat. pl. **βόεσσι** and acc. **βόας:** Lat. bos, a cow, bullock, ox; pl. cattle; shield covered with ox-hide.

βοῶπις, ιδος, ἡ, (βοῦς, ὤψ,) ox-eyed, large-eyed, beautiful.

βρέμω, to roar, B 210; to clash.

Βριάρεως, ὁ, a giant called by gods Bri-a′-reus, by men Æ-gæ′on, A 403: lit. Strong One.

βριερός, ή, όν, Ion. of βριαρός, (βριάω,) strong, robust.

βρίθω, to be weighed down or be heavy with weight.

Βρισεύς, Ion. gen. ῆος, ὁ, Bri-sæ′-us, priest and father of Hip′-po-da-mi′-a, A 302.

Βρισηίς, ίδος, ἡ, daughter of Bri-sæ′-us, Hip′-po-da-mi′-a, A 184.

βροτόεις, εσσα, εν, (βροτός,) spattered or covered with blood, bloody.

βροτολοιγός, ον, (βροτός, λοιγός,) ruinous to mortals or men.

βροτός, οῦ, ὁ, a mortal; as adj., Lat. mortalis, mortal, app. to a god.

Βρυσειαί, ῶν, αἱ, Bry-se′-æ, a town of La-co′-ni-a; in B 583, some texts read Βρυσεάς.

βωμός, οῦ, ὁ, (βαίνω,) mound, step, stand; a raised place on which to place the sacrifice, altar.

Βῶρος, ου, ὁ, Bo′-rus.

βωτιάνειρα, ας, adj., (βόσκω, ἀνήρ,) man-nourishing, fruitful.

Γ.

γαῖα, Hom. for γῆ, Ep. gen. ης, ἡ, Lat. *terra, earth, ground,* A 245; *land, country,* A 254; is it equal to Lat. *tellus?*

γαίω, *to exult;* used in part. with dat., κύδεῖ γαίων, *exulting in his strength,* A 405.

γάλοως, οω, ἡ, Lat. *glos, a sister-in-law;* -ῳ dat. sing. and nom. pl.

γαμβρός, οῦ, ὁ, (γάμος,) *a marriage connection* in opp. to connection by natural ties, *son-in-law,* etc.

γάμος, οv, ὁ, *a marriage; the married state.*

γάρ, conj., Lat. *enim, for, since, as,* never the first word in the sentence; it is used to introduce a reason or explanation, — *what, why, O that:* γάρ is often used in questions and wishes to express a *vague idea of uncertainty* that the question or wish explains; also, to strengthen the wish or question.

γαστήρ, τέρος, ἡ, *the belly.*

γέ, encl. particle, Lat. *quidem,* has many meanings, which are often difficult to render; *at all events, at least; true; well, then; indeed, too; even;* γέ is often used to strengthen an oath; used with pronouns, as ὅγε, which see.

γέγαα, Ep. 2 pf. of γίγνομαι, Ep. part. γεγαώς, B 866.

γέγωνα, 2 pf. from poet. stem γων with present sense; see Grammar: *to speak audibly, shout, call out and be heard; to be heard, sound; to proclaim* or *declare, publish.*

γείνεαι, Ep. for γείνηαι, aor. mid. subj. of foll.

γείνομαι, Lat. *nasci, to be born;* aor. *to bring forth; beget;* Lat. *gignere.*

γελάω; Ep. parts, pres. γελόω, pres. part. όωντες, ώοντες, impf. γελοίων, or γελώων; aor. pass. ἐγελάσθην: Lat. *rideri, to laugh, laugh at, deride,* B 270.

γελοίος, Ep. for γέλοιος, adj., (γέλως,) Lat. *ridiculus, laughable, causing laughter,* B 215; *humorous, sportive.*

γέλως, ωτος, ὁ, Ep. dat. γέλῳ, Ep. acc. γέλω, (γελάω,) Lat. *risus, laughter, a laugh; joke.*

γενεή, ῆς, ἡ, (γίγνομαι,) Ion. for γενεά, *birth; descent, origin, birth,* B 707; *generation,* A 250; *race; descendants.*

γενέθλη, ης, ἡ, *origin, birth, stock, original stock; birth-place* or *place from which anything comes, home.*

γένειον, ου, τό, (γένυς,) Lat. *mentum, the chin.*

γενετή, τῆς, ἡ, (γίγνομαι,) *birth.*

γένος, εος, τό, (γίγνομαι,) Lat. *genus, race, lineage, family, generation;*

birth, age, Γ 215, similar to Lat. *aetas; nation; generation; kind; sex, gender.*

γέντο, only this form is found, *he seized* or *took.*

γεραιός, ά, όν, (γέρων,) Lat. *senex, old, aged, venerable; the venerable old man,* A 35: irreg. compar. and sup., γεραίτερος, γεραίτατος.

γέρανος, ου, ή, *crane,* Γ 3.

γεραρός, ά, όν, (γεραίρω, γέρων,) compar. Lat. *venerandus, augustus, reverend, august,* Γ 170, 211.

γέρας, αος, τό, nom. pl. Ep. γέρα contr. from γέρεα, Lat. *praemium, reward, prize, gift of honor,* A 118, 167; *prerogative;* γέρας θανόντων, *last honors of the dead.*

Γερήνιος, ου, ό, *Ge-re′-ni-an,* applied to *Nestor,* from Ge-re′-ni-a the city of his birth, B 336.

γερούσιος, a, ον, (γέρων,) *of old men, belonging to old men.*

γέρων, οντος, ό, Lat. *senex, old man,* A 358, *an elder, principal one; a member of the council,* Lat. *senator;* adj. *old, aged.*

γέφυρα, as, ή, *a dam* or *dike, mound of earth; space between two hostile lines of battle.*

Γῆ, ῆς, ή, Lat. *Tellus, Earth.*

γηθέω, f. ήσω, 2 pf. γέγηθα, (γαίω,) Lat. *gaudēre, rejoice.*

γηθοσύνη, ης, ή, (γηθέω,) *gladness, delight.*

γῆρας, αος, dat. γήραϊ, τό, compare Lat. *senecta, senectus, old age.*

γηράσκω and γηράω; f. άσω; aor. ἐγήρασα; 2 aor. ἐγήραν; pf. γεγήρακα: (γῆρας:) Lat. *senescere, to begin to grow old* or *aged, show marks of age; to become infirm from old age:* trans. in aor., *cause to grow old and infirm.*

γίγνομαι, f. γενήσομαι; 2 aor. ἐγενόμην, iter. 3 sing. (ἐ)γενέσκετο; pf. γεγένημαι; 2 pf. γέγονα, Ep. γέγαα, pl. γέγαμεν, γεγάατε, γεγάασι, inf. γεγάμεν; aor. pass. ἐγενήθην: *to have been born, be alive, to become, come to pass, to be; to be born,* Lat. *nasci; to occur; was* or *arose,* A 49; *to be,* Lat. *esse;* compare Lat. *gigni, oriri, fieri.*

γιγνώσκω; f. γνώσομαι; 2 aor. ἔγνων, sub. γνῶ, -ῷς, -ῷ, Ep. subj. γνώω, opt. γνοίην, imperat. γνῶθι, inf. γνῶναι, Ep. γνώμεναι, part. γνούς; pf. ἔγνωκα; aor. pass. ἐγνώσθην: Lat. *noscere, to see, perceive, obtain knowledge of, know; to discover, understand; to mark;* with the gen. *know of; form an opinion; to decree.*

γλάγος, εος, τό, (γάλα,) Lat. *lac, milk.*

Γλαῦκος, ου, ό, *Glau′-cus,* leader of the Ly′-ci-ans.

γλαυκῶπις, ιδος, acc. -ιδα and -ιν, ή, (γλαυκός, ὤψ,) *with blue eyes;* as epith. of Mi-ner′-va, *fierce eyed.*

Γλαφυραί, ων, αί, *Glaph′-y-ræ,* a town of Thes′-sa-ly, B 712.

γλαφυρός, ά, όν, (γλάφω,) *hollowed; deep; smoothed, well-wrought.*

Γλίσας, αντος, ή, *Gli′-sas,* a city of Bœ-o′-ti-a.

3

γλουτός, οῦ, ὁ, *the buttock.*

γλυκύς, εῖα, ύ, Lat. *dulcis, sweet, agreeable to the taste,* A 598; *agreeable, pleasing, sweet,* A 249, B 453, compare Lat. *acceptus, gratus, jucundus, dulcis; dear; kind-hearted, gentle :* compar. reg. ; also irreg., γλυκίων, γλύκιστος.

γλυφίς, ίδος, ἡ, *the notch at the end of an arrow, an arrow.*

γλῶσσα, ης, ἡ, Lat. *lingua, tongue,* B 489; *language, dialect,* B 804.

γνύξ, (γόνυ,) adv., *with bended knee.*

γνῶ, -ῷς, -ῷ, 2 aor. subj. of γιγνώσκω, which see.

γνωτός, adj., (γιγνώσκω,) Lat. *notus, known;* as subst., *friend, one that is known,* Lat. *cognatus,* Γ 174.

γοάω ; Ep. forms, pres. inf. γοήμεναι, part. γοόων, impf. ἔγοον and γοάσκον, (γόος,) *to mourn, wail;* also, *to mourn for* anything.

γονή, ῆς, ἡ, (γίγνομαι,) *a young one, a child; progeny, race; birth;* also, *the womb whence the race originates.*

Γονόεσσα, ης, ἡ, Go-no-es'-sa.

γόνος, ὁ or ἡ, (γίγνομαι,) *a young one, a child, anything that has been begotten; birth; race; anything that is produced by natural growth from a parent germ.*

γόνυ, -νατος, τό; nom., acc., and voc. sing. γόνυ, all other cases are from stem γονατ: Ep. forms, except nom., acc., and voc. sing., are from stem γουν: Ion. and poet. forms, with these exceptions, are from stem γουνατ : Lat. *genu, the knee.*

γόος, ου, ὁ, *a demonstration of grief, weeping, moaning.*

Γόρτυν, υνος, ἡ, Gor'-tyn, a city of Crete.

γουνάζομαι, f. άσομαι, (γόνυ,) *to clasp the knees of another in passionate entreaty;* Lat. *supplicare, to implore, supplicate, beseech.*

Γουνεύς, έως, ὁ, Gu'-ne-us, leader of the Æ-ni-a'-nes, B 748.

γουνός, οῦ, ὁ, Ion. (γόνος,) Lat *uber, fertile land.*

Γραῖα, ας, ἡ, Græ'-a, a town of Bœ-o'-ti-a, B 498.

γράφω ; f. ψω ; aor. ἔγραψα ; 2 pf. γέγραφα, mid. γέγραμμαι ; aor. pass. ἐγράφθην, 2 aor. pass. ἐγράφην : Lat. *scribere, to mark, engrave, mark with a sharp instrument,* also, *mark with a pencil* or *brush, draw, draft, write, write down.*

γρηῦς and γρηύς, gen. γρηός, Ion. and poet. for γραῦς, γραός, ἡ, *old woman,* Lat. *anus.*

γύαλον, ου, τό, *a hollow* or *depression; hollow in the land, a valley; hollow of the hand;* Hom. applies it to armor.

Γυγαίη λίμνη, *the* Gy-gæ'-an Lake ; *nymph of this lake,* B 865.

γυῖον, ου, τό, pl. in Hom., Lat. *membra, the limbs, the lower limbs,* Γ 34.

γυμνός, ή, όν, *not clad, uncovered, naked, without clothing,* also, *without arms, without means of defence, defenceless; uncovered, exposed.* .

γυναιμανής, ές, (γυνή, μαίνομαι,) *having inordinate love for women*, Γ 39, of Par'-is.

γυνή, γυναικός, acc. αῖκα, voc. γύναι, Lat. *femina, a woman*, Γ 171 ; *wife*, Lat. *uxor; a concubine; a female*, Lat. *femina; woman*, as opp. to a goddess.

Γυρτώνη, ης, ἡ, *Gyr-to'-ne.*

γύψ, -πός, ὁ, *a vulture.*

Δ.

δα-, intensive prefix.

δαήμων, ον, gen., ονος, *knowing.*

δαήρ, έρος, voc. δᾶερ, gen. pl. δαέρων, ὁ, Lat. *levir, a husband's brother.*

δαί, after interrog., *then, so, indeed*

δαιδάλεος, α, ον, *skilfully wrought.*

δαιδάλλω, *to work skilfully, elaborate, decorate.*

δαίδαλος, η, ον, *skilfully wrought;* see foreg.

Δαίδαλος, ου, ὁ, *The Cunning Worker, Dœd'-a-lus.*

δαΐζω, f. ξω, aor. ἐδάιξα, (δαίω,) *to cleave, split, divide*, Β 416 ; *to pierce through.*

δαιμόνιος, adj., (δαίμων,) *of a divinity, influenced by a divinity for good or ill; divine, of divine nature;* Hom. uses in voc., and in such cases it is often foll. by a term of *respect or reproach, noble sir!* Β 190; *luckless man!* Β 200.

δαίμων, ονος, ὁ, ἡ, (δαίω,) Lat. *numen, a divinity*, Α 222 ; *god or goddess, goddess*, Γ 420 ; *fortune, fate ; a divine power, causing fate or chance, either good or ill; a devil*, this meaning of the word applies in the New Testament.

δαίνυμι, f. δαίσω, aor. ἔδαισα, (δαίω,) *to divide or assign shares, give a feast :* mid. Lat. *epulari, to feast, feast upon, banquet.*

δαίς, τος, ἡ, δαιτύς, (δαίω, to divide,) Lat. *epulae, a repast, meal, banquet*, Α 424; compare Lat. *convivium, dapes, epulum ; food ; food* that constitutes the meal.

δαΐς, ΐδος, ἡ, (δαίω, to kindle,) *a burning brand, a torch;* by meton., *war.*

δαιτύς, ύος, ἡ, see δαίς.

δαΐφρων, ον, ονος, (δαΐς, φρήν,) see Lat. *bellicosus, warlike in mind, bold*, Β 23: *knowing, prudent*, Lat. *prudens;* in this sense δαΐφρων is practically a diff. word, having another deriv., (δάω, an obsol. verb, φρήν,) *learned in mind.*

δαίω, *to kindle, set in a blaze;* pass. *to be kindled*, hence *to burn*, Lat. *ardēre.*

δαίω, compare Lat. *dividere, distribuere, partiri, dirimere, dispertire, to divide, portion out, distribute;* mid., *distribute.*

δάκνω, Ep. 2 aor. inf. δακέειν, *to sting, bite, to give a sharp bite; to bite.*

δάκρυ, υος, τό, Hom. for δάκρυον, Lat. *lacrima, a tear.*

δακρυόεις, εσσα, εν, *weeping; tearful.*

δάκρυον, see δάκρυ.

δακρυχέων, ουσα, ον, (δάκρυ, χέω,) Lat. *lacrimans, letting tears fall, weeping.*

δακρύω, f. ύσω, (δάκρυ,) Lat. *lacrimare, to shed tears;* pf. pass. *to be subject to tears, be sorrowful, tearful:* as a trans. verb, *lament anything.*

δάμαρ, αρτος, ἡ, (δαμάω,) Lat. *uxor, a wife; married woman.*

δαμάω, Ep. 3 pl. -όωσι; f. Ep. σσω; Ep. aor. (ἐ)δάμασσα; aor. pass. ἐδμή-θην; 2 aor. ἐδάμην, Ep. inf. δαμημέν(αι), part. δαμείς, *having been subdued,* Γ 429; δαμήῃς, *thou mightst be subdued,* Γ 436: Lat. *domare, to tame, bring into subjection, subdue,* A 61; *to yoke in marriage, give as wife:* pass. *to be subdued, subject to, obey,* Γ 183; Γ 301, *ravished.*

Δαναοί, ων, οἱ, *the Greeks; descendants of Dan'-a-us.*

δάος, εος, τό, (δαίω, *to kindle,*) *a burning brand: a fire.*

δάπεδον, ου, τό, (δα-, πέδον,) Lat. *solum, the ground, earth, soil; the ground or floor of a room,* Lat. *pavimentum.*

Δαρδάνια, ας, ἡ, *Dar-da'-ni-a, Troy.*

Δαρδανίδης, ου, ὁ, *a son of Dar'-da-nus.*

Δάρδανος, ου, ὁ, *Dar'-da-nus,* founder of Dar-da'-ni-a and the Tro'-jan race; as adj. *Tro'-jan;* see Classical Dictionary.

Δάρης, ητος, ὁ, *Da'-res,* one of the Tro'-jans.

δάσασθαι, aor. mid., see δατέομαι.

δασμός, οῦ, ὁ, (δάσασθαι, see Hadley and Allen, 520 D, 4,) Lat. *distributio, division; distribution of booty,* Lat. *distributio praedae.*

δατέομαι, f. δάσομαι; parts are formed from stem δα-; for Lat. see δαίω, (*to divide,*) *to divide; to tear or cut in pieces,* Lat. *dissecare; to distribute.*

Δαυλίς, ιδος, ἡ, *Dau'-lis,* a town of Pho'-cis, B 520.

δαφοινός, όν, (δα-, φοινός,) *very red, blood-red.*

δάω, f. δαήσομαι, pf. δεδάηκα, *to learn:* causal, like Lat. *docēre,* in 2 aor. δέδαε, *to teach;* see διδάσκω: 2 aor. ἐδάην, subj. Ep. δαείω, inf. δαῆναι and Ep. δαήμεν(αι).

-δε, encl., joined to a demon. to streng. it; joined to proper nouns to denote *motion towards;* ἅλαδε, *to the sea.*

δέ, *but;* may sometimes be rendered *and, again, also;* conjunctive particle with an adversative force, and is weaker than ἀλλά; μέν . . . δέ, *on one hand . . . on the other, as well . . . as;* in passing from one thing to another, *and, furthermore:* compare Lat. *sed, autem, verum.*

δέγμενος, Ep. 2 aor.; see δέχομαι.

δέδηε, δεδήει, 3 sing. 2 pf. and plup. of δαίω, to burn, Lat. exarsit.

δεδμήατο, Ion. 3 pl. plup. pass. of δαμάω, which see.

δεδμημένος, perf. pass. part. of δαμάω, which see.

ἐεδοκημένος, Ep. pf. part., see δέχομαι, watching sharply for.

δειδήμων, ον, ονος, (δείδω,) Lat. timidus, fearful, timid, cowardly, Γ 56.

δειδίσσομαι, f. ίξομαι, (δείδω,) Lat. terrēre, terrify: pass. to be terrified, fear, B 190, see Lat. trepidare.

δείδοικα, Ep. for δέδοικα, pf. of δείδω.

δείδω; f. δείσομαι; aor. ἔδεισα; pf. δέδοικα, with pres. signif.: 2 pf. δέδια, pl. δέδιμεν, δεδίασι, subj. δεδίω, opt. δεδιείην, imperat. δέδιθι, inf. δεδιέναι, part. δεδιώς, 2 plup. 3 du. ἐδεδίτην, 3 pl. ἐδέδισαν: Ep. forms, aor. ἔδδεισα, pf. and 2 pf. δείδοικα, δείδια, with pres. signif., pl. ἐδείδιμεν, ἐδείδισαν: compare with the different meanings of this word, Lat. verēri, timēre, metuere; to fear, be afraid: with μή, fear lest, fear it is; with μὴ οὐ, to fear it is not: with acc. fear anything, stand in awe of; with inf., to fear to do anything.

δείκνυμι; f. δείξω, Ion. δέξω; 2 pf. δέδειχα; to show, let see, point out; display, make evident: mid., to set before; to make clear, tell, point out, explain; prove; to receive kindly.

δειλός, ή, όν, (δείδω,) compare Lat. timidus, ignavus, cowardly: bad; miserable, Lat. miser.

δεῖμα, ατος, τό, (δείδω,) dread, alarm; that which causes fear, a terror.

δεινός, ή, όν, (δέος, δείδω,) Lat. horrendus, dreadful, dread, terrible, fearful; powerful, mighty; great, vast; wondrous, strange; venerable: adv. δεινόν, terribly, Γ 342.

δεῖπνον, ου, τό, (deriv. uncertain, perhaps δαίω,) compare Lat. epulae, convivium, dapes, epulum, coena, a meal, repast: the chief meal, B 381; food; fodder, B 383; ἄριστον is the early meal, δόρπον is the late meal: in Hom. often the first meal, as breakfast.

δειρή, ῆς, ἡ, Lat. cervix, the neck, throat.

δέκα, Lat. decem, ten.

δεκάκις, adv., tenfold.

δεκάς, άδος, ἡ, (δέκα,) Lat. decuria, a company of ten; ten.

δέκατος, η, ον, (δέκα,) Lat. decimus, tenth.

δέκτο, 3 sing. Ep. 2 aor. of δέχομαι.

δέμας, τό, frame, body, build of body, A 115; as acc. of specification, in stature; it is applied to the living body, see σῶμα; see, also, φυή.

δέμνιον, ου, τό, a bed, couch.

δένδρεον, ου, τό, Ion. for δένδρον, Lat. arbor, tree.

δεξιός, ά, όν, Lat. dexter, right, on the right; dexterous, handy; shrewd; propitious.

δεξιτερός, A 501, poet. and compar. in form for foreg.; old dat. δεξιτερῆφι.

δέος, Hom. δεῖος, ους, τό, see Lat. *timor, fear ; a terror, that which inspires terror ; awe.*

δέπας, αος, τό, *drinking-cup, goblet, chalice.*

δέρκομαι, f. δέρξομαι, 2 aor. ἔδρακον, pf. δέδορκα, (is Lat. *tueri* the equivalent of this word?) *to look* or *see ; to gleam* or *shine out*, of light; *to see the light of day* or *life, to live :* trans. *be aware of, know ; behold.*

δέρω ; f. δερῶ ; aor. ἔδειρα ; pf. δέδαρμαι ; aor. pass. ἐδάρθην ; 2 aor. pass. ἐδάρην : *to strip off the hide, skin, flay,* A 459 ; *to flay by stripes, to cudgel :* Ion. δείρω.

δέσμα, ατος, τό, (δέω,) *anything used for binding, a fetter ; band for the head.*

δεσμός, ου, ὁ, (δέω,) Lat. *vinculum, fetter, bond ; a cord* or *cable for binding* or *hitching ; bonds.*

δεῦρο, δεῦτε, adv., Lat. *huc, hither ! come here !* of time, *hitherto.*

δεῦτε, imperat. adv., *this way.*

δεύτερος, α, ον, Lat. *secundus, second ; second, inferior ;* neu. as adv., with αὖ, αὖτις, *secondly, again, then again, a second time, next,* Lat. *iterum.*

δεύω, iter. impf. δεύεσκον, *wet,* B 471 ; *drench, soak ; to fill up with liquid ; to shed* or *cause to flow, pour.*

δεύω, Ep. for δέω, f. δευήσω, *to miss, want, lack,* Γ 294 ; *be lacking in ; be inferior.*

δέχομαι, Ion. δέκομαι ; f. ξομαι and redupl. f. δεδέξομαι ; Ep. 2 aor. ἐδέγμην ; pf. δέδεγμαι ; *take ; receive, accept,* Lat. *accipere ; to receive favorably* or *graciously, entertain ; to take in good part ; await and receive the attack ; to choose* or *approve ; to watch and wait for.*

δέω, f. δήσω, aor. ἔδησα, pf. δέδεκα, aor. pass. ἐδέθην, Lat. *ligare, to tie, fasten, bind, make fast ; to fetter, chain, restrain ; hinder ;* Lat. *vincire :* mid., *bind one's self* or *for one's self.*

δή, particle, stric. of time, marks the idea as being immediately present or obvious to the mind ; it also marks connection ; it com. follows the word to which it belongs ; it allows a great variety of renderings : *now, indeed, in particular, already, forthwith, directly,* compare Lat. *jam, nunc ; then ; so,* Lat. *igitur ;* δὴ οὗτοι, *these then ;* καὶ δὴ καί, *and what is more,* καὶ δή, *well, suppose ;* it gives *urgency to imperative expressions,* ἄγε δή *come now,* μὴ δή *not by any means, I pray, only, do but ;* it renders *pron's.* and *particles more definite,* ὃς δή *the particular one who,* σὺ δή *you of all persons,* ἐμὲ δή *me in particular* or *one like me,* ὡς δή or ἵνα *that it may be just so,* ὁποῖος δή *of whichever particular sort,* οὕτως δή *just so,* οἷα δή, ὡς δή, ἅτε δή *inasmuch as* or *in that,* τί δή *just what ?* or *what now ?* εἰ δή *if indeed* or *really ;* it strengthens a sup., μέγιστος δή *the very greatest, assuredly;* it streng. the force of an adj., μόνος δή *all alone;* in irony *of course, pretended.*

δηθά, adv., *for a long time.*

δηθύνω, (δηθά,) *to tarry, linger.*

δήιος, η, ον, Ep. for **δάιος** ; *hostile,* B 415, 544.

δηιοτής, ῆτος, ἡ, *the strife of battle, battle, deadly conflict.*

δηιόω, many parts from δηο-, *to treat with hostility, cut down, kill; destroy.*

Δηίφοβος, ου, ὁ, *De-iph'-o-bus.*

δηλέομαι, f. ήσομαι, Lat. *delēre, to hurt; to harm; violate,* Γ 107 ; *to lay waste.*

Δημήτηρ, τερος and τρος, ἡ, (δῆ = γῆ, μήτηρ,) Lat. *Ce'-res, De-me'-ter,* goddess of agriculture.

δημοβόρος, ον, (δῆμος, βορά,) *devouring the people, robbing the people of their possessions.*

δημογέρων, οντος, ὁ (δῆμος, γέρων,) *elder of the people, chief.*

Δημοκόων, ωντος, ὁ, *De-moc'-o-on.*

δῆμος, ου, ὁ, *a tract of country; country, the inhabitants of the country,* Γ 50 ; *common people,* B 188, Lat. *plebs; the people in their social relations,* Lat. *populus; a body of citizens in their political capacity,* democracy, popular government, Lat. *civitas.*

δημός, οῦ, ὁ, *the fat of the body.*

δήν, adv., Lat. *diu, long, for a long time; long time ago.*

δηρός, ά, όν, (δήν,) *long, lasting,* B 298 ; *too long:* also, neu. as an adv.

δηῶν, contr. part. pres. of **δηιόω,** which see.

διά, prep.: with the gen., Lat. *per, through; amidst, among; during, throughout; because of, arising from, on account of; every;* διὰ πολλοῦ, *at a distance; by; after,* διὰ χρόνου, *after an interval:* with the acc., *throughout, through; aiming at; on account of, because of,* Lat. *propter:* in compo. *through, in two, across; partly; between; thoroughly; with; against; apart:* as adv. *entirely.*

διαδατέομαι, (διά, δατέομαι,) *to divide* or *distribute.*

διαθρύπτω, f. ψω, (διά, θρύπτω,) *to shatter, break, break in pieces,* Γ 363 ; *to weaken:* mid., *to take on airs; to be proud* or *vain.*

διαίνω, *to moisten; to weep.*

διακοσμέω, f. ήσω, (διά, κοσμέω,) *arrange,* B 476 and 126, *put in order, muster:* mid., *set in order.*

διακρίνω; f. νῶ ; aor. διέκρινα ; pf. διακέκρικα ; aor. pass. διεκρίθην, older form διεκρίνθην, Ep. inf. διακρινθήμεναι : (διά, κρίνω :) Lat. *discernere, separate,* B 475, *part, divide,* B 387 ; *distinguish; decide.*

διάκτορος, ου, ὁ, (διάγω,) *guide, conductor, messenger.*

διαλέγομαι, (διά, λέγομαι,) *to talk with.*

διαμάω, f. *ήσω*, aor. *διήμησα*, (διά, ἀμάω,) *to cut through.*

διαμετρέω, f. *ήσω*, (διά, μετρέω,) *to measure through* or *off*, Γ 315 ; *to portion out.*

διαμετρητός, ή, όν, Lat. *metatus, measured*, Γ 344.

διαμπερές, (διά, ἀναπείρω,) *completely through, through and through, entirely, wholly.*

διάνδιχα, (διά, ἀνά, δίχα,) adv. *in two ways;* with *μερμηρίζειν, deliberate between two opinions*, A 189.

διαπέρθω ; f. *ἐρσω* ; 2 aor. *διέπραθον*, A 367, Ep. inf. *διαπραθέειν* : (διά, πέρθω:) *to utterly ruin ; sack*, B 691 ; *ravage ;* compare Lat. *perdere, pessumdare, pervertere, evertere.*

διαπέτομαι, see διίπταμαι.

διαπορθέω = διαπέρθω.

διαπράσσω, Ion. *διαπρήσσω*, f. *ξω*, (διά, πράσσω,) Lat. *conficere, to accomplish, finish, complete ; to succeed in, effect.*

διαπρό, (διά, πρό,) adv., *right through, in a thorough manner, thoroughly.*

διαρραίω, f. *αίσω*, aor. *διέρραισα*, (διά, ῥαίω,) *to ruin, utterly destroy ;* see Lat. words after διαπέρθω.

διασεύομαι, Ep. 2 aor. *διεσσύμην, to fly* or *rush through.*

διατμήγω, Ep. for διατέμνω, formed regularly, 2 aor. act. and pass. *διετμαγ-, to cut through, cleave, divide, sever, cut in two*, Lat. *dissecare.*

διατρίβω, (διά, τρίβω,) *to rub between* or *on ; to rub* or *wear away, waste, put off.*

διατρυφείς, 2 aor. pass. part. of διατθρύπτω.

διδάσκω ; f. *διδάξω* ; poet. aor. *ἐδιδάσκησα* ; 2 pf. *δεδίδαχα* : Lat. *docēre, to teach, instruct :* see δάω.

δίδωμι, f. *δώσω*, aor. *ἔδωκα*, (what verbs have their aor. in *κα*?) 2 aor. *ἔδων*, pf. *δέδωκα*, aor. pass. *ἐδόθην* ; Ep. forms, pres. inf. *διδόμεν(αι)*, *διδοῦναι*, aor. inf. *δόμεν(αι)* ; Ion. forms, 2 and 3 sing. pres. *διδοῖς(θα)*, *διδοῖ* ; Lat. *dare, to give, bestow, present ; grant*, Γ 322 ; *to devote ; give up ; decree ; inflict ; deliver up ; pay ; to offer, offer to give* another ; *to permit ; to give to wife ; to allow* or *cause that ;* intrans. *to devote one's self :* Hom. imperat. *δίδωθι*, f. *διδώσω.*

διέξειμι, Ep. inf. *διεξίμεναι*, (διά, ἐξ, εἶμι,) *to go out through* anything.

διεξίμεναι, see διέξειμι.

διέπω, f. *ψω, to manage, accomplish*, A 166 ; *to arrange, order*, B 207 ; compare with Lat. *administrare, gubernare.*

διέρομαι, Hom. διείρομαι, *to question diligently* or *closely*, A 550.

διέρχομαι ; f. *διελεύσομαι* ; 2 aor. *διῆλθον* ; 2 pf. *διελήλυθα*, Ep. *διειλήλουθα* : Lat. *pertransire, to go through*, Γ 198 ; *go across ; reflect upon.*

διέσσυτο, Ep. 2 aor. 3 sing. of **διασεύομαι**.

διέτμαγεν, 2 aor. Ep. 3 pl. of **διατμήγω**, which see.

διέχω, (διά, ἔχω,) trans. *to hold apart, separate; stretch across:* intrans., *to hold quite through; to stand separate* from anything; *to go across, intervene, come in between.*

δίζημαι, *to go in search of, seek.*

διῆται, sub. of **δίω**.

δίπταμαι = **διαπέτομαι**, (διά, πέτομαι,) *to fly through* or *away.*

διίστημι; f. διαστήσω; aor. διέστησα; 2 aor. διέστην; pf. διέστηκα: (διά, ἵστημι:) trans. in pres., f., and aor. *to set apart, place apart, divide:* intrans. in 2 aor., pf., plup., *to stand aloof, part from each other, separate; to differ, quarrel,* A 6 ; *to stand at intervals.*

δικάζω, (δίκη,) *to decide, give a decision.*

δικασπόλος, ου, ὁ, (δίκη, πολέω,) *lawgiver, minister of justice, judge,* A 238.

δινεύω and **δινέω**, tenses are formed from each stem, (δίνη,) *to cause anything to turn rapidly around, turn round, twirl, drive in a circle; to roam.*

δινήεις, εσσα, εν, *whirling; rounded.*

δινωτός, ή, όν, (δινόω,) *turned, made with the lathe, rounded, worked.*

διογενής, ές, (Δίς, γένω,) *sprung from Jove, Jove-born.*

Διόθεν, adv., *from Jove.*

Διομήδης, εος, ὁ, *Di-o-me'des,* B 567, king of Ar'-gos and one of the bravest of the Greeks before Troy.

δῖος, α, ον, (Δίς,) *godlike, divine; noble, trusty, excellent; mighty; wonderful.*

Δῖος, ου, ὁ, *Di'-us,* a son of Pri'-am.

διοτρεφής, ές, (Δίς, τρέφω,) *nourished-by-Jove.*

δίπλαξ, ακος, ἡ, *double mantle.*

δίπτυχος, ον, (δίς, πτυχή,) *double, folded together,* A 461 ; *twofold.*

δίσκος, ου, ὁ, (δικεῖν,) Lat. *discus, quoit; a large tray.*

δίφρος, ου, ὁ, *a chariot-board for two, war chariot,* Γ 262 ; acco. to deriv. *that which carries two,* short. from διφόρος; (δίς, φέρω;) *travelling chariot; a seat,* Γ 424.

δίχα, (δίς,) prep. with gen., Lat. *sine* with abl., *without; separate from, different from; contrary to.*

δίχα, (δίς,) adv., *in two parts, in two; at differences, asunder, contrarily, in an opposite way.*

δίψα, ης, ἡ, *thirst;* also, *longing.*

δίω, *to flee; to fear, be afraid:* also, *to drive away.*

διώκω, leng. 2 aor. ἐδιώκαθον, see Hadley and Allen's Gram. 494, (δίω,) *to* *hunt, follow persistently, seek for, drive; to drive away, put to flight:* also, *to hasten, make haste.*

Διώνυσος, ου, ὁ, *Di-o-ny'-sos,* Lat. *Bac'-chus.*

Διώρης, εος, ους, ὁ, *Di-o'-res,* chief of the E-pe'-i.

δμη-, see **δαμ-.**

δμήθεις, aor. pass. part. of **δαμάω,** which see.

δμωή, ῆς, ἡ, (δαμάω,) *a woman slave.*

δνοπαλίζω, f. ίξω, (δονέω,) *to shake* or *fling about.*

δοιή, ῆς, ἡ, *doubt, uncertainty;* δοιῇ ἐν, *in perplexity.*

δοιώ, *both, two.*

δοκέω, *to think, conjecture, fancy, conceive:* also, *to appear* or *seem* so and so.　Some of the parts are formed as if from the stem δόκ.

δολιχόσκιος, ον, (δολιχός, σκιά,) *casting long shadows.*

δολόμητις, ιος, and -μήτης, ου, ὁ, (δόλος, μῆτις,) *wily, crafty.*

Δολοπίων, ονος, ὁ, *Do-lo-pi'-on,* one of the Tro'-jans.

δόλος, ου, ὁ, *a bait; a deceit, an artful trick;* Lat. *dolus, artifice, treachery.*

δολοφρονέων, ουσα, ον, (δολόφρων, (δόλος, φρήν),) *wily-minded.*

δόμος, ου, ὁ, (δέμω,) Lat. *domus, a building, house, habitation; hall; room; home; household.*

δονακεύς, έως, ὁ, (δόναξ,) *a dense growth of reeds, thicket.*

δόρπον, ου, τό, *the evening meal, supper.*

δόρυ, ρατος, Ep. gen. **δούρατος** and **δουρός,** other Ep. and Ion. forms in δουρ-, dat. pl. ασι and εσσι; *the trunk of a tree that has been cut; timber, ship-timber, beam,* Lat. *trabs,* Γ 61, *a ship; shaft of spear, a spear,* Β 382, Lat. *hasta.*

δουκαίδεκα, Lat. *duodecim, twelve.*

δόσκον, Ep. 2 aor. of **δίδωμι,** which see.

δούλη, ης, ἡ, Lat. *serva, female slave,* (one born in bondage.)

δούλιος, α, ον, (δοῦλος,) *of slavery* or *a slave.*

Δουλίχιον, ου, τό, *Du-lich'-i-um,* **Δουλιχιόνδε,** *to Du-lich'-i-um.*

δουλιχόδειρος, α, ον, Hom. form, (δολιχός, δειρή,) *long-necked.*

δούρα, δούρ-, Ep. forms from **δόρυ.**

δουρικλυτός, ή, όν, Hom. form, (δόρυ, κλυτός,) Lat. *hasta inclitus, renowned for the spear.*

δράγμα, ατος, τό, (δράσσω,) *a handful, a handful of grain in a reaper's hand, sheaf.*

δραγμεύω, (δράγμα,) *to gather grain into bundles.*

δράκων, οντος, ὁ, (δρακεῖν, 2 aor. inf. of δέρκομαι,) Lat. *draco, dragon, large serpent; serpent.*

δρεπάνη, ης, ἡ, (δρέπω,) *a hook for reaping.*

Δρύας, αντος, ὁ, *Dry'-as,* one of the Lap'-i-thae, Α 263.

δρῦς, νός, and ύος, acc. ῦν, η, Lat. *quercus*, *an oak*, *a tree strong and sturdy with age*; *any tree good for timber*.

δρυτόμος, ον, (δρῦς, τεμεῖν, 2 aor. inf. of τέμνω,) *cutting* or *felling timber*.

δύναμαι, f. δυνήσομαι, aor. ἐδυνησάμην, pf. δεδύνημαι, aor. pass. ἐδυνήθην, Lat. *posse*, *to be able*, *strong enough to*; *to be worth*.

δύναμις, εως, ἡ, (δύναμαι,) *potency*, *strength*; *ability*, *faculty*, *aptitude*; *force*, *power*; *value*.

δύνω or δύω; f. δύσω; aor. ἔδυσα; 2 aor. ἔδυν; pf. δέδυκα: trans. in f. and aor., *to put anything on another*: intrans. in other tenses; *to enter*, *go into*; of sun, *go into the sea*, *set*; *go under*, *sink in*; *come upon* or *over*; *to put on one's self*, as clothes, armor, etc.

δύο, Ep. δύω, Lat. *duo*, *two*.

δυσ-, *mis-*, *un-*, prefix implying *bad*, *ill*; streng. the meaning.

δυσάμμορος, ον, (δυσ-, ἄμμορος,) *very miserable*, *wretched*, *ill-fated*.

δυσηχής, ές, (δυσ-, ἠχέω,) *ill-sounding*, *fearful to hear*.

δυσκλεής, ές, (δυσ-, κλέος,) *of bad report* or *fame*, *inglorious*, see Lat. *infamis*.

δυσμενής, ές, (δυσ-, μένος,) *ill disposed*, *hostile*.

Δύσπαρις, ιδος, ὁ, *hateful* or *ill-fated Par'-is*, Γ 39.

δύστηνος, ον, *most miserable*, *ill-fated*, *most unhappy*; *miserable*.

δυσχείμερος, ον, (δυσ- χεῖμα,) Lat. *hiemalis*, *wintry*.

δύω = δύο, which see.

δυώδεκα, (δύο, δέκα,) Lat. *duodecim*, *twelve*.

δυωδέκατος, ον, *twelfth*, A 493, shorter δωδέκατος.

δῶ, τό, Ep. for δῶμα, *any house*; *abode*, *dwelling*, A 426; *a room* or *part of the house*.

δωδέκατος, Lat. *duodecimus*, see δυωδέκατος.

Δωδώνη, ης, ἡ, *Do-do'-na*, the seat of an oracle of Ju'-pi-ter surrounded by oaks sacred to him.

δώῃ, δώῃσι, Ep. 3 sing. 2 aor. subj. of δίδωμι, which see.

δῶμα, ατος, τό, (δέμω,) *any house*; *abode*; *a room* or *part of the house*; *household*.

Δώριον, ον, ἡ, *Do'-ri-um*, B 594.

δῶρον, ου, τό, (δίδωμι,) Lat. *donum*, *a gift*, Γ 54; *tribute*, *votive offering*.

E.

ἕ, Lat. *se*, acc. 3 sing. pron., *him*, *her*, *it*; this form is encl. but the Ep. form ἕε is not encl.: see οὗ.

ἔα for εἴα, 3 sing. impf. ἐάω.

ἔα, Ion. for ἦν impf. of εἰμί.

ἐάγην, 2 aor. pass. of ἄγνυμι.

ἐανός, ή, όν, (ἕννυμι,) to be put on and worn; pliant, light.

ἐανόν, οῦ, ὁ, (ἕννυμι,) a rich robe, robe of state, Γ 419.

ἔαρ, ρος, τό, Lat. ver, the spring-time.

ἔασι(ν), Ep. for εἰσί(ν).

ἔασκον, iter. impf. of ἐάω, Β 832.

ἔαται for ἦνται, pres. 3 pl. of ἧμαι, which see.

ἐάω, ἐῶ, Ep. contr. εἰῶ, εἰῶσι, Ep. for ἐῶσι 3 pl.; impf. εἴων; f. ἐάσω; aor. εἴασα, Ep. ἔασα; pf. εἴακα: to permit, allow, let; let alone; leave; heed not.

ἐγγέγαα, Ep. 2 pf. of ἐγγίγνομαι, (ἐν, γίγνομαι,) Lat. innasci, to come into being in, grow in, come about in; to take place in, occur in; to appear in.

ἐγγυαλίζω, f. ξω, (ἐν, γύαλον,) Lat. in manus tradere, put into the hollow of the hand, give into one's charge, Β 436.

ἐγγύθι, (ἐγγύς,) adv., near to, close by, near at hand.

ἐγγύς, adv., Lat. prope, near, soon; of place and time, may be used with the gen., dat., or without case; of numbers, nearly; compar. ἐγγίων, sup. ἐγγίστος, also reg. forms.

ἐγείρω; also, poet. pres. ἔγρω, ἔγρομαι; f. ἐγερῶ; aor. ἤγειρα; Ep. forms in ἐγρε-; pf. ἐγήγερκα; aor. pass. ἠγέρθην, Ep. 3 pl. ἔγερθεν: Lat. excitare, to arouse, awaken, stir up, Β 440, excite, raise or erect; awaken from the dead.

ἔγκατα, ων, τά, in pl., sing. not in use, the intestines, bowels.

ἔγκειμαι, (ἐν, κεῖμαι,) to lie wrapped up in; to be in, be concerned in: also, to be interested greatly in, be strongly interested against, urge, press hard against.

ἐγκέφαλος, ον, (ἐν, κεφαλή,) within the head; as subst. brain, Lat. cerebrum, Γ 300, stric. adj. with μυελός.

ἐγκονέω, to be quick and prompt, hasten.

ἔγνω, see γιγνώσκω.

ἔγρεο, 2 aor. imperat. mid. of ἐγείρω, which see.

ἐγχείη, ης, ἡ, (ἔγχος,) lance.

ἐγχεσίμωρος, ον, fighting with the spear.

ἐγχέσπαλος, ον, (ἔγχος, πάλλω,) wielding the spear.

ἔγχος, εος, τό, Lat. hasta, spear, made of two parts, αἰχμή, the head, and δόρυ, shaft.

ἐγχρίμπτω, (ἐν, χρίμπτω,) to make approach, bring near; to push or dash against; to attack.

ἐγώ, Ep. ἐγών, Lat. ego, I; Ep. gen. ἐμεῖο, ἐμέο, ἐμεῦ, (encl. μευ,) ἐμέθεν; Ep. du. νῶϊ, νῶϊν; Ep. nom. pl. ἄμμες; Ep. gen. pl. ἡμείων, -έων; Ep. dat. ἄμμι(ν); Ep. acc. ἄμμε, Ion. ἡμέας; ἔγωγε, I for my part.

ἐδάην, 2 aor. of δάω, which see.

ἔδδεισα, Ep. for ἔδεισα, aor. of δείδω, which see.

ἐδητύς, ύος, ἡ, (ἔδω,) *food.*

ἕδος, εος, τό, (ἕζομαι,) gen. pl. ἑων, A 534, Lat. *sedes, a place for sitting, seat; an abode; foundation; sitting, act of sitting.*

ἕδρα, ας, ἡ, Ep. ἕδρη, ης, (ἕζομαι,) *seat of any kind; dwelling-place, abode; abode of the gods; a sitting; a foundation.*

ἔδυν, 2 aor., 1 sing. and 3 pl., of δύω.

ἔδω; f. ἔδομαι; pf. ἐδήδα, Ion. impf. ἔδεσκον; see ἐσθίω, 593, 3, Hadley and Allen's Gram.: Lat. *edere, to eat, devour, consume.*

ἐδωδή, ῆς, ἡ, *food.*

ἕεδνα, Ep. for ἕδνα, τά, *suitor's presents, marriage gifts; presents to the bride's father and relations; the bride's dower :* these were usu. *cattle.*

ἐείκοσι(ν), Ep. for εἴκοσι(ν); Lat. *viginti, twenty.*

ἐεικοστός, Ep. for εἰκοστός, ἡ, όν, Lat. *vicesimus, twentieth.*

ἐεισάμενος, Ep. aor. part. of εἴδω.

ἐέλδωρ, Ep. for ἔλδωρ, τό, *wish, desire; a longing desire.*

ἐελμ-, see εἰλέω.

ἐέργαθον, Ep. for ἔργαθον, which is poet. 2 aor. of εἴργω, and that is Att. for ἔργω, in Hom. usu. ἐέργω, see Lat. *includere, to confine, keep in; to include; to coerce;* also, *to keep off, shut out, keep out,* Lat. *arcēre, to hinder, prohibit.*

ἐέργει, see ἔργω.

ἐερμένος, pf. part., see εἴρω.

ἕζομαι, f. ἑδοῦμαι, trans. aor. εἶσα, (*to put, place, lay,*) as if from pres. ἕζω, *to sit down, seat one's self;* see ἱδρύω.

ἕηκε, Ep. for ἧκε, aor. 3 sing. of ἵημι.

ἑῆος, gen. mas. of ἑύς, which see.

ἔθ' = ἔτι, B 344.

ἔθειρα, ας, ἡ, Lat. *coma, hair of the head; the mane of a horse* or *the horsehair crest of a helmet,* Lat. *juba equorum.*

ἐθέλω, f. ἐθελήσω, aor. ἠθέλησα, pf. ἠθέληκα, *to wish, will, desire,* B 391, A 112, 554; see note on B 247; *able; to be wont.*

ἔθεν, Ep. gen. for οὗ, *of him* or *her.*

ἔθνος, εος, τό, *company, host; swarm, flock; a tribe, race, nation, people,* Lat. *natio.*

ἔθορον, 2 aor. of θρώσκω, which see.

ἔθω, 2 pf. εἴωθα, *to be accustomed.*

εἰ, Ep. αἰ, Lat. *si, if;* εἰ γάρ, mostly in wishes, *for if, O if! for even if! O that!* Lat. *utinam.*

εἰαμενή, ῆς, ἡ, *low land, moist land, meadow* or *pasture.*

εἰαρινός, ἡ, όν, Ep. for ἐαρινός, (ἔαρ,) Lat. *vernus, of spring.*

εἴαται, εἴατο, Ep. for ἕαται, ἕατο used as 3 pl. pres. and impf. of ἧμαι.

εἰ δέ, *but if.*

εἰδ' ἄγε, *come! come then! come on! come go!*

εἶδος, εος, τό, (εἴδω,) Lat. *species, external appearance, that which is seen; the manner; a form or sort;* Γ 124 *as to form.*

εἴδω, ἴδῶ, Lat. *videre;* the pres. act. is obsol., ὁράω, being used instead; f. ὄψομαι, or εἴσομαι and εἰδήσω from εἴδω: aor. εἰσάμην, Ep. ἐεισάμην; 2 aor. εἶδον; Ion. ἴδεσκον, Ep. inf. ἰδέειν, inf. mid. ἰδέσθαι; pf. ἑώρακα, 2 pf. οἶδα, ὄπωπα; aor. pass. ὤφθην: *to see:* mid. and pass. *seem, appear,* Lat. *vidēri:* 2 pf. οἶδα, Lat. *novi,* is used like pres. *I know,* because *I have seen;* 2 plup. like impf., *he knew,* Β 409, 213; 2 aor. imperat. ἰδοῦ is used as an exclamation, *lo! see!* Lat. *ecce.*

εἰδώς, part. of οἶδα.

εἴθε, Ep. αἴθε, interj., Lat. *utinam, would that!*

εἴκοσι(ν), Ep. ἐείκοσι(ν), Lat. *viginti, twenty.*

εἰκοσινήριτος, ον, (εἴκοσι, νήριτος,) *fully twenty-fold.*

εἴκω, Hom. impf. 3 sing. εἶκε, f. εἴξω, 2 pf. ἔοικα, *to be like* or *likely; appear, seem, seem good; to be fitting, right:* the pres. is obsol., used in 2 pf. and 2 plup. with the sense of the pres. and impf.; *very much like,* Γ 158; *being like,* Α 47; in Hom. ἐοικώς is found as adj., *right, fitting:* see Hadley and Allen's Gram. 402, D. 7.

εἴκω, Ion. iter. aor. εἴξασκε, poet. 2 aor. εἴκαθον, *to yield, retreat, fall back; to give up and obey, submit: to yield, yield the superiority.*

εἰλαπίνη, ης, ἡ, compar. Lat. *epulum, comissatio, a splendid feast* or *banquet.*

Εἰλέσιον, ου, τό, *I-le'-si-um,* a town of Bœ-o'-ti-a, Β 499.

εἰλέω, leng. forms of εἴλω, εἴλλω, ἴλλω; impf. εἴλεον; f. εἰλήσω; aor. εἴλησα, ἔλσα; aor. pass. εἰλήθην; 2 aor. pass. ἐάλην: Ep. forms, impf. 3 sing. ἐόλει, ἐείλει, aor. inf. ἐέλσαι, pf. mid. ἔελμαι, plup. ἐόλητο: *to roll tight; to press hard, crowd together, confine, shut in; restrain,* Β 294; *to urge violently on, strike, smite:* pass. *to be crowded together; to cower, crouch; collect themselves together* as in close array.

εἰλήλουθα, Ep. for ἐλήλυθα, 2 pf. of ἔρχομαι, which see.

εἰλίπους, adj. for decl. see πούς, (εἰλέω, πούς,) *slowly trailing the feet,* of oxen.

εἷλον, 2 aor. of αἱρέω, which see.

εἰλύω, Lat. *involvere, to wrap up, wrap round, envelop, cover.*

εἶμα, εἴματος, τό, (ἕννυμι,) compare Lat. *vestis, vestitus, vestimentum, amictus, amiculum, cultus, habitus; a garment, cloak; dress, clothing.*

εἰμί, Lat. *esse;* Ep. forms in the present are 2 sing. εἶς and ἐσσί, pl. εἰμέν, 3 pl. ἔασι; Ep. forms of impf. ἦα, ἔα, and ἔον or ἔσκον, 2 sing. ἔησθα, 3 sing. ἦεν, ἤην, ἔσκε, Γ 180, 3 pl. ἔσαν; Ep. subj. 1 sing., ἔω, εἴω, 3 sing. ἔῃ, ἔῃσι, 3 pl. ἔωσι; Ep. opt. ἔοιμι, ἔοις, ἔοι; Ep. imperat. ἔσο, ἔσσο; Ep. inf. ἔμ(μ)εν(αι), ἔμμεν, ἔμεν; Ep. part. ἐών, ἔουσα, ἔον: f.

ἔσομαι, Ep. f. ἔσσομαι, 3 sing. ἔσσεται, ἐσσεῖται, Β 393: the pres. indicat.
is encl. except 2 pers. sing. and Ep. 3 sing. ἔασι: *to be, to exist, to live;*
with inf. *to be possible,* Β 393, *to be permitted, to be proper;* with gen., *to
spring from, originate with, to be of,* (as being part of a whole,) *to be of,*
(denoting ownership.)

εἰμι, Lat. *ire:* Ep. 2 sing. εἶσθα: Ep. forms in the impf. are sing. ἤϊα,
ἤϊον, 3 sing. ἤϊε contr. ἤε, pl. ἤομεν, 3 pl. ἤϊσαν or ἤϊσαν, ἤϊον, ἤσαν,
ἴσαν: Ep. forms in the subj. 2 sing. ἴησθα, 3 sing. ἴησι, pl. ἴομεν: Ep.
opt. 3 sing. ἰείη, εἴη, ἴε: Ep. inf. ἴμ(μ)εν(αι): Ep. f. and aor. mid.
εἴσομαι, εἰσάμην: *to go;* ἴε, went, Γ 383, *return =* f. in Γ 305; *go away;*
with f. inf. *to go to do anything; to fly; to sail,* Α 482; *go through,*
with διά, Γ 61; *go forward; come hither,* Γ 390.

εἰν, poet. for ἐν, which see.

εἰνάτερες, αἱ, *wives of brothers.*

εἴνατος, η, ον, Ep. for ἔννατος, (ἐννέα,) Lat. *nonus, ninth.*

εἴνεκα, Hom. for ἔνεκα, prep. with gen., *because of.*

εἰνοσίφυλλος, ον, (ἔνοσις, φύλλον,) *quivering with foliage* or *leaves, leaf-
shaking.*

εἴξασκε, Ion. aor. 3 sing. from εἴκω, which see.

εἰο, Ep. for οὗ, *of him.*

εἴπερ, (εἰ, πέρ,) *if indeed, if only, if at all events, if however.*

εἶπον, a 2 aor. form to which a pres. λέγω, φημί, or ἀγορεύω, (and rare.
in Hom. εἴρω,) is supplied; f. ἐρέω, contr. ἐρῶ; aor. εἶπον or εἶπα; pf.
εἴρηκα or εἴρημαι; aor. pf. ἐρρήθην; Ep. inf. εἰπέμεν(αι); ἔειπεν, Β 59;
iter. form εἴπεσκον; Ep. imperat. 2 pl. ἔσπετε: *to speak, say, tell.*

εἴποτε, (εἰ, πότε,) adv., Lat. *si quando, if ever.*

εἴ πως, *if in any way.*

Εἰρέτρια, ας, ἡ, poet. for Ἐρέτρια, *E-re'-tri-a,* a town of *Eu-bœ'-a.*

εἴρη, ης, ἡ, (εἴρω,) *a meeting-place.*

εἰρήνη, ης, ἡ, Lat. *pax, peace, quiet, tranquillity.*

εἴριον, ου, τό, (εἶρος; wool,) Lat. *lana, wool.*

εἰροκόμος, ον, (εἶρος, κομέω,) *dressing wool, spinning; wool-working,* Γ 387.

εἰροπόκος, ον, (εἶρος, πόκος,) *fleeced-with-wool, wool-producing.*

εἰρύαται, see ἐρύομαι.

εἴρω, *to say, speak, tell,* see ἐρέω.

εἰς, ἐς, prep. with acc., *towards, into, to:* of place, *into,* Lat. *in,* opp. to
ἐξ; *at, upon, on, in, by,* with verbs expressing *rest;* with a hostile
sense, *against,* Lat. *contra:* of time, *till, until, up to; for; during:* with
numerals, *to, at,* Β 379 *but if ever we shall be of one counsel; up to, as
many as, about:* of purpose, *for, for the purpose of:* in other relations,
in regard to, for; εἰς τί, *why?* ἐς ὅ, *wherefore;* ἐς χρόνον, *till aftertime:*
in compo. *into, to, in.*

εἶς, μία, ἕν, gen. ἑνός, μιᾶς, ἑνός, Lat. *unus, a, um, one, one alone, only one.*

εἶσα, see ἕζομαι and ἵζω.

εἰσαγείρω or ἐσαγείρω; f. εἰσαγερῶ; aor. εἰσήγειρα; pf. εἰσαγήγερκα; aor. pass. εἰσηγέρθην, Ep. pl. εἰσήγερθεν: (εἰς, ἀγείρω:) *to collect into, assault* or *gather into.*

εἰσαναβαίνω, for prin. parts see ἀναβαίνω, (εἰς, ἀνά, βαίνω,) *to go up into* or *to, to mount.*

εἶσατο, Ep. aor. 3 per. of εἶμι and εἴδω.

εἰσαφικνέομαι, (εἰς, ἀφικνέομαι,) *to arrive at* or *come into.*

εἰσβαίνω, for prin. parts see βαίνω, (εἰς, βαίνω,) *to go into; to go on board, embark; enter:* causal in aor. *to make to go into,* A 310 ἐς βῆσε, *made to go in.*

εἰσέρχομαι, for prin. parts see ἔρχομαι, (εἰς, ἔρχομαι,) compare Lat. *inire, intrare, introire, ingredi, to go into, come into, arrive at; go* or *come upon.*

εἴσεται, see εἶμι and οἶδα.

ἴσκω, (ἴσος,) Lat. *assimilare, to make like; to liken, think like; to see resemblance; to compare; to judge.*

εἰσνοέω, (εἰς, νοέω,) see Lat. *animadvertere, to remark, notice.*

εἰσόκε(ν), (εἰς, ὅ, κε,) Lat. *dum, donec, until; so long as.*

εἰσοράω, Ep. εἰσορόω; f. εἰσόψομαι; 2 εἰσεῖδον: (εἰς, ὁράω:) Lat. *adspicere, to look at, view, behold; look on with respect* or *admiringly; gaze upon.*

ἶσος, η, ον, Ep. for ἴσος, Lat. *aequus, par, alike, proportionate, equal; equal = equally divided,* A 468.

εἰστίθημι, for prin. parts see τίθημι, (εἰς, τίθημι, Lat. *imponere, to put in* or *into.*

εἴσω, ἔσω, adv., (εἰς,) Lat. *intra, intus, into, within,* Γ 322, with acc. and gen., it seems to have partly the force of a prep.; *inside, in.*

εἴ τε, ... εἴ τε, or (Hom.) ἢ καί, *either, ... or,* Lat. *sive, ... sive, whether, ... or.*

εἴωθα, 2 pf. ἔθω with pres. sense, *to be won'.*

εἴων, impf. of ἐάω.

εἴως, Ep. for ἕως.

ἐκ, before vowels ἐξ, Lat. *e* or *ex, out from* a position *in, from out of, away from;* prep. with the gen., of place, *away from, forth from, from, from among, without, beyond:* of time, ἐξ οὗ A 6, Lat. *ex quo, from the time, since; from* or *out of = after:* of origin or cause, *afar from* as opp. to ὑπό, *springing from,* A 63 *is from; because of:* in phrases, ἐκ πολλοῦ, *from a great distance;* ἐξ ἴσου, *from* (or *on*) *an equality;* ἐκ πολλοῦ χρόνου, *long ago:* in compo., *from out, off, away.*

Ἑκάβη, ης, ἡ, *Hec'-u-ba,* Pri'-am's wife.

ἑκάεργος, ὁ, (ἑκάς, ἔργω,) *working from far, far-working,* epith. of Apollo.

ἕκαθεν, adv., (ἑκάς,) *from far; far away.*

ἑκάς, (ἐκ,) adv, Lat. *longe, afar off; far from, away from,* with gen. of separation.

ἕκαστος, η, ον, Lat. *unusquisque, each one;* Lat. *quisque, every, every one, each.*

ἑκάτερθε(ν), for ἑκατέρωθε(ν), adv., Lat. *utrimque, on both sides, from each side.*

ἑκατηβελέτης, Α 75, = ἑκατηβόλος, Α 370, (ἑκάς, βάλλω,) *far-throwing, far-darting;* as subst. an epith. of Λ-pol'-lo, the *Far-darter.*

ἑκατόγχειρος, ον, (ἑκατόν, χείρ,) *hundred-handed.*

ἑκατόμβη, ης, ἡ, (ἑκατόν, βοῦς,) *a hecatomb, an offering of a hundred oxen; a great sacrifice.*

ἑκατόμβοιος, ον, (ἑκατόν, βοῦς,) *worth a hundred oxen.*

ἑκατόμπολις, ι, εως, (ἑκατόν, πόλις,) *with a hundred cities.*

ἑκατόν, indecl., Lat. *centum, a hundred.*

ἕκατος, ον, ὁ, (ἑκάς,) *far-shooting* or *far-darting,* = ἐκηβόλος, ον, (ἑκάς, βάλλω,) epith. of Apollo.

ἐκβαίνω; f. ἐκβήσω, ἐκβήσομαι; aor. ἐξέβησα; 2 aor. ἐξέβην; pf. ἐκβέβηκα: (ἐκ, βαίνω:) Lat. *exire, to go out of, go out; alighted,* Γ 113; *to disembark,* Α 439; *depart from; turn out:* f. act. and aor. have causal signif. *to make to go out of* or *disembark,* Α 438.

ἐκβάλλω, f. ἐκβαλῶ, 2 aor. ἐξέβαλον, pf. ἐκβέβληκα, (ἐκ, βάλλω,) Lat. *ejicere, to cast forth; to expel, drive out, banish; to put out of the ship* or *cause to disembark; let fall,* Lat. *fundere; strike out,* Lat. *excutere; hew out; to put forth a word* or *utter; throw away, reject; send out; lose.*

ἐκγέγαα, poet. for ἐκγέγονα, 2 pf. of ἐγίγνομαι, inf. ἐκγεγάμεν, part. ἐκγεγαώς, ἐκγεγαυῖα, Γ 418.

ἐκγελάω; Ep. forms, ·λόω and participles ·λόωντ- and ·λόοντ-, forms in ·λοίω-: *to laugh out loud.*

ἐκγίγνομαι; f. ἐκγενήσομαι; 2 aor. ἐξεγενόμην; 2 pf. ἐκγέγονα, poet. ἐκγέγαα: (ἐκ, γίγνομαι:) Lat. *enasci, to grow out of* or *from, be born of, descend from; to be allowable,* Lat. *licet.*

ἔκδηλος, ον, (ἐκ, δῆλος,) Lat. *evidens, evident, conspicuous, perfectly evident.*

ἐκδίδωμι, for prin. parts see δίδωμι, (ἐκ, δίδωμι,) Lat. *edere, to give out; give back, return,* Lat. *reddere; give up, surrender,* Γ 459, Lat. *tradere; to let* or *hire out.*

ἐκδύνω, 2 aor. ἐξέδυν, pf. ἐκδέδυκα, (ἐκ, δύνω,) *to throw off, put off,* as a garment; *to get rid of;* same in mid.: ἐκδύω, f. ἐκδύσω, aor. ἐξέδυσα, *to take* or *strip off from another,* as a garment.

ἐκεῖνος, Ion. κεῖνος, η, ον, (ἐκεῖ,) Lat. *ille,* demon. pron. *that, that one* or *thing;* ἐκεῖνος and οὗτος have the same relation and uses as Lat. *ille* and *hic;* ἐκείνῃ, adv. *there; in that way.*

ἐκέκαστο, 3 sing. plup. of καίνυμαι, has an impf. sense.

ἐκηβολία, as, ἡ, (ἑκάς, βάλλω,) skill in shooting from far, archery.

ἐκηβόλος, ον, (ἑκάς, βάλλω,) far-throwing, far-darting, epith. of Apollo; as subst. Far-darter, A 96.

ἐκκαθαίρω, f. ἐκκαθαρῶ, aor. ἐξεκάθηρα, (ἐκ, καθαίρω), Lat. purgare, to cleanse out, thoroughly clear out, B 153 ; clear off.

ἐκ-και-δεκά-δωρος, ον, sixteen hands long or high.

ἐκκαλέω, f. έσω, (ἐκ, καλέω,) Lat. evocare, to call out, evoke ; incite.

ἐκκατεῖδον, (ἐκ, κατά, εἶδον, 2 aor. of ὁράω,) to look down from above.

ἐκλανθάνω, f. ἐκλήσω, 2 aor. ἐξέλαθον, Ep. redupl. 2 aor. ἐκλέλαθον, 2 pf. ἐκλέληθα, intrans. in pres., 2 aor., to lie hid, completely escape notice : trans. in aor. Ep. redupl. 2 aor., make to quite forget, also, the rare pres. ἐκληθάνω is trans.

ἐκλέλαθον, B 600, (ἐκ, λανθάνω,) see foreg.

ἐκμυζάω, (ἐκ, μυζάω,) to suck any thing out.

ἔκπαγλος, ον, (ἐκπλαγῆναι,) frightful, horrible, dreadful, A 146 : adv. ἐκπάγλως, exceedingly ; terribly.

ἐκπέμπω, (ἐκ, πέμπω,) Lat. emittere, to send forth ; to dismiss or drive off ; to bring or cause to come out.

ἐκπέρθω, f. ἐκπέρσω, (ἐκ, πέρθω,) to sack, destroy utterly.

ἐκπίπτω, f. ἐκπεσοῦμαι, 2 aor. ἐξέπεσον, Ep. 2 aor. ἔκπεσον, pf. ἐκπέπτωκα, (ἐκ, πίπτω,) Lat. excidere, to fall out from ; to lose, be deprived of : to be driven out, expelled, banished, Lat. ejici ; to come forth, escape or depart from ; issue.

ἐκπρεπής, ές, (ἐκπρέπω,) distinguished, conspicuous ; in bad sense unbecoming.

ἐκσαόω, Δ 12, see ἐκσώζω.

ἐκσεύομαι, pf. ἐξέσσυμαι, (ἐκ, σεύω,) Lat. erumpere, to rush forth B 809, hurry away from.

ἐκσπάω, (ἐκ, σπάω,) to draw or take out, pull out.

ἐκσώζω, f. σω, Ep. ἐκσαόω, to keep from harm, guard ; Δ 12, rescue.

ἔκτανε, 3 sing. 2 aor. of κτείνω ; ἔκταν, Ep. = ἔκτασαν, 3 pl. aor.

ἐκτελέω, Ep. impf. ἐξετέλειον ; f. ἐκτελέσω, Ep. ἐκτελέω ; Ep. aor. -εσσ- ; aor. pass. -λέσθην : to bring to completion, finish ; achieve ; compare with this Lat. absolvere, perficere, terminare, consummare.

ἐκτέμνω, Ion. ἐκτάμνω, Γ 62, f. ἐκτεμῶ, 2 aor. ἐξέταμον, pf. ἐκτέτμηκα, aor. pass. ἐξετμήθην, to cut out, to hew trees out of a forest ; to cut out, fashion.

ἔκτοθι, (ἐκτός), outside of, out from.

Ἐκτόρεος, of Hec'-tor.

ἐκτός, (ἐκ,) adv., without.

ἕκτος, η, ον, (ἕξ), Lat. sextus, the sixth.

ἐκτός, (ἐκ,) prep. with gen., *out of, away from, beyond, separate from, apart from.*

Ἕκτωρ, ορος, ὁ, *Hec′-tor,* eldest son of Pri′-am, slain by A-chil′-leus.

ἑκυρά, ᾶς, ἡ, Hom. -ή, *mother by law.*

ἑκυρός, οῦ, ὁ, Lat. *socer, father-in-law.*

ἐκφαίνω, f. φανῶ, aor. ἐξέφηνα, aor. pass. ἐξεφάνθην, (ἐκ, φαίνω,) Lat. *in lucem edere, to bring into light, expose, show forth; to reveal, make known.*

ἐκφέρω, for parts see φέρω, (ἐκ, φέρω,) Lat. *efferre, to bear out* or *forth, carry off, bear away; put forth, put forward, bring on, produce; to carry out* or *finish; to put forth into public* or *proclaim, declare, make public.*

ἐκχέω, f. ἐκχεῶ; aor. ἐξέχεα, Ep. ἐξέχευα; (other Ep. forms in -χυ-;) pf. ἐκκέχυκα; aor. pass. ἐξεχύθην: Lat. *effundere, to pour out; to spill; to lose; waste, squander:* pass. *to be poured out, stream out, gush forth; spread abroad.*

ἑκών, ἑκοῦσα, ἑκόν, Lat. *sponte, willing, voluntary, of one's own will* Γ 66 ; *intentionally, deliberately.*

ἔλαιον, ου, τό, (ἐλαία,) Lat. *olivum,* same as *oleum, olive-oil, fat.*

ἔλασα, Ep. for ἤλασα, aor. of ἐλαύνω, 3 sing. ἔλασσε, Ep. and Ion. iter. 3 sing. ἐλάσασκε.

ἐλαστρέω, Ep. for ἐλαύνω, which see.

ἐλατήρ, ῆρος, ὁ, (ἐλαύνω,) *one that drives, charioteer.*

ἐλαύνω, f. ἐλάσω, contd. ἐλῶ, Ep. ἐλάσσω and ἐλόω; aor. ἤλασα, Ep. ἔλασ(σ)α ; pf. ἐλήλακα ; aor. pass. ἠλά(σ)θην : rare poet. pres. ἐλάω ; iter. aor. 3 sing. ἐλάσασκε ; aor. mid. Ep. 2 sing. ἐλάσαιο : *to set in motion; drive on; to drive away* or *off,* Α 154, Lat. *abigere, to steal cattle; to drive, crowd into a narrow place, harass, press; to push a* weapon into or against, hence *to wound, strike, hew, thrust, cut; to beat* or *draw out metal,* (does Lat. *ducere* have this meaning?) *forge; to draw out:* as intrans., *to ride, go, advance, march,* in which senses Xen′-o-phon uses the word in his A-nab′-a-sis.

ἔλαφος, οῦ, ὁ, ἡ, Lat. *cervus, a deer;* a term for *a coward,* Α 225.

ἐλαφρός, adj., Lat. *levis, not heavy, light, not weighing down; light in movement, quick, alert, agile; light of mind.*

ἐλεαίρω, poet. for ἐλεέω, (ἔλεος,) iter. impf. ἐλεαίρεσκον, Lat. *misereri, to take pity on, feel pity for.*

ἐλεγχείη, ης, ἡ, (ἐλέγχω,) *reproach, insult, that which causes disgrace.*

ἐλεγχής, ές, (ἔλεγχος,) irreg. sup. ἐλέγχιστος, Β 285, *open to reproach, disgraceful, shameful, likely to be reproached; cowardly.*

ἔλεγχος, τό, (ἐλέγχω,) *disgrace, shame, cowardice, dishonor;* compare Lat. *dedecus, probrum, opprobrum.*

ἐλέγχω, f. ξω, pf. pass. ἐλήλεγμαι, Att. redupl., *to affect with shame, treat contemptuously, despise, dishonor ; to accuse, reproach ; to demonstrate, convict, convince ;* compare Lat. *convincere, arguere ; to inquire into, examine.*

ἐλεέω, f. ήσω, (ἔλεος,) Lat. *misereri, to pity,* see ἐλεαίρω.

ἐλεεινός, ή, όν, (ἔλεος,) Lat. *miserabilis, pitiable, miserable :* neu. pl. also as adv., *pitifully.*

ἐλελίζω, Ep. for ἐλίσσω, f. ίξω, Ep. aor. ἐλέλιξα, Ep. aor. pass. ἐλελίχθην, *to whirl ; to wheel* or *rally* soldiers : as causal, *to make to shake,* A 530: pass. *to tremble :* mid. *to wind one's self round,* B 316.

ἐλελιξάμενος, B 316, aor. mid. part. of foreg.

'Ελένη, ης, ἡ, *Hel'-en,* wife of Men-e-la'-us, see Classical Dictionary.

"Ελενος, ου, ὁ, *El'-e-nus,* a son of Pri'-am.

ἐλεόθρεπτος, ον, (ἕλος, τρέφω,) *marsh-grown, growing in the marshes,* B 776.

ἐλεός, οῦ, ὁ ; also, -όν, οῦ, τό, *a table for cutting meat, dresser.*

ἐλεύθερος, α, ον, *free, not enslaved.*

ἐλέφας, αντος, ὁ, *an elephant ;* also, *ivory from the elephant.*

'Ελεφήνωρ, ορος, ὁ, *El-e-phe'-nor,* chief of the A-ban'-tes, B 540.

'Ελεών, ῶνος, ὁ, *E'-le-on,* a town of Bœ-o'-ti-a, B 500.

'Ελικάων, ονος, ὁ, *Hel-i-ca'-on,* a Tro'-jan, son of An-te'-nor.

'Ελίκη, ης, ἡ, *Hel'-i-ce,* a city of A-cha'-ia, B 575.

ἑλίκωψ, ωπος, ὁ, ἡ, (ἕλιξ, ὤψ,) *with quick-rolling eyes ;* fem. ἑλικῶπις, A 98, *quick-glancing ; rolling-eyed,* A 389 ; a mark of activity and spirits.

ἕλιξ, ικος, ἡ, (ἑλίσσω,) Lat. *vortex, that which has been twisted* or *wound round, something coiled, a whirl of water* or *wind.*

ἐλίσσω, Ep. εἱλίσσω ; ἑλίξω ; aor. εἵλιξα ; pf. ἐλήλιγμαι ; aor. pass. εἱλίχθην : Lat. *volvere, to turn about* or *round and round, turn, revolve* in the mind ; *to whirl, put in rapid motion ; to roll, coil, twist :* intrans. *to go quickly about :* mid. and pass. *to turn one's self quickly round ; rally ; turn at bay ; turn one's self this way and that ; to be engaged.*

ἑλκεσίπεπλος, ον, (ἕλκω, πέπλος,) *dragging a robe,* (Lat. *peplum,*) *wearing a long robe.*

ἑλκέω, *to drag around, treat badly, misuse ; to rend.*

ἑλκηθμός, οῦ, ὁ (ἑλκέω,) *a dragging away, ill treatment.*

ἕλκος, εος, τό, Lat. *vulnus, plaga, a wound ; a running sore, sore, ulcer,* B 723, Lat. *ulcus.*

ἕλκω, f. ἕλξω, ἑλκύσω ; aor. εἷλξα, εἵλκυσα, Ep. ἕλξα ; aor. pass. εἱλκύσθην ; pf. εἵλκυσμαι, Ep. inf. ἑλκέμεν(αι) B 165 : Lat. *trahere, to draw ; to draw ships seaward* B 165, Lat. *naves deducere ; to drag ; to draw a sword* or *bow; tear; to hoist* or *stretch sails; to tug at; to quaff; to attract;* of balance, *to draw down, to weigh.*

'Ελλάς, άδος, ή, *Hel'.-las,* a city of Thes'-sa-ly, founded by Hel'len; (Ἕλλην;) in gen. *Greece.*

ἐλλεδανός, οῦ, ὁ, (εἰλέω,) *band of straw.*

Ἕλλην, ηνος, ὁ, *Hel'-len,* son of Deu-ca'-li-on, and founder of Hel'-las; his descendants were the Ἕλληνες, the Greeks.

'Ελλήσποντος, ου, ὁ, (Ἕλλη, πόντος,) *the Hel'-les-pont.*

ἕλος, εος, τό, *low marshy ground, meadow.*

Ἕλος, ους, τό, *He'-los,* a town of La-co'-ni-a, so called from its marshes, (ἕλος,) B 584; from this is *He'-lot,* a town of E'-lis, B 594.

ἔλπω, Ep. mid. ἐέλπομαι, 2 pf. ἔολπα as pres., 2 plup. ἐώλπειν as impf., Hom. ἐώλπεα; causal in pres. act., Lat. *in spem adducere, to make to hope, to awaken hope in another:* intrans. in mid., 2 pf., 2 plupf., *to hope, expect; apprehend, fear; think; believe.*

ἕλσαι, aor. inf. of εἴλω, see εἰλέω.

ἐλύω, (εἴλω or εἰλέω,) *to wrap up, roll about, cover.*

ἕλωρ, ωρος, τό, (ἑλεῖν, 2 aor. of αἱρέω,) compare Lat. *captura, praeda, capture, game, spoil.*

ἐλώριον = ἕλωρ, (see deriv. of ἕλωρ,) *booty, spoil; prey,* A 4, compare Lat. *praeda, manubiae, spolia, exuviae, rapina.*

ἐμβαίνω; for parts see βαίνω; (ἐν, βαίνω;) *to enter, step into* or *on; to go into* or *on, step up on to, mount, walk upon,* compare Lat. *incedere, ingredi; to go on board; embark; enter upon a thing:* trans. in aor. ἐνέβησα, *to cause to enter; cause to go upon, cause to walk in.*

ἐμβάλλω, f. ἐμβαλῶ, for parts see βάλλω, (ἐν, βάλλω,) Lat. *immittere, injicere, to throw into, put into* or *in, lay on, lay in; to infuse, inspire;* with dat., *to put into the mind; to lay to* a thing; *to throw at; to introduce; rush into, attack.*

ἐμβασιλεύω, f. σω, (ἐν, βασιλεύω,) *to rule among* or *in.*

ἐμέθεν, ἐμέο, ἐμεῖο, ἐμεῦ, μεῦ encl., Ep. for ἐμοῦ, which see.

ἔμεν(αι), Ep. for εἶναι, Lat. *esse.*

ἔμεν(αι), Ep. inf. of ἵημι.

ἔμμεν(αι), (Lat. *esse,*) Ep. inf. of εἰμί, which see.

ἔμμορα, 2 pf. of μείρομαι, which see.

ἐμός, ή, όν, Lat. *meus, my, mine;* τὸ ἐμόν or τἀμά = τὰ ἐμά, *my affairs.*

ἐμπάσσω, f. άσω, (ἐν, πάσσω,) *to sprinkle in; to weave in,* Γ 126, Lat. *intexere.*

ἔμπης, Ep. for ἔμπας, (ἐν, πᾶς,) adv., *on the whole, at any rate; yet, notwithstanding,* Lat. *tamen.*

ἐμπίπλημι, or **ἐμπίμπλημι,** f. λήσω, (ἐν, πίμπλημι,) *to fill up entirely; to fill completely full of.*

ἐμπίπτω, f. ἐμπεσοῦμαι, 2 aor. ἐνέπεσον, (ἐν, πίπτω,) to come upon, charge upon ; to burst into.

ἔμπλην, (ἐμπελάζω,) adv. Lat. juxta, close by, near, B 526.

ἐμπνείω, poet. for -νέω, f. -νεύσομαι, (ἐν, πνέω,) to breathe upon, to blow upon ; to breathe into or inspire : intrans. to breathe or live.

ἐμπρήθω, see ἐνιπρήθω.

ἐμφύομαι, 2 aor. ἐνέφυν, pf. ἐμπέφυκα, intrans., to cling, cling fast, A 513, ἐμπεφυυῖα clinging closely, to be fixed in, see Lat. innasci : ἐμφύω, f. ύσω, aor. ἐνέφυσα, trans., to implant, fix, inspire.

ἐν, poet. ἐνί, εἰν, prep. with dat., Lat. in, with abl. in, amongst ; on, at, upon ; before one's face, see Lat. coram ; with, by ; during, within ; ἐν χρόνῳ, in time, at length : in compo., in, on, at, near ; into, against ; except in compo. ἐν does not express the idea of motion : as adv. therein, in addition, besides, among.

ἐναίρω, f. ἐναρῶ, aor. ἐνηράμην, compare Lat. occidere, perdere, spoliare, to kill, slay in battle, also destroy ; injure.

ἐναίσιμος, ον, (ἐν, αἶσα,) from or by destiny, according to fate, and so fitting, just ; favorable, B 353.

ἐναλίγκιος, ον, (ἐν, ἀλίγκιος,) Lat. similis, similar.

ἐναντίβιος, ον, (ἐν, ἀντί, βία, or ἀντίβιος,) striving against, opposing.

ἐναντίος, α, ον, (ἐν, ἀντίος,) opposite ; before the face : adv. ἐναντίον, against, contrary or opposed to ; before, in presence of.

ἔναρα, τά, Lat. spolia, spoils from the slain.

ἐναρίζω, f. ίξω, Ep. aor. ἐνάριξα, (ἔναρα,) Lat. spoliare, to strip off spoils ; to slay.

ἐναρίθμιος or ἐνάριθμος, ον, (ἐν, ἀριθμός,) taken in the reckoning, of account, of value, B 202 ; numbered among.

ἔνατος, Hom. form εἴνατος, η, ον, (ἐννέα,) Lat. nonus, ninth.

ἔνδεκα, οἱ, αἱ, τά, (ἔν, δέκα,) Lat. undecim, eleven.

ἐνδέξιος, α, ον, to the right ; ἐνδέξια as adv., from the left hand even to the right, A 597 ; propitious, of good omen, good, Lat. dexter.

ἐνδέω, f. ήσω, aor. ἐνέδησα, (ἐν, δέω,) Lat. illigere, to fasten to or bind on to ; involve, B 111.

ἐνδίεσαν, 2 aor. 3 pl. of ἐνδίημι, (deriv. uncertain, perhaps ἐν and δίω,) to follow persistently, pursue.

ἔνδοθι, (ἔνδον,) Lat. intus, within ; of members of a family, at home.

ἔνδον, (ἐν,) adv., Lat. intus, within ; within doors or at home.

ἐνδύω, ἐνδύνω, ἐνδύομαι, f. ἐνδύσω, aor. ἐνέδυσα, 2 aor. ἐνέδυν ; ἐνδύνω = ἐνδύομαι, and 2 aor. are intrans.: trans. Lat. induere, to put on to one, as clothes or armor, to put on or dress in : intrans., to enter.

ἔνειμι, (ἐν, εἰμί,) Lat. in esse, to be in, within or at home, be among, remained in, A 593 ; to be permitted or possible.

ἕνεκα, poet. Ep. **εἵνεκα, εἵνεκεν, ἕνεκεν,** prep. with gen., Lat. *causa, because of; for, on account of, as concerns, regarding; by.*

ἐνενήκοντα, οἱ, αἱ, τά, (**ἐννέα,**) Lat. *nonaginta, ninety.*

ἐνέπω, ἐννέπω; f. **ἐνισπήσω, ἐνίψω;** 2 aor. **ἔνισπον;** *to tell, declare, relate; announce; report; speak.*

Ἐνετοί, ῶν, οἱ, *the En'-e-ti,* a tribe living in Paph-la-go'-ni-a.

ἐνήρατο, aor. mid. Ep. 3 sing. of **ἐναίρω,** which see.

ἔνθα, (**ἐν,**) adv., of place, Lat. *ibi, there; whither,* A 610; *hither, thither,* Lat. *illuc; where; ἔνθα καὶ ἔνθα,* B 812, *on this side and on that, on every side:* of time, *then,* B 308; *when; thereupon.*

ἔνθαδε, adv., Lat. *illuc, thither;* Lat. *hic, here.*

ἔνθεν, (**ἔνθα** *there,* Lat. *ibi,*) adv., Lat. *illinc, from that place; then, so then, therefore.*

ἐνί, poet. for **ἐν,** which see.

ἔνι = **ἔνεστι.**

ἐνιαυτός, οῦ, ὁ, (**ἔνος,**) Lat. *annus, a year; a period of time, an age.*

Ἐνιῆνες, ων, οἱ, *Æ-ni-a'-nes,* a Thes-sa'-lian tribe.

ἐνιπρήθω, Hom. for **ἐμπρήθω;** aor. **ἐνέπρησα,** A 481; (**ἐν, πρήθω;**) Lat. *inflare, to fill with wind, inflate; to kindle, burn.*

ἐνίπτω; f. **ἐνίψω;** Ep. 2 aor. **ἠνίπαπον** B 245 and Γ 427, **ἐνένιπον:** Lat. *objurgare, to scold, chide, reproach; to announce.*

Ἐνίσπη, ης, ἡ, *E-nis'-pe,* a town of Ar-ca'-di-a.

ἔνισπον, see **ἐνέπω.**

ἐνίσσω, *to upbraid, chide; abuse.*

ἔνατος, incorrect for **ἔνατος,** which see.

ἐννέα, Lat. *novem, nine.*

ἐννεάβοιος, ον, (**ἐννέα, βοῦς,**) *worth nine oxen or kine.*

ἐννεα-και-δεκα, Lat. *novemdecim, nineteen.*

ἐννῆμαρ, (**ἐννέα, ῆμαρ,**) adv., *nine days long.*

Ἔννομος, ου, ὁ, (**ἐν, νόμος,**) lit. *within the limits of the law,* i.e., *lawful, upright; En'-no-mus,* a Tro'-jan ally.

ἔννυχος, ον, = **ἐννύχιος,** adj., (**ἐν, νύξ,**) Lat. *noctu, nightly, by night.*

ἐννύω, ἔννυμι; f. **ἔσω:** Ep. forms f. **ἔσσω;** aor. **ἔσσα** and **ἑσσάμην,** 3 sing. **ἕσσατο;** pf. 2 pers. **ἔσσαι;** plup. 3 sing. **ἕεστο,** other Ep. forms from (ε)εσ(σ)-: Lat. *vestire, to put on to another person, put on:* mid. *put on or cover one's self, put on:* pass. *to be clad in;* Γ 57, *thou hadst put on or been clothed with thy tunic of stone* = *hadst been buried.*

ἐνοπή, ῆς, ἡ, (**ἐνέπω,**) *a shout, cry, call, the battle-shout,* Γ 2; *voice; sound.*

ἐνόρνυμι; f. **ἐνόρσω;** (**ἐν, ὄρνυμι;**) *to excite or stir up in:* **ἐνῶρτο,** 2 aor. pass. Ep. 3 sing. *to begin among.*

ἔντεα, ων, τά, *utensils, instruments;* with δαιτός, *table-furniture;* with νηός, *rigging of a ship; trappings; armor,* Γ 339, *arms.*

ἐντίθημι, for parts see τίθημι, Lat. *imponere,* (ἐν, τίθημι,) *to put into, introduce into, inculcate, infuse into.*

ἐντός, (ἐν,) adv., Lat. *intus, within, inside:* as a prep. with gen., *in, within; at this side.*

ἔντοσθε(ν), *from inside.*

ἐντροπαλίζομαι, *to turn constantly about.*

'Ενύαλιος, ου, ὁ, ('Ενυώ,) *the warlike,* A'-res.

ἐνύπνιον, ου, τό, neu. of ἐνύπνιος, (ἐν, ὕπνος,) as subst., Lat. *insomnium* (what is the difference between this and *somnium ?*) *that which is seen during sleep, a dream:* as adv., *in sleep,* B 56.

'Ενυώ, όος, ἡ, *E-ny'-o,* war-goddess.

ἐξάγω, for parts see ἄγω, (ἐξ, ἄγω,) Lat. *educere, to lead out, lead out of* or *forth; to bring out* or *forward, to lead on; to carry off, drive off; perform; drive away:* seemingly intrans., *go out.*

'Εξάδιος, ου, ὁ, *Ex-a'-di-us,* one of the Lap'-i-thae, A 264.

ἐξαίνυμαι, (ἐκ, αἴνυμαι,) *to carry away.*

ἐξαιρέω, (ἐκ, αἱρέω,) for parts see αἱρέω, *to take from, take away* or *out of, remove, take away; to select; to lay in ruins.*

ἐξακέομαι, (ἐκ, ἀκέομαι,) *to heal fully, cure, soothe.*

ἐξαλαπάζω, f. ξω, *to destroy.*

ἐξαλέομαι, (ἐκ, ἀλέομαι,) *to look upon suspiciously, avoid.*

ἐξάλλομαι, tenses formed from stem -αλ-, see Hadley and Allen's Gram. 518, 3, (ἐκ, ἄλλομαι,) *to leap forth, leap out from, spring up out of; leap* or *jump up, to be prominent; to come about.*

ἐξαναλύω, f. ύσω, (ἐκ, ἀναλύω,) Lat. *liberare, to loose, set entirely free.*

ἐξανίημι, f. ἐξανήσω, (ἐκ, ἀνίημι,) *to send* or *let go forth, dismiss from.*

ἐξαπατάω, f. ήσω, (ἐκ, ἀπατάω,) Lat. *decipere, to deceive fully.*

ἐξαπίνης, *suddenly, of a sudden.*

ἐξάπτω, f. ψω, (ἐκ, ἅπτω,) *to tie to, hang to.*

ἐξαρπάζω; f. άσω, άξω; (ἐξ, ἁρπάζω;) *to carry off by force, snatch away; to snatch* or *rescue from, save.*

ἔξαρχος, ου, ὁ, (ἐκ, ἄρχω,) *one who begins; a leader, a chief.*

ἐξάρχω, f. ξω, (ἐκ or ἐξ, ἄρχω,) *to commence, make a beginning, begin; lead.*

ἐξαυδάω, f. ήσω, (ἐξ, αὐδάω,) *to utter, speak out,* see Lat. *eloqui.*

ἐξαῦτις, for ἐξαῦθις, (ἐξ, αὖτις,) adv., Lat. *rursus, again, once again; back again.*

ἐξείης, poet. for ἐξῆς, (ἔξω,) adv., Lat. *deinceps, in order, one after another, in succession.*

ἐξεῖπον, (ἐξ, εἶπον,) *to speak out, proclaim, declare ; betray, divulge.*

ἐξελαύνω, for parts see ἐλαύνω or ἐλάω, (ἐκ, ἐλαύνω,) see Lat. *expellere, to drive from, drive out, expel ; to lead out* or away on an expedition ; *to beat out* or *work metals.*

ἐξελεῖν, 2 aor. of ἐξαιρέω, which see.

ἐξέλκω ; tenses are formed from stems -ελκ- and -ελκυ-, see Hadley and Allen's Gram., 503, 19, (ἐκ, ἕλκω,) *to draw out, save;* also, *to prolong, extend.*

ἐξεναρίζω, (ἐκ, ἐναρίζω,) *to strip entirely, ruin, destroy, kill.*

ἐξερέω, (ἐξ or ἐκ, ἐρέω,) a f., the pres. being supplied by other verbs, *to speak out, declare.*

ἐξέρχομαι, for parts see ἔρχομαι, (ἐκ, ἔρχομαι,) *to come* or *go out of* or *through, go out* or *come to an end.*

ἐξηγέομαι, f. ήσομαι, *to direct, lead, conduct ; to govern ; to lead on ; to show* or *teach ; to be leader of; to narrate.*

ἐξήκοντα, (ἔξ,) Lat. *sexaginta, sixty.*

ἐξίημι, f. ήσω, Ep. 2 aor. inf. ἐξέμεν, *to dismiss, send forth :* mid. *remove, put away ; to put off* or *send from one's self,* A 469.

ἐξοίχομαι, (ἐκ, οἴχομαι,) *to be out, be gone out.*

ἐξονομάζω, f. ἄσω, (ἐξ, ὀνομάζω,) *to speak out, proclaim, spoke the word and called him by name,* A 361.

ἐξονομαίνω, (ἐξ, ὄνομα,) Γ 166, Lat. *nomine vocare, to name, mention by name.*

ἐξονομοκλήδην, (ἐκ, ὄνομα, καλέω,) adv., *calling-by-name.*

ἐξορούω, f. σω, (ἐξ, ὀρούω,) Lat. *exsilire, to jump* or *spring out,* Γ 325.

ἔξοχος, ον, (ἐξέχω,) *being above, prominent ; distinguished,* with gen., *distinguished of* or *above,* Γ 227, Β 480.

ἐξυπανίστημι, (ἐξ, ὑπό, ἀνά, ἵστημι,) *to cause to come* or *start up ;* intrans. in 2 aor. act., **ἐξυπανέστη,** Β 267, *started up from the back under the sceptre.*

ἕο, Ep. for οὗ, gen. of pers. pron. *his, of him.*

ἔοικα, Ion. οἶκα, pres. εἴκω obsol., pf. with sense of pres., *to be like,* Ep. 3 du. εἴκτον, Att. also Hom. part. εἰκώς, υῖα, ός, Ion. οἰκώς ; Ep. plup. 3 pl.

ἐοίκεσαν, Ep. pass. 3 sing. ἤϊκτο: *to be like ; to be fitting, be right ;* ἔοικε, *it is seemly, right ; to appear, seem,* part. ἐοικώς as adj., *proper, right, fitting, just.*

ἔολπα, part. 2 pf. of ἔλπω, which see.

ἔοργα, Ion. pf. of ἔρδω, which see.

ἑός, ή, όν, Ep. for ὅς, ή, ὄν, (ἕ,) possessive adj. pron., Lat. *suus, his, her* or *hers, their.*

4

ἐπαγείρω, (ἐπί, ἀγείρω,) f. γερῶ, compare Lat. *colligere, congregare, to collect, bring together.*

ἐπαιγίζω, f. σω, (ἐπί, αἶγίς,) *to rush violently on to.*

ἐπαινέω, f. ἔσω, (ἐπί, αἰνέω,) see Lat. *approbare, to consent* or *agree to, approve,* Β 335, Γ 461 ; *to laud, praise,* Lat. *laudare.*

ἐπαίσσω, f. αἶξω, (ἐπί, ἀίσσω,) *to rush upon* or *against ; assault, assail, attack ;* compare Lat. *adoriri, invadere.*

ἐπαίτιος, ον, (ἐπί, αἰτία,) *culpable, blamed, blamable.*

ἐπακούω, aor. ἐπήκουσα, (ἐπί, ἀκούω,) with acc. and gen., *to hearken to, hear* Γ 277, *attend to ; hear and obey,* Β 143.

ἔπαλξις, εως, ἡ, (ἐπαλέξω,) *works of defence, parapet, breastwork ; a defence.*

ἐπαμείβω, f. ψω, (ἐπί, ἀμείβω,) *to change, exchange, alternate :* mid. *to alternate.*

ἐπαμύνω, (ἐπί, ἀμύνω,) *to come to one's assistance, aid.*

ἐπανίστημι, f. στήσω, aor. ἐπανέστησα, (ἐπί, ἀνίστημι,) compare with Lat. *excitare, to cause to rise, excite, raise, set up :* intrans. in 2 aor. ἐπανέστην, pf. ἐπανέστηκα, *to rise up, to rise and stand up ; rise in.*

ἐπαπειλέω, f. ἤσω, (ἐπί, ἀπειλέω, Lat. *minari* in one of its senses,) *to threaten ; to add threats ; to menace besides.*

ἐπαρήγω, f. ἤξω, (ἐπί, ἀρήγω,) *to come to any one's assistance, succor,* Α 408.

ἐπαρκέω, (ἐπί, ἀρκέω,) *to ward off from ; hinder ; to furnish* or *provide enough.*

ἐπάρχω, f. ξω, (ἐπί, ἄρχω,) *to govern* or *rule,* the act. is not found in Hom.: mid. *to begin anew ;* Α 471 *having begun again with the cups,* i.e. *having again filled the cups for distribution.*

ἐπάσαντο, see πατέομαι.

ἐπασσύτερος, α, ον, (ἐπί, ἄσσον,) *one close upon the next, in rapid succession* or *one quick upon another,* Α 383, *crowded together,* compare Lat. *alter post alterum, creber, frequens.*

ἐπαυρίσκομαι, f. ἐπαυρήσομαι, 2 aor. Hom. inf. ἐπαυρέμεν, 2 aor. Hom. mid. subj. 2 sing. ἐπαύρηαι ; *to take a portion* of anything ; *taste of ; touch, hit ; reach* or *attain to ; enjoy :* mid. *to take to one's self* of anything ; *to suffer, enjoy,* Α 410.

ἐπέδραμον, 2 aor. of ἐπιτρέχω, which see.

ἐπεί, Hom. also ἐπειή, (ἐπί,) conj., *after ; since, when, seeing that ; after that,* Lat. *postquam : since, because, for the reason that :* with particles, with ἄρ or ἄρα, *when* or *since therefore ;* Hom. ἐπεί κε, see ἄν ; with περ, *seeing that ;* αὐτάρ ἐπεί, *yet when ;* with γε, *since at all events ;* with δή, *since now, when now, since that, after that,* Lat. *postquam ;* with τοι or ᾖ, *since indeed.*

ἐπείγω, f. ξω, aor. ἤπειξα, aor. pass. ἠπείχθην, Lat. *urgēre, to press hard upon* or *down, to push, press, urge, oppress; to press hard in pursuit, pursue; to drive, urge,* or *hurry forward, quicken, accelerate:* as seemingly intrans., *to urge one's self along, make haste:* mid., *to urge on for one's own benefit:* pass. *to be pressed on* and *so to hurry.*

ἐπειή, (ἐπεί, ἤ,) see ἐπεί.

ἔπειμι, f. ἐπέσομαι, (ἐπί, εἰμί,) *to be on, upon,* or *over, remain on,* B 259 ; *to be after* or *remain.*

ἔπειμι, inf. ἐπιέναι, Hom. pr. indic. 2 sing. εἶσθα ; Ep. impf. ἐπήϊα or ἤϊον, ας, ε, pl. ἐπῇομεν, 3 pers. ἤϊσαν, ἦσαν, ἤϊον ; f. ἐπιείσομαι ; (ἐπί, εἶμι, Lat. *ire,) to go to, go towards; to come to* or *towards, approach, come near; to come upon; to come* or *go against, attack, assail; to come on* or *come,* ὁ ἐπιών *the one coming,* i.e. *the one coming first,* τὸ ἐπιόν *what comes* or *occurs, follows, succeeds; to pass* or *go over; to go through* or *over.*

Ἐπειοί, ῶν, οἱ, *the E-pe'-i,* inhabitants of E'-lis.

Ἐπειός, οῦ, ὁ, *E-pe'-us,* see Classical Dictionary.

ἔπειτα, (ἐπί, εἶτα,) adv., Lat. *deinde, then, afterwards, thereupon, directly after, next in order; so then, therefore;* and *yet, still;* with ὁ, ἡ, τό, *the following.*

ἐπέκειντο, impf. 3 pl. of ἐπίκειμαι, *to be put* or *laid on, be placed on, be brought to* and *closed; to be heavy upon, press a request.*

ἐπενήνοθε, (ἐπί, ἐνήνοθε,) 3 sing. 2 pf., pres. or impf. in sense ; there is no pres. in use from this stem ; *to be grown upon, be upon, grew thereon.*

ἐπέοικε, (ἐπί, ἔοικε,) impersonal pf. from ἐπείκω, which is obsol., *it is like; it is becoming, it is fitting, is not fitting,* A 126 ; *it suits, pleases,* or *is agreeable.*

ἐπέπιθμεν for ἐπεποίθειμεν, pl. plup. of πείθω.

ἐπερέφω, (ἐπί, ἐρέφω,) *to roof over, cover with garlands,* A 39.

ἐπερρώσαντο, 3 pl. aor. of ἐπιρρώομαι.

ἐπερύω, f. ύσω, aor. ἐπείρυσα, (ἐπί, ἐρύω,) *to draw towards* or *upon; to bring to:* mid. *to draw on to one's self.*

ἐπέρχομαι, for parts see ἔρχομαι, (ἐπί, ἔρχομαι,) *to go to, come to, arrive at, approach; to come on* or *occur; to come* or *fall upon, to come unexpectedly, surprise; to move against; to come on* or *forward; to traverse; to occur to one.*

ἐπεσβόλος, ον, (ἔπος, βάλλω,) *throwing words, talking foolishly, impudent,* B 275.

ἐπευφημέω, f. ήσω, *to shout approval; to praise in song.*

ἐπεύχομαι, f. ξομαι, (ἐπί, εὔχομαι,) *to pray, to invoke, supplicate; to call down curses upon another,* with dat.; *to exult* or *boast.*

ἔπεφνον, Ep. 2 aor. of φένω.

ἐπέχω, f. ἐφέξω, for other parts see ἔχω, (ἐπί, ἔχω,) *to have upon, hold upon or at, apply to, have or hold towards, keep to or on, have, keep, hold; to keep at or striving for; to have control of; to offer to; to hold in check, hold from, restrain,* also, *to hold one's self from or stop, leave off; to keep close to; to hold to or assail.*

ἐπημύω, f. ύσω, (ἐπί, ἡμύω,) *to bow down, bend down,* B 148.

ἐπήν, (ἐπεί, ἄν,) conj. *when, after, as soon as, whenever,* see Hadley and Allen's Gram., 1055, 5.

ἔπηξα, aor. of πήγνυμι.

ἐπηπύω, (ἐπί, ἠπύω,) *to call out encouragingly to, encourage.*

ἐπήρατος, ον, (ἐπί, ἐράω,) *to be lovable, loved, pleasant.*

ἐπήτριμος, ον, (ἐπί, ἤτριον,) *on the warp* or *closely woven; compact, thronged with people.*

ἐπί, *on, upon,* prep. with all the oblique cases: with gen. *at, amid, among, by, upon, in, near by; over; to, towards; before,* Lat. *coram, with reference to;* with numbers *by,* as ἐπί τριῶν *by threes, by, according to;* temporal, *in, during, in the time of:* with dat., *at, on, close upon, upon, in; after; thereupon; against; over and above, besides; in the hands of; because of, for, with one eye to:* with acc., *to, towards; against; among, throughout; for; upon, as to; over, extending over; according to, by;* τὸ ἐπ' ἐμέ, *as regards me;* ἐπ' ὅσσον, *how far;* ἐπὶ πολύ, *to a great extent;* ἐπὶ τὸ πολύ, *for the most part;* ἐπὶ τόσσον, *so far, so large, so much;* ἐπὶ τί, *for what? wherefore;* ἐπὶ χρόνον, *for a time;* with numbers, *up to, about, nearly;* temporal, *during, till:* in compo. denotes *on, upon, at; toward, against; after, unto;* often it cannot be translated.

ἐπιβαίνω, for parts see βαίνω, (ἐπί, βαίνω,) *to go upon, mount; to arrive at, come to; walk upon, be on; to come* or *fall upon* in attack, *assail; to come upon, find.*

ἐπιβάσκω, (ἐπί, βάσκω,) Hom. trans. of ἐπιβαίνω, B 234 ἔμεν poet. inf., *to lead* the sons of the Greeks or *cause them to go* into evils.

ἐπιβρίθω, (ἐπί, βρίθω,) *to lie heavily on, press upon.*

ἐπιγίγνομαι, for parts see γίγνομαι, (ἐπί, γίγνομαι,) *to come into existence* or *happen on* or *after, come after; to come* or *fall upon, assault.*

ἐπιγνάμπτω, f. ψω, (ἐπί, γνάμπτω,) Lat. *flectere, to bend, turn; to bend to one's will, prevail on, to bend* or *restrain the spirit,* A 569.

ἐπιγράφω, for parts see γράφω, (ἐπί, γράφω,) *to make a scratch upon, mark, write on:* see Eng. Ep'-i-graph.

Ἐπίδαυρος, ου, ὁ, ἡ, *Ep-i-dau'-rus,* a town of Ar'-go-lis.

ἐπιδεής, ές, poet. and Ion. -δευής, ές, (ἐπιδέομαι,) *wanting, lacking, defective; falling short of.*

ἐπιδέξιος, ον, (ἐπί, δεξιός,) on or *towards the right:* as adv., ἐπιδέξια, on the right, auspiciously B 353, in seeking omens the Greeks faced to the north.

ἐπιδεύομαι, Hom. for ἐπιδέομαι, (ἐπιδέω, *to be in want of,*) *to lack, to want,* B 229.

ἐπιδίδωμι, see δίδωμι, (ἐπί, δίδωμι,) *to give in addition.*

ἐπιδινέω, f. ήσω, (ἐπί, δινέω,) *to whirl,* having *whirled* Γ 378 : mid. *to revolve in the mind,* Lat. volvere animo.

ἐπίδρομος, ον, *capable of being run over* or *upon, capable of being scaled.*

ἐπιδύω and **ἐπιδύνω,** f. ύσω, (ἐπί, δύω,) *to sink* or *set upon;* B 413 *to go down* or *set,* Lat. occidere.

ἐπιείκελος, ον, (ἐπί, εἴκελος,) *like.*

ἐπιεικής, ές, (ἐπί, εἰκός,) *seemly, meet, becoming; suitable.*

ἐπιέλπομαι, Ep. for ἐπέλπομαι, (ἐπί, ἔλπω,) Lat. sperare, *to hope; to expect.*

ἐπιέννυμι, Ion., (ἐπί, ἔννυμι,) aor. ἐπίεσα, Ion. pf. pass. part. ἐπιειμένος, *clad in,* A 149 ; compare with Lat. *induere, to put on in addition, put on ·* mid., *to put on one's self.*

ἐπίηρα, neu. pl. adj. ; *agreeable* things, A 572, 578.

ἐπιθαρσύνω, (ἐπί, θαρσύνω,) *to encourage.*

ἐπιθρώσκω, (ἐπί, θρώσκω,) *to leap upon; to jump* or *spring forward; leap upon insultingly.*

ἐπίκειμαι, (ἐπί, κεῖμαι,) *to lie upon, rest upon, be upon; to be set to* or *closed.*

ἐπικερτομέω, (ἐπί, κερτομέω,) *to mock at, vex, annoy.*

ἐπικίδνημι, (ἐπί, κίδνημι,) *to strew upon;* pass., *to be spread over* or *diffused.*

ἐπίκλησις, εως, ἡ (ἐπικαλέω,) *an added name, a surname, nickname, a name; a bad name* or *insult.*

ἐπίκλοπος, ον, (ἐπί, κλοπή, κλοπός,) *addicted to thieving, given to theft; sly, furtive; cunning, crafty.*

ἐπικλώθω, (ἐπί, κλώθω,) *to spin out,* or *allot.*

ἐπικουρέω, f. ήσω, (ἐπίκουρος,) see Lat. auxiliari, *to aid, succor, help,* in war ; *to aid, render assistance.*

ἐπίκουρος, (ἐπί, κοῦρος,) *aiding;* in Hom. as subst., *one who aids, an auxiliary;* see Lat. auxiliator.

ἐπικραιαίνω, Ep. for foll.

ἐπικραίνω, f. κρανῶ ; Ep. aor. -κρ(ή)ηνα (ἐπί, κραίνω,) compare Lat. efficere, perficere, *to bring about, fulfil, accomplish.*

ἐπικρήηνον, Ep. aor. imperat. of foreg., A 455.

ἐπιλανθάνω, for parts see λανθάνω, (ἐπί, λανθάνω,) *to cause to forget :* also, intr. *to be unnoticed* or *out of notice.*

ἐπὶ . . . λείβε, Α 462, see ἐπιλείβω.

ἐπιλείβω, (ἐπί, λείβω,) to pour out a libation upon.

ἐπιλεύσσω, f. λεύσω, (ἐπί, λεύσσω,) to look forwards or to ; after τόσσον τίς τ', Γ 12, any one sees before himself so much.

ἐπιμαίνομαι, (ἐπί, μαίνομαι,) to be greatly or desperately in love with.

ἐπιμαίομαι, (ἐπί, μαίομαι,) to make great efforts after, strive for ; to take hold of.

ἐπιμέμφομαι, f. ψομαι, (ἐπί, μέμφομαι,) to blame, find fault with : intrans., blame or be dissatisfied because of, with gen., Α 65, Β 225 ; complain.

ἐπιμιμνήσκω, f. μνήσω, (ἐπί, μιμνήσκω,) to remind of, remind : mid. and pass. to bear in mind, remember, call to mind.

ἐπιμύζω, (ἐπί, μύζω,) Δ 23, to grumble at.

ἐπινέμω, f. εμῶ, εμήσω ; aor. ἐπένειμα, (ἐπί, νέμω,) compare Lat. distribuere, partiri, dividere, to allot, share among, portion out.

ἐπινεύω, f. νεύσω, (ἐπί, νεύω,) Lat. annuere, to nod forwards, nod to, expressing promise, command, confirmation, assent, approval, etc. ; to nod assent or command ; to promise by a nod, Α 528.

ἐπίορκος, ον, (ἐπί, ὅρκος,) Lat. perjurus, perjured ; neu. as adv., falsely, Γ 279.

ἐπιπάσσω, f. άσω, (ἐπί, πάσσω,) Lat. inspergere, to strew or sprinkle over or upon.

ἐπιπείθομαι, f. πείσομαι, (ἐπί, πείθομαι,) pass., to yield to persuasion, hence be persuaded ; to put confidence in, trust, Β 341 Ep. sync. 2 plup., hence to yield to in the sense of to obey.

ἐπιπλέω, Ion. and Ep. ἐπιπλώω ; f. πλεύσομαι ; Ion. aor. part. ἐπιπλώσας ; Ep. 2 aor. ἐπέπλων, (ἐπί, πλέω,) to sail away upon, Α 312.

ἐπιπλώσας, Ion. aor. part. of foreg.

ἐπιπνείω, Hom. for ἐπιπνέω, f. νεύσομαι, (ἐπί, πνέω,) Lat. inspirare, adspirare, to blow upon, breathe upon or into ; inspire, animate, incite ; encourage ; to breathe prosperously upon, prosper, favor.

ἐπιπροΐημι, (ἐπί, προΐημι,) to send out to.

ἐπιπροέμεν, Ep. 2 aor. inf. of foreg.

ἐπιπωλέομαι, (ἐπί, πωλέομαι,) Lat. obire, to go over ; walk around ; to review, look over, inspect, Γ 196.

ἐπιρρέω, f. ῥεύσομαι, (ἐπί, ῥέω,) to flow over, Β 754 ; to stream towards.

ἐπιρρώομαι, f. ῥώσομαι, aor. ἐρρωσάμην, (ἐπί, ῥώομαι,) to roll or flow down upon ; to fall waving down from the immortal head, Α 529, ἐπερρώσαντο aor.

ἐπισ(σ)εύω, (ἐπί, σεύω,) to urge against, send upon, set in motion against, let loose upon : pass., to hasten to ; to attack.

ἐπίσκοπος, ου, ὁ, (ἐπισκοπέω (ἐπί, σκοπέω),) *one who watches over and protects, a watch.*

ἐπισπεῖν, 2 aor. inf. of ἐφέπω.

ἐπισ(σ)είω, (ἐπί, σείω,) *to shake* or *brandish at* or *against.*

ἐπισσεύω, Ep. for ἐπισεύω.

ἐπίσταμαι, Ion. 2 sing. and 3 pl. ἐπίστῃ, ἐπιστέαται, Ion. imperat. ἐπίστασο; impf. ἠπιστάμην, Hom. without aug.; f. ἐπιστήσομαι; aor. pass., ἠπιστήθην, (ἐπί, ἴσαμι for ἴσημι,) *to know, to understand,* B 611; with direct object, *to have full knowledge of, know, to be skilful in.*

ἐπιστενάχομαι, for ἐπιστένω, (ἐπί, στένω,) *to sorrow about, grieve for, mourn over.*

ἐπιστένω, see ἐπιστενάομαι.

ἐπιστέφω, f. ψω, (ἐπί, στέφω,) *to crown :* mid. A 470, *to crown (fill to the brim).*

ἐπιστρέφω, f. ψω, 2 aor. pass. ἐπεστράφην, (ἐπί, στρέφω,) *to turn round to, having turned himself to,* Γ 370 ; *to correct,* i. e. *turn from an error ; to turn :* intrans., *to turn round* or *any way ; to turn and come back.*

Ἐπίστροφος, ου, ὁ, *E-pis'-tro-phus.*

ἐπισφύριον, ου, τό, (ἐπί, σφυρόν,) *a tie* or *clasp to fasten the greaves,* Γ 331, *ancle-clasps ; an ancle-covering.*

ἐπιτέλλω, f. τελῶ, aor. ἐπέτειλα, pf. ἐπιτέταλκα, (ἐπί, τέλλω,) *to put upon, charge, impose, enjoin, to add* A 25 ; *to command* B 802, *to give orders to* B 643, ἐπετέταλτο, 3 sing. plup., *it had been entrusted.*

ἐπιτετράφαται, perf. pass. Ion. 3 pl. of ἐπιτρέπω, B 25.

ἐπιτηδές, (ἐπί, τάδε,) adv., *sufficient for the purpose,* A 142 ; *purposely.*

ἐπιτίθημι, f. ἐπιθήσω, aor. ἐπέθηκα (What three verbs take κ in the aor. ?), pf. ἐπιτέθεικα, 2 aor. pass., ἐπεθέμεν, (ἐπί, τίθημι,) Lat. *imponere, to put upon, place upon, lay upon, impose ; to turn towards, apply to, set on ; to enjoin, charge, command : to put to* or *close to anything ; to add ; to impose a penalty :* mid., *to put upon one's self,* and so *to give the attention to* or *engage in.*

ἐπιτοξάζομαι, (ἐπί, τοξάζομαι,) *to shoot at.*

ἐπιτρέπω, ψω ; aor. ἐπέτρεψα ; 2 aor. ἐπέτραπον, mid. ᾽πετραπόμην ; aor. pass. ἐπετράφθην ; 2 aor. pass. ἐπετράπην, pf. pass. -τετρα-: (ἐπί, τρέπω,) *to turn to ; to give up to, hand over, put into one's hands ; to leave as an inheritance to ; give up, to concede to, yield to ;* Lat. *concedere ; to permit.*

ἐπιτρέχω, for parts see τρέχω, Hadley and Allen's Grammar, 539, 5 (ἐπί, τρέχω,) *to run up to, rush upon ; to go after ; to run* or *spread out over.*

ἐπιτροχάδην, adv., (ἐπιτροχάζω,) *glibly, briefly,* Γ 213.

ἐπιφέρω, for prin. parts see **φέρω**, (ἐπί, φέρω,) Lat. *inferre, to put upon, impose, lay* or *bring upon,* A 89, Γ 132; *to do violence to, assail;* to *bring against* or *impute to; to offer:* mid. *to bring with one's self.*

ἐπιφλέγω, (ἐπί, φλέγω,) *to set on fire, burn,* B 455; *to make brilliant,* see Lat. *illustrare; to inflame, rouse, excite;* intraus. *to blaze forth, shine.*

ἐπιφράζω, f. σω (ἐπί, φράζω,) *to say* or *declare in addition to* or *after:* mid. and pass. *to think; to think upon; invent, contrive; to observe, recognize;* Ep. opt., ἐπιφρασσαίατο, B 282.

ἐπιχθόνιος, adj., (ἐπί, χθών,) *on the earth, earthly:* as subst. *a mortal.*

ἔπλεο and **ἔπλευ,** 2 sing. 2 aor. mid. of **πέλομαι,** A 418.

ἐποίσω, see **ἐπιφέρω.**

ἐποίχομαι, f. χήσομαι, (ἐπί, οἴχομαι,) compare Lat. *accedere, invadere, to go* or *come to* or *towards;* also *to approach with hostile intent, attack,* A 50; *to go throughout* or *round, go to each one in turn,* A 383; *tø go about* a task; A 31, *to go about* or *be occupied at the loom,* Lat. *percurrere telam.*

ἔπορον, see **πόρον.**

ἐπορούω, f. ούσω, (ἐπί, ὀρούω,) *to rush upon* or *at,* Γ 379; *attack; to come quickly upon.*

ἔπος, εος, τό, *a word,* A 77; *that which has been spoken,* A 108; *discourse, narrative, speech,* Γ 83; *song, story; prophetic utterance; promise; meaning of an utterance;* compare Lat. *vox, verbum, dictum.*

ἐποτρύνω, (ἐπί, ὀτρύνω,) *to drive on, rouse up against, rouse up.*

ἐπουράνιος, α, ον, (ἐπί, οὐρανός,) *of heaven, pertaining to heaven, celestial.*

ἔπραθον, 2 aor. of **πέρθω.**

ἔπω, f. ἔψω; 2 aor. ἔσπον; mid. ἑσπόμην; see Hadley and Allen's Gram., 508, 13; Ep. 2 aor. imperat. mid. σπεῖο : *to be busy about, occupied with:* mid. *to follow,* i. e. Lat. *sequi,* B 675, Γ 376, 447; *to go with* or *attend,* A 424; *to obey; to follow,* i. e. *to belong to,* Γ 255; *to follow with hostile intent, pursue; to follow with the understanding, understand.*

ἔραμαι, Ep. 2 pl. ἔρασθε : *to be in love with; long for; desire,* with gen.

ἐρατεινός, ή, όν, (ἐρατός, ἐράω,) *lovely, amiable, charming; pleasing,* Γ 175.

ἐρατός, ή, όν, (ἐράω,) poet. for ἐραστός, *longed for, beloved; lovely, charming.*

ἔ(ε)ργαθον, Ep. 2 aor. of εἴργω, see ἔργω.

ἔργον, ου, τό, (ἔργω, *to work,*) *work; employment, pursuit; deed, something done;* Lat. *opus,* as opp. to ἔπος, (*something spoken,*) A 395, *achievements,* B 338, Γ 130; *task, business,* B 436; *husbandry, work in field; property, possessions, tilled fields,* B 751; *a thing,* A 294; *works, doings,* A 573, Γ 321; *a hard work.*

ἔργω, in Hom. words are usu. from stems ϝέργ-, ϝ(ε)ρχ-, (ει)(ει)ργ-, Lat. *in-*

cludere, to keep in, confine, keep close, cut off from liberty ; also, in the sense of *to keep out from, debar, prohibit, cut off :* Ep. and Ion. 3 pl. endings -αται, -ατο : Β 617.

ἔργω, obsol. in pres., f. ἔρξω ; aor. ἔρξα ; 2 pf. ἔοργα, part. ἐοργώς ; *to do work, to do, perform ;* with ἱερά, *to perform rites of sacrifice,* Lat. *sacra, facere :* ἔρδω is used as a pres.

ἔρδω, see foreg.

ἐρεβεννός, contr. ἐρεμνός, ή, όν, ("Ερεβος,) see Lat. *furvus, gloomy, obscure, dark.*

ἐρεείνω, *to question, to ask.*

ἐρεθίζω, f. ίσω, aor. ἠρέθισα, (ἐρέθω,) *to excite, provoke, irritate, to enrage.*

ἐρέθω, *to enrage, to distress.*

ἐρείδω, f. ἐρείσω, pf. ἐρήρεισμαι, 3 sing. plupf. pass. ἠρήρειστο Γ 358, *to lean one thing against another ; to support ; to press against* or *upon ; to support firmly, stay ; fix firm ; fix on ; to press upon firmly* or *fix into ; rest upon ; to lean* or *press upon ; to contend against ; withstand, beset ; to press against hard* or *push to close quarters, struggle against :* intrans. *to crowd together ; to fall to ; to go to work :* mid. and pass. *to support one's self on,* i. e. *lean on ;* ἐρεισάμενος, *having planted himself ; had been fixed = stuck fast,* Γ 358 ; *to strive among themselves* or *one against another.*

ἐρείομεν, see ἐρέω.

ἐρείπω, f. ἐρείψω, aor. ἤρειψα, 2 aor. ἤριπον, 2 pf. ἐρήριπα, aor. pass. ἠρείφθην, Lat. *evertere, demoliri, to throw down, overturn, destroy :* intrans. in 2 aor. and 2 pf., *to fall down.*

ἐρεμνός, see ἐρεβεννός.

ἐρέπτομαι, *to feed upon, eat,* Β 776.

ἐρέουσα, Β 49, *about to announce,* Ep. part. from ἐρῶ.

ἐρέτης, ου, ὁ, (ἐρέσσω,) Lat. *remex, a rower.*

ἐρετμός, οῦ, ὁ, and ἐρετμόν, οῦ, τό, (ἐρέσσω,) Lat. *remus, an oar.*

'Ερεχθεύς, έως, ὁ, *E-rech'-the-us,* king and national hero of Ath'-ens, Ep. gen. ῆος.

ἐρέω, Ep. for ἐρῶ, f. with no pres. form ; pres. is supplied by λέγω, φημί, and ἀγορεύω ; Hadley and Allen's Gram., art. 539, 8 and D 8 : *say, speak ; tell, announce, promise ; to order to :* in Hom. as pres. for ἔρομαι, εἴρομαι, ἐρείομεν, Α 62, Ep. for ἐρέωμεν, subj. pl., *to ask.*

ἔρημος, adj., *lone, desolate, forsaken ; bereft* or *destitute of, forsaken by,* with gen. of separation.

ἐρητύω, f. ύσω ; aor. ἐρήτυσα, iter. aor. ἐρητύσασκα ; Lat. *reprimere, to hinder, hold back, prevent, withhold, restrain,* Α 192, Β 99 ἐρήτυθεν, pass. Ep. 3 pl., *were restrained.*

ἐρι-, prefix streng. the signif. of the word.

ἐριβῶλαξ, ακος, ὁ, ἡ, (ἐρι-, βῶλος,) *abounding in clods, fertile;* Lat. *fertilis.*

ἐρίβωλος, ον, = foreg.

ἐρίγδουπος, ον, *loud-sounding.*

ἐριδαίνω, f. ἐριδήσω, (ἔρις,) *to contend, dispute, quarrel.*

ἐρίζω, f. ἐρίσω; aor. ἤρισα, (ἔρις,) *to contend, wrangle, fight; to contend or vie with any one;* Ion. iter. impf. ἐρίζεσκον.

ἐρίηρος, ον, (ἐρι-, ἄρω, assumed root of ἀραρίσκω,) *close-fitting, closely attached, strongly attached, faithful.*

ἐριθηλής, ές (ἐρι-, θάλλω,) *luxurious, very productive, rich, very fruitful.*

ἔριθος, ὁ, ἡ, (deriv. not certain,) *any common day-servant; reaper of the harvest-field; wool-workers,* of domestics, esp. of women.

ἐρικυδής, ές, (ἐρι-, κῦδος,) *very glorious.*

ἐρινεός, οῦ, ὁ, *the wild fig-tree.*

ἐριούνιος, ου, ὁ, or ἐριούνης, (ἐρι-, ὀνίνημι), *most useful, helper,* epith. of Mer'-cu-ry.

ἔρις, ιδος, dat. ἔριδι, acc. ἔριν, ἔριδα, ἡ, *strife, dispute, contention,* A 8; *friendly debate* or *rivalry; zeal:* E'-ris, *goddess of strife,* personification of strife.

ἔρισμα, ατος, τό, (ἐρίζω,) *an occasion of dispute.*

ἐρίτιμος, ον, (ἐρι-, τιμή,) *of great value, highly prized, honored, precious.*

ἕρκος, εος, τό, (ἔργω,) *a fence, hedge, enclosure; a wall* or *fence to court-yard* or *garden; the wall* or *barrier-line of teeth,* hence *the teeth; a protection, defence, bulwark,* A 284.

ἕρμα, ατος, τό, *anything to support and steady, prop, stay,* A 486; *foundation,* hence *that upon which a vessel may be stranded;* also, in the sense of *occasion:* also, *an earring, necklace, chain.*

Ἑρμῆς, Ep. gen. έω, Ep. nom. Ἑρμείας, gen. είαο, ὁ, Lat. *Mer-cu'-ri-us, Her'-mes, messenger of the gods;* see Classical Dictionary.

Ἑρμιόνη, ης, ἡ, *Her-mi'-one,* a city of Ar'-go-lis.

ἔρξω, see ἔργω.

ἔρομαι, Ion. εἴρομαι; ἐρείομεν, Ep. for ἐρέωμεν, pl. subj. from ἐρέω, which see; f. ἐρήσομαι, 2 aor. ἠρόμην, Ep. imperat. ἔρειο; Ion. parts from εἰρ- : *to ask, to interrogate, to question* or *ask,* A 332, 62, 553; *inquire for* or *into; to consult; to ask about; to look into, seek to know, examine; to question any one about:* compare with Lat. *rogare, interrogare, percontari.*

ἔρρίγα, 2 pf. of ῥιγέω.

ἔρος, old form for ἔρως, ὁ, *love* Γ 442, *desire* A 469.

ἔρρω, f. ἐρρήσω, *to walk with a halting gait; to fall into ruin.*

ἐρσήεις, see ἐερσήεις.

ἐρύγμηλος, η, ον, *bellowing very loudly, bellowing.*

Ἐρυθῖνοι, ων, οἱ, *Er-y-thi'-ni,* in Paph-la-go'-nia.

Ἐρυθραί, ῶν, αἱ, *Er'-y-thræ,* a city of Bœ-o'-ti-a.

ἐρύκω, f. ξω, aor. ἤρυξα, Ep. 2 aor. (ἐ)(ή)ρύκακον, (ἐρύω,) *to restrain,* Γ 113, *hold back, detain ; ward off, keep away,* Lat. *arcēre ; keep in check, control, govern, manage.*

ἔρυμα, ατος, τό, (ἐρύω,) *a defence, protection.*

ἐρύω, Ep. εἰρύω ; f. ἐρύσω, Ep. f. mid. ἐρύσσομαι ; Ep. aor. εἴρυσ(σ)α, Lat. *trahere, draw, pull, drag along ; to drag* or *carry off with force, take away violently, plunder ; to trail, drag about, drag along ; pull :* mid. *to draw up to one's self ; to draw to one's self, to protect, to keep, respect,* A 216 ; *to ward off.*

ἔρχομαι ; f. ἐλεύσομαι ; 2 aor. ἦλθον ; 2 pf. ἐλήλυθα, Ep. εἰλήλουθα : *to go, come, arrive, return ; to march ;* used with cognate words, ὁδὸν ἐλθέμεναι A 151, *to go a journey ; go to the tent,* A 322 ; with gen. *to go through ;* how does it differ from Lat. *venire ?*

ἐρωέω, f. ήσω, aor. ἠρώησα, *to burst out* A 303, *gush out.*

ἐρωέω, f. ήσω, with gen. *to cease from, draw away from :* trans. *to drive back.*

ἐρωή, ῆς, ἡ, *a violent and powerful motion ; sweep, force,* Γ 62.

ἔρως, Γ 442, see ἔρος.

ἐς, see εἰς.

ἐσ- or εἰσ-, in compo. *into.*

ἐσαθρέω or εἰσα-, f. ήσω, (ἐς or εἰς, ἀθρέω,) *to look into ; might behold,* Γ 450.

ἔσαν, Ep. for ἦσαν, see εἰμί.

(ἐ)ἐσάωσα, aor. of σαόω, Ep. for σώζω, *to save,* which see.

ἐσθλός, ή, όν, *good ; honorable, noble ; brave ; glorious ; strong ; clever, kind ; rich.*

ἔσθω, Lat. *edere, to eat up, consume,* Ep. for ἐσθίω, which see for parts.

ἐσκίδναντο, see σκίδνημι.

ἔσκον, see εἰμί.

ἕσπερος, ον, ὁ, Lat. *vesper, evening ;* hence sometimes *the West, Hes'-pe-rus.*

ἔσπετε, 2 pl. Ep. imperat. of εἶπον for εἴπετε.

ἑσπόμην, 2 aor. of ἕπομαι, see ἕπω.

ἐσσεύοντο, see σεύω.

ἐσσί, Ep. for 2 sing. of εἰμί.

ἔσσο, Ep. imperat. of ἕννυμι.

ἐσσυμένως, *rapidly, eagerly, hastily, vehemently,* Γ 85.

ἐστίθημι = εἰστίθημι.

ἐσχατάων, όωσα, Ep. for ἰσχατάων, (ἔσχατος,) part., *being about the limit* or *border, being on the frontier* or *boundary.*

ἔσχον, 2 aor. of ἔχω.

ἑταῖρος, ου, ὁ, Ep. ἔταρος, οιο, Lat. *sodalis, companion, mate, associate, fellow, comrade; a confidential friend, companion-in-arms, an assistant.*

ἐτεός, ά, όν, Lat. *verus, actual, true, real;* ἐτεόν as adv., *truly* B 300, *actually, in fact.*

ἕτερος, a, ον, Lat. *alter, the other* (of two); *one;* ἕτερον, . . . ἑτέρην, Γ 103, *one,* . . . *the other,* Lat. *alter,* . . . *alter; other, opposite, different:* often it is used in dat. as adv. like ἑτέρως, *in another way, otherwise, differently, in another place.*

ἑτέρωθεν, (ἕτερος,) *from the other side; on the other side.*

ἑτέρωσε, (ἕτερος,) adv., *another way, in another direction, elsewhere.*

ἐτέταλτο B 643, see ἐπιτέλλω.

Ἐτεωνός, οῦ, ὁ, *E-te-o'-nus,* a town of Bœ-o'-ti-a.

ἐτήτυμος, ον, leng. poet. form from ἔτυμος, Lat. *sincerus, true, tried, not false, real; truthful;* ἐπήτυμον adv., A 558, *in truth, truly.*

ἔτι, adv., Lat. *adhuc, even, as yet, even to this, still; still more, yet further, yet longer, still; furthermore, besides, yet,* Lat. *praeterea.*

ἔτλην, 2 aor. of τλάω.

ἑτοιμάζω, f. άσω, (ἕτοιμος,) *to make ready, prepare, provide:* mid. *to prepare for one's self* or *for one's own benefit.*

ἔτος, εος, τό, Lat. *annus, year.*

ἐτώσιος, ον, *fruitless, vain, ineffectual* Γ 368, *useless.*

εὖ, also Ep. ἐΰ, adv., (neu. of ἐΰς, *good,*) *well, prosperously, rightly, properly,* opp. to κακῶς, *ill; skilfully, fortunately, luckily; happily, easily, carefully, quite well,* εὖ πάντες or πάντα, *all together:* εὖ πᾶς, *quite all;* with ἔχειν, *to be well off:* as subst. τὸ εὖ, *the right, good fortune:* in compo. εὖ retains the gen. meanings already given, and also expresses *greatness, facility, increase, abundance; well, well-minded,* A 73.

εὗ, Ion. gen. of 3 pers. pron. for οὗ, Lat. *sui.*

Εὐαίμων, ονος, ὁ, *Eu-æ'-mon.*

Εὔβοια, Ion. gen. ης, ἡ, *Eu-bœ'-a,* an island of the A-ban'-tes.

εὔδμητος, ον, Ep. ἐΰδμητος, (εὖ, δέμω,) *well-built.*

εὕδω; Ep. imp. εὗδον, iter. εὕδεσκον: Lat. *dormire, to sleep; rest; be quiet; to sleep the sleep of death.*

εὐειδής, ές, Γ 48, (εὖ, εἶδος,) *well-formed, beautiful.*

(εὔ)(ἐΰ)ζωνος, ον, (εὖ, ζώνη,) *well-girded, beautifully girdled; girt for action, active; unencumbered,* Lat. *expeditus.*

εὐηκής, ες, (εὖ, ἀκή,) *well edged* or *pointed, very sharp.*

Εὐηνός, οῦ, ὁ, *Eu-e'-nus.*

εὔκηλος, ον, Lat. *securus, quiet, at ease,* A 554, *unmolested, tranquil, free from fear.*

εὐκλείη, Ep. for **εὔκλεια,** ας, ἡ, (ἐύ, κλεῖα, acc. pl. of κλέος,) Lat. *splendor nominis, a good report, good name, good renown.*

εὐκνήμις, δος, ὁ, ἡ, Ep. **ἐυκνή-,** A 17, (εὖ, κνημίς,) *well-greaved, well-booted.*

εὐκτίμενος, η, ον, (εὖ, κτίζω,) *well-built ; well-laid-out* or *planned ; well-made.*

ἐύκτιτος, ον, Ep. for **εὔκτιστος** = foreg.

εὐλή, ῆς, ἡ, *a very small worm, maggot, that which breeds in wounds.*

Εὔμηλος, ου, ὁ, *Eu-me'-lus,* a Thes-sa'-li-an ; stric. *having many sheep,* (εὖ, μῆλον.)

ἐυμμελίης, ὁ, (εὖ, μελία,) adj., *carrying a good ashen spear.*

εὐναιετάων, ουσα, ον, B 648 ; (εὖ, ναιετάω,) *well-situated, pleasant to dwell in ; well-inhabited.*

εὐναιόμενος, η, ον, (εὖ, ναίω,) = foreg., A 164.

εὐνάω, f. ήσω, aor. εὔνησα, pf. εὔνημαι, aor. pass. εὐνήθην, (εὐνή,) *to put to sleep, lull to rest, soothe, quiet, still; to place in ambush :* mid. and pass. *to put one's self to rest* or *sleep, go to bed ; to lie with,* in sexual intercourse, B 821, Γ 441.

εὐνή, ῆς, ἡ, Ep. gen. sing. and pl. **εὐνῆφι,** Lat. *cubile, a bed, couch, bedstead, a resting-place,* εὐνήθεν, *from the couch ; marriage-bed,* either *wedlock* or *unlawful cohabitation ; bedding :* in pl. εὐναί, *mooring-stones* used as anchors.

ἐύνητος, Ep. for **εὔνητος,** ον, (εὖ, νέω,) *well-woven, of good workmanship.*

εὖνις, ιος, ὁ and ἡ, *deprived of, bereft of,* with gen.

ἐύξεστος, ον, Ep. for **εὔξεστος,** (εὖ, ξέω,) *well smoothed* or *polished, very smooth.*

εὔξοος, Ep. **ἐύξοος,** ον, Ep. gen. ἐύξου, (εὖ, ξέω,) = foreg.

εὔπεπλος, ον, (εὖ, πέπλος,) *well-robed, well-dressed.*

εὔπηκτος, ον, or **ἐύπηκ-,** (εὖ, πήγνυμι,) *well-joined, strong, well-put-together, firm, well-built.*

ἐυπλεκής, ές, Ep. **ἐυπλεκής,** B 449, (εὖ, πλέκω,) *well-woven, well-plaited* or *twisted.*

ἐυ(or εὐ)πλοκαμίς, ῖδος, fem. adj. with **εὐπλόκαμος,** ον, (εὖ, πλόκαμος,) *with beautiful tresses.*

εὔπρηστος, ον, (εὖ, πρήθω,) *well-blowing.*

εὑρίσκω ; f. εὑρήσω ; 2 aor. ηὗρον and unaugm. εὗρον ; 2 aor. (ηὑ)(εὑ)ρόμην ; pf. (ηὕ)(εὕ)ρηκα ; aor. pass. (ηὑ)(εὑ)ρέθην : *to find accidentally, light upon, find out, discover ; to invent, devise, think of,* Lat. *invenire ; to get, obtain,* Lat. *reperire :* mid. *to find for one's own benefit, get.*

Εὖρος, ου, ὁ, Lat. *Eu-'rus, the South-East wind.*

ἐυρρείος, Ep. gen. of **ἐυρρεής,** ές, (εὖ, ῥέω,) *well-flowing.*

εὐρνάγυιος, α, ον, (εὐρύς, ἀγυιά,) *broad-streeted*, of great cities.

Εὐρύαλος, ου, ὁ, *Eu-ry'-a-lus*, see Classical Dictionary.

Εὐρυβάτης, ου, ὁ, *Eu-ryb'-a-tes*, name of two heralds.

Ευρυδάμας, αντος, ὁ, *Eu-ryd'-a-mas*.

εὐρυκρείων, οντος, ὁ, (εὐρύ, κρείων,) *wide-ruling*, epith. of A-ga-mem'-non.

εὐρύοπα, nom. for εὐρυόπης, (εὐρύ, ὄψομαι,) *far-seeing*; acc. of εὐρύοψ, (εὐρύ, ὄψ, Lat. *vox*,) *far-thundering*; Hom. epith. of Jove.

Εὐρύπυλος, ου, ὁ, *Eu-ryp'-y-lus*, a Thes-sa'-li-an prince, B 736; a chief from Cos.

εὐρυρέων, ουσα, ον, (εὐρύ, ῥέω,) *wide-flowing*.

εὐρύς, εὐρεῖα, Ion. εὐρέα, εὐρύ; gen. mas. and neu. -έος, fem. -είας; dat. -ἐι; acc. -ύν, Ep. -έα; Lat. *latus, broad, extended, ample, wide, far-extending*; εὐρύτερος, *broader; spacious, wide-spread*; Γ 227, *broad shoulders*.

Εὔρυτος, ου, ὁ, *Eu'-ry-tus*, see Classical Dictionary.

εὐρύχορος, ον, Ep. for εὐρύχωρος, (εὐρύ, χῶρος,) Lat. *spatiosus, spacious, extensive*.

ἐΰς, Ep. ἠΰς B 653, gen. ἐῆος, acc. ἐΰν, gen. pl. ἐάων, *good; good in the fight, courageous, daring, brave; noble*.

εὔσελμος, ον, Ep. ἐΰσ(σ)ελμος, (εὖ, σέλμα,) *well furnished with rower's benches, well-rowed; well-equipped*.

εὖτε, poet. and Ion. for ὅτε, Lat. *quum, when, as, then, since*; εὖτ' ἄν, with subj. like ὅταν, *when, as often as, in case, whenever*; for ἠΰτε, Γ 10, *as, just as*.

εὐτείχεος, ον, and εὐτειχής, ές, (εὖ, τεῖχος,) *well-walled, strongly fortified*; also Hom. -χητος.

Εὔτρησις, ιος, ἡ, *Eu-tre'-sis*, a village of Bœ-o'-ti-a.

ἐΰτροχος, ον, Ep. for εὔτροχος, (εὖ, τροχός,) *well-rounded, having good wheels, easy-running, swift*, of chariots, etc.

εὔτυκτος, ον, (εὖ, τεύχω,) *well-constructed, well-built*.

Εὔφημος, ου, ὁ, (εὖ, φήμη, φημί,) lit., *of good prophetic voice, of happy omen; Eu-phe'-mus*.

εὐφραίνω, Ep. ἐϋφραίνω; f. ανῶ, Ep. νέω; Ep. aor. εὔφρηνα; (εὔφρων (εὖ, φρήν)): *to gladden, delight, cheer, render cheerful* or *happy*.

ἐϋφρονέων, Ep. for εὐφρονέων, (εὖ, φρονέω,) *well-disposed*, A 73, B 78, *well-thinking, kind and wise*.

ἐΰφρων, Ep. for εὔφρων, ον, (εὖ, φρήν,) Lat. *laetus, cheering* Γ 246, *gladdening, comforting, making merry; happy and light, gay, light*.

εὐφυής, ές, (εὖ, φυή, φύω,) *having good growth*, both of body and mind; *of fine figure; well-disposed; of good mind*.

εὐχετάομαι, *to pray to, supplicate, entreat; to brag, boast*.

εὔχομαι; Hom. impf. εὐχόμην; εὔξομαι; Lat. precari, to pray, offer prayer, supplicate; to vow: as trans. to pray for; to pray to, beseech, implore, supplicate: with μέγα, to pray aloud and earnestly; to vow, promise solemnly; to vow loudly or confidently; to boast, brag, Lat. gloriari, A 91, B 82; to declare.

εὖχος, εος, τό, (εὔχομαι,) an object of prayer, anything prayed for, an offering to secure an answer to one's prayer; something prized.

εὐχωλή, ῆς, ἡ, (εὔχομαι,) Lat. votum, precatio, a prayer, petition, vow, A 65; a boast, a matter of boasting, B 160.

εὐώδης, ες, (εὖ, ὄδωδα, pf. of ὄζω,) fragrant, sweet-scented.

ἔφαλος, ον, (ἐπί, ἅλς,) Lat. maritimus, by the sea, on the sea.

ἐφάπτω, f. ἐφάψω, (ἐπί, ἅπτω,) to bind or fasten on to: pass. to be attached to, hang over, be fastened to, impend, B 15 like Lat. imminet: mid. to touch, lay hold of, seize.

ἔφαγον, B 317, see ἐσθίω.

ἐφέζομαι, f. ἐφεδοῦμαι, (ἐπί, ἕζομαι,) to sit one's self upon; to sit by; aor. act. ἐφεῖσα, to place or set one on anything, put or lay upon.

ἐφέπω; impf., Ep. ἔφεπον, iter. ἐφέπεσκον; f. ἐφέψω; 2 aor. ἐπέσπον, (ἐπί, ἕπω,) inf. ἐπισπεῖν: Lat. persequi, to pursue, follow after, closely or upon; to press closely, urge; to follow an occupation, manage; to traverse; to follow up, seek out: mid. to follow or accompany; to follow in the sense of to obey.

ἐφέστιος, ον, (ἐπί, ἑστία,) on the hearth, by one's own hearth; having a house in a place, at home, B 125; with verbs of motion, to one's hearth: as subst. οἱ ἐφέστιοι, the household gods, Lat. Penates.

ἐφετμή, ῆς, ἡ, (ἐφίημι,) an order, injunction, a command, Hom. gen. pl. -έων, A 495.

ἐφευρίσκω, f. ἐφευρήσω, 2 aor. ἐφεῦρον, (ἐπί, εὑρίσκω,) to find, light upon, come upon, find by chance; to find out, understand, discover, detect, Lat. invenire.

ἐφίημι; inf. ἐφιέναι; impf. 3 sing. ἐφίει; f. ἐφήσω; aor. ἐφῆκα, Ep. ἐφέηκα, (what verbs have their aor. in κα?); 2 aor. imperat. ἔφες, Ep. subj. ἐφείω and opt. ἐφείην: Lat. immittere, to send to or against, A 382, hurl or launch at; to impel, urge, excite against; to set on; with χεῖρας, to lay hands upon; to place upon, Lat. imponere; cause to fall on; to permit; to let go; to give up: mid. to enjoin, give in charge, Lat. mandare, to strive for, long earnestly after; to allow one to do.

ἐφίστημι, for parts see ἵστημι, also, Hadley and Allen's Grammar, 500, 1, (ἐπί, ἵστημι). Like ἵστημι, the compd. is trans. (or causal) in certain tenses and intrans. in certain others: the pres., impf., f. and aor. are trans.; the 2 aor., pf., and f.pf. are intrans.: trans. see Lat. collocare juxta, to place anything on or over, rest on or by; to set up, cause to come *about; to cause to stand* or *stop, hence, to make to cease:* intrans. *to take one's stand on* or *over,* hence, *to be over* or *upon; to be opposite, be near to, be near.*

ἐφοράω; impf. ἐφεώρων; for parts see ὁράω; Ion. and Hom. parts, pres. ἐπορἀω, f. ἐπόψομαι *to look on,* and ἐπιόψομαι *to choose,* impf. 3 sing. ἐπώρα: (ἐπί, ὁράω:) *to look at, look to; to look over,* Γ 277; *to observe, look upon, survey, behold; to watch over; to superintend, pick out.*

ἐφορμάω, f. ἥσω, (ἐπί, ὁρμάω,) *to stir up* or *incite against, rouse against,* Lat. *excitare contra,* Γ 165; *to excite, rouse, impel, provoke,* Lat. *excitare:* also, seemingly intrans., *to rush upon:* (lit. *to urge one's self against:*) mid. and pass. *to be urged, impelled, stirred up, to have a strong inclination; to rush on,* Lat. *irruere; to rush against, attack; to hurry.*

ἐφύπερθε(ν), (ἐπί, ὑπέρ, θεν,) adv., *from over;* also, *above.*

Ἐφύρη, ης, ἡ, *Eph'-y-ra,* the name of several towns.

ἔχαδον, Δ 24, 2 aor. of χανδάνω, which see.

Ἐχέμ(μ)ων, ονος, ὁ, *E-che'-mon.*

ἐχεπευκής, ές, (ἔχω, πεύκη,) of darts, arrows, etc., *sharp, pointed, sore, bitter,* of a plague, A 51.

Ἐχέπωλος, ου, ὁ, *Ech-e-po'-lus,* slain by An-til'-o-cus.

ἔχεσκον, iter. impf. of ἔχω, which see.

ἔχευα, Ep. aor. from χέω, which see.

ἔχθιστος, η, ον, sup. of ἐχθρός, (ἔχθος,) compar. ἐχθίων, *most detested, most odious.*

ἐχθοδοπέω, f. ἥσω, (ἐχθοδοπός,) *to cause hatred, to be hateful towards* or *offend,* A 518.

ἔχθος, εος, τό, Lat. *odium, hatred,* Γ 416.

ἐχθρός, ά, όν, (ἔχθος,) *detested, hateful, hated; hostile to, inimical,* Lat. *inimicus:* see ἔχθιστος, compar. ἐχθίων; reg. forms for compar. and sup. are also found.

Ἐχῖναι, ῶν, αἱ, *a group of islands in the I-o'-ni-an sea.*

ἔχω; impf. εἶχον, Ep. ἔχον, iter. ἔχεσκον; f. ἕξω, σχήσω; 2 aor. ἔσχον, Ep. inf. σχέμεν, poet. indicat. ἔσχεθον, poet. 3 pl. mid. opt. σχοίατο; pf. ἔσχηκα, Hom. ὄχωκα; Hom. plup. mid. 3 pl. ἐπώχατο: trans. *to hold, have, keep,* compare the meanings here given with Lat. *tenēre, habēre, possidēre: to hold, keep, hold fast, have in the power; to grip, grasp, to get hold of with the mind, understand; to have* A 356, *possess, be possessed of;* οἱ ἔχοντες, *those having possessions, the rich; to hold, keep;* with ποδός, χειρός, etc., *to hold by the foot, hand,* etc.; *let him have,* Γ 282; .*to hold anything* (as a horse, etc.) *on its course,* hence *to turn, guide, drive,* Γ 263; *to retain; to hold together; to hold to, close; to enclose; to imply; to bear, carry, to shut out, hold back, withhold, restrain, check; to hold up, bear up; to occupy; to keep away, avert; to hold a* position, sustain, stand, Lat. sustinēre; to hold fast; to understand; to dwell in, inhabit; to protect, guard, keep safe; to have the means or power to do, to be in a condition to do, to be able: to aim, direct to; to cause; to wear, to make: intrans. to keep one's self, be so and so, be in a certain state whether of body or mind, persist; to hold in the sense of to go; εὖ ἔχει, it goes well; to remain; to stand firm or upright; to point to; to be or hold one's self about anything, be busied about; to keep on: mid. to hold one's self fast to, hold on by, cling to; to be closely attached to; to border on or be next to; to claim for one's self and take; to conduct or control one's self, comport one's self; to wear; to hold (one's self) back from, cease, Lat. abstinēre; to resist, withstand, stand; hold the ground; to let be; σχέο, σχέσθε, hold!

ἐών, Hom. for ὤν, pres. part. of εἰμί.

ἐῷ, dat. of ἐός, Ion. and Ep. for ὅς poss. adj. his or her.

ἕως, Ep. εἵως Γ 291, and εἷος, Lat. donec and quamdiu, whilst A 193, when, as long as, during; Lat. quoad, till, until Γ 291; = Lat. ut, in order that, for the sake of.

Z.

ζα-, intens. prefix.

ζάθεος, adj., (ζα-, θεός,) Lat. divinus, sacer, very divine, holy, sacred, of localities favored by the gods, does not apply to living beings.

ζάκοτος, ον, (ζα-, κότος,) Lat. furiosus, valde iracundus, very wrathful, furious, angry, Γ 220.

Ζάκυνθος, ου, ἡ, Za-cyn'-thus, an island in the I-o'-ni-an sea.

ζείδωρος, ον, (ζειά, δῶρον,) Lat. fertilis, grain-giving, fruitful.

Ζέλεια, ας, ἡ, Ze-le'-a, a town near I'-da.

ζεύγνυμι; impf. 3 pl. (ἐ)ζεύγνυ(σαν)(ον); f. ζεύξω; aor. ἔζευξα; aor. pass. ἐζεύχθην, 2 aor. pass. ἐζύγην: Lat. jungere, to put to, join, yoke together, couple together; to unite; to join or bar, make fast; to bridge, Lat. jungere ponte; to join in marriage, Lat. jungere matrimonio: mid. and pass. to put to or join for one's self or benefit, to wed, to be married.

ζευγνύω = ζεύγνυμι.

ζεῦγος, εος, τό, (ζεύγνυμι,) Lat. jugum, a pair of beasts yoked together for work, a yoke of oxen or horses, also, a cart or anything drawn by the yoke and so used for the whole; things yoked together or united.

Ζεύς, gen. Διός, dat. Διί, acc. Δία; also poet. Ζήν, gen. Ζηνός, dat. Ζηνί, acc. Ζῆνα, Ζῆν', voc. Ζεῦ: Lat. Ju'-pi-ter, Zeus, father and king of gods and men, Ζεῦ πάτερ, from these two words is derived Lat. Ju'-pi-ter; for a full description see Classical Dictionary.

ζέφυρος, ου, ὁ, Lat. *zephyrus, the north-west wind, the west wind.*

Ζήν, Ζῆν', see Ζεύς.

ζυγόν, οῦ, τό, Lat. *jugum, the yoke,* which was only a cross-bar to which the beasts were attached; *a cross-bar; the bench for rowers* in a ship, *cross-beam; the transverse piece of a lyre.*

ζωγρέω, (ζωός, ἀγρεύω,) *to take living,* hence, *to take as prisoner and not kill in battle* as was the custom; *to resuscitate.*

ζῶμα, ατος, τό, (ζώννυμι,) *anything bound around, the garment bound under the armor, inner dress.*

ζώνη, ης, ἡ, (ζώννυμι,) Lat. *cingulum, balteus, zona, a girdle, waist band, the low outside girdle worn by women; the part of the body covered by the girdle, the waist,* B 479.

ζωός, ή, όν, (ζώω for ζάω,) Lat. *vivus, living, alive;* ζώς, acc. ζών, rare forms for ζωός.

ζωστήρ, ῆρος, ὁ, (ζώννυμι,) Lat. *cingulum, balteus, the girdle with which an armor is bound to the body.*

ζώω, Ep. for ζάω, Lat. *vivere, to live; living.*

H.

ἦ, adv.: *to confirm,* Lat. *certe, profecto, in truth, assuredly, certainly, to be sure, without doubt, verily;* with γάρ, *for truly,* A 293; with δή, *surely then,* A 518; with μήν, Ep. μάν, Ion. μέν, *a strong asseveration, that you will boldly defend me* A 77, *but certainly with words* A 211; *to introduce and streng. an oath,* etc.; see ἦ τοι; τίη = τὶ ἦ, *why (then):* interrog. (also, ἦε, ἠέ,) Lat. *utrum? an? num?* ἦ οὐ *nonne? do you indeed? is it that? what? can it be?* often untranslated; used in both parts of disjunc. questions, *do,* etc.? . . . *or?*

ἦ, 3 sing. impf. of ἠμί, the only form used by Hom., Lat. *ait, he said.*

ἤ, Ep. ἠέ, interrog., disjunc., and compar. conj.: interrog., in indirect double questions, Lat. *utrum . . . an,* ἤ . . . ἤ *whether . . . or,* A 190–192, also εἰ = ἤ; *to introduce direct questions like* Lat. *an, and cannot always be rendered:* disjunc., *or,* Lat. *aut,* ἤ . . . ἤ, Lat. *aut . . . aut, vel . . . vel, either . . . or,* A 27; ἤ *may be repeated several times as in* A 138: compar., *than,* Lat. *quam.*

ἠβαιός, ά, όν, Lat. *parvus, little, small.*

ἡβάω, f. ἥσω, (ἥβη,) Lat. *pubescere, to attain the age of puberty* or *manhood, possess the full vigor of man, be in the prime of young-man-hood; to be young and vigorous with the impulses of youth.*

ἥβη, ης, ἡ, Lat. *pubertas, puberty, the age of manhood; youthful vigor, ripe-*

ness of age, manly vigor and strength; the fire, passion, and mirth of youth, spirit of youth; a company of young men.

ἠγάθεος, η, ον, (ἄγαν, θεός,) sacred, hallowed, most holy, very divine, of places, islands, etc.

ἠγάσσατο, Hom. 3 sing. aor. of ἀγάομαι, see ἄγαμαι.

ἡγεμονεύω, f. σω, (ἡγεμών,) Lat. praeire, to go before, precede; Lat. regere; with ὁδόν, to point out the way: trans. to conduct, lead, Lat. ducere; with gen. to command, with. dat. once B 816.

ἡγεμών, όνος, ὁ, Lat. dux, a leader; chief; a guide; a commander; one who is first to do or act, Lat. princeps, actor.

ἡγέομαι, f. ἡσομαι, aor. ἡγησάμην, (ἄγω,) to go before, guide, lead the way, conduct, Lat. praeire; point out, lead; to be first, be chief; to think, believe, Lat. opinari: trans., Lat. ducere, to lead as a general or commander, and so to command, govern, with gen.; to lead in the sense of to go in advance of or before, with dat.

ἠγερ(ε)θ(ο)-, Hom. from ἀγείρομαι, to be gathered together, assemble themselves, congregate.

ἤγερθεν, see ἀγείρω.

ἡγητήρ, ῆρος, ὁ = ἡγεμών; (ἡγέομαι;) Lat. dux, ductor, a guide, leader, chief, commander.

ἡγητής, οῦ, ὁ, see ἡγητήρ.

ἡγήτωρ, ορος, ὁ, see ἡγητήρ.

ἠδέ, (ἤ, δέ), and, besides, also; ἠδὲ καί, and besides; foll. and answering to ἠμέν, as, also; ἠδὲ ἔτι, and yet; ἠδὲ, ... καί, both, ... and.

ἤδεα, Ion. plup. of οἶδα.

ἤδη, adv., Lat. jam, now, directly, at present, already, at once, presently; ἤδη νῦν, A 456, even now or already now, now at least Γ 98, A 260 for already at one time.

ἦδος, εος, τό, (ἡδύς,) pleasure A 576, enjoyment; profit, gain.

ἡδυεπής, ες, (ἡδύς, ἔπος,) Lat. suaviloquens, speaking agreeably, pleasant-spoken.

ἡδύς, ἡδεῖα, Ion. ἡδέα, ἡδύ; compar. both in -ίων, -ιστος, and -τερος, -τατος; compare with Lat. jucundus, suavis; sweet, pleasant; pleasant, acceptable, welcome: ἡδύ is also used as adv.

ἠείδειν, Ep. plpf. of οἶδα, see εἴδω and Hadley and Allen's Grammar, 491, 6.

ἠέλιος, ὁ, poet. and Hom. for ἥλιος, (ἕλη,) Lat. sol, sun; day, daylight; personified as a god seeing all things Γ 104 and 277; rising sun, sunrise, the East: Ἤλιος or Ἡέλιος is the father of the Hē-li'-a-dæ and Hē-li'-a-des, see Classical Dictionary.

ἦεν, Lat. erat, see εἰμί, impf., Ep. 3 sing.

ἠέπερ, poet. for ἤπερ.

ἠερέθομαι, *to hang fluttering over, floating, float, flutter;* Γ 108, the minds of young men *are fickle,* Lat. *inconstans.*

ἠέριος, α, ον, Ep. for ἀέριος, (ἀήρ,) *when vapor* or *mist covers the earth* A 497, *at early morn, early, at dawn,* Lat. *matutinus; in the air,* Lat. *aërius.*

ἠέρος, Ep. gen. of ἀήρ, which see.

ἠερόφωνος, ον, (ἀηρ, φωνή,) *sounding through air, loud.*

'Ηετίων, ωνος, ὁ, *E-e'-ti-on,* the name of several heroes of Hom.

ἠήρ, see ἀήρ.

ἠθεῖος, α, ον, (ἦθος,) *honored;* in Hom. usu. in voc. and used by a younger brother to an elder, *honored Sir, respected Sir.*

ἦθος, εος, τό, (ἔθος,) *a frequented place, haunt, abode; custom, anything common.*

ἦιε, see εἶμι.

ἠίθεος, ου, ὁ, *an unmarried youth.*

ἦιξα, aor. of ἀίσσω, which see.

'Ηιόνες, ων, αἱ, *E-i'-o-nes, the Banks,* a port town of Ar'-go-lis, see ἠιών.

ἠίχθην, aor. pass. of ἀίσσω, Γ 368.

ἠιών, όνος, ἡ, Lat. *litus, sea-shore, strand, coast, beach; a bank of a river,* Lat. *ripa.*

ἦκα, aor. of ἵημι, see Hadley and Allen's Grammar, 429.

ἦκα, adv., *softly, in a low tone, mildly,* Γ 155; *a little, carefully, gently;* compare Lat. *leniter, quiete, placide.*

ἠλακάτη, ης, ἡ, *a distaff* or *staff from which the flax was drawn, spindle,* also came to be applied to *a reed* though not used for a distaff; *a shaft.*

ἠλάσκω, Lat. *vagari, to wander, roam about; to swarm about:* an Ep. form for ἀλάομαι. '

ἠλέκτωρ, ορος, ὁ, *the shining sun.*

ἡλικία, ας, ἡ, (ἧλιξ,) Lat. *aetas, age; the age of manhood, manhood, prime of life; youth with its impulses.*

ἥλιος, see ἠέλιος.

'Ἦλις, ιδος, ἡ, *E'-lis,* a district on the west coast of the Pel'-o-pon-ne'-sus.

ἧλος, ου, ὁ, *a nail, stud,* for ornament on swords, etc.

ἤλυθον, Ep. and uncontd. for ἦλθον, 2 aor. of ἔρχομαι, Lat. *veni.*

'Ηλώνη, ης, ἡ, *E-lo'-ne,* a city near Mt. O-lym'-pus.

ἠμαθόεις, εσσα, εν, Ion. for ἀμαθόεις, (ἄμαθος,) Lat. *arenosus, sandy,* B 77.

ἧμαι, ἧσαι, ἧται or ἧσται, du. ἧσθον, pl. ἥμεθα, ἧσθε, ἧνται, Hom. 3 pl. εἵατ(αι)(ο); imperat. ἧσο, ἧσθω; inf. ἧσθαι; part. ἥμενος; impf. ἥμην, ἧσο, ἧστο, du. ἧσθον, ἀσθην, pl. ἥμεθα, ἧσθε, ἧντο, Ion. ἕατο, Ep. εἵατο; subj. and opt. are wanting; found only in pres. system: Lat. *sedēre, to be seated,* Γ 153, *to sit;* with a part. A 134, *to sit wanting: to sit still, remain.*

ἦμαρ, ατος, τό, poet. and Hom. for ἡμέρα, day, Lat. dies; ἐπ' ἤματι, Lat. quotidie, daily, every-day, day-by-day; as adv., by day; the time of the year, season, as summer time: ἦμαρ ἐλεύθερον, day of freedom.

ἤμβροτον, 2 aor. of ἁμαρτάνω, which see.

ἡμεῖς, ἄμμες; ἡμείων, -έων; ἄμμι(ν); ἄμμε: see ἐγώ.

ἠ-μέν, ... ἠ-δέ, (ἤ, μέν,) poet. for καί ... καί, Lat. et, ... et, both, ... and, both, ... as well, as well, ... as also; if, ... or whether; either, ... or, Lat. vel, ... vel, sive, ... sive.

ἡμέρη, Ion. for ἡμέρα, ας, ἡ, Hom. ἦμαρ, which see, see Lat. dies, tempus tempestas, a day or the light of day, day as opp. to night.

ἡμέτερος, α, ον, (ἡμεῖς,) Lat. noster, our, ours.

ἡμι-, Lat. semi-, prefix meaning half-.

ἡμίονος, ὁ, ἡ, (ἡμι-, ὄνος,) a half-ass; a mule, Lat. mulus.

ἡμίσεες, pl. of ἥμισυς, εια, υ, adj., Lat. semis, half; the neu. is freq. used as subst., a half.

ἡμιτελής, ές, (ἡμι-, τέλος,) half complete; δόμος ἡμιτελής, a house (household) but half complete or wanting its master or mistress.

ἦμος, conjunctive adv., Lat. quando, quum, when, during, as, so long as, while.

ἡμύω, f. σω, aor. ἤμυσα, (α euph., μύω,) to incline, bend, bow down, droop; nod; ἡμύει ἀσταχύεσσι, it droops with its ears of corn, B 148; to sink, go to ruin.

ἤν, uncontr. ἐάν, conditional conj., if, Lat. si; whether.

ἠνεμόεις, εσσα, εν, (ἄνεμος,) Lat. ventosus, windy, breezy; exposed to winds, elevated.

ἡνία, ας, ἡ, Lat. frenum, a rein, bridle.

ἡνίοχος, ου, ὁ, (ἡνία, ἔχω,) one that holds reins, a driver.

ἡνίπαπε, 3 sing. 2 aor. of ἐνίπτω.

Ἠνοπίδης, ου, ὁ, son of E'-nops.

ἀντέω, Ion. for ἀντάω, which see.

ἦντο, see ἧμαι.

ἠνώγεα, Ion. plupf. from ἄνωγα, which see.

ἤπειρος, ἡ, Lat. continens, the main land as opp. to islands; land as opp. to the sea, and so an island.

ἤπερ, poet. ἠέπερ, (ἤ, περ,) Lat. quam, than, as.

ἠπεροπεύς, έως, Ion. -ῆος, ὁ, Lat. deceptor, impostor, a cheat, deceiver.

ἠπεροπευτής, οῦ, ὁ, Γ 39, = foreg.

ἠπεροπεύω, f. σω, Lat. fallere, to cheat, overreach, deceive; seduce.

ἠοῖος, α, ον, (Ἠώς,) relating to the morning, in the morning, morning; hence in the east where morn first appears, eastern, relating to the east, compare Lat. oriens, orientalis; used as a subst., the morn.

ἤπιος, α, ον, see Lat. lenis, placidus, mild.

ἦρα, neu. pl., *that which is pleasing, agreeable;* with φέρειν, *do a kindness; to show a favor, do kind offices,* A 578, Lat. *obsequium praestare Jovi.*

'Ηρακλείδης, ου, ὁ, *descendant of Her'-cu-les.*

'Ηράκλειος, Ep. 'Ηρακλήειος, η, ον, *of Her'-cu-les, Her-cu'-le-an.*

ἤραρον, 2 aor. of ἀραρίσκω, which see.

ἤρατο, 3 sing. aor. mid. of αἴρω.

ἠρᾶτο, impf. 3 sing. of ἀράομαι, which see.

"Ηρη, Ion. for "Ηρα, ἡ, Lat. *Juno, He'-ra,* both sister and wife of Zeus, see Classical Dictionary.

ἠρήρειστο, 3 sing. plup. pass. of ἐρείδω.

ἦρι, adv. *early,* Lat. *mane.*

ἠριγένεια, ας, ἡ, (ἦρι, γένω,) *early-born, child of early morn,* epith. of 'Ηώς.

ἤριπον, 2 aor. of ἐρείπω.

ἥρως, ωος, *a hero,* Lat. *heros;* in Hom. not only of warriors, but a term of respect for the *free and honored;* later meanings not here given.

ἤσκειν, contr. 3 sing. impf. of ἀσκέω, Γ 388, *to work* or *fashion.*

ἦσο, see ἧμαι.

ἦ- τε or ἦ τε, *surely, certainly, doubtless.*

ἦ τοι, conj.; *now; certainly, surely, verily, truly,* A 140, Lat. *certe;* foll. by ἤ, *either, . . . or; either, surely.*

ἦτορ, ορος, τό, used in the nom. and acc., *the heart,* Lat. *pectus;* usu. not as an organ of the body but *the heart, the power of thought,* Lat. *mens, mind, feelings,* A 188, the seat of all the emotions of the mind.

ηὔδα, 3 sing. impf. from αὐδάω.

ἠΰκομος, Ep. for εὔκομος, (εὖ, κόμη,) Lat. *pulchras comas habens, beautiful-haired, fair-haired.*

ἠΰς, see ἐΰς.

ἠΰτε, Ep. for εὖτε, *as, as also, like as, so as, like;* B 87, ἠΰτε = ὡς, ὅτε, *as when.*

"Ηφαιστος, ου, ὁ, *He-phais'-tus,* Lat. *Vul-ca'-nus,* the god of fire and of the art of working metals requiring the aid of fire; see Classical Dictionary: by metonymy, *fire.*

ἧφι, Ep. for ᾗ, see ὅς.

ἠχή, ῆς, ἡ, Lat. *sonus; a sound; a noise, clamor, tumult of a crowd,* B 209; *sound of the waves; hum.*

ἠχήεις, εσσα, εν, (ἠχή,) Lat. *resonans, sonorous, echoing, resounding, roaring.*

ἧχι, Ep. for ᾗ, Lat. *ubi, where.*

ἠώς, ἠόος, dat. ἠόι, acc. ἠόα; contr. forms ἠοῦς, ἠοῖ, ἠῶ; ἡ: Lat. *aurora, dawn of day, early morning; day,* Lat. *dies; day-light; the east,* Lat. *oriens;* 'Ηώς, E'-os, *the goddess of morn,* Lat. *Au-ro'-ra.*

Θ.

θάλαμος, ου, ὁ, a room, an inner room, chamber; a woman's chamber, bed-room, chamber of the mistress, Γ 423, Lat. cubiculum; a store-room, room for weapons and other goods; inner part of the ship.

θάλασσα, ας, ἡ, (ἅλς,) Lat. mare, the sea; the Med'-i-ter-ra'-ne-an is under-stood when any particular sea is mentioned, see map of the world as known to Hom.

θαλάσσιος, adj., (θάλασσα,) Lat. marinus, belonging to or of the sea, by the sea, in the sea.

θάλεα, τά, (θαλεῖν, 2 aor. of θάλλω,) those things that cheer the heart.

θαλερός, ά, όν, (θαλεῖν, 2 aor. of θάλλω,) Lat. florens, floridus, blooming; fresh, vigorous, strong; rich; copious, large, abundant.

θάλος, εος, τό, a young and tender twig or shoot; a shoot as a production of like kind.

Θάλπιος, ου, ὁ, Thal'-pi-us, a chief of the E-pe'-i.

θαλπωρή, ῆς, ἡ, (θάλπω,) a warming, a cheering, an encouraging; pleasure, comfort.

Θαλυσιάδης, ου, ὁ, son of Tha-lys'-i-us.

θαμβέω, f. ήσω, pf. τεθάμβηκα, (θάμβος,) Lat. obstupescere, to be amazed, Α 199, Γ 398; to gaze upon with astonishment, to marvel at.

θάμβος, εος, τό, Lat. stupor, wonder, astonishment.

θαμέες, (θαμά,) poet. adj. found only in pl., Lat. frequentes, crowded, close, thick, frequent, in great numbers.

θάμνος, ου, ὁ, (θαμινός,) a shrub, bush, thicket, copse.

Θάμυρις, ιδος or ιος, ὁ, Tham'-y-ris, a bard.

θανατόνδε, (θάνατος, δέ encl.,) adv., see Lat. ad mortem, to death.

θάνατος, ου, ὁ, (θνήσκω,) Lat. mors, death; Death, twin-brother of Sleep; θανατόνδε, to death.

θαρσαλέος, α, ον, (θάρσος,) Lat. audax, bold, resolute, confident, courageous, also, daring, rash, foolhardy, also, impudent.

θαρσέω, f. ήσω, (θάρσος,) Lat. confidere, to be daring, be bold; to be confident, assured; to be over-bold; to be presumptuous; to believe, confide in.

θάρσος, εος, τό, Lat. fiducia, good courage, courage, confidence, readiness; bad courage, temerity, presumption, see Lat. audacia.

θάσσων, compar. of ταχύς, Lat. celerior.

θαῦμα, ατος, τό, (θάομαι,) Ion. forms θῶμα or θώϋμα; Lat. res mira, an object to excite wonder and prob. admiration.

θαυμάζω; iter. impf. εσκον; Ep. f. άσσομαι; aor. ἐθαύμασα; pf. τεθαύμακα; aor. pass. ἐθαυμάσθην: (θαῦμα:) Lat. mirari, admirari; to wonder, *to be amazed, be astonished; to behold with wonder*, with acc.; *to look upon with admiration, admire.*

Θαυμακία, ας, ἡ, *Thau-ma'-ci-a*, a town of *Mag-ne'-si-a.*

θεά, ᾶς, ἡ, fem. of θεός, Lat. *dea, a goddess;* A 280, *the goddess mother.*

Θεανώ, οῦς, ἡ, *The-a'-no*, wife of An-te'-nor, sister of Hec'-u-ba.

θείνω; f. θενῶ; aor. ἔθεινα; 2 aor. ἔθενον: *to strike, dash.*

θεῖος, α, ον, (θεός,) Lat. *divinus, of the gods, appointed by the gods, divine, sacred, holy, godlike; glorious, excellent, eminent, extraordinary; consecrated to a god.*

θέμις, ἡ; Hom. and Ep. gen. θέμιστος, and dat. θέμιστι, acc. θέμιν, and in Hom. Θέμιστα; Att. gen. Θέμιτος and Θέμιδος; Ion. gen. Θέμιος: (τίθημι:) *right, law, justice*, Lat. *jus, concessum est, fas est, that which is right by common consent and by the law of nature and reason*, θέμις ἐστί, *it is right, fitting, proper:* in pl. *decrees, institutions, ordinances; the rights of rule, privilege, authority*, B 206; *just tributes, taxes; suits; courts of justice; sentences of a court.* Hom. uses it as prop. n. *The'-mis*, the goddess of right, *Justice*, Lat. *Dea juris.*

-θεν, particle affixed to nouns denoting motion *from* as opp. to -δε *to* or *towards*, but originally the gen. termination : θεόθεν, *from the gods.*

θεοειδής, ες, (θεός, εἶδος,) *of divine form, godlike* B 623, *of godlike beauty.*

θεοείκελος, ον, (θεός, εἴκελος,) Lat. *deo similis, like a god, godlike*, A 131.

θεοπροπέω, (θεοπρόπος, (θεός, πρέπω),) *to prophesy*, part. θεοπροπέων, *prophesying*, Lat. *vaticinans.*

θεοπροπία, ας, ἡ, A 385, and θεοπρόπιον, ου, τό, A 85, Lat. *vaticinatio, prophecy, prediction of future events.*

θεός, οῦ, ὁ, Lat. *deus, a god; deity*, Lat. *numen;* θεόφιν, Ep. gen. and dat. sing. and pl.

θεράπων, οντος, ὁ, *a servant, an attendant;* of free service as opp. to δοῦλος *a slave; a companion (of lower rank) in arms.*

θερμός, adj., (θέρω,) (see Eng. *thermal*,) Lat. *calidus, hot, heated, glowing, warm; boiling-hot;* also, *vehement, ardent, rash, precipitate, hasty;* also, *ready to do.*

θέρος, εος, τό, (θέρω,) Lat. *aestas, the warm season of the year, summer; the heat of summer; summer fruit, harvest, fruit, crop.*

Θερσίτης, ου, ὁ, *Ther-si'-tes*, a detested and scurrilous Greek, B 212.

θέσκελος, ον, (θεός, ἴσκω,) *godlike, noble, excellent; marvellous, wonderful;* always of inanimate objects; θέσκελα ἔργα, Γ 130, *wonderful works;* neu. as adv., Lat. *mirum in modum, wonderfully.*

Θέσπ(ει)(ι)α, ας, ἡ, and -πιαί pl., *Thes'-pi-æ*, a city of Bœ-o'-ti-a.

θεσπέσιος, adj., (θεός, ἔπος,) *divinely spoken, god-spoken; unspeakable, astonishing, extraordinary, vast*, B 670; *wondrous, excellent; spoken or* sent by a god, B 600; dat. fem. sing., θεσπεσίη, as adv., Lat. divina voluntate, by divine ordering, B 367; divine, godlike.

Θεσσαλός, οῦ, ὁ, Thes'-sa-lus, son of Her'-cu-les.

Θεστορίδης, ου, ὁ, son of Thes'-tor, Cal'-chas.

Θέτις, ιδος, ἡ, The'-tis, one of the Ne-re'-ids and mother of Achil'-les. See Classical Dictionary.

θέω, Ep. θείω; iter. impf. θέεσκον; f. θεύσομαι: Lat. currere, to run; to hasten; of birds, to fly; of anything circular or, if not circular, that runs in a continuous line ever returning to the same point, though not in motion.

Θῆβαι, ων, αἱ, also Θήβη, ης, ἡ, Thebes, the name of several cities mentioned by Hom.

θήγω, f. θήξω, aor. ἔθηξα, pf. τέθηγμαι, aor. mid. imperat. θηξάσθω B 382, Lat. acuere, to whet, sharpen; also, to excite, provoke; stimulate.

θηέομαι, f. ἡσομαι; Ep. forms, impf., 3 sing. θηεῖτο, other parts in -ηευ-: to look at, behold; to look at with admiration, admire.

θήῃς, 2 aor. subj. Ep. 2 sing. of τίθημι, which see.

θῆλυς, adj., εια, υ, and υς, υ, Ep. fem. parts θήλεα, etc.; Lat. femineus, of female sex, female, feminine, of the gentler sex; womanish, effeminate; tender, delicate; fruitful.

θήν, Ep. particle, encl. surely, yet, then, truly, so then, see Lat. sane.

θήρ, θηρός, ὁ, Lat. fera, a wild beast of prey.

θήρη, Ion. for θήρα, ας, ἡ, (θήρ,) Lat. venatio, the chase of wild animals, also, the results of the chase, captured game; any ardent pursuit.

θηρητήρ, τῆρος, ὁ, Ep. for θηρατής, see θηρήτωρ.

θηρήτωρ, ορος, ὁ, Ion. for θηρατής, οῦ, ὁ, (θηράω,) Lat. venator, one that follows the chase, a hunter.

Θησεύς, έως, ὁ, The'-seus, the national hero of Ath'-ens.

θίς, θινός, Ep. ὁ, Lat. cumulus, a heap of sand on the sea-shore; the strand, beach, Lat. litus; a heap of anything.

Θίσβη, ης, ἡ, This'-be, a city of Bœ-o'-ti-a.

θνήσκω; the parts are formed from θνα- and θαν-; Ep. f. inf. θανέεσθαι; 2 aor. Ep. inf. θανέειν: pf. τέθνηκα; 2 pf. pl. τέθναμεν, τεθνᾶσι, opt. τεθναίην, etc., Hom. imperat. τέθναθι, τεθνάτω, inf. τεθνάναι, Hom. inf. τεθνάμεν(αι), part. τεθνεώς, Hom. gen. -νηότος as also -ηῶτος, fem. -ηυίης: Lat. moriri, to die; to perish.

θνητός, adj., (θνήσκω,) Lat. mortalis, mortal, subject to death.

Θόας, αντος, ὁ, Tho'-as.

θοός, ή, όν, (θέω,) Lat. velox, celer, quick, prompt, rapid, active; sharp, projecting, pointed, of rocky points as they shoot out into the sea: θοῶς, adv. quickly.

θόρε, 2 aor. Ep. 3 sing. of θρώσκω, which see.

5

θοῦρος, ου, ὁ, (θορεῖν, 2 aor. of θρώσκω,) *leaping and rushing, bounding, vehement.*

Θοών, ωνος, ὁ, *Tho'-on,* killed by U-lys'-scs.

θρασυμένων, ονος, (θρασύς, μένω,) *bravely-waiting.*

θρασύς, εῖα, ύ, Lat. *audax, bold, hardy, resolute, courageous, brave, daring: fool-hardy, rash.*

θρέξασκον, aor. Ion. 3 pl. of τρέχω, f. θρέξω and δραμοῦμαι, aor. ἔθρεξα, 2 aor. ἔδραμον, pf. δεδράμηκα; Ion. and poet. forms, f. δραμέομαι and δράμομαι, 2 pf. δέδρομα; for forms in τρεχ- and δραμ- see Hadley and Allen's Grammar, 539, 5: Lat. *currere, to move rapidly, run.*

θρέπτρα, ων, τά, *the returns of children to parents.*

θρέψα, poet. aor. of τρέφω.

Θρήϊξ, ικος, ὁ, uncontr. for Θρῇξ, *Thra'-cian,* B 595.

θρηνέω, (θρῆνος, (θρέω)) *to weep aloud, bewail.*

θρῆνυς, νος, ὁ, *a footstool, a bench.*

θρίξ, τριχός, ἡ, Lat. *capillus, the hair or beard; bristles, hair, fur, wool.*

θρόνα, ων, τά, pl. of θρόνον, *flowers, flower work, embroidery.*

Θρόνιον, ου, τό, *Thro'-ni-um,* a town of the Lo'-cri-ans.

θρόνος, (see Eng. *throne,*) ου, ὁ, Lat. *thronus, a seat, a stool* or *chair; an arm-chair, chair of state; the king's power, royal power, the throne.*

Θρύον, ού, τό, (θρύον, *a reed, a rush,*) *Thry'-um,* a city of E'-lis; Θρυόεσσα πόλις, *a city among the reeds,* a term given on account of the situation.

θρώσκω, f. θοροῦμαι, 2 aor. ἔθορον, compare Lat. *salire, to spring, leap, leap forward;* trans. *to leap upon, cover,* i. e. *impregnate.*

θυγάτηρ, gen. θυγατέρος, contr. θυγατρός; Ep. acc. θύγατρα; voc. θύγατερ; Ep. dat. pl. θυγατέρεσσι: Lat. *filia, a daughter.*

Θυέστης, ου, ὁ, *Thy-es'-tes.*

θυμαλγής, ές, (θυμός, ἀλγέω,) *causing the soul to grieve, sorrowful.*

Θυμοίτης, ου, ὁ, *Thy-mœ'-tes,* a Tro'-jan chief.

θυμολέων, ὁ, (θυμός, λέων,) *lion-hearted, fearless, brave.*

θυμός, οῦ, ὁ, (θύω,) *life, animal life,* Lat. *anima; the soul, heart, the immortal part* (as seat of the emotions, *anger, appetite, desire,* etc.), *the disposition, nature, mind, thought, will, resolve, purpose,* Lat. *animus.*

θυμοφθόρος, ον, (θυμός, φθείρω,) *destroying life, deadly.*

θύνω, (θύω,) *to rush hastily along* B 446, *charge.*

θύραζε, θύρασδε, adv., *to* or *without the door.*

θύρετρον, τό, compare Lat. *ostium, janua, gate, door;* pl. *folding-doors,* Lat. *fores.*

θύρη, Ion. for θύρα, ας, ἡ, *door,* compare Lat. *ostium, janua;* frequent. in Hom. in pl. *folding-doors; gate; entrance; a dwelling.*

θυρωρός, οῦ, ὁ, ἡ, (θύρα, οὖρος,) *a guarder of the gate.*

θύσανος, ου, ὁ, (θύω,) *a tuft, tassel;* in pl. *tassels, fringe.*

Θύσθλα, ων, τά, (θύω,) *utensils used in the worship of Bac'-chus.*

θύω, f. θύσω, *to rush* or *dart along; to be furious, to rage, storm,* Lat. *saevire; of water, to surge, rush.*

θύω, f. θύσω, *to offer sacrifice, slay and sacrifice* a victim, *sacrifice; to celebrate with a sacrifice.*

θώρηξ, ηκος, ὁ, Ion. for θώραξ, Lat. *thorax, lorica, a cuirass, a coat of mail consisting of breastplate and back piece; the chest, breast,* Lat. *pectus; breastwork, outer wall.*

θωρήσσω, f. ξω, (θώραξ,) *to put on a cuirass* or *breastplate, to arm, put on armor:* mid. and pass. *to arm one's self, be armed,* Γ 340 *were armed.*

I.

ἰάλλω, f. ἰαλῶ, aor. ἴηλα, compare Lat. *emittere, jacere, to send* or *cause to go out* or *forth.*

Ἰάλμενος, *I-al'-me-nus,* a chief of the Bœo'-tians.

ἰάχω, ἰαχέω, f. ἰαχήσω, 2 pf. ἴαχα, (ἰά,) Lat. *clamare, to cry out* or *aloud, shout,* B 333; *to proclaim; of inanimate objects, to resound, clang, re-echo, ring, twang, roar, hiss,* (as hot iron in water,) *crackle,* Lat. *strepere.*

Ἰαωλκός, οῦ, ἡ, *I-ol'-cus,* a town of *Thes'-sa-ly,* home of Ja'-son, poet. for Ἰωλκός.

Ἰδαῖος, ου, ὁ, *I-dæ'-us,* a name of two Tro'-jans; one a herald, Γ 248.

ἰδέ, Ion. and Ep. for ἠδέ, Lat. *et, and,* Γ 194.

ἰδέειν, ἰδεσκον, ἰδεσθαι, see εἴδω.

Ἴδη, ης, ἡ, Ion. for Ἴδα, *I'-da,* a mountain near Troy; Ἴδηθεν, adv. of place, *from I'-da.*

ἴδηαι, Ep. 2 sing. 2 aor. mid. of εἴδω, Γ 130.

ἰδνόω, f. ώσω, Lat. *incurvare, to bend, bend down* or *back, curve;* pass. B 266, *bend himself, writhe.*

Ἰδομενεύς, έως, ὁ, *I-dom'-e-neus,* son of Deu-ca'-li-on and leader of the Cre'-tans.

ἰδρείη or -ρίη, Ion. for ἰδρεία, ας, ἡ, (ἴδρις,) Lat. *scientia, science, knowledge, experience, dexterity.*

ἰδρόω, f. ώσω, Lat. *sudare, to sweat, perspire; reek with sweat,* B 388.

ἰδρύω, f. ύσω, pf. ἴδρυμαι, aor. pass. ἰδρύθην, ἰδρύνθησαν, Γ 78, (ἵζω,) causal of ἕζομαι, which see, *to cause to sit down,* B 191, Lat. *sedēre facio, to seat; to establish, pitch, fix, set up, to dedicate;* pass. *to sit, be seated; to be placed, be situated.*

ἰδυῖα, Ep. for εἰδυῖα, 2 pf. part. fem. of εἴδω, Lat. *sciens.*

ἴε, 3 sing. impf. of εἶμι.

ἱερεύς, έως, ὁ, Ion. ἱρεύς, ῆος, (ἱερός,) Lat. sacerdos, *a priest, a sacrificial priest.*

ἱερεύω, Ion. and Ep. ἱρεύω, iter. impf. ἱρεύεσκον, (ἱερός,) Lat. sacrificare, *to offer, sacrifice* B 402, *to slay for sacrifice, slaughter; to perform the duties of a priest.*

ἱερήϊον or ἱρή-, Ion. for ἱερεῖον, ου, τό, (ἱερός,) *a victim for the sacrifice, a sacrifice.*

ἱερόν, Ion. ἱρόν, οῦ, τό, neu. of foll., Lat. sacrum, *anything sacred* or *consecrated to the gods; a sacrifice, victim, temple;* in pl. *offerings, victims,* Lat. victimae, *sacred rites* A 147, *entrails of a slaughtered victim.*

ἱερός, adj., Ion. ἱρός, ή, όν, Lat. sacer, *of the gods; holy, divine, sacred, hallowed, inviolable;* a general term, *holy* temple, *sacred* grove, *holy* war, *holy* city, island, etc., *under the protection of a divinity.*

ἱζάνω, (ἵζω,) Lat. facere sedēre, *to make* or *cause to sit, seat:* intrans. *to sit; to settle down,* Lat. sidere.

ἵζω; iter. impf. ἵζεσκον; Hom. causal aor. εἷσα, Lat. sedēre facio, *to seat, place, make to sit:* usu. intrans. Lat. sidere, *to sit* B 53, *take a seat; to sit still;* of an army, *to encamp:* causal, *to make to sit, bid be seated;* if βουλήν be used, in B 53, *to hold a council.*

Ἰηλυσός, οῦ, ὁ, Ion. for Ἰα-, *I-al'-y-sus,* a city of Rhodes.

ἵημι, ἵης and ἱεῖς, ἵησι, du. ἵετον, pl. ἵεμεν, ἵετε, ἱᾶσι and ἱεῖσι Γ 152: impf. ἵην and ἵειν (Hom.), ἵης or ἵεις, ἵη or ἵει, pl. ἵεμεν, ἵετε, Æol. 3 pl. ἵεν for ἵεσαν: subj. ἱῶ, ἱῆς, etc.; opt. ἱείην or ἵοιμι, etc.; imperat. ἵει, ἱέτω; inf. ἱέναι, Ep. ἱέμεν(αι); part. ἱείς, ἱεῖσα, ἱέν: f. ἥσω: aor. ἧκα, Ep. ἕηκα: 2 aor. du. εἷτον, -την, pl. εἷμεν, -τε, -σαν; 2 aor. subj. ὧ, etc.; opt. εἵην, etc.; imperat. ἕς, ἕτω, etc.; inf. εἷναι; part. εἵς, εἷσα, ἕν: pf. εἷκα: mid. and pass. ἵεμαι, subj. ἵωμαι, opt. ἱείμην or ἱοίμην: aor. ἡκάμην: 2 aor. εἵμην: pf. εἷμαι: aor. pass. εἵθην and ἕθην: Lat. mittere, *to put in motion, to send, send forth; to send out, emit, discharge; to make to go; to cast, send forth, hurl, throw, let fly, let fall, shoot;* used with the gen. of the per. or thing aimed at or striven for; *to let flow forth, to loose, let flow:* mid. *to cast one's self, to hasten, to put one's self in motion, to impel one's self,* and so *to feel impelled* or *inclined, to long for; to endeavor to, strive after.*

ἰητήρ, ῆρος, ὁ, Ep. for ἰατήρ, poet. for ἰατρός, *a surgeon, physician.*

Ἰθάκη, ης, ἡ, *Ith'-a-ca,* an island off the western coast of Greece, and the birthplace and home of U-lys'-ses.

Ἰθακήσιοι, *Ith'-a-cans.*

ἴθι, imperat. of εἶμι, Lat. age, *come, go;* as adv. *come on!* often with ἄγε.

ἰθύνω, f. νῶ, Hom. for εὐθύνω, (εὐθύς,) *to straighten, cause to be straight, guide in a direct line; to direct, govern, rectify.*

ἰθύς, εῖα, ύ, Lat. *rectus, in a straight* or *direct line, straight; honest, upright, straightforward.*

ἰθύς, ύος, ἡ, *an impulse of the mind; an intention* or *undertaking, an enterprise, an effort.*

'Ἰθώμη, ης, ἡ, *I-tho'-me,* a stronghold of Thes'-sa-ly.

ἱκάνω, Ep. for ἵκω, Lat. *adire, to arrive at* or *come to, reach.*

'Ἰκάριος, α, ον, ("Ικαρος,) *I-ca'-ri-an,* 'Ικάριος πόντος, part of the Æ-ge'-an Sea where I'-ca-rus was drowned.

ἵκελος, η, ον, poet., (εἴκω,) Lat. *similis, like.*

'Ἰκετάων, ονος, ὁ, *Hic-e-ta'-on,* a brother of Pri'-am.

ἱκέτης, ου, ὁ, (ἱκέσθαι, 2 aor. of ἱκνέομαι,) Lat. *supplex, one who comes* or *goes as a suppliant for aid, a suppliant, a petitioner;* also, *one who receives the suppliant, a protector.*

ἵκμενος, *aiding* or *favoring arrival,* hence ἵκμενος οὖρος, *a fair breeze, a favoring wind* A 479, Lat. *ventus secundus.*

ἵκω, (ἱκνέομαι,) Ep. 2 aor. ἷξον, Lat. *venire, to come;* Lat. *ire, go;* Lat. *adsequi, to arrive at, go to, reach; comes,* A 166; with ὑπότροπον, *to return.*

ἰλαδόν, (ἴλα for ἴλη,) adv., Lat. *turmatim, in crowds, in troops, in companies; in large numbers.*

ἵλαος, ον, Lat. *propitius, gracious, placable, propitious,* A 583; Lat. *benignus, mild, kind, gentle, gracious, good-natured.*

ἱλάσκομαι, Ep. f. ἱλάσσομαι, aor. Ep. part. A 100 *having propitiated,* (ἵλαος,) compare Lat. *placare, propitiare; to propitiate, render gracious, make propitious, to render favorable to one's self, reconcile, conciliate,* A 472 *were appeasing the God with song.*

"Ἰλιος, ου, ἡ, or "Ιλιον, ου, τό, *Il'-i-os* or *Il'-i-um, Troy,* the city founded by I'-lus, the home of Pri'-am, capital of the Tro'-jan plain.

ἱμάς, άντος, ὁ; Ep. dat. pl. ἱμάντεσσι: Lat. *lorum, a thong, a leathern strap* or *rope: the latch-string; helmet-strap going under the chin,* Γ 371; *a whip-lash, a whip;* in pl. *straps, the straps of a harness,* hence *a harness, a network of straps, reins;* the word has a general application to things made of thongs; *the girdle* of Aph-ro-di'-te; *the cestus of boxers* made of leathern straps wound round the hand and forearm, Lat. *caestus.*

ἱμάσσω, f. ἱμάσω, (ἱμάς,) *to whip, lash; to strike.*

'Ἰμβρασίδης, ου, ὁ, *son of Im'-bra-sus.*

"Ἰμβρος, ου, ἡ, *an island in the* Æ-ge'-an Sea.

ἱμείρω, (ἵμερος,) *to desire eagerly, long for, yearn after.*

ἴμεν(αι), Ep. for ἰέναι, inf. of εἶμι, Lat. *ire.*

ἱμερόεις, εσσα, εν, (ἵμερος,) Lat. *amabilis, exciting love and desire, lovable, charming, delightful.*

ἵμερος, ου, ὁ, Lat. *desiderium, an earnest longing for any desired object, longing, desire.*

ἱμερτός, ή, όν, (ἱμείρω,) *longed for, desired, lovely.*

ἵνα, conj. introducing final clauses, Lat. *ut, that, in order that;* introduces the subj. mood ; it may introduce the opt. mood instead of the subj. after historical tenses : adv. Lat. *ubi, where; why?* ἵνα περ, *to what end;* ἵνα μή, *lest.*

ἰνίον, ου, τό, (ἴς,) *the back of the neck,* stric. *the back muscles of the neck.*

ἴξαλος, ον, *springing,* of the chamois and wild goat.

ἴξον, see ἵκω.

ἰός, οῦ, ὁ, (deriv. uncertain, perhaps ἵημι, or ἰέναι *to go,*) Lat. *sagitta, an arrow.*

ἱππεύς, έως, Ion. gen. ῆος, ὁ, (ἵππος,) *one fighting from a chariot, a charioteer* or *driver of horses to the chariot distinct from the warrior who fights from the chariot ; a horseman, rider,* Lat. *eques; a knight.*

ἱπποχαίτης, (ἵππιος, χαίτη,) *with long horse-hair.*

ἱππόβοτος, ον, (ἵππος, βοτός verbal of βόσκω,) Lat. *equis pascendis aptus, pastured by horses, horse-nourishing.*

Ἱπποδάμεια, ας, ἡ, *Hip'-po-da-mi'-a.*

ἱππόδαμος, ον, (ἵππος, δαμάω,) Lat. *equorum domitor, horse-taming,* of Tro'-jans.

ἱππόδασυς, obsol. mas., ἱπποδάσεια, (ἵππος, δασύς,) *with heavy horse-hair plume, thick set with horse-hair,* Γ 369 ; *of a plumed helmet.*

Ἱππόθοος, ου, ὁ, *Hip-poth'-o-us.*

ἱπποκορυστής, οῦ, ὁ, (ἵππος, κορύσσω,) *one who prepares* or *equips horses, one who is equipped with horses,* and so *one who uses horses, a horseman; horse-equipping* B 1.

Ἱππόλοχος, οῦ, ὁ, *Hip-pol'-o-chus.*

ἵππος, ου, ὁ, ἡ, Lat. *equus, a horse.*

ἱππότης, ου, ὁ, Ep. ἱππότα, (ἵππος,) Lat. *eques, a horseman, a driver of horses, charioteer;* of Nes'-tor, B 336 ; *a knight.*

ἵππουρις, ιδος, fem. adj., (ἵππος, οὐρά,) *of a horse-tail (crest); plumed with horse-tail.*

ἵπτομαι, f. ἵψομαι, *to oppress, afflict ; to hurt ; to inflict punishment;* of gods A 454, and kings B 193.

ἵρηξ, contr. of ἱέρηξ, Ion. of ἱέραξ, ηκος, ὁ, Lat. *accipiter, a hawk.*

Ἶρις, ιδος, ἡ, *I'-ris,* messenger goddess of the gods to men.

ἱρόν, see ἱερόν.

ἰσάζω, (ἴσος,) *to equalize.*

Ἴσανδρος, ου, ὁ, *I-san'-der.*

ἰσόθεος, ον, (ἴσος, θεός,) Lat. *deo par, equal to a god; godlike, divine.*

ἴσος, η, ον ; Ep. ἴϊσος ; compare Lat. *par, aequus; like, equal;* τὸ ἴσον or τὰ ἴσα, *equality, equal share, reparation;* ἴσα καί, *just as; equally portioned out* or *divided; equal, even, level:* adv. ἴσως, also, neu. sing. and pl., Lat. *pariter, equally, in an equal manner.*

ἵστημι ; f. στήσω ; aor. ἔστησα ; 2 aor. ἔστην ; pf. ἔστηκα ; aor. pass. ἐστάθην : the trans. tenses are the pres. system, f., aor.: the intrans. tenses are 2 aor., 1 pf. system, f.pf.; the same distinction prevails in the compds.: Hom. and Ep. forms, iter. 3 sing. impf. ἵστασκε, aor. 3 pl. ἔστασαν Β 525, inf. ἐστάμεν(αι); iter. 2 aor. στάσκον, 3 sing. στάσκε, and 3 pl. ἔσταν Α 535, inf. στήμεν(αι), 2 and 3 sing. subj. στήῃς, στήῃ, and pl. στέωμεν and στείομεν ; pf. inf. ἐστάμεν(αι), part. ἐστ(ε)(α)ώς : Lat. *collocare;* trans. *to erect, cause to stand, set up, place, locate; to cause to rise* Β 151 ; *to place in the balance, weigh off; to set in order, arrange; to establish; to set up* or *begin,* Lat. *excitare;* with νῆα, *to bring to a standstill, to land; to check, stop:* intrans. *to stand, to to be standing still,* Β 170 ; *to stand up,* Α 533, 535 ; *to be in a certain state; to remain fast* or *fixed, stand firm; to begin,* as a month.

Ἰστίαια, ας, ἡ, *His-ti-æ'-a,* a town of Eu-bœ'-a.

ἱστίον, τό, (ἱστός,) *that which has been woven,* Lat. *textum; sail,* Lat. *velum.*

ἱστοδόκη, ης, ἡ, (ἱστός, δέχομαι,) Α 434, *a mast-holder, mast-receiver, a rest for the mast when lowered.*

ἱστός, ὁ, (ἵστημι,) Lat. *malus, a mast of a ship;* the web-beam of an upright loom, a loom itself Α 31 ; *the warp, web, the woven cloth.*

ἴστωρ, ορος, ὁ, ἡ, (ἴσημι,) *knowing, having knowledge of, knowing right.*

ἴσχω for ἔχω, found in the pres. system, Lat. *retinēre, to hold, hold firm; withhold, keep back, restrain, keep from;* intrans. *to hold* (one's self) *back, to stop:* mid. *to restrain one's self, stay.*

ἴτυς, υος, ἡ, (deriv. uncertain,) *the extreme edge of a round body.*

Ἴτων, ωνος, ἡ, *I'-ton,* a town of Thes'-sa-ly.

ἰυγμός, οῦ, ὁ, (ἰύζω,) *a shout,* either of pain or pleasure.

ἴφθιμος, adj., (ἶφι,) compare Lat. *validus, robustus, strong, vigorous; brave, valiant, mighty,* Α 3.

ἶφι, Ep. adv., Lat. *fortiter, valiantly, bravely* Α 151, *strongly, nobly, stoutly; with might* or *violence,* Lat. *vi.*

Ἴφικλος, ου, ὁ, *Iph'-i-clus.*

Ἴφιτος, ου, ὁ, *Iph'-i-tus,* of Pho'-cis.

ἴψαο, aor. 2 sing. of ἴπτομαι.

K.

καγχαλάω, Hom. and Ep. parts καγχαλοω-, Γ 43 ; Lat. *cachinnari*, also, compare with *ridēre, to laugh loudly* or *exultingly, exult*.

κάδ = **κατά** before δ.

Κάειρα, ας, fem. adj. *Ca'-ri-an*.

καθάπτω, f. ψω, aor. καθῆψα, (κατά, ἅπτω,) Lat. *annectere, to fasten on to, tie to, to put on*: mid. *to fasten upon, seize ; to accost*, Lat. *compellare, to soothe* A 582 ; *to revile, abuse ; to upbraid*, Lat. *reprehendere ; to lay hold of* with hostile intent ; *to call as witness*, Lat. *antestari*.

καθέζομαι, f. καθεδοῦμαι, (κατά, ἕζομαι,) Lat. *considere, to seat one's self, sit down ; to tarry, loiter ;* with πρόχνυ, *to settle down upon the knees ; to settle down*.

καθεῖσα, Ep. aor. of **καθίζω**.

καθεύδω, f. καθευδήσω, (κατά, εὕδω,) Lat. *dormire, to sleep, to slumber,* A 611 ; *to lie down to slumber ; to be at rest*.

κάθημαι, κάθησο, inf. καθῆσθαι, part. καθήμενος, Lat. *sedēre, to sit down, sit ; to establish one's self ; to be inactive, idle*.

καθίζω ; f. καθίσω ; aor. ἐκάθισα, Ep. καθεῖσα in trans. sense : (κατά, ἵζω,) Lat. *sedēre jubeo*, trans. *to cause to sit ; to make* or *constitute ; to put in a certain condition, to convoke and hold :* intrans. *to sit down, seat one's self, sit ; to settle down*.

καθίημι, for parts see ἵημι, and Hadley and Allen's Grammar 476, (κατά, ἵημι,) compare Lat. *submittere, emittere, to send* or *let down, put down, cause to go down, lower, let go down ; to let one's self down*, i. e. *to come down*.

καθύπερθε(ν), (κατά, ὕπερθε,) Lat. *desuper, down from above ; above ; beyond*.

καί, conj. *and, even, also, as ; and*, Lat. *et*, see τε ; καί . . . καί, *both . . . and*, Lat. *et . . . et*, a repetition not found in Ep., see τε ; *as well as ;* καὶ δέ, *and yet, besides ;* καὶ μέν, *and yet, certainly, surely ;* καὶ δή, *and even, even now, already*, A 161 ; καί τε, *and besides, also ;* καὶ δὴ καί, *and in particular also ; also, even*, used to draw particular attention and to mark emphasis, and also to modify the force of words and clauses ; καὶ ταῦτα, *and that, and besides ;* καὶ περ or Hom. καί . . . περ, with part. *though, although ;* καὶ μᾶλλον, Lat. *etiam magis, and more, even more ;* καὶ εἰ, Lat. *et si, etiamsi, and if, even if ;* καὶ οἵ, *and they ;* καὶ γάρ, *for even, for also, for*, Lat. *etenim*.

Καινείδης, ου, ὁ, *son of Cæ'-neus, Co-ro'-nus*.

Καινεύς, έως, ὁ, *Cæ'-neus*.

καίνυμαι, pf. κέκασμαι, Lat. *superiorem esse, to be superior ; excel, surpass,* Lat. *excellere.*

καίριος, adj., (καιρός,) *taking place at the proper time; in just the right place,* hence, of wounds, *fatal, mortal.*

καίω ; f. καύσω ; Ep. aor. (ἔ)κεια, Hom. (ἔ)κηα ; aor. pass. ἐκαύθην ; 2 aor. ἐκάην, Ep. inf. καήμεν(αι): Lat. *cremare, to burn, set in a blaze; to consume:* pass., Lat. *ardēre, to be lighted, to be in a blaze, burn, blaze.*

κακκείοντες, Hom. and Ep. part. from κατακείω.

κακός, ή, όν : compar. κακίων, χείρων, ἥσσων ; sup. κάκιστος, χείριστος, ἥκιστος ; but Ep. compar. κακώτερος is also found ; *feebler ; less honorable ; worse :* Lat. *malus, improbus, evil, bad, cowardly, worthless, wicked, worthless* or *bad of its kind ; bad at one's trade ; unlucky ; vile, low, mean, malicious ; of low estate ; useless ; mischievous, injurious ; fatal :* as neu. subst., Lat. *malum, evil, mischief, pest, misfortune, woe, damage, distress, loss, injury, hurt :* in compo. expresses *hurtful ; too-, very,* Lat. *nimis :* adv. κακῶς, Lat. *male, badly, ill, insolently* A 25.

κακότης, ητος, ἡ, (κακός,) *badness ; wickedness,* Γ 366 ; Lat. *malum, evil, misfortune, pain, suffering ; cowardice* B 368, Lat. *ignavia.*

κάκτανε, 2 aor. Ep. imperat. of κατακτείνω, which see.

κακώτερος, Ep. for κακίων, see κακός.

καλέω ; iter. impf. καλέεσκον, pass. 3 pl. καλεῦντο, Ep. inf. καλήμεν(αι); f. καλέσω, Ep. καλέω ; Ep. aor. (ἐ)κάλεσσα ; pf. κέκληκα ; aor. pass. ἐκλήθην ; f. mid. καλέσομαι ; poet. aor. mid. καλεσσάμην ; Ep. plup. 3 pl. κεκλήατο ; f. pass. κληθήσομαι ; f. pf. κεκλήσομαι : Lat. *vocare, to call, call upon, summon ; to invoke ; to invite,* Lat. *invitare ; to call by name, address ; to name, summon, call,* Lat. *nominare :* pass. *to be called, to pass for.*

καλήτωρ, ορος, ὁ, (καλέω,) Lat. *calator, a herald, crier.*

καλλι-, a prefix giving the idea of *beautiful.*

Καλλίαρος, ου, ἡ, *Cal-li'-a-rus,* a town in Lo'-cris.

καλλιγύναιξ, αικος, adj., (καλλι-, γυνή,) Lat. *pulchris mulieribus abundans, of beautiful women.*

καλλίζωνος, ον, (καλλι-, ζώνη,) *having a beautiful girdle.*

καλλιπάρῃος, ον, (καλλι-, παρειά,) Lat. *pulchras genas habens, having beautiful checks* A 143.

καλλίρροος, ον, (καλλι-, ῥέω,) *beautifully-flowing, smooth-flowing.*

κάλλιστος, see καλός.

κάλλιφ', Ep. for κατέλιπε, see καταλείπω.

κάλλος, εος, τό, (καλός,) Lat. *pulchritudo, beauty* Γ 392 ; *a beauty.*

καλός, ή, όν, Lat. *pulcher, beautiful* A 473 ; τὸ καλόν, *moral excellence* or *virtue*, Lat. *honestum ; auspicious, favorable ; good, noble, upright :* compar. καλλίων, sup. κάλλιστος : adv. καλῶς and neu. καλόν.

Κάλυδναι νῆσοι, αἱ, *the Ca-lyd'-nae Islands*, near the coast of Ca'-ri-a ; νῆσος, Lat. *insula, island.*

Καλυδών, ῶνος, ἡ, *Cal'-y-don*, a city of Æ-to'-li-a.

καλύπτρη, Ion. for καλύπτρα, ας, ἡ, *a veil for a woman's head, woman's head-dress, veil.*

καλύπτω, f. ύψω, Ep. aor. κάλυψα ; aor. pass. ἐκαλύφθην, Lat. *tegere, to cover, cover up, conceal; to envelop, overshadow ; to veil,* Lat. *velare,* Γ 141 *having veiled.*

Κάλχας, αντος, ὁ, *Cal'-chas,* (*one who searches out, a searcher,*) a Greek secr.

κάμαξ, ακος, ἡ, *a long pole,* and so *a spear, a pole* or *prop for vines.*

Κάμειρος, ου, ὁ, *Ca-mi'-rus,* a city of Rhodes.

καμμονίη, Ep. for καταμονή, which see.

κάμνω ; f. καμοῦμαι ; 2 aor. ἔκαμον, Ep. κέκαμον and subj. κεκάμω and part., acc. pl., καμόντας Γ 278 *the dead ;* pf. κέκμηκα, Hom. and Ep. part. κεκμηώς : Lat. *fatigari, to be weary, to be fatigued, to be weary from toil, exhausted ; to be troubled :* trans. Lat. *elaborare, to labor hard at, work out with much pains and labor, to work out carefully.*

κάμπτω, f. μψω, *to bend ; turn, deflect, change the direction ; to bend the mind.*

καμπύλος, η, ον, (κάμπτω,) Lat. *curvus, inflectus, bent, curved, crooked.*

κάνειον, Ion. for κάνεον, ου, τό, (κάννη,) *a basket made of reeds, a basket for bread,* used at the sacrifices.

Καπανεύς, έως, ὁ, *Cap'-a-neus.*

Καπανηιάδης, ου, ὁ, son of *Cap'-a-neus.*

καπνίζω, f. ίσω, (καπνός,) *to make smoke, produce smoke ; to kindle a fire,* Β 399 ; *to smoke.*

κάπετος, ου, ἡ, (σκάπτω,) *any place dug out, trench, hole.*

καπνός, οῦ, ὁ, Lat. *fumus, smoke.*

κάππεσον, Ep. 2 aor. of καταπίπτω.

κάρ, καρός, τό, *the hair ; ἐν καρὸς αἴση, but as a hair;* short. for κάρα, Ion. κάρη, τό, indecl., the *head, ἐπὶ κάρ, headlong,* and like κεφαλή, (Lat. *caput,*) may mean *a person; κατὰ κρῆθεν,* (Hom. gen.,) *from the head down, wholly;* another form κράς, gen. κρατός.

Κάρ, ρός, ὁ, *a Ca'-ri-an.*

καρδίη, Ion. for καρδία, poet. κρα- Α 395, ης, ἡ, Lat. *cor, the heart,* as centre of the *anima* or life ; *the heart* Α 225, *mind, thought, reason,* Α 395, *the seat of the emotions.*

κάρη κομόωντες, (κομόων Ep. part. from κομάω,) οἱ, *long-haired,* an epith. applied to the A-chai'-ans.

κάρηνον, ου, τό, (κάρη,) *the head, summit ; a peak, citadel* B 117 (on the highest part of the city was the citadel).

καρπάλιμος, ον, (ἁρπάζω,) Lat. *rapidus, rapid, swift, quick ;* adv. *καρπαλίμως, rapidly, forthwith* A 359.

καρπός, ου, ὁ, Lat. *frux, fruit ; the fruit, return, enjoyment* or *profit of a thing,* Lat. *fructus:* also, *the wrist,* Lat. *carpus.*

καρτερός, see **κρατερός**.

κάρτιστος, η, ον, Hom. and Ep. for **κράτιστος**, irreg. sup. of ἀγαθός, Lat. *validissimus, strongest, most powerful, mightiest ; bravest,* Lat. *fortissimus ; best, most superior, most excellent,* Lat. *optimus.*

Κάρυστος, ου, ἡ, *Ca-rys'-tus,* a town of Eu-bœ'-a.

κασίγνητος, ου, ὁ, (κάσις, γεννάω,) *a brother ; any blood relation,* Lat. *consanguineus ; a child of a brother* or *sister :* as adj. *fraternal.*

Κάσος, ου, ἡ, the island *Ca'-sus.*

Κασσάνδρα, ας, ἡ, *Cas-san'-dra.*

κασσίτερος, ου, ὁ, Lat. *stannum, tin.*

Κάστωρ, ορος, ὁ, *Cas'-tor,* brother of Pol'-lux, Γ 237 ; see Classical Dictionary.

κατά, prep. used with gen. and acc.: with gen. *down from ; down towards, to, upon* or *over, down into ; upon ; against :* with acc. *down, down through* or *over, through, throughout,* in which sense freq. used by Hom., *at, by, on, about, over, among ;* of time, *during, in the course of :* in other relations, *with, according to ;* κατὰ πάντα, *according to all, generally ;* καθ᾽ ἕνα, *one by one ;* κατ᾽ ἔπος, *word by word, accurately ;* in the region of, on ; κατὰ σφέας, *by themselves ; for the sake of ; after ; concerning ;* κατὰ μῆνα, *every month ; because of ;* καθ᾽ ἑαυτόν, *by himself, alone ; in the midst of ; about :* in compo. *down, against,* also has a *strengthening* influence : as adv. *down.*

καταβαίνω, for prin. parts see **βαίνω**, 2 aor. subj. Ep. and Hom. pl. *καταβείομεν*, aor. mid. indicat. Ep. and Hom. 3 sing. *κατεβήσετο* and Ep. and Hom. imperat. *καταβήσεο*, (κατά, βαίνω,) Lat. *descendere, to descend, go down, step down ; to go down from ; to go down to ;* also, as trans. *to descend, to go down* along.

καταβάλλω, for prin. parts see **βάλλω**, 2 aor. Ep. 3 sing. *κάββαλε*, (κατά, βάλλω,) Lat. *dejicere, to throw* or *cast down ; to overthrow, destroy, ruin,* Lat. *evertere ; to let fall, drop down,* Lat. *effundere ; to put down and leave ; to strike down, slay, shoot down, conquer ; to put down ; to let down ; to pay down :* mid. *to lay as foundation, institute.*

καταδαίω, (κατά, δαίω,) *to tear in small pieces,* κατά . . . δάσονται.

καταδάπτω, f. άψω, (κατά, δάπτω,) Lat. *lacerare, to tear in pieces ; tear and devour,* as of wild beasts.

καταδέω, f. δήσω, (κατά, δέω,) Lat. *alligare, to bind firmly; hamper, hinder, stop; to put in confinement; to convict.*

καταδύ(ν)ω; f. ύσω; aor. κατέδυσα, 2 aor. κατέδυν; pf. καταδέδυκα: trans. in pres. καταδύω, f. καταδύσω, aor. κατέδυσα, Lat. *mergere, to cause to sink, immerse, sink:* intrans. in the form καταδύνω, 2 aor. κατέδυν, pf. καταδέδῡκα, Lat. *occidere, to sink, go under, go down* or *set,* of the sun; *to enter, go down into,* Lat. *intrare.*

καταθάπτω, (κατά, θάπτω,) *to bury.*

καταθνήσκω, for parts see θνήσκω, (κατά, θνήσκω,) see Lat. *mori, to die off;* in past tenses *to be dead.*

καταθνητός, ή, όν, (κατά, θνητός (θνήσκω),) Lat. *mortalis, subject to death, mortal.*

καταθρώσκω, f. θοροῦμαι, 2 aor. ἔθορον, (κατά, θρώσκω,) *to jump down.*

κατακαίω, Ep. inf. κατακαιέμεν; f. κατακαύσω; Ep. aor. κατέκηα; aor. pass. κατεκαύθην; 2 aor. pass. κατεκάην: Lat. *comburere, to burn, to burn to ashes; burn out.*

κατακαλύπτω, f. ψω, (κατά, καλύπτω,) Lat. *occulere, to cover up, hide, envelop, disguise.*

κατάκειμαι, (κατά, κεῖμαι,) *to lay one's self down, repose; to be laid up.*

κατακείω, Ep. subj. pl. κατακείομεν, Ep. part. κακκείοντες Α 606, *to desire to lie down.*

κατακοιμάω, f. ήσω, (κατά, κοιμάω,) Lat. *consopire, to put to sleep;* pass. *to fall asleep, to sleep.*

κατακοσμέω, (κατά, κοσμέω,) *to set in regular order, arrange.*

κατακρύπτω, f. κρύψω, Ep. forms κακκρύπ-, (κατά, κρύπτω,) Lat. *occultare,* trans. *to hide, hide away, keep concealed;* intrans. *to practise deception, conceal* in appearance, *dissemble, cloak, disguise,* Lat. *dissimulare.*

κατακτείνω; f. κτενῶ, Ep. and Hom. κτανέω, Ion. κτανῶ; 2 aor. κατέκτανον, Ep. κατέκταν, 3 sing. κατέκτα, Ep. imperat. κάκτανε, Ep. inf. κτάμεν(αι), Ep. part. κατακτάς; aor. pass. κατεκτάθην, Ep. 3 pl. κατέκταθεν; 2 pf. κατέκτονα: (κατά, κτείνω:) Lat. *necare, to kill, slay.*

καταλείπω, f. ψω; for parts see λείπω, Ep. forms are pres. καλλ-, (κατά, λείπω,) Lat. *relinquere, to leave behind, leave; leave by will* or *as a heritage; to forsake, abandon,* Lat. *deserere; to give up; to allow.*

καταλήθομαι, (κατά, λήθομαι,) *to forget wholly.*

καταλύω, f. ύσω, (κατά, λύω,) Lat. *dissolvere, to loosen, dissolve, to end; to relinquish, give up; to put down; to cancel; to abolish, disband; destroy; to unyoke, unharness:* mid. *to desist from, to be reconciled to.*

καταμάρπτω, (κατά, μάρπτω,) *to seize, take hold of.*

καταμονή, ῆς, ἡ, (καταμένω,) *a remaining firm, firmness, ability to stand.*

κατανεύω, f. νεύσομαι, Ep. aor. part. καννεύσας, (κατά, νεύω,) Lat. *anuere,* to nod in assent, grant by a nod; to confirm a promise of anything by a nod, Lat. *nutu aliquid confirmare.*

καταπατέω, (κατά, πατέω,) to tread down.

καταπέσσω, f. πέψω, (κατά, πέσσω,) to boil down, to digest, suppress or keep under A 81.

καταπέφνῃ Γ 281, redupl. 2 aor. subj. 3 sing. of **καταφένω,** Lat. *interimere,* may kill.

καταπίπτω; f. πεσοῦμαι; 2 aor. κατέπεσον, Ep. κάππεσον; pf. καταπέπτωκα: (κατά, πίπτω:) Lat. *decidere,* to fall down; to fall, Lat. *procumbere.*

καταπλήσσω, f. ξω, aor. κατέπληξα, 2 aor. pass. κατεπλ(ά)(ή)γην, (κατά, πλήσσω,) Lat. *percellere,* to strike down; to strike with terror or amazement, Lat. *obstupefacere;* to confound: pass. to be stricken with amazement or terror, Γ 31 was smitten in his heart.

καταπτώσσω, (κατά, πτώσσω), == **καταπτήσσω,** from which Ep. and Ion. parts are formed, Ep. 2 aor. part. -πτακών, to cower down as from fear, be or lie crouched down, be in a crouching posture.

καταρρέζω, f. ξω, Ep. aor. κατέρεξα, Ep. fem. part. καρρέζουσα, (κατά, ῥέζω,) Lat. *permulcēre,* to stroke, caress.

κατατείνω, f. τενῶ, aor. κατέτεινα, pf. τέτακα, Lat. *tendere,* to stretch, tighten, draw tight, Γ 261; to strain: intrans. to exert one's self and make every effort, to strive earnestly.

καταρρέω, parts. formed from stem -ῥ(ε)υ-, see Hadley and Allen's Grammar 512,5, (κατά, ῥέω,) to flow or rush down.

κατασβέννυμι, f. έσω, (κατά, σβέννυμι,) to put completely out, extinguish fully.

κατασμύχω, (κατά, σμύχω,) to burn down with a smouldering fire.

καταστορέννυμι, f. έσω, (κατά, στορέννυμι,) to spread down upon, cover with; to spread, strew.

κατατίθημι; f. θήσω; aor. κατέθηκα; 2 aor. κατέθην, Ep. sync. forms κατθε-, Ep. subj. καταθει-; for other forms see **τίθημι:** (κατά, τίθημι:) Lat. *deponere,* to place or lay down; to pay down: mid. to lay down for one's own benefit, lay up, lay aside; to put away.

καταφαγέειν, contr. -γεῖν, 2 aor. inf. of **κατεσθίω,** which see.

καταφέρω, for parts see **φέρω,** (κατά, φέρω,) to bear down.

καταφλέγω, (κατά, φλέγω,) to burn down, destroy with fire.

καταφυλαδόν, (κατά, φυλή,) adv., Lat. *tributim,* by tribes.

καταχέω, f. χεῶ, aor. κατέχεα, aor. pass. κατεχύθην: Ep. forms, pres. καταχεύω; aor. κατέχευα; 2 aor. pass. κατεχύμην, 3 sing. and pl. ἔχυτο, ἔχυντο: (κατά, χέω:) Lat. *defundere,* to pour down; to shower down; to shed or let fall upon or over, Lat. *offundere;* to melt down; to throw down: mid. to let flow down; to cause to be melted.

κατέδω, (κατά, ἔδω,) Ep. form for κατεσθίω, to eat up, which see.

κατείβω for καταλείβω, for parts see λείβω, (κατά, λείβω,) to shed or let run down.

κάτειμι, for parts see εἰμι, (κατά, εἰμι,) Lat. descendere, to descend, go down, flow down; to return, come back, Lat. revertere.

κατειρύω, Ion. of κατερύω, f. ύσω, (κατά, ἐρύω,) compare Lat. detrahere, deducere, to draw down.

κατέκταθεν, see κατακτείνω.

κατερείπω, (κατά, ἐρείπω,) to dash down, overthrow, ruin.

κατερύκω, f. ύξω, (κατά, ἐρύκω,) see Lat. detinēre, to detain, poet. form κατερυκάνω.

κατεσθίω; f. κατέδομαι; 2 aor. κατέφαγον; pf. κατεδήδοκα, Ep. 2 pf. κατέδηδα : (κατά, ἐσθίω :) Lat. devorare, to devour, eat up.

κατευνάω, f. νήσω, Ep. 3 pl. aor. pass. κατεύνασθεν Γ 448, (κατά, εὐνάω,) Lat. sopire, to put to rest or lull to sleep: pass. to be put to sleep, to fall asleep, Lat. dormire.

κατέχω, poet. 2 aor. κατέσχεθον, for other forms see ἔχω, also, Hadley and Allen's Gram. 508,16 and D 16, (κατά, ἔχω,) Lat. retinēre, detinēre, to detain, hold back, restrain, check, also, possess; to keep, hold, occupy; to take possession of, seize; to hold for residence; to cover Γ 419; to hide; with κεφαλήν, to bend over: intrans. to hold, stop; to happen; to prevail, have the advantage, have sway.

κατηρεφής, ές, (κατά, ἐρέφω,) well covered, covered, covered over, vaulted or arched.

κατήφεια, Hom. -είη, as, ἡ, (κατηφής (κατά, φάος),) Lat. vultus, demissus, the act of casting the eyes down; dejection, sadness, sorrow; disgrace, Γ 51, Lat. dedecus.

κατηφέω, f. ήσω, (κατηφής (κατά, φάος),) to be dejected or downcast, be sad, through grief or shame.

κατίσχω, a pres. = κατέχω, Lat. detinēre, retinēre, to hold in, check; to steer; to hold: (seemingly) intrans. to (hold one's course to or) come upon: mid. to keep: see κατέχω.

κατοίσομαι, see καταφέρω.

Καΰστριος, ου, ὁ, the Ca-ys'-ter, a river of Ly'-di-a.

κέ(ν), Hom. for ἄν encl. ἄν (Hom. κέ(ν) encl.) in independent clauses is foll. by the past tenses of the indicat. (Hom. sometimes uses it with f. to mark the event as contingent) mood to mark an action as depending upon some supposition that has not been fulfilled, and by the opt. mood to express possibility; in dependent clauses ἄν or κέ(ν) is foll. by the subj. mood. Hom. uses ἄν or κέ(ν) with subj. in independent clauses to indicate futurity. Hom. often omits ἄν or κέ(ν) from positions in which it would naturally belong. It is also used with ἄν ; in relative and conditional clauses which have the subj. it is often repeated : with the indicat., with the f. to mark the event as contingent or looked for, A 175, *who will honor me ;* with the impf. and aor. to denote customary *action ;* in conclusion with a past tense when the condition is a false one : with the subj.; for the f. indicat. A 184 ; with subj. of wish or expectation ; in hypothetical relative sentences, in many subordinate clauses, and in cases of past uncertainty : with the opt.; to denote concession ; with the opt. to denote f. or pres. time ; to ask questions : see ἄν.

Κεάδης, ου, ὁ, *son of Ce'-as.*

κεατ-, Ep. and Ion. forms from κεῖμαι, which see.

(σ)κεδάννυμι, Hom. aor. ἐκέδασσα, Hom. aor. pass. ἐκεδάσθην, Lat. *dissipare, disperse, break up, burst.*

κεδνός, ή, όν, (κῆδος,) *careful, prudent, provident ;* also, *meriting care, cared for, dear* to one bestowing the care ; *valued, held in great regard.*

κεῖθεν, Ep. and Ion. adv. for ἐκεῖθεν, (κεῖνος,) Lat. *illinc, thence, from that place.*

κεῖθι, Ep. for ἐκεῖθι, adv. Lat. *illic, there.*

κεῖμαι, κεῖσαι, κεῖαι, κεῖται, Ion. κέεται, κεῖσθον, κείμεθα, κεῖσθε, κεῖνται, Ep. and Hom. κέαται and κείαται, Ion. κέονται ; impf. ἐκει-, iter. 3 sing. κέσκετο, Hom. 3 pl. (ἐ)κέατο, κέλατο ; subj. κέωμαι, Hom. 3 sing. κῆται ; opt. κεοίμην ; imperat. κεῖσο, -σθω ; Hom. κεε- for κει-; f. κείσομαι: Lat. *jacēre, to be laid, lie down, lie at rest, remain inactive, lie idle* or *at ease, rest, lie dead, lie neglected ; to be situated ; to be fixed in a position, to be laid up, stored ; to be deposited ; to lie in ruins.*

κεῖνος, η, ο, for ἐκεῖνος, which see.

κεινός, ή, όν, poet. for κενός, Lat. *inanis, vacuus, empty.*

κεῖσε, Ep. for ἐκεῖσε, adv., Lat. *illuc, thither, to that place ;* see κεῖθι.

κεκαδών, 2 aor. Ep. part. of χάζομαι, which see.

κέκασμαι, pf. pass., but having sense of the pres. tense ; see καίνυμαι.

κεκαφηώς, E 698, pf. part., Ep. from κάπτω, *to gasp ;* stric. *to eat with greed* or *quickly.*

κέκλετο, 2 aor. Ep. 3 sing. of κέλομαι, which see.

κεκλήατο, see καλέω.

κεκληγώς, see κλάζω.

κέκλιμαι, see κλίνω.

κέκλυθι, κέκλυτε, Ep. redupl. 2 aor. of κλύω.

κεκρύφαλος, ου, ὁ, (κρύπτω,) see Lat. *reticulum, a small net for a woman's hair ; the purse of a hunter's ne ;* also, *the throat-latch of a bridle ; the second stomach of ruminants.*

κέλαδος, ου, ὁ, compare Lat. *strepitus, tumultus, clamor, a loud noise* like the noise of rushing wind and waters ; a clear *loud noise, a tumultuous noise, the din of conflict, a cry* or *shouting.*

κελάδω, (κέλαδος,) Hom. uses only part., *to sound loud, make a loud noise* as of rushing waters.

κελαινεφής, ές, (κελαινός, νέφος,) *dark-clouded, shrouded with clouds.*

κελαινός, ή, όν, Lat. *niger, dark.*

κέλευθος, ου, ἡ, neu. also, in pl., Lat. *callis, path, track, way ; the course of life ; an outgoing ; a journey, travelling,* Lat. *iter.*

κελεύω, f. σω, (κέλλω,) *to put in motion, urge on ;* compare Lat. *jubēre, imperare, praecipere, mandare, to order* B 50, 74, *command ; to incite ;* with acc. and inf.; with dat. *to call out to,* B 50.

κέλομαι ; f. κελήσομαι ; poet. 2 aor. (ἐ)κεκλόμην : (κέλλω:) poet. *to urge on, encourage ; to exhort,* Lat. *hortari ; command ; to call to.*

κέν, see κέ.

κενεός, ή, όν, poet. and Hom. for **κενός**, Ion. **κεινός**, Lat. *inanis, vacuus, empty ; void, fruitless, futile, vain :* neu. as adv., κενεά, κενεόν B 298, *to no purpose, vainly, in vain :* Hom. κεινός Γ 376.

Κένταυρος, ου, ὁ, (κεντέω,) *a Cen'-taur, a Piercer* or *Spearman ;* the Cen'-taurs were a savage race of horsemen in Thes'-sa-ly ; later they were thought to be half man and half horse.

κέντωρ, ορος, ὁ, (κεντέω,) *one who goads* or *urges on a team, a driver.*

κέονται, see κεῖμαι.

κεραΐζω, (κέρας,) *to plunder, to ravage ; to destroy, kill,* B 861.

κεραίω, Ep. for **κεράννυμι**, *to mix.*

κεραμεύς, έως, ὁ, Lat. *figulus, a potter.*

κεραοξόος, ον, (κέρας, ξέω,) *scraping* or *polishing horn, working horn.*

κεραός, ά, όν, (κέρας,) *horned ; of horn.*

κέρας ; gen. κέρατος, Ep. κέραος, Ion. κέρεος ; Ion. dat. κέρεϊ ; Ep. dat. pl. also κεράεσσι ; the Ion. does not use the forms with τ ; τό : Lat. *cornu, a horn ; that which is made of horn ; horn ; a drinking horn ; a horn for blowing ; a branch of a river ; an arm of the sea ; wing of an army ; a promontory, mountain peak ; sail-yard ; any projection* or *arm,* etc.

κερδαλεόφρων, ον, (κερδαλέος, φρήν,) *eager for gain, crafty,* A 149 ; *crafty-minded.*

κερδίων, κέρδιον, ονος, compar., sup. κέρδιστος, η, ον, (κέρδος,) Lat. *utilius, more profitable,* Γ 41 ; *more lucrative ; more helpful, better ;* from obsol. positive.

κερδοσύνη, ης, ἡ, (κέρδος,) *craftiness, cunning, prudence, shrewdness.* Do Lat. *astutia* and *dolus* convey the meanings of this word ?

κέρκις, ιδος, ἡ, (κέρκω,) *a weaver's comb* or *stay* used to make the web or threads close ; also, *the shuttle, the web worked with the shuttle;* from its shape *any quill for playing on a musical instrument.*

κερτομέω, f. ήσω, (κέρτομος,) Lat. *conviciari, to wound by cutting expressions, taunt, mock, tease.*

κερτόμιος, ον, (κέαρ, τέμνω,) *heart-cutting, cutting by sarcasm, heart-wounding; mocking;* A 539 *taunting* or *sharp-cutting* (*words*).

κευθάνω, Hom. for κεύθω, which see.

κεῦθος, εος, τό, (κεύθω,) see Lat. *latebra, any place of concealment, a secret place, a retired place; a hole, cave, a depth.*

κεύθω, see κευθάνω ; f. κεύσω ; aor. ἔκευσα (Hom.) ; 2 aor. (ἔ)κυθον, Ep. subj. κεκύθω ; 2 pf. κέκυθα (as pres.) : Lat. *celare, occultare, occulere, to hide, conceal; to hide away from danger,* Lat. *abscondere; to disguise, keep secret:* intrans. *to be concealed, to be out of sight.*

κεφαλή, ῆς, ἡ, Lat. *caput, the head; the upper part, the summit; life,* a use com. in Lat. (*caput*) and Eng.; by synecdoche for *the whole person; a man, an individual,* Lat. *homo; the principal personage,* Lat. *princeps;* Γ 273 ; *the sum, conclusion, the chief point of a matter,* Lat. *summa, conclusio.*

Κεφαλλήν, ῆνος, ὁ, *a Ce-phal-le'-ni-an,* in pl. a gen. name for the followers of U-lys'-ses.

κεχαροίατο, see χαίρω.

κῆδος, εος, τό, Lat. *sollicitudo, care, solicitude, concern; trouble, anxiety, affliction; mourning,* Lat. *luctus; funeral obsequies; a relationship by marriage, a marriage connection.*

κήδω, iter. impf. κήδεσκον, f. κηδήσω, ἐκήδησα, irreg. f. pf. κεκαδήσ-, 2 pf. κέκηδα ; trans. in pres.; *to cause any one anxiety, to trouble, to annoy:* intrans. *to be troubled* or *distressed;* with gen. *to be distressed* or *troubled concerning, be anxious* or *care for,* A 196.

κηλε(ι)ος, ον, (καίω,) compare Lat. *ardens, splendens, burning, brilliant.*

κῆλον, ου, τό, Lat. *telum ligneum, the wooden shaft of an arrow.*

Κήρ, gen. Κηρός, dat. Κηρί, acc. Κῆρα, ἡ, sometimes pl. Κῆρες, *the Goddess of Fate; Death* Γ 454, *Fate; Destiny, Doom; the Goddess of Evil; Evil, Disease, Misfortune, Disgrace;* B 302, Κῆρες θανάτοιο, *the Fates of death.*

κῆρ, (contd. from κέαρ,) κῆρος, uncontr. κέαρος, τό, Lat. *cor, heart; the heart,* corresponding to our use of the word "*heart*," compare Lat. *animus, mens.*

Κήρινθος, ου, ἡ, *Ce-rin'-thus,* a town of Eu-bœ'-a.

κῆρυξ, υκος, ὁ, (γῆρυς,) Lat. *praeco, a herald;* the herald summoned the assembly of the people, carried messages, (Lat. *caduceator,*) proclaimed war or peace, regulated the order at trials, and performed many duties that with us devolve upon *a sheriff* or *marshal :* the sign of their office was a wand ; and, as at the present day, with one carrying a flag of truce, or with one sent on business from one army to another, they were safe from personal violence.

κηρύσσω, f. ξω, aor. ἐκήρυξα, 2 pf. κεκήρυχα, Lat. *praedicare, to perform the duty of herald; to make publicly known, proclaim as herald; to call together as herald; to call on* or *summon ; to cause to be sold, proclaim for sale.*

κητώεις, εσσα, εν, *having ravines,* epith. of La-ce-dæ'-mon ; *spacious*

Κηφισίς, ίδος, ἡ, *Ce-phi'-sis,* a lake in Bœ-o'-ti-a.

Κηφισός, οῦ, ὁ, *the Ce-phi'-sus,* a river of Bœ-o'-ti-a.

κηώδης, ες, (καίω,) Lat. *fragrans,* (see, also, *bene olens,*) *sweet-smelling.*

κηώεις, εσσα, εν, Lat. *fragrans, fragrant, perfumed, scented,* Γ 382 ; see foreg.

κιθαρίζω, f. ίσω, (κίθαρις,) *to play on a harp.*

κίθαρις, ιος, ἡ, Lat. *cithara, the lyre, the harp ; the art of playing the harp.*

κιθαριστύς, ύος, ἡ, (κιθαρίζω,) *the art of playing the lyre,* also, *the act of playing the harp.*

κικλήσκω, poet. for **καλέω,** which see, Lat. *vocare, to call ; to call upon,* Lat. *invocare ; to call by name, nominate,* Lat. *nominare ; to summon ; to accost.*

Κίκονες, ων, οἱ, *the Cic'-o-nes,* a Thra'-ci-an tribe.

Κίλιξ, ικος, ὁ, *a Ci-li'-ci-an.*

Κίλλα, ης, ἡ, *Cil'-la,* a town sacred to A-pol'-lo, Α 38, 452.

κινέω, f. ήσω, aor. (ἐ)κίνησα, (κίω,) Lat. *movēre, to set in motion, move, stir, disturb, urge, incite, provoke, make angry ;* κινηθέντος, Α 47, in a mid. sense, *as he moved along ; cause to begin, commence, originate, to be the author of ; to change ; to move to emotion, excite.*

κίρκος, ου, ὁ, *a species of hawk* that describes circles in the air ; hence, also, *a circle.*

κιχάνω, f. κιχήσομαι ; aor. 3 sing. κιχήσατο ; 2 aor. ἔκιχον : μι- forms from stem κιχε ; impf. ἐκίχην, 2 sing. ἐκίχεις, 3 du. κιχήτην, pl. (ἐ)κίχημεν ; Ep. subj. κιχείω Α 26, Γ 291 ; Ep. opt. κιχείην Β 188 ; inf. κιχῆναι, Ep. κιχῆμεν(αι), part. κιχείς, κεχμένος : Lat. *invenire, to find, overtake, attain, light upon ; to reach,* Lat. *adsequi.*

κίω, subj. Ep. pl. κίομεν, Lat. *ire, to go,* Α 348, Β 509 ; pres. indicat. obsol.

κλαγγή, ῆς, ἡ, (κλάζω,) Lat. *clangor, a quick and loud sound, a clang, a twang, shout of men, the loud and shrill cry of birds of prey* esp. *the eagle, the cry* or *noise of beasts, the baying of a dog, the grunting of swine ; noise,* Γ 5 ; κλαγγηδόν, adv., *with a noise,* Β 463.

κλάζω ; f. κλάγξω ; Ep. 2 aor. ἔκλαγον ; 2 pf. with signif. of pres. κέκλαγγα, Hom. part. κεκληγώς, gen. -οντος, as if from a 2 pf. κέκληγα : Lat. *clangere, to make* or *utter any loud, quick sound, to clang ; to screech ;* of dogs, *to bark ; to rush,* of a flying arrow ; A 46, *to rattle, clash,* Lat. *stridēre ; to roar ;* of men, *to cry out loudly, shout,* Lat. *vociferari ; to make a noise in any of the senses of* κλαγγή.

κλαίω ; f. κλαύσομαι, κλαήσω, and κλαιήσω ; aor. ἔκλαυσα ; pf. κέκλαυμαι and -αυσμαι : Lat. *plorare, to weep, deplore, bemoan, lament :* trans. *to mourn, sorrow for.*

κλαυθμός, οῦ, ὁ, (κλαίω,) *a lamentation, a wailing.*

κλαῦσε, aor. Ep. 3 sing. of κλαίω, which see.

κλειτός, ή, όν, (κλείω,) Lat. *inclitus, renowned, famous, fine, splendid, excellent,* A 447.

κλέος, τό ; Ep. κλει- ; Lat. *fama, a rumor, report ; fame, renown, glory, honor,* Lat. *gloria.*

κλέπτης, ου, ὁ, (κλέπτω,) Lat. *fur, a thief,* Γ 11.

κλέπτω ; f. ψω ; aor. ἔκλεψα ; 2 pf. κέκλοφα ; aor. pass. ἐκλέφθην, 2 aor. ἐκλάπην : Lat. *furari, to steal ; to do anything by stealth ; to conceal, disguise ; to seduce, deceive,* Lat. *fallere ; to mislead ; = to practise deceit,* A 132.

Κλεωναί, ῶν, αἱ, *Cle-o'-næ,* a town in Ar'-go-lis.

κληίς, ίδος, ἡ, Ion. for κλείς, *that with which the door was closed ; a key ; a bolt* or *bar, a hook ; the claviele.*

κλῆρος, ου, ὁ, Lat. *sors, a lot* of any description, *a portion assigned by lot ; the act of casting* or *drawing lots ; an inheritance,* Lat. *hacreditatis pars.*

κλίνω ; f. κλινῶ ; aor. ἔκλινα ; pf. κέκλικα, mid. κέκλιμαι Γ 135 ; aor. pass. ἐκλί(ν)θην ; 2 aor. pass. ἐκλίνην : Lat. *clinare, to make to incline ; to incline one thing against another, to lean one thing against another,* Lat. *inclinare ; to bend, bend down ; to cause to turn,* and so *to rout* an army ; *to turn aside, turn away,* Lat. *deflectere, avertere ; to make to recline :* pass. *to be bent ; to lean* or *rest upon* Γ 135 ; *to recline* or *lie down ; to slope* or *incline,* of places ; *to wander.*

κλισία, ας, Ion. -ίη, ης, ἡ, (κλίνω,) Lat. *tabernaculum, a place for reposing, a lodge, a tent, hut, shed, cabin ; a rural dwelling ; a chair, a couch ;* κλισίηθεν, *from the hut.*

κλισμός, οῦ, ὁ, (κλίνω,) *a reclining chair.*

κλονέω, (κλόνος,) *to put into confusion, drive before in confusion, agitate, push before.*

Κλονίος, ου, ὁ, *Clo'-ni-us,* leader of the Bœ-o'-tians.

κλῦθι, Hom. 2 aor. imperat. of κλύω.

Κλυμένη, ης, ἡ, *Clym'-e-ne,* an attendant of Hel'-en, Γ 144 ; lit. *famous.*

Κλυταιμνήστρα, as, ἡ, *Clyt-em-nes'-tra,* wife of Ag-a-mem'-non, sister of Hel'-en.

Κλυτίος, ου, ὁ, *Cly'-tius,* son of La-om'-e-don, Γ 147.

κλυτόπωλος, ον, (κλυτός, πῶλος,) *famed for horses.*

κλυτός, (κλύω,) adj., Lat. *clarus, inclitus, heard of, renowned, famous, illustrious; splendid, beautiful, fine.*

κλυτοτέχνης, ου, ὁ, (κλυτός, τέχνη,) Lat. *arte clarus,* one *famous for his art, renowned artist.*

κλυτότοξος, ον, (κλυτός, τόξον,) *renowned of the bow.*

κλύω ; Ep. 2 aor. imperat. κέκλυθι, κέκλυτε Γ 86 ; Lat. *exaudire, to hear, attend to, give ear to, to hearken ;* with gen. *to hear* in the sense of *to obey,* Lat. *obedire ; to hear, find out by report.*

κλωμακόεις, εσσα, εν, (κλῶμαξ,) *rocky, rough.*

κνέφας, αος, τό, *darkness, obscurity, twilight, dusk ;* poet. dat. κνέφει.

κνήμη, ης, ἡ, Lat. *tibia, crus, the calf of the leg, the leg between the knee and ankle.*

κνημίς, ῖδος, ἡ, (κνήμη,) Lat. *ocrea, a greave.*

κνημός, οῦ, ὁ, (κνήμη,) *the side of a mountain, the side* or *sloping part of a mountain.*

κνίσα, ης, ἡ ; Ep. κνίσ(σ)η ; *the fat, the fat-caul in which the thighs of the victim were wrapped up and burned* A 460 ; *the smoke, steam, and odor of a burning sacrifice,* Lat. *nidor.*

Κνωσός, οῦ, ὁ, *Cno'-sus,* a city of Crete.

κοῖλος, η, ον, Lat. *cavus, concavus, hollowed, hollow, concave ; excavated ; extending into.*

κοιμάω, Ion. -έω, f. ήσω, Lat. *sopire, to lull to rest, put to bed ; to calm, lull, soothe, still, quiet :* mid. and pass. *to lay one's self down to rest ; to be put to rest, sleep, rest, to die* or *sleep the sleep of death.*

κοιρανέω, f. ήσω, (κοίρανος,) Lat. *dominari, to be ruler* or *commander, hold command* or *rule :* as trans. *to govern, rule, lead.*

Κοίρανος, ου, ὁ, *Cœr'-a-nus.*

κοίρανος, ου, ὁ, Lat. *dominus, a ruler, master ; commander,* Lat. *imperator.*

κολεόν, οῦ, τό, Ion. κουλεόν, (κοῖλος,) Lat. *vagina, a scabbard.*

κόλπος, ου, ὁ, Lat. *sinus, bosom, fold* or *swell of garment, hollow, bay, the womb.*

κολῳάω, Ion. -έω, f. ήσω, (κολῳός (κολοιός),) *to brawl with loud vociferation,* B 212.

κολώνη, ης, ἡ, Lat. *collis, a hill ; a burial mound,* Lat. *tumulus.*

κολῳός, οῦ, ὁ, (κολοιός,) Lat. *tumultus, the noise of scolding and strife, a noisy wrangling, brawling.*

κομάω, Ep. part. κομόων B 542 ; f. ήσω, (κόμη,) *to cultivate long hair, to
  let the hair grow long; to be vain, haughty, proud,* as long hair was a
  sign of rank ; of horses, *to have long manes;* of trees, etc., *to have
  foliage.*

κόμη, ης, ἡ, Lat. coma, *the hair of the head, foliage, leaves; the tail of a comet.*

κομίζω, f. ίσω, aor. (ἐ)κομίσ(σ)α, pf. κεκόμισμαι, aor. pass. ἐκομίσθην,
  (κομέω,) Lat. curare, *to take care of, attend to, provide for ; to save or
  rescue; to transport, carry away, bear off,* Γ 378 ; *to pick up, gather in ;
  to bring, import :* mid. *to carry with one; to carry off; to get; to take
  away; to receive hospitably; to recover; to rescue.*

κοναβίζω, f. ίσω = **κοναβέω,** f. ήσω, (κόναβος,) Lat. resonare, *to resound,
  re-echo* B 334, *clash.*

κονία, ας, Ep. **κονίη,** ἡ, (κόνις,) Lat. pulvis, *dust ; fine powder ; sand,* Lat.
  arena ; *ashes,* Lat. cineres ; wrestlers sprinkled their bodies with fine
  sand.

κόνις, ιος, ἡ, Lat. pulvis, *dust, ashes or their dust.*

κονίσ(σ)αλος, ου, ὁ, (κόνις,) *dust, a cloud of dust* Γ 13.

κόπρος, ου, ἡ, *excrement, manure ; any filth ;* also, *the place where dung is,
  the stable* or *barn-yard.*

κόπτω, f. ψω, 2 pf. κέκοφα and Ep. part. κεκοπώς, *to beat, strike, pound ; to
  hammer out, forge anything ; to cut ; to strike down, knock down, hew
  down* or *fell men or trees, cut down* or *slay, kill ; to cut into* or *off, lop
  off ; to cut up* or *chop ; to strike* or *injure, wound, mutilate.*

κορέννυμι, f. κορέσω, aor. ἐκόρεσα, aor. pass. ἐκορέσθην ; Ep. forms, f. κορέω,
  aor. -εσσ-, Ion. pf. κεκόρημαι with Ep. and Ion. part. κεκορηώς having
  pres. sense ; (κόρος ;) Lat. satiare, saturare, *to satisfy, fill* (with gen.),
  satiate.

Κόρινθος, ου, ἡ, *Cor'-inth.*

κόρση, ης, ἡ, *the temple ; the hair.*

κορυθάιξ, ικος, ὁ, (κόρυς, ἀίσσω,) *with waving helmet.*

κορυθαίολος, ον, (κόρυς, αἰόλος,) *with waving helmet,* Γ 83, B 816.

κόρυς, υθος, ἡ, (κάρα,) Lat. galea, *a helmet, a helmet and crest ; the crown
  of the head.*

κορύσσω, f. ύξω, (κόρυς,) Lat. galea armare, *to equip* or *arm with the helmet ; to arm,* Lat. armare ; B 273 *to fit out, prepare for.*

κορυστής, οῦ, ὁ, *one that wears a helmet, a fighting-man.*

κορυφή, ῆς, ἡ, (κόρυς,) Lat. vertex, cacumen, *the top, crest, uppermost part ;
  the top of the head, crown, head.*

Κορώνεια, ας, ἡ, *Cor-o-ne'-a,* a city of Bœ-o'-ti-a.

κορώνη, ης, ἡ, Lat. cornix, *a crow, sea-crow, cormorant ; a door-handle* or
  anything curved like a crow's beak, the extremity of a bow.

κορωνίς, ίδος, ή, (κορώνη,) *crooked-beaked, curved, crooked,* epith. of ships : as subst. *anything curved ; a wreath, garland,* Lat. *corona ; a crooked pen-flourish at the end of a chapter* or *book, the end.*

Κόρωνος, ου, ὁ, *Co-ro'-nus.*

κοσμέω, f. ήσω, (κόσμος,) Lat. *instruere, to arrange, set in order, regulate, equip, marshal, prepare ; to deck, embellish,* Lat. *ornare.*

κοσμήτωρ, ορος, ὁ, (κοσμέω,) *one who arranges, a marshaller, commander.*

κόσμος, ου, ὁ, (κομέω,) Lat. *ordo, order, regulation, institution, arrangement ; good order, discipline ; an ornament, attire, embellishment, decoration,* Lat. *ornamentum, decus ; the world,* Lat. *mundus, the universe,* from the perfect order.

κοτέω, Ep. 2 pf. part. κεκοτηώς, (κότος,) *to be angry at,* Lat. *irasci ;* Lat. *invidēre, to envy, grudge.*

κότος, ου, ὁ, Lat. *ira, anger ; envy, jealousy,* Lat. *invidia ; grudge, animosity, ill-will, hatred.*

κοτύλη, ης, ή, Lat. *cavum, a hollow ; a small drinking-cup ; a measure* containing about a half-pint of liquid, also, *a dry measure ; the socket* in the hip-joint.

κουλεόν, see **κολεόν.**

κούρη, ης, Ion. for **κόρη,** fem. of **κοῦρος** or **κόρος,** Lat. *puella, a young girl, maid, damsel,* A 111 *maiden* ⸗ *virgin ; daughter, a young wife.*

κουρίδιος, α, ον, (κοῦρος,) *bridal,* A 114 *lawful wife, lawfully wedded ; bridal, nuptial.*

κοῦρος, ου, ὁ, Ion. for **κόρος,** *a youth, boy,* Lat. *puer ; son ; servant at the sacrifice ;* also in pl., *soldiers,* A 473 ; *noble.*

κραδίη, see **καρδία.**

κραίνω, Hom. and Ep. **κραιαίνω ;** f. κρανῶ ; aor. ἔκρανα, Ep. ἔκρηνα, Ep. imperat. κρήηνον and inf. κρῆηναι ; aor. pass. ἐκράνθην : Lat. *perficere, to achieve, accomplish, complete, fulfil, bring about :* intrans., Lat. *regnare, to be king ; to come to an end.*

κραιπνός, ή, όν, *rushing, rapid ; quick, fleet ; with hot haste, vehement.*

Κρανάη, ης, ή, *Cran'-a-e,* an island where Par'-is first took Hel'-en.

κραναός, ή, όν, (κράνον,) Lat. *asper, rough, rocky, stony ;* Γ 201, *very rugged.*

Κράπαθος, ου, ή, *Crap'-a-thus,* an island.

κραταιός, ά, όν, (κράτος,) poet., Lat. *potens, validus, strong, powerful.*

κρατερός, ά, όν, poet. **καρτερός,** (κράτος,) *strong, mighty ; brave, valiant,* Lat. *fortis, hard, violent, harsh :* adv. κρατερῶς, *mightily.*

κρατέω, f. ήσω, (κράτος,) *to be powerful, to have power ; to rule,* Lat. *dominari ;* with dat. *to bear sway among ;* with gen. *to have power over, become* or *be master of, have in his power, conquer, rule over ;* with acc.

to surpass, Lat. *excellere* or *praestare*, *vanquish*, Lat. *vincere* ; *to hold fast*, *seize* : intrans. *to prevail*, *last*.

κράτος, εος, τό, poet. **κάρτος,** Lat. *robur, vis, potentia, might, power, force, strength, violence; rule, sovereignty, dominion,* Lat. *imperium; victory,* Lat. *victoria.*

κρατός, see **κάρ.**

κρείσσων, ον, gen. ονος, Ion. **κρέσσων,** irreg. compar. of ἀγαθός, which see, Lat. *viribus praestantior, stronger, more powerful, mightier; nobler, better, braver,* Lat. *melior; greater; superior.*

κρείων, οντος, fem. **κρείουσα,** stric. part. *ruling,* Lat. *regnator; a ruler, chief, lord;* epith. of persons of superior rank, esp. of Ag-a-mem′-non.

κρήγυος, ον, Lat. *gratus, utilis, good, helpful, agreeable,* A 106 ; *true.*

κρήδεμνον, ου, τό, (κράς, δέω,) *a band for the head; a head-dress made to serve as veil, a veil; battlement; cover of a jar or vessel.*

κρηῆναι, see **κραίνω.**

Κρήθων, ωνος, ὁ, *Cre′-thon.*

κρήνη, ης, ἡ, Lat. *fons, a fountain, well, spring; source.*

Κρής, Κρητός, ὁ, *a Cre′-tan;* **Κρήτη,** ης, ἡ, *Crete,* Γ 233 **Κρήτηθεν,** *from Crete.*

κρητήρ, ῆρος, ὁ, Hom. and Ep. for **κρατήρ,** (κεράννυμι,) Lat. *crater, a mixing vessel in which the wine and water were mixed; the crater of a volcano.*

κρίνω, f. **κρινῶ,** aor. ἔκρινα, pf. κέκρικα, aor. pass. ἐκί(ν)θην, Lat. *cernere, to put asunder, part, separate, divide; to choose, select,* Lat. *eligere; to choose* in the sense of *to decide; to judge of, criticise; explain; to examine in a court of justice;* hence, also, *to condemn :* mid. and pass. *to select for one's self* or *one's own benefit, choose; to be selected, to be the chosen one; to dispute, fight,* B 385 *that we may contend,* lit. *decide among ourselves.*

Κρῖσα, ης, ἡ, *Cri′-sa,* a city of Pho′-cis.

κροαίνω, poet. word with sense of **κρούω,** *to stamp* or *tread with the hoof,* as an active horse.

κροκόπεπλος, ον, (κρόκος, πέπλος,) *with saffron-colored robe* or *mantle.*

Κροκύλεια, ων, τά, *Croc-y-le′-a,* a part of Ith′-a-ca.

Κρονίδης, ου, ὁ, *son of Cro′-nos, Zeus,* A 552 ; also **Κρονίων,** ιωνος.

Κρόνος, ου, ὁ, *Cro′-nos,* Lat. *Sa-tur′-nus,* father of Zeus.

κρόταφος, ου, ὁ, *the temple, side of the forehead and face.*

κρουνός, ου, ὁ, *the fountain-head* or *source.*

κρυερός, ά, όν, (κρύος,) Lat. *gelidus, icy, chilling.*

κρυπτάδιος, adj., (κρύπτω,) Lat. *clandestinus, occultus, clandestine, secret, hidden, concealed.*

κρύσταλλος, ου, ὁ, (κρύος,) Lat. *glacies, ice.*

Κρῶμνα, ης, ἡ, *Crom'-na,* a place in Paph-la-go'-ni-a.

κτάμεν(αι), see κτείνω.

κτεάτεσσι(ν), Ep. dat. pl., Lat. *bonis, goods, property, possessions.*

Κτέατος, ου, ὁ, *Cte'-a-tus,* one of the E-pi'-i.

κτείνεσκον, iter. impf. of foll.

κτείνω ; f. κτενῶ, Hom. and Ep. κτενέω and κτανέω ; aor. ἔκτεινα ; poet.
    2 aor. ἔκτανον, poet. ἔκταν and 3 pl. ἔκταν, Ep. subj. κτέω and pl. κτέω-
    μεν, Ep. inf. κτάμεν(αι); Ep. part. κτάς, Ep. mid. ἐκτάμην ; pf. ἔκταγκα,
    ἔκτακα ; 2 pf. ἔκτονα ; aor. pass. ἐκτάνθην, Hom. ἐκτάθην, Ep. 3 pl.
    ἔκτανθεν : Lat. *interficere, to slay, kill.*

κτερίζω, f. ριῶ, (κτέρεα,) *to perform the last sacred rites.*

κτῆμα, ατος, τό, (κτάομαι,) Lat. *possessio, a possession, piece of property;*
    in pl. *goods, possessions, treasures, riches.*

κτῆσις, εως, ἡ, (κτάομαι,) *a gaining, getting ; property gained, possessions,*
    Lat. *possessio.*

κτῖλος, ου, Lat. *aries, a ram.*

κυάνεος, α, ον, (κύανος,) *dark blue, steel-blue ; dark.*

κυβιστάω, f. ήσω, *to plunge head foremost ; to throw one's self on the head,*
    tumble heels over head, turn a somersault.

κυβιστητήρ, τῆρος, ὁ, (κυβιστάω,) *one who tumbles* or *plunges head foremost,*
    a plunger.

κυδαλίμος, ον, (κῦδος,) Lat. *gloriosus, glorious, famous.*

κυδιάνειρα, fem. adj., (κῦδος, ἀνήρ,) Lat. *viros honestans, man-ennobling.*

κυδιάω, (κῦδος,) Ep. part. κυδιόων, Lat. *gloriari, to be puffed up with pride,*
    to be proud, exult.

κύδιστος, η, ον, (κῦδος,) Lat. *gloriosissimus, most renowned ; greatest.*

κυδοιμός, οῦ, ὁ, compare Lat. *tumultus, strepitus, clamor, tumult, uproar,*
    din, of battle.

κῦδος, εος, τό, Lat. *gloria, decus, honor, distinction, pride, glory, re-*
    nown.

κύκλος, ου, ὁ, also τά in pl., Lat. *orbis, circulus, a circle, a ring, a cir-*
    cumference; anything round, a wheel; a shield, as being round ; *a*
    place where the people met ; root of Eng. *cycle.*

κυκλόσε, (κύκλος,) adv., *around in a circle.*

κυκλοτερής, ές, (κύκλος, τείρω,) *rubbed into round form, round.*

κύκνος, ου, ὁ, Lat. *cycnus* or *cygnus, a swan;* metaph. *a poet.*

κυλίνδω, f. λίσω, *to roll.*

Κυλλήνη, ης, ἡ, *Cyl-le'-ne,* a chain of mountains in Ar-ca'-di-a.

κῦμα, ατος, τό, (κύω,) *a swell ; a wave, billow,* Lat. *fluctus, unda ; the*
    fœtus in the womb.

κυνέη, ης, ἡ, (κύων,) Lat. *pellis canina, a dog-skin ; a soldier's dog-skin cap,* hence *any leathern cap for soldiers,* hence *a helmet,* Lat. *galea.*

κυνέω, f. also κύσ(σ)ω, Ep. aor. (ἔ)κυσ(σ)α, Lat. *osculari, to kiss ; to earnestly plead with, implore.*

Κῦνος, ου, ἡ, *Cy'-nus,* a port of Lo'-cris.

κυνώπης, ου, ὁ, (κύων, ὤψ,) lit. *having dog's eyes, dog-eyed,* and so *fierce-eyed ; the impudent, audacious, shameless one;* κυνῶπις, Γ 180, fem.

Κυπαρισσήεις, εντος, ἡ, *Cyp-a-ris-se'-is,* a town of E'-lis.

κυπάρισσος, ου, ἡ, Lat. *cupressus, cypress.*

κύπελλον, ου, τό, (κύπη,) Lat. *cupella, a large drinking-cup, goblet.*

κύπτω, f. κύψω, 2 p. κέκυφα, *to bend the head, stoop down, bow the head and body.*

Κύτωρος, ου, ἡ, *Cy-to'-rus,* a town of Paph-la-go'-ni-a.

κυρτός, ή, όν, Lat. *curvus, curved, bent,* curved = *deformed* B 218.

κύρω and **κυρέω**; parts are formed from both words; f. κύρσω, κυρήσω; aor. ἔκυρσα, ἐκύρησα : Lat. *incidere, nancisci ;* with gen. *to touch, find, attain, reach, extend to, arrive at, secure, obtain ;* with dat. *to light upon, attain, fall upon* or *in with, encounter,* Γ 23 ἐπὶ σώματι κύρσας *having come upon ;* with acc. *to get, find, obtain :* intrans. *to occur, come to pass, turn, chance.*

κύστις, εως, ἡ, (κύω,) *a bladder,* and so *a bag.*

Κύφος, ου, ἡ, *Cy'-phus,* a town of Thes'-sa-ly.

κύω, see **κυνέω**.

κύων; all cases but nom. and voc. sing. are from stem κυν-; κυνός, dat. κυνί, acc. κύνα, voc. κύον, pl. κύνες, gen. κυῶν, κυσί, acc. κύνας; Ep. κύνεσσι; dat. pl. ὁ, ἡ ; Lat. *canis, a dog, bitch ;* the gen. senses of the word were the same as with us, both for good and bad ; *sea-dog ; dog-star.*

κωκυτός, οῦ, ὁ, (κωκύω,) Lat. *fletus, a wailing, lamenting, weeping;* as pr. name, *the Co-cy'-tus,* the river of lamenting in the Infernal regions.

κωκύω, f. ύσω, compare Lat. *lamentari, flēre, plorare, to cry bitterly, lament, wail.*

Κῶπαι, ων, αἱ, *Co'-pæ,* a town of Bœ-o'-ti-a.

κώπη, ης, ἡ, (κάπτω,) Lat. *remus, the handle of an oar, an oar* or *rudder ;* and so, *any handle ; the sword handle,* Lat. *manubrium ; the handle of a key ; the handle of a mill.*

Κῶς, ἡ ; Ep. **Κόως** : see Hadley and Allen's Grammar, 161 ; *Cos,* an island.

6

Λ.

λᾶας contr. **λᾶς, λᾶος,** dat. **λᾶϊ,** acc. **λᾶαν** contr. **λᾶν,** pl. **λᾶες,** gen. **λάων,** dat. **λάεσι,** Ep. **λάεσσι,** poet. for **λίθος,** Lat. *lapis, saxum, stone; a rock.*

Λᾶας, ας, ἡ, *Las,* a town on the La‧co′‧ni‧an gulf.

λάβρος, ον, Lat. *vehemens, vehement, boisterous; furious, turbulent; greedy.*

λαγχάνω, f. **λήξομαι,** 2 aor. **ἔλαχον,** 2 pf. **εἴληχα,** aor. pass. **ἐλήχθην;** Ep. and poet. forms, 2 aor. **ἔλλαχον,** 2 pf. **λέλογχα:** see Lat. *sortiri, sortes ducere, to receive by drawing lots, draw lots; to receive, obtain, get, obtain possession of, have for a share* or *by assignment,* with both acc. and gen.

λαγωός, οῦ, ὁ, ἡ, Lat. *lepus, a hare.*

Λαερτιάδης, ου, ὁ, *son of La‧er′‧tes, U‧lys′‧ses,* the king of Ith′‧a‧ca.

λάζομαι, Hom. = **λαμβάνω,** Lat. *prehendere, to take, grasp, hold;* **γαῖαν ὀδάξ,** *to take the earth with the teeth, bite the dust.*

λαθικηδής, ές, (**λαθεῖν** 2 aor. of **λανθάνω**), **κῆδος,**) *driving away care, care-banishing.*

λάθρη or **ῃ,** adv., (**λαθεῖν,**) Lat. *clam, secretly, stealthily;* with gen. *hidden from.*

λαι-, intensive prefix.

λάϊν(ε)ος, α, = **ον, λάϊνος, η, ον,** (**λᾶας,**) Lat. *lapideus, of stone, stone, stony.*

λαιψηρός, ά, όν, (**λαι-,** **αἰψηρός,**) *light of foot, swift of foot, swift, agile.*

Λακεδαίμων, ονος, ἡ, *La′‧ce‧dæ′‧mon.*

λαμβάνω; f. **λήψομαι;** 2 aor. **ἔλ(λ)αβον,** iter. **λάβεσκον,** Hom. inf. mid. **λελαβέσθαι;** 2 pf. **εἴληφα,** Ion. pf. **λελάβηκα;** aor. pass. **ἐλήφθην:** Lat. *accipere, prehendere, to take hold of, grasp; to seize, lay hold of, take possession of; to receive; to obtain, gain, acquire, procure; to take and carry off,* Lat. *capere; to catch, overtake; to take in and grasp with the mind, comprehend; to reach; to take* in the sense of *to win;* often used with gen. in the sense of *to take hold of (a part).*

λαμπετάω, poet. for **λάμπω,** found only in Ep. part. **λαμπετόων** Α 104, Lat. *splendēre, lucēre, to shine, flash.*

Λάμπος, ου, ὁ, *Lam′‧pus.*

λαμπρός, ά, όν, (**λάμπω,**) Lat. *splendidus, luminous, shining, radiant, brilliant; clear; fresh; evident, open;* of men, *renowned, splendid, glorious,* Lat. *clarus.*

λάμπω, f. **μψω,** Lat. *lucēre, splendēre, to emit light, shine, be brilliant,* *gleam, be radiant; to blaze; to be clear:* Eng. *lamp* is from λάμπας which is from λάμπω.

λανθάνω, older form λήθω; iter. impf. ἐλήθεσκον; f. λήσω; aor. ἔλησα; 2 aor. ἔλαθον, Ep. 2 aor. λέλαθον; 2 pf. λέληθα; aor. pass. ἐλήσθην: Lat. *latēre, to lie hidden, escape notice, to remain concealed, be unseen:* trans. in aor. and Ep. 2 aor., and sometimes in rare pres. ληθάνω and (ἐπι)λήθω, *to cause one to forget:* mid., also pass., *to forget,* Lat. *oblivisci.*

λάξ, adv., *by* or *with the heel.*

Λαοδάμεια, as, ἡ, *La-od'-a-mi'-a.*

Λαοδίκη, ης, ἡ, *La-od'-i-ce,* the name of two women, the daughters of Pri'-am and Ag-a-mem'-non.

Λαόδοκος, ου, ὁ, *La-od'-o-chus.*

Λαοθόη, ης, ἡ, *La-oth'-o-e.*

Λαομέδων, οντος, ὁ, *La-om'-e-don.*

Λαομιδοντιάδης, ου, ὁ, *son of La-om'-e-don,* Pri'-am ; Lam'-pus.

λαός, οῦ, ὁ, Lat. *populus, the people, the multitude, crowd; the army, troops,* Lat. *exercitus, the soldiery.*

λαπάρη, ης, ἡ, Ion. for λαπάρα, Lat. *ilia, the part of the body above the hips and below the ribs, loins.*

Λάρισ(σ)α, ης, ἡ, *La-ris'-sa,* B 841.

λάρναξ, ακος, ἡ, *a chest* or *coffer, an urn, a closet.*

λάσιος, adj., Lat. *villosus, hairy, shaggy, having long wool, woolly ; rough with bushes, bushy.*

λάσκω, the parts are formed from the stem λακ(ε)-, *to sound, ring; to creak, crash, crack ; to yelp, bark ; to shout, scream, bellow, cry out.*

λαυκανίη, ης, ἡ, Lat. *gula, guttur, the throat.*

λαφύσσω, f. ύξω, (λάπτω,) *to devour greedily, swallow with greed, eat inordinately.*

λάχε, Ep. 2 aor. from λαγχάνω, which see.

λάχνη, ης, ἡ, *woolly hair* or *down, thin, downy hair* B 219.

λαχνήεις, εσσα, εν, Lat. *lanuginosus, woolly, hairy, shaggy,* B 743.

λέγω ; f. λέξω ; aor. ἔλεξα ; pf. mid. λέλεγμαι ; aor. pass. ἐλέχθην ; Ep. 2 aor. pass. ἐλέγμην: Lat. *colligere, to put in order, gather, collect, pick up, to select, choose* or *gather,* Lat. *deligere ; to recount, reckon up, narrate,* Lat. *enumerare ; to speak, relate* or *tell,* Lat. *narrare, declare* (φράζω is a stronger word), *command, speak* or *discuss* B 435, Lat. *dicere, mean ; to put to lie down,* mid. and pass. *to lie down* or *recline.*

λειαίνω, f. λειανέω, Ep. word, (λεῖος,) Lat. *polire, to make smooth, polish ; to reduce in size ; to tone down.*

λείβω, aor. ἔλειψα, *to pour,* usu. like Lat. *libare, to pour a libation, pour,*

pour a drink offering, Λ 463 ; *to shed, let fall* or *flow,* Lat. *fundere :* mid. and pass. *to flow, melt, be dissolved;* also, *to be wet* as with a pouring.

λειμών, ῶνος, ὁ, (λείβω,) Lat. *pratum, a meadow, a piece of moist, grassy land;* λειμωνόθεν, adv., *from the meadow.*

λεῖος, a, ον, Lat. *levis* or *laevis, smooth, even.*

λείπω ; f. λείψω ; 2 aor. ἔλιπον ; 2 pf. λέλοιπα ; pf. mid. λέλειμμαι ; aor. pass. ἐλείφθην ; 2 aor. pass. ἐλίπην: Lat. *linquere, to leave, leave behind, forsake, resign, abandon :* mid. *to leave behind one, bequeath :* pass. *to be left, be forsaken ; to remain, linger ;* with gen. *to be left without, behind, wanting, weaker than,* or *inferior to,* etc.: intrans. *to fail.*

λειριόεις, εσσα, εν, (λείριον,) Lat. *liliaceus, of a lily, lily-like, lily-colored; delicate, charming,* Γ 152, Lat. *suavis.*

λέκτρον, ου, τό, (λέγω,) Lat. *lectus,* see also, *cubile, a bed ; marriage-bed.*

λεληκώς, pf. part. from λάσκω, which see.

λελιημένος, η, ον, stric. part. from λελίημαι, compare Lat. *rapidus, ardent, eager, enthusiastic, hasty.*

Λεοντεύς, έως, ὁ, *Le-on'-teus,* a suitor of Hel'-en.

λεπταλέος, a, ον, poet. word, (λεπτός,) Lat. *tenuis, subtilis, thin, delicate, frail.*

λεπτός, ή, ον, (λέπω,) *stripped of the husk; thin, sleek, frail, slight, fine, lank,* both in a good sense and a bad sense, see Lat. *subtilis, tenuis* (what is the exact signif. of *tenuis,* good or bad ?); *attenuated, narrow, small, of no importance, trivial, trifling.*

λέπω, f. ψω, Lat. *delibrare, to strip off the husks, skin, hull,* or *bark, peel off.*

Λέσβος, ου, ἡ, *Les'-bos,* an island off the coast of A'-si-a Mi'-nor.

λευκάσπις, ιδος, adj., (λευκός, ἀσπίς,) *with white shield.*

Λεῦκος, ου, ὁ, *Leu'-cus,* a Greek.

λευκός, ή, όν, Lat. *albus, white, hoary, bright, shining white, bright, gleaming ; fair ; happy,* Lat. *jucundus.*

λευκώλενος, ον, (λευκός, ὠλένη,) *with white elbows, white-armed,* epith. of women.

λεύσσω, *to look ;* Lat. *adspicere, vidēre, see, behold.*

λεχεποίη, ης, ἡ, (λέχος, ποία,) *with a bed in the grass; situated in a grassy meadow.*

λέχος, εος, τό, (λέγω,) *a bed, couch, bedstead; a nuptial bed,* and so *marriage.*

λέων, οντος, ὁ, Ep. dat. pl. λείουσι for λέουσι, Lat. *leo, a lion ;* metaph. *a destruction.*

λήγω, f. ξω, Lat. *desinere facio, to cause to cease, stay from :* intrans. and usu. with gen. *to cease from, leave off,* Lat. *cessare.*

λίγδην, (λίξω,) adv., *grazing, scraping the surface.*

λήθη, ης, ή, (λήθω, see λανθάνω,) Lat. *oblivio, oblivion, forgetfulness, a forgetting* B 33.

Λῆθος, ου, ὁ, *Leth'-us.*

λήθω, older form of λανθάνω, which see.

λήϊον, ου, τό, Lat. *seges, a crop of corn; a field and crop.*

Λήϊτος, ου, ὁ, *Le'-i-tus,* chief of the Bœ-o'-tians.

Λῆμνος, ου, ή, *Lem'-nos,* an island. It was held sacred to Vul'-can because of a volcano; see Classical Atlas.

Λητώ, contr. gen. οὖς, acc. Λητώ, voc. Λητοῖ, ή, Lat. *Latona, Leto,* mother of A-pol'-lo and Di-a'-na by Zeus.

λιάζομαι, *to go aside, swerve* or *bend to the side;* Lat. *secedere, to retire, give way, withdraw, recede; to bend down, sink.*

λιαρός, ά, όν, Lat. *tepidus, tepid, lukewarm; mild, agreeable,* compare Lat. *mitis, placidus, lenis.*

λιγέως, adv. of λιγύς.

λίγξε, only form found of λίγγω, *twanged.*

λιγύς, εῖα, ύ, *sharp, penetrating, clear, shrill, thrilling; sweet, agreeable:* λιγέως, adv., *loudly, clearly.*

λιγύφθογγος, ον, (λιγύς, φθογγή,) *clear-toned, loud-sounding,* epith. of heralds, B 50.

λίζω, *to scratch, wound slightly.*

λίην, Ion. for λίαν, adv., Lat. *nimis, valde, admodum, too much, very much, exceedingly; certainly, surely, gladly, fully.*

λίθος, ου, ὁ, Lat. *lapis, a stone, stone; a rock; stone* in nearly all the senses in which we are accustomed to use the word; in certain signifs. the word is fem.; *a stone* used in playing draughts; *a stone* for anchor; *a rostrum,* usu. built of stone: compare Lat. *saxum, lapis, rupes, cautes, scopuli, calculus.*

Λικύμνιος, ου, ὁ, *Li-cym'-ni-us.*

Λίλαια, ας, ή, *Li-læ'-a,* a town of Pho'-cis.

λιλαίομαι, Lat. *cupere, desiderare, to desire earnestly, crave, desire;* with gen. *to be eagerly desirous of,* Γ 133.

λιμήν, ένος, ὁ, Lat. *portus, a sea-port, harbor; a refuge;* in pl. also *inlets.*

λίμνη, ης, ή, Lat. *palus, stagnum, lacus, a pool of standing water formed by the overflowing of a river or the sea,* and so *the sea,* Lat. *mare; lake, marsh.*

Λίνδος, ου, ή, *Lin'-dus,* a town of Rhodes.

λινοθώρηξ (Ion. form), ηκος, ὁ, ή, (λίνον, θώραξ,) Lat. *lineum thoracem habens, wearing a linen cuirass.*

λίνον, ου, τό, Lat. *linum,* (stem of Eng. *linen,*) *flax, that which was made of flax; flaxen yarn, a cord* or *thread made of flax; a linen net, linen cloth, a sail made of flax, sail-cloth;* metaph. *the thread* of destiny.

Λίνος, ου, ὁ, *Li'-nos,* a minstrel; *the lay* or *song* of Li'-nos.

λιπαρός, ά, όν, (λίπας,) Lat. *pinguis, fat, greasy, anointed, shining; rich, fruitful, fat, opulent, wealthy.*

λίσσομαι, iter. impf. λισσέσκετο; aor. ἐλισάμην, 2 aor. ἐλιτόμην: Lat. *precari, supplicare, to pray, beseech, entreat.*

λιτανεύω, f. εύσω; Ep. parts are formed from ἐλλιταν-; (λιτή;) compare Lat. *obsecrare, precari, supplicare, supplex orare, to ask as a suppliant, beseech, pray, entreat:* stem of Eng. *litany.*

λοετρόν, Ep. for λουτρόν, οῦ, τό, (λοέω,) Lat. *lavacrum, a place for bathing, a bath;* also, *the water used for bathing, bath-water.*

λοιβή, ῆς, ἡ, (λείβω,) Lat. *libatio, the act of pouring out, a pouring out, a libation,* used as having only a religious sense.

λοίγιος, ον, (λοιγός,) Lat. *perniciosus, pernicious, deadly, fatal* A 518.

λοιγός, οῦ, ὁ, Lat. *pernicies, exitium, death, destruction, ruin.*

λοιμός, οῦ, ὁ, Lat. *pestis, a plague* A 61.

Λοκροί, ῶν, οἱ, *the Lo'-cri-ans.*

λούω, f. σω, aor. pass. ἐλούσθην; many parts are formed from the uncontd. form λοέω, from Ep. λουέω, and from a form λόω; Lat. *lavare, to wash.*

λόφος, ου, ὁ, Lat. *cervix, the back of the neck, the neck; a ridge of mountains* or *hills,* Lat. *jugum, a hill,* Lat. *collis; the crest of a helmet,* Lat. *crista in galea; a tuft of hair on the crown.*

λοχάω, f. ήσω; Ep. parts λοχόω-; (λόχος;) intrans., Lat. *insidiari, to be in ambush;* trans. *to lie in ambush* or *wait for.*

λόχος, ου, ὁ, (λέγω,) see Lat. *insidiae, a place of ambush, the place where the ambush are in waiting,* also, *the chosen men placed in ambuscade* and *the act of waiting for the purpose of attack; a fixed division of infantry:* A 227 λόχονδε, *to ambush.*

λυγρός, ά, όν, Lat. *miserabilis, tristis, pitiable, sad; hurtful,* Lat. *perniciosus; worthless, cowardly, weak, contemptible.*

Λύκαστος, ου, ὁ, *Ly-cas'-tus,* a town of *Crete.*

Λυκάων, ονος, ὁ, *Ly-ca'-on.*

λυκηγενής, ές, (λύκη, γένος,) *light-born,* epith. of A-pol'-lo.

Λυκία, ας, ἡ, Ion. Λυκίη, *Lyc'-i-a,* a division of A'-si-a Mi'-nor; Λύκιοι, ων, οἱ, *the Lyc'-i-ans.*

Λυκόοργος, ου, ὁ, *Ly-cur'-gus.*

λύκος, ου, ὁ, Lat. *lupus, a wolf.*

Λύκτος, ου, ἡ, *Lyc'-tus,* a city of Crete.

λύμα, ατος, τό, Lat. *purgamentum, dirt* or *uncleanness* taken off by washing; in a moral sense, *disgrace; vile outcast.*

Δυρνησσός, οῦ, ἡ, *Lyr-nes'-sus*, a town of Mys'-i-a. .

λύσιος, adj., (λύω,) *ransoming, delivering.*

λύω, f. λύσω ; aor. ἔλυσα ; pf. λέλυκα ; plup. contr. Ep. opt. 3 sing. λελῦτο ; aor. pass. ἐλύθην, Ep. 3 pl. λύθεν ; Hom. and Ep. 2 aor. mid. as pass. (ἐ)λύμην : Lat. *solvere, laxare, to loosen, untie, unfasten, release* A 20, *slacken, deliver up, dismiss, dissolve, undo, set at liberty; break down, destroy; slay, kill; put down; to release for a ransom; to atone* : mid., *to loosen for one's self, set free; to ransom,* A 13, Lat. *redimere.*

λωβάομαι, f. ήσομαι, Lat. *contumeliam inferre, to maltreat, abuse, insult; to abuse by blows, mutilate, injure in person,* Lat. *mutilare.*

λώβη, ης, ἡ, Lat. *contumelia, maltreatment, ill treatment, outrage, insult,* whether by word or act ; *a disgrace, shame,* Lat. *opprobrium, dedecus,* Γ 42.

λωβητήρ, ῆρος, ὁ, (λωβάομαι,) *one who maltreats, a slanderer, abusive reviler* B 275 ; *a vile wretch; a murderer, destroyer.*

λωβητός, ή, ον, (λωβάομαι,) *misused;* also, *abusing, abusive, acting insultingly.*

λωίων, λώιον, gen. ονος, ὁ, ἡ, τό ; = **λωίτερος,** sup. **λώιστος** ; Lat. *melior, better;* Hom. compar. and sup. of ἀγαθύς.

λωτός, οῦ, ὁ, Lat. *lotus, a kind of clover for horses,* B 776 ; *lotus,* a sweet fruit as large as the olive, and resembling the date in taste, *the jujube* of north Af'-ri-ca.

M.

μά, Lat. *profecto, certe, vero,* a particle used, in declarations and oaths, with acc., **μὰ Δία,** *by Zeus;* foll. *val* it is affirmative, ναὶ μὰ τόδε σκῆπτρον A 234 ; foll. οὐ, negative.

Μάγνης, ητος, ὁ, *a Mag-ne'-sian.*

μαζός, οῦ, ὁ, Lat. *mamma, a breast, a teat, nipple.*

Μαίανδρος, ου, ὁ, *Mæ-an'-der,* a river of A'-si-a Mi'-nor, noted for its windings ; hence Eng. *meander.*

μαιμάω, f. ήσω ; Ep. forms, 3 pl. -μώωσι, part. -μώων ; *to desire earnestly; to be agitated with eagerness.*

μαινάς, άδος, ἡ, (μαίνομαι,) *frenzied; causing frenzy;* also subst., *a raving woman; a Bac'-chan-te; a woman under the influence of a passion.*

μαίνομαι, f. μανήσομαι, aor. ἔμηνα (trans. tense, *to make furious*), 2 pf. μέμηνα, 2 aor. pass. ἐμάνην, (μάω,) Hom. uses pres. and impf. ; see Lat. *insanire, to be frenzied, rage, rave, be furious; to be crazed by drink, be drunk; to be under a strong inspiration or in any passion.*

μάκαρ, fem. μάκα(ι)ρ(α), αρος, ὁ, Ep. dat. pl. μακάρεσσι, Lat. *beatus*, *blessed*, in pl. *the gods;* of men, *happy, blest, fortunate, wealthy*, Lat. *felix*, in pl. *the blessed*, i. e. *the dead*.

Μάκαρ, ος, ὁ, *Ma'-car*, king of Les'-bos.

μακρός, ά, όν, (μᾶκος,) *long*, both of space, Lat. *longus*, and time, Lat. *diuturnus, longus;* of space, *far-distant, of great extent, long*, also *high* and *deep*, Lat. *altus*, neu. as adv. Γ 81 *far = loudly;* of time, *long, enduring, tedious*.

μάλα, a streng. adv., compar. μᾶλλον, sup. μάλιστα, Lat. *valde, vehementer, very much, exceedingly; very, quite;* A 217 *even though very greatly;* Γ 214 *very clearly; certainly, very, no doubt:* compar., Lat. *magis, potius, more, so much the more, more strongly, to a greater degree, too much;* sometimes used with another compar. : sup. Lat. *maxime, imprimis, most, mostly, most strongly, particularly, by far;* with numbers, *about;* καὶ μάλιστα, *most surely;* sometimes with other superlatives, *especially*, B 57, *especially most nearly*, B 220 *especially most hateful*.

μαλακός, ή, όν, Lat. *mollis, soft, delicate, tender, gentle; indolent, careless, easy; effeminate, feeble*, Lat. *mollis, effeminatus*.

μάλιστα, μᾶλλον, see μάλα.

μάν, affirm. particle, Ep. for μήν.

μανθάνω, f. μαθήσομαι, 2 aor. ἔμαθον, pf. μεμάθηκα; in Hom. 2 aor. (ἐμ)μάθ-; Lat. *discere, to learn, find out, receive information about; to learn* or *find out by asking; to comprehend* a thing, *grasp* the idea, *see into* or *understand* (the aor. has this sense; for what has been *learned* is supposed to be *known* or *understood*) ; also, *to seek information about*.

μαντεύομαι, f. σομαι, (μάντις,) Lat. *vaticinari, to foretell, prophesy; to conjecture, surmise; to consult an oracle*, Lat. *oraculum consulere*.

μάντις, εως, Ion. ιος, ὁ, (μαίνομαι,) Lat. *vates, haruspex, hariolus*, a *prophet, diviner, seer; ἡ, prophetess*.

μαντοσύνη, ης, ἡ, (μάντις,) Lat. *vaticinandi ars, the art, gift*, or *knowledge of divination*, A 72.

μαρμαίρω, Lat. *resplendēre, coruscare, to shine, sparkle* = *bright* Γ 397, *gleam, flash, to emit a twinkling light*, of metal and eyes.

μαρμάρεος, α, ον, (μαρμαίρω,) *flashing* or *reflecting back light, bright; of marble*, from the same stem as Eng. *marble*, Lat. *marmor*.

μάρναμαι, Lat. *pugnare, to fight; to contend, wrangle, quarrel*, A 257, Γ 307 ; *to toil*.

μάρπτω, f. -ψω, ἔμαρψα ; compare. Lat. *prehendere, capere, to lay hold of, take, grasp, catch, seize; to touch, reach*, Lat. *attingere; to overtake*.

μάρτυρος, ου, ὁ, Ep., Lat. *testis, a witness :* hence Eng. *martyr.*

Μάσης, ητος, ὁ, *Ma'-ses, a town of Ar'-go-lis.*

μαστίζω, f. ίξω, (μάστιξ,) Lat. *flagellare, to scourge.*

μάχαιρα, as, ἡ, *a knife, short and broad, worn as a side-arm, and also used at sacrifices* Γ 271 ; *a dagger, a bent sword, while* ξίφος was the *straight sword.*

Μαχάων, ονος, ὁ, *Ma-cha'-on,* son of Æs-cu-la'-pi-us, skilled in the art of healing.

μάχη, ης, ἡ, Lat. *pugna, acies, a fight, conflict, battle ;* also *a single battle, a duel ; a contest for the prize, a friendly contest ; a contention, quarrelling ; the battle-field.*

μάχομαι, Hom. μαχέομαι, Ep. and Hom. part. μαχειόμενος and -εούμενος ; iter. impf. μαχέσκετο ; f. Ep. and Hom. -εσ(σ)ομαι and -ήσομαι ; Hom. aor. ἐμαχ(ε)(η)σάμην : (μάχη :) Lat. *pugnare, to contend in battle, to fight ;* with σύν with the dat., see σύν ; *to quarrel* A 8, *dispute,* Lat. *contendere ; to strive in friendly contest,* such as games ; κατά with acc., *by, against.*

μάψ, adv., Lat. *frustra, to no purpose, in vain ; rashly, thoughtlessly,* Lat. *temere ; recklessly, inconsiderately,* Lat. *incassum,* B 214.

μάω, act. obsol. except in 2 pf. system, μέμαα, du. μέματον, pl. μέμαμεν, 3 pl. μεμάασι, 3 sing. imperat. μεμάτω, part. μεμαώς B 818, -υῖα, gen. ῶτος, pl. -ῶτες and -αότες, plup. 3 pl. μέμασαν ; Lat. *vehementer cupere, to desire ardently, to greatly desire, to make great effort for ; to wish to be ; to press forward ; to seek.*

μεγάθυμος, ον, (μέγας, θυμός,) Lat. *magnanimus, great or high-minded.*

μεγαίρω, f. μεγαρῶ, aor. ἐμέγηρα, (μέγας,) *to regard as large, feel something to be greater or better than we would like another to enjoy, envy* (Lat. *invidēre), grudge, refuse :* also intrans., *to oppose, object, find fault.*

μεγαλήτωρ, ορος, ὁ, ἡ, (μέγας, ἦτορ,) Lat. *magnanimus, courageous, great-hearted.*

μέγαρον, ου, τό, (μέγας,) *a large room* or *hall, chief room, dining-hall, women's apartment, bed-chamber ;* in pl. *rooms,* and so *house, palace,* Lat. *aedes ; the inner recess of a temple, temple.*

μέγας, μεγάλη, μέγα ; μεγάλου, ης, ου ; acc. μέγαν, μεγάλην, μέγα ; compar. μείζων, ον, gen. ονος ; sup. μέγιστος: Lat. *magnus, great,* used in a variety of applications ; *mighty, powerful ; great, vast ; high ; spacious ; strong ; important, weighty ; excessive ;* of sounds, *great = loud, long :* neu. as adv., *exceedingly, greatly* B 480, A 517, and 78, *very much,* Lat. *valde ;* with compar., *much, far,* Lat. *multo ;* with sup., *greatly, by far,* B 82, Lat. *longe :* adv., μεγάλως ; also μεγάλα, A 450.

μέγεθος, εος, τό, (μέγας,) Lat. *magnitudo, greatness, largeness, size, magnitude; height.*

Μέγης, ητος, ὁ, *Me'-ges*, chief of the Du-lich'-i-ans, and nephew of U-lys'-ses.

μέγιστος, see μέγας.

μεδέων, ονος, ὁ, *one that rules and protects, a guardian;* stric. Lat. *imperium tenens, having rule, ruling;* Γ 276, Ἴδηθεν μεδέων, *ruling from I'-da,* where he (Zeus) had an altar.

Μεδεών, ῶνος, ὁ, *Me'-de-on,* a town of Bœ-o'-ti-a.

μέδομαι, f. μεδήσομαι, *to give care and attention to; to be mindful of, have a care for.*

μέδων, οντος, ὁ, *a lord, one who governs* : = μεδέων.

Μέδων, οντος, ὁ, *Me'-don,* a brother of A'-jax.

μεθείω, see μεθίημι.

μεθέμεν, see μεθίημι.

μεθήμων, ον, gen. ονος, (μεθίημι,) Lat. *remissus, negligens, careless, negligent.*

μεθίημι, pres. 2 and 3 sing. -ιεῖς, -ιεῖ; Ep. impf. 3 pl. μεθίεν; Ep. inf. μεθιέμεν(αι); f. μεθήσω; Ep. aor. μεθέηκα; 2 aor. Ep. subj.: μεθείω, Ep. inf. μεθέμεν: trans., Lat. *dimittere, to let go, dismiss, release, throw, let go* or *lay aside; to let flow* or *drop; to give up, yield; to neglect, forgive :* intrans., *to become indifferent* or *careless; to cease* or *desist from, to leave,* with gen.

μεθομιλέω, f. ήσω, (μετά, ὁμιλέω,) *to mix with, keep company with.*

μειδάω and μειδιάω, f. ήσω, Ep. part. μειδόων, Lat. *subridēre, to smile.*

μείλινος, poet. for μέλινος, η, ον, Lat. *fraxineus, of ash.*

μειλίχιος, α, ον, μείλιχος, ον, (μειλίσσω,) Lat. *mitis, soft, mild, placid, gentle, quieting, gracious, winning.*

μείρομαι, 2 pf. ἔμμορα Α 278, pass. εἵμαρμαι: *to receive one's share;* with gen., Α 278, *has never obtained such honor as his portion.*

μείς, Ion. for μήν, ὁ, Lat. *mensis, a month.*

μείων, μεῖον, gen. ονος, see μικρός.

μέλαθρον, ου, τό, (μέλας,) *the cross-beam under the roof, black with smoke; ceiling, roof;* also, *a house.*

μελαίνω, f. μελανῶ, (μέλας,) *to cause to become black, blacken.*

μέλας, μέλαινα, μέλαν; gen. mas. and neu. -ανος, fem. μελαίνης; dat. -ανι and -αίνῃ, pl. -ασι; compar. μελάντερος, άντατος: Lat. *niger, dark, black; gloomy;* neu. as subst., *the dark.*

Μελέαγρος, ου, ὁ, *Me-le-a'-ger.*

μέλι, ιτος, τό, Lat. *mel, honey.*

Μελίβοια, ας, ἡ, *Mel-i-bœ'-a,* a town of Thes-sa'-lian Mag-ne'-si-a.

μελίη, ης, ἡ, Ion. form, Lat. *fraxinus*, *the ash ; the ashen shaft of a spear*, and so *the spear itself*.

μελιηδής, ες, (μέλι, ἡδύς,) *sweet as honey ; agreeable*.

μέλινος, see **μείλινος**.

μέλισσα, ης, ἡ, (μέλι,) Lat. *apis*, *a bee*.

μελίφρων, ονος, ὁ, ἡ, (μέλι, φρήν,) *pleasant to the soul*.

μέλλω, f. μελλήσω, com. used with inf. expressed or understood, *to be about* or *intend to do anything ; to be destined to do, have to, must ; to be likely ; to continue intending to do ; to put off, delay*.

μέλπω, f. ψω, Lat. *cantare, cantu celebrare*, *to celebrate in song* ; intrans.,
- *to play, dance,* or *sing ;* with Ἄρηι, *to dance agreeable to Mars* = *to fight bravely* or *on foot*.

μέλω, f. μελήσω, 2 pf. 3 sing. μέμηλε, Lat. *curae esse*, *to be a care* ; impersonal use, *it is a care*, Lat. *curae est*, and in this use often joined with gen. and dat. cases ; *to be an object of interest* or *concern :* trans., *to take care of*.

μέμαα, see **μάω**.

μέμηλε, see **μέλω**.

μέμονα, 2 pf. of poet. verb μαίομαι, with sense of pres., *to wish earnestly, yearn, design ;* from stem of obsol. pres.

μέμυκα, pf. of **μυκάομαι**, which see.

μέν, orig. = **μήν**, an intensive particle, *indeed*, Lat. *quidem ;* com. answered by the correlative δέ, μέν . . . δέ, Lat. *quidem . . . sed, indeed . . . but*, also, Lat. *et . . . et, quum . . . tum, both . . . and, as well . . . as, on the one hand . . . on the other ;* ὁ μέν . . . ὁ δέ, *this . . . that, the one . . . the other ;* μέν may be answered by other particles than δέ, as ἀτάρ, αὖθις, αὐτάρ, ἀλλά, etc. ; often μέν cannot be rendered by any English word : other uses, ἐγὼ μέν *I at least*, μέν που *doubtless, indeed*, μὲν (ἅ)ρα *since then*, μέν γε *yet, however, nevertheless, certainly*, μὲν οὖν = μενοῦν *so then* or *yes indeed*, μὲν δή *now then* or *however* with εἰ or νῦν *if then* or *now certainly*, καὶ μέν *and truly*, οὐ μέν *not indeed*, ἀτὰρ μέν *but indeed*, οὐδὲ μὲν οὐδέ *not by any means ; in truth, yet, indeed, nevertheless*, Lat. *quidem, profecto ; now*.

μενεαίνω, (μένος,) something like Lat. *cupere*, but stronger, *to desire eagerly, to long earnestly for ;* with gen., *to long for ; to be angry*, Lat. *irasci*.

Μενέλαος, ου, ὁ, (μένω, λαός,) *Me-ne-la'-us*, brother of Ag-a-mem'-non and husband of Hel'-en ; by deriv., *one who withstands the people*.

μενεπτόλεμος, ον, (μένω, πόλεμος,) *steadfast* or *standing firm in battle*.

Μενεσθεύς, Ion. gen. ῆος, ὁ, (μένω,) *Me-nes'-theus*, son of Pe'-teus and leader of the A-the'-nians ; by deriv., *one who abides*.

Μενέσθης, ουs, ὁ, *Me-nes'-thes, a Greek.*

Μενοιτιάδηs, ου, αο, εω, ὁ, son of *Me-noe'-ti-us, Pa-tro'-clus*, A 307.

μένοs, εοs, τό, *something* like Lat. *robur*, though in more act. sense, *might, strength, power, force; fierceness;* of the blood as *vital force, life,* Γ 294 ; *spirit, temper,* or *disposition, purpose, courage,* Lat. *mens;* B 536, Γ 8, *breathing strength* or *animated with courage ; anger, fury,* B 387, *wrath ; ardor.*

μένω, iter. impf. (ε)μένεσκον ; f. μενέω, contr. ῶ ; aor. ἔμεινα ; pf. μεμένηκα : Lat. *manēre, to stay, remain, wait; to stand the ground, remain firm ; to persist; to stay, linger, dally ; to remain, continue; to be unchanged :* trans., *to wait for* or *await, expect,* Lat. *exspectare ;* in hostile sense, *to await, sustain, resist, withstand,* Lat. *sustinēre.*

μερμηρίζω, f. ίξω, *to ponder anxiously; to ponder, consider, deliberate,* B 3, Lat. *deliberare, meditari; to be distracted by doubt :* trans., *to devise.*

μέροψ, οπος, ὁ, (μείρομαι, ὄψ,) Lat. *divisam vocem habens, having the power of dividing the voice, articulately speaking,* epith. of men as opp. to brutes, which have not such power ; hence = Lat. *homines* B 285.

Μέροψ, οπος, ὁ, (μείρομαι ὄψ,) lit. *having the power of dividing the voice, articulately speaking, having the power of speech; Me'-rops,* prince of Per-co-'te.

μέρω, μέρομαι, see μείρομαι.

μεσ(σ)ηγύ(s), (μέσος,) adv., Lat. *in medio, in between, in the midst; meanwhile, in the meantime, in the interval,* compare Lat. *interim, interea ; between.*

Μέσθλης, ουs, ὁ, *Mes'-thles.*

μέσον, see μέσσος.

μέσ(σ)οs, η, ον, Lat. *medius, middle, intermediate, in the midst; middling, medium, moderate :* neu. as subst., μέσον (τό), *the middle, common ground; ἐς μέσον τιθέναι, to place in the midst* as a prize, hence *to offer as a prize,* Lat. *in medio ponere; μέσον ὑπέρ, half way.*

Μέσση, ηs, ἡ, *Mes'-sa,* a harbor town of La-co'-ni-a.

Μεσσηίs, ίδος, ἡ, *Mes-se'-is,* a spring in Thes'-sa-ly.

μετά, after its subst. μέτα, prep. *among:* with gen., *with, amidst, along with, in common with, with the aid:* with dat., poet. use, *among, amid, with:* with acc., whether of time, place, or order, *after,* **μετὰ ταῦτα**, *after these things, in the course of; next, behind;* of motion, *into* or *among* Α 423, Γ 264, *toward, after, for, in pursuit of; in; according to:* adv., Lat. *postea, afterwards; among:* in compo., *sharing with, between, amongst, during, towards, after, from one to other, back.*

μεταδρομάδην, (μετά, δραμεῖν (see τρέχω,)) adv., *immediately after.*

μετακιάθω, (μετά, κιάθω,) Lat. *sequi, to follow; to go over,* Lat. *transire.*

μεταλλάω, f. ήσω, (μετά, ἄλλα,) Lat. *sciscitari, to seek after* other things, *to search ; to question, inquire about,* Lat. *percontari.*

μεταμάζιος, ον, (μετά, μαζός,) *betwixt the breasts, on the chest.*

μεταξύ, (μετά,) adv., *between* A 156 ; *after, meanwhile ;* prep. with gen., *between, during.*

μεταπρέπω, (μετά, πρέπω,) Lat. *excellere, to be conspicuous* or *prominent among,* B 481.

μετατρέπω, f. ψω, (μετά, τρέπω,) Lat. *convertere, to turn about, turn back :* mid. *to turn one's self around and look after, to turn and care for,* hence *regard* A 160.

μετάφημι, impf. μετέφην, 2 aor. μετεῖπον, Ep. μετέειπον, (μετά, φημί,) *to speak among, address,* A 58 *rising up among them addressed them;* B 411, Γ 303, *spoke among.*

μεταφράζομαι, f. άσομαι (μετά, φράζομαι,) Lat. *postea considerare, to consider afterwards, will consider* A 140.

μετάφρενον, ου, τό, (μετά, φρήν,) *the part between the shoulder-blades and behind the diaphragm, the back.*

μετέειπε(ν), see μετάφημι.

μέτειμι, f. μετέσομαι, (μετά, εἰμί,) Lat. *interesse, versari inter, to be with* or *among, associate with ; intervene.*

μετέρχομαι, for parts see ἔρχομαι, (μετά, ἔρχομαι,) *to go* or *come between* or *among ; to come* or *go among for the sake of attacking,* hence *attack* or *assail ; to pass from one to other, go among ; to go for* or *in search of, strive for, endeavor to attain, follow, go after* or *to find ; to go* or *look after, take care of, pursue ; to go for; to come upon; to desire earnestly ; to come to* with supplications, *go to and entreat, entreat.*

μετόπισθε(ν), adv., Lat. *pone, behind, backwards; from behind,* Lat. *a tergo ;* Lat. *post, postea, afterwards :* prep. w. gen., Lat. *pone, post, after, behind.*

μετοχλίζω, f. ίσω, (μετά, ὀχλίζω,) *to remove by means of a lever, move away ;* μετοχλίσσειε, aor. opt. Ep. 3 sing.

μέτωπον, ου, τό, (μετά, ὤψ,) *between the eyes ; the forehead, the front of the head ;* hence *the front.*

μεῦ, see ἐγώ.

μή, a prohibitory particle, similar to Lat. *ne, that not, lest, not,* and differs from οὐ in being used in case of an *expressed* or *implied condition,* or in an independent clause with the indicat. or opt. containing a *wish* or *command,* οὐ being an *absolute neg.,* Lat. *non.* μή is used with the subj.

and imperat. A 26, in independent sentences with the indicat. and opt. to express a wish, B 259 and 260, in dependent sentences with the indicat. and opt. to express a condition or purpose, with a part. when it expresses a condition. μή is found with the aor. subj. used as imperat.: after verbs of fearing μή and μὴ οὐ are used with the subj.: used after final conj., *that not :* in questions implying a neg. answer, Lat. *num :* μή γε, *not at least ;* μήτι, *not in any manner;* μὴ γάρ, *certainly not.*

μηδέ, (μή, δέ,) adv., Lat. *ncc, ncque, and* or *but not, not at all, nor; not even,* Lat. *ne . . . quidem ;* μηδέ . . . μηδέ, *neither . . . nor ;* B 259 and 260, . . . *nor.*

μηδείς, -δεμία, -δεν, gen. μηδενός (mas. and neu.), μηδεμιᾶς, fem., (μηδέ, εἷς,) Lat. *nullus, not one, none :* neu., Lat. *nihil, nothing;* as adv., *in nothing.*

μήδομαι, f. μήσομαι, (μῆδος,) compare Lat. *deliberare, cogilare, meditari, to devise, plot, plan, contrive ; resolve, counsel ; bring about, execute.*

μῆδος, εος, τό, in pl. μήδεα, Lat. *consilia, devices, counsels, plans.*

Μηθώνη, ης, ἡ, *Mc-tho'-ne,* a city of Thes'-sa-ly.

μήκετι, (μή, ἔτι,) adv., Lat. *non amplius, no longer, no further ;* B 259, *may the head no longer.*

Μηκιστεύς, έως, ὁ, Hom. gen. ῆος and έος, *Mc-cis'-teus.*

μηλοβοτήρ, ῆρος, ὁ, (μῆλον, βόσκω,) *a feeder of sheep, a shepherd.*

μῆλον, ου, τό, Lat. *pecus, pecoris,* (which *pecus* is here meant, *pecoris* or *pecudis ?*) in Hom. gen. *a sheep ; a goat ;* in pl., *flocks of small cattle,* as *sheep and goats.*

μήν, Ep. μάν, streng. particle, Lat. *profecto, certainly, in truth, yea, then, indeed ;* ἦ μήν, *yes certainly :* καὶ μήν, *and certainly :* ἄγε μήν, *go then, on then;* μὴ μήν, *certainly not.*

μήν, μηνός, ὁ, see μείς.

μήνιμα, ατος, τό, (μηνίω,) *the occasion of anger.*

μῆνις, ιος, ἡ, Lat. *ira, wrath, anger,* A 1.

μηνίω, f. ίσω, (μῆνις,) Lat. *succensēre, irasci, to be angry* B 769, A 488; with dat., *to be angry towards.*

Μηονίη, ης, ἡ, *Mæ-o'-ni-a,* afterwards called *Ly'-di-a ;* Μηονίς, ἡ, adj., *Mæ-o'-nian ;* οἱ Μήονες, *inhabitants of Mæ-o'-ni-a.*

μήποτε, (μή, ποτέ,) conj. ; Lat. *ne quando, lest at any time.*

μήπως, Lat. *ne quo modo, lest in some manner, lest somehow, that not in any way ; lest perchance,* Lat. *ne forte ; whether or not, whether perhaps.*

μηρά = μηρία, τά, (μηρός,) *the thigh-bones which, wrapped in fat, were burned on the altar.*

Μηριόνης, ου, ὁ, *Me-ri'-o-nes,* a Cre'-tan hero.

μηρός, οῦ, ὁ, Lat. *femur, femen, the ham, the fleshy part of the thigh.*

μήτε, (μή, τέ,) μήτε ... μήτε, Lat. *nec ... nec, neither ... nor;* standing alone, *and not*, Lat. *neve.*

μήτηρ, ἡ, gen. μητρός, dat. μητρί, acc. μητέρα, voc. μῆτερ, dat. pl. μητράσι; Hom. uncontracted forms μητερ-; Lat. *mater, mother; that which produces*, or *brings forth, producer;* γῆ μήτηρ, *producing* or *mother earth.*

μητιάω, f. άσω, (μῆτις,) see Lat. *deliberare, to deliberate, meditate, revolve in mind; plan, arrange, execute.*

μητίετα, Ep. for μητιέτης, ου, ὁ, (μῆτις,) Lat. *consultor, an adviser, counsellor.*

μητίομαι, f. ίσομαι, (μῆτις,) *to devise, plan, contrive, invent,* Γ 416.

μῆτις, ιος, ἡ, Ep. dat. μήτι, Lat. *consilium, wisdom, penetration, shrewdness; skill; expedient; proposal.*

μήτις, μήτι, gen. -τινος, neg. pron., (μή, τίς,) Lat. *nequis, nullum, no one;* stric., *lest any one:* neu. as adv., *that by no means, lest by any means.*

μήτρως, ωος, ὁ, acc. -ωα Β 662, (μήτηρ,) Lat. *avunculus, a maternal uncle; a maternal relation.*

μῆχος, εος, τό, *a device, expedient; help, means; remedy, aid.*

μία, see εἷς.

μιαίνω, f. μιανῶ, aor. ἐμίηνα, pf. μεμίαγκα, aor. pass. ἐμιάθην, *to stain, color, stain over; to contaminate, pollute:* stem of μίασμα, Eng. *miasma.*

μιαιφόνος, ου, (μιαίνω, φένω,) *stained with blood,* hence *stained by murder.*

μίγνυμι, f. μίξω; aor. ἔμιξα, 2 aor. mid. 3 sing. ἔμικτο; pf. pass. μέμιγμαι; aor. pass. ἐμίχθην, Ep. 3 pl. ἔμιχθεν, Ep. inf. μιχθήμεν(αι) ; 2 aor. pass. ἐμίγην, Ep. 3 pl. μίγεν, Ep. inf. μιγήμεν(αι) : forms are also formed from μίσγω Γ 270, iter. impf. μισγέσκετο : Lat. *miscēre, to mix liquids,* Γ 270 *to mix the wine* of the two parties; also used, in other relations, *to mix, mingle together; to make acquainted with, bring in contact with, bring together :* mid. and pass., *to come in contact* or *to mingle with; to have social relations with, to associate with, to have sexual intercourse with; to reach; to live with;* also used in a hostile sense.

Μίδεια, poet. for Μίδεα, ας, ἡ, *Mid'-e-a*, a town of Bœ-o'-ti-a.

μικρός, α, ον, Lat. *parvus, little, small, mean, insignificant;* compar., μείων, Lat. *minor, less,* Γ 193 μείων κεφαλῇ *less = shorter (in stature) by a head:* other irreg. forms of compar. are also found.

Μίλητος, ου, ἡ, *Mi-le'-tus*, name of two cities, one in I-o-'ni-a, the other in Crete.

μιλτοπάρῃος, ον, (μίλτος, παρειά,) *cheeks colored with vermilion, red-cheeked;* of ships, *painted red on bows or sides.*

μιμνάζω, (μίμνω, poet. for μένω,) *to keep staying, to remain,* (does Lat. *permanēre* express the same idea?) *to wait for, expect,* Lat. *exspectare :* μιμνάζω, *to keep staying,* but μίμνω = μένω, *to stay* or *remain.*

μιμνήσκω, f. μνήσω, aor. infin. act. and mid. imperat. μνῆσαι, iter. 3 sing. mid. μνησάσκετο, (μνάω,) Lat. *commonefacere, to remind, put others in mind:* mid. and pass., with gen., *to remember* or *bethink one's self of,* Lat. *recordari; to recall to mind* or *remind one's self, bear in mind, remember,* Lat. *in memoriam revocare, meminisse; to mention,* Lat. *memorare; to give attention to, to be mindful of* or *for,* Lat. *curare.*

μίμνω, poet. redupl. and sync. form for μένω.

μίν, encl., Ion. and Hom. acc. sing. for ἕ or ἑέ, Lat. *eum, eam, id, him, her, it;* with αὐτόν, etc., *-self.*

Μινύειος, α, ον, pr. adj. from Μινύαι, οἱ, *Min'-y-an.*

μίνυνθα, adv., Lat. *paululum, a little; a little while, a short time,* Lat. *parumper, paulisper.*

μινυνθάδιος, α, ον, Lat. *parum durans, brief, of short duration.*

μίσγω, see μίγνυμι.

μιστύλλω, f. τυλῶ, *to cut up* (meat) *into small bits for roasting.*

μίτρη, Ep. for μίτρα, ας, ἡ, *a broad linen belt,* worn next the person under the θώραξ; being covered on the outside with metallic scales or plates, it was an additional protection to the thighs and lower part of the abdomen; *a girdle; a band for the head.*

μιχθείς, aor. pass. part. of μίγνυμι.

μνάομαι, Lat. *uxorem petere, to woo, court;* also, *to solicit, seek after.*

μνάομαι, Ep. for μιμνήσκομαι, *to remember.*

μνῆσαι, see μνησάσκετο, μιμνήσκω.

μνωόμενος, -ώοντο, Ep. part. for μνώμενος and Ep. 3 pl. impf. for μνῶντο of μνάομαι.

μογέω, f. ἥσω, aor. ἐμόγησα, (μόγος,) Lat. *laborare, to toil, labor; to suffer from toil, be in distress; to labor at* or *do with difficulty; to suffer* or *undergo;* μογέοντες, *weary.*

μόγις, (μόγος,) adv., Lat. *vix, with labor, laboriously, with difficulty, hardly.*

μόγος, ου, ὁ, *toil, trouble, difficulty, distress, hardship; pain.*

μόθος, ου, ὁ, *the tumult of conflict, din, battle, strife.*

μοῖρα, ας, ἡ, Ion. gen. and dat. in η, (μείρομαι,) Lat. *pars, partis, part, portion, share; one's portion of the booty, one's lot in life, destiny,* Lat. *sors, fatum,* also *fate* or *destruction* Γ 101; κατὰ μοῖραν, *according to share, justly, rightly; one's due, that which is right; a party; any division.*

μοιρηγενής, ές, (μοῖρα, γένος,) *favored at birth,* Γ 182, *born with good fate* or *destiny.*

μόλπη, ης, ἡ, (μέλπω,) *a dance with music and song; sport, play,* accompanied with dance and song; *song.*

μολών, οῦσα, ον, 2 aor. part. of βλώσκω, which see.

(ἔμ)μορε, see μείρομαι.

μορμύρω, leng. from μύρω, Lat. *murmurare, to murmur* or *produce the deep roar of the ocean.*

μόρος, ου, ὁ, (μείρομαι), = μοῖρα, *appointed lot, destiny, that which has been allotted ; fate, doom, a lot not desired, misfortune, death.*

μόρσιμος, ου, ὁ, (μόρος,) see Lat. *fatalis, decreed by fate, fated ; doomed to destruction* or *death beforehand, doomed.*

μοῦνος, Ion. for μόνος, η, ον, Lat. *solus, alone, solitary ; single, one, sole, only,* Lat. *unicus, lone, lonely, desolate ;* neu. as adv., *merely, only.*

Μοῦσα, ης, ἡ, Lat. *Mu′-sa*, *the Muse*, goddess of music and the other fine arts, one of the nine Mu′-ses, see Classical Dictionary.

μοχθίζω, f. ίσω, *to toil ; to suffer.*

Μύγδων, ονος, ὁ, *Myg′-don*, king of Phryg′-i-a.

μυελός, ου, ὁ, *the marrow* of the bones, *the rich part within the bone, the inner-most part,* hence *the brain ;* as applied to rich and nourishing food, *the marrow* or *fatness.*

μυθέομαι, iter. impf. μυθέσκοντο, f. ήσομαι, (μῦθος,) *to speak, say ; report, tell ; speak of, name.*

μῦθος, ου, ὁ, Lat. *verbum, a word, discourse, speech, that which is spoken ; plan, counsel, opinion,* Lat. *consilium ; a conversation, talk,* Lat. *sermo ; a request, command, advice ; the matter* or *subject of mention.*

μυῖα, ης, ἡ, Lat. *musca, a fly.*

Μυκάλη, ης, ἡ, *Myc′-a-le*, a promontory on the coast of I-o′-ni-a.

Μυκαλησσός, οῦ, ἡ, *Myc-a-les′-sus*, a town of Bœ-o′-ti-a.

Μυκήνη, ης, ἡ, *My-ce′-ne*, home ot Ag-a-mem′-non.

μυκάομαι, f. ήσομαι, Ep. parts are formed as if from μύκω ; of animals, *to emit a deep sound, bellow, growl, roar ; to creak ; resound.*

μυκηθμός, οῦ, ὁ, (μυκάομαι,) *a low, hollow sound ; a bellowing, lowing, roaring.*

Μύνης, ητος, ὁ, *My′-nes.*

Μυρίνη, ης, ἡ, *My-ri′-na*, an Am′-a-zon.

μυρίος, α, ον, Lat. *innumerus, innumerable, countless, numberless ; vast,* Lat. *immensus ; infinite, endless,* Lat. *infinitus :* stem of Eng. *myriad.*

Μυρμιδόνες, οἱ, *Myr′-mi-dons*, a tribe of Thes′-sa-ly, and led by A-chil′-les.

Μύρσινος, ου, ἡ, *Myr′-si-nus*, a town in Elis.

μύρω, Lat. *fluere, to flow ; to fall* or *run in drops,* Lat. *stillare ;* with acc., *to lament any one, sorrow for :* mid. *to be melted into tears :* stem of Eng. *myrrh.*

Μυσός, οῦ, ὁ, *a Mys′-i-an.*

μυχοίτατος, η, ον, and μύχατος, η, ον, irreg. Hom. sups of μύχιος, (μυχός,) see, also, Hadley and Allen's Grammar, 255 D, *farthest, most remote ; innermost, most retired.*

μύω, f. ύσω, *to be closed, shut up ; to have the eyes* or *lips closed, close the eyes* or *lips : to close*, in both trans. and intrans. senses : stem of μυστήριον, Eng. *mystery*.

μῶλος, ου, ὁ, *labor ; labor* or *tumult of battle*, Lat. *pugnae tumultus ; war, struggle ;* B 401, μῶλον Ἀρηος, *the danger of war*.

μωμέομαι, Ion. for μωμάομαι, f. ήσομαι, (μῶμος,) Lat. *vituperare, reprehendere, to blame, chide, reproach*.

μῶνυξ, υχος, ὁ, ἡ, (μόνος, ὄνυξ,) *having solid hoofs, not cloven-hoofed*.

N.

ναί, Lat. *nae, ita, etiam, sane, verily, yea, truly, yes*.

ναιετάω, iter. impf. ναιετάσκον, -άεσκον; Hom. contr. part. ναιετάωσα, -όωσα : (ναίω :) Lat. *habitare, to inhabit, dwell ; to be, to exist ; to be situated*, Lat. *situs est*.

ναίω, iter. impf. ναίεσκε B 758, *to dwell ;* of places, *to be located, situated,* or *lie :* trans., *to inhabit ; to give for a home,* causal in Ep. ᾳor., *to cause to dwell* == *to settle one ;* hence, mid. and pass. *to settle one's self* or *be settled, dwell*.

Νάστης, ου, ὁ, *Nas'-tes*, leader of the Ca'-ri-ans.

Ναυβολίδης, ου, ὁ, *son of Nau'-bo-lus*, Iph'-i-tus.

ναῦς, see Ion. νηῦς.

ναύτης, ου, ὁ, (ναῦς,) *a sailor, a mariner, one who goes by a ship, one who manages a ship*.

ναῦφι(ν), see νηῦς.

νεαρός, ά, όν, (νέος,) Lat. *recens, recent, fresh ; young*, Lat. *tener*.

νέατος, η, ον, Ion. νείατος, *last, extreme ; lowest ; latest*.

νεβρός, οῦ, ὁ, Lat. *cervi pullus, a young deer, fawn*.

νέεσσι(ν), see νηῦς.

νειαίρη, ης, Ion. for νειαίρα, ας, ἡ, Lat. *inferior, lower ;* νειαίρη γαστήρ, *the lower part of the belly* or *the abdomen :* stric. fem. adj., irreg. compar. of νέος, *new, newer,* and from that *lower*.

νεικείω, Ep. for νεικέω; Ion. iter. impf. νεικείεσκον B 221 ; f. νεικέσ(σ)ω ; aor. ἐνείκεσα, Ep. νείκεσσεν Γ 38 : (νεῖκος :) Lat. *rixari, to quarrel, contend, bicker, dispute ;* trans., Lat. *objurgare, to rail at, reprove, inveigh against, upbraid* B 221, Γ 38, *vex, criminate, irritate*.

νεῖκος, εος, τό, Lat. *altercatio, jurgium, a dispute, quarrel, lawsuit, dissension, difficulty ; the cause of the quarrel ; abusive language, invective*.

νεῖμα, see νέμω.

νειός, οῦ, ἡ, (νέος,) *newly ploughed land, new land*.

νεκρός, οῦ, ὁ, *a dead body ; a carcass,* Lat. *cadaver ; a corpse,* Lat. *corpus.*

νέκταρ, αρος, τό, Lat. *nectar, potus deorum, the drink of the gods,* was red and fragrant.

νεκτάρεος, adj., (νεκτάρ,) Lat. *nectareus, like nectar, scented with nectar,* Γ 385 *fragrant ; divine ; beautiful, sweet.*

νεκύς, υος, ὁ, Ep. dat. pl. νεκύεσσι(ν) or νέκυσσι(ν), see Lat. *corpus, cadaver, a corpse, dead body ;* adj., *dead.*

νεμεσάω, contr. -σῶ, Ep. -σσάω Γ 410 ; f. -σήσ(σ)ω, (νέμεσις,) Lat. *indignari, to be justly indignant at something not deserved, to be vexed with ; to think unseemly, censure :* mid. and pass. *to be indignant at one's self ;* Β 223, νεμέσσηθεν, Ep. aor. pass. 3 pl. *were enraged :* verbal adj., Γ 410 *reprehensible.*

νεμεσίζομαι, used in pres. system, (νέμεσις,) *to be indignant at injustice ; to be angry with* or *at ; to fear* or *stand in awe of ; to be ashamed.*

νέμεσ(σ)ις, εως, ἡ, (νέμω,) Lat. *justa indignatio, just indignation at injustice* or *any undeserved good fortune of another ; censure, envy ; disgrace : that which causes indignation* Γ 156.

νεμεσσητός, Ep. verbal adj. from νεμεσάω, Γ 410.

νέμω, f. νεμῶ, aor. ἔνειμα or Ep. νεῖμα, pf. νενέμηκα, aor. pass. ἐνεμήθην, Lat. *distribuere, to distribute ; dispense, assign :* mid. *to divide among themselves, hold in possession, use ; to occupy, inhabit,* Lat. *incolere.*

νέμω, Lat. *pascere, to put out to graze, drive to pasture :* mid. *to feed, graze, feed upon,* Lat. *pasci ; enjoy,* Lat. *frui.*

νέομαι, or **νεῦμαι ;** used in pres. system with f. signif. ; Lat. *abire, to go away ; go back ; to go, come,* Lat. *ire, venire :* 2 sing. νεῖαι ; νει-, νε-.

νέος, adj., Lat. *novus, new, recent, fresh ; unexpected ; young,* as subst. in pl. νέοι, Α 463, *young men,* Lat. *juvenes,* also in sing. νέος, *a youth,* Lat. *puer ; youthful :* adv. νέον, Lat. *nuper, lately, now, again.*

νέος, see **νηῦς.**

νεοσσός, οῦ, ὁ, (νέος,) *a newly born animal,* esp. a young bird, Lat. *pullus, a chick, nestling ;* in pl. *young bees,* Lat. *apes.*

νεούτατος, ον, (νέος, οὐτάω,) *newly* or *recently wounded.*

νέρθε(ν), adv., *below, underneath ; from under :* also, prep. with gen., *under,* Lat. *sub* with abl.

Νεστόρεος, α, ον, (Νέστωρ,) *Nes-to'-re-an.*

Νέστωρ, ορος, ὁ, *Nes'-tor,* king of Py'-lus.

νευρή, ῆς, ἡ, Ion. for νευρά, *a sinew ; a bowstring* made of sinew ; *any string made of sinews.*

νεῦρον, ον, τό, Lat. *nervus, a sinew ; nerve, strength, power ; a bowstring* or *string of a musical instrument* made of sinews ; *any cord* or *string made of sinews.*

νεύω, Lat. *innuere, to nod ; nod assent to,* Lat. *nutu confirmare ;* with κεφαλήν, *to bow down the head, hang the head ;* Γ 337, *to nod, hang* or *bend down ; decline.*

νεφέλη, ης, ἡ, (νέφος,) Lat. *nubes, nebula, a cloud ;* see ἄχος.

νεφεληγερέτης, Ep. -έτα, Hom. gen. -αο, ὁ, (νεφέλη, ἀγείρω,) Lat. *nubes cogens, the gatherer of clouds, cloud-compeller,* epith. of Zeus.

νέφος, εος, τό, Lat. *nebula, nubes, a cloud, a mist* or *fog, a thick mass of clouds ; a cloud,* metaph. as we are accustomed to use the word, of the brow, of sorrow or anger, of death, etc.

νη-, a neg. prefix.

νηγάτεος, η, ον, Lat. *nuper factus, newly made.*

νήδυμος, ον, of ὕπνος, *profound, deep, sweet, refreshing.*

νηδύς, ύος, ἡ, Lat. *venter, uterus, the belly, stomach, womb.*

νήιος, η, ον, (νηῦς for ναῦς,) *of a ship ;* δόρυ νήιον or simply νήιον, *ship-timber,* Γ 62.

Νηλεύς, Ep. gen. ῆος, ὁ, *Ne'-leus,* son of *Nep'-tune,* father of Nes'-tor.

νηλ(ε)ής, ές, (νη-, ἔλεος,) *pitiless* Γ 292, *ruthless, merciless, relentless ;* with ἦμαρ, *the day of death ; irresistible.*

νημερτής, ές, (νη-, ἁμαρτάνω,) *unerring, true, infallible ;* νημερτέα εἰπεῖν, *to speak the truth.*

νηός, οῦ, ὁ, Ion. for ναός, Lat. *aedes, a temple, the abiding-place of a god.*

νηός, see νηῦς.

νηπιαχεύω, f. εύσω, (νηπίαχος, poet. for νήπιος,) *to act like a child, be childlike.*

νηπίαχος, Β 338, ον, poet. for νήπιος, ον, Lat. *puerilis, silly, childish.*

νήπιος, adj., (νη-, ἔπος,) Lat. *infans, speechless, without speech,* also *childish, foolish ; feeble, helpless ;* as subst., *young, offspring.*

Νηρή, poet. for **Νηρηίς**, ίδος, ἡ, which is Ion. for **Νηρείς**, *a daughter of Ne-re'us, a Ne-re'-id* or *sea-nymph,* fifty in number, found in pl.

Νήριτον, ου, τό, *Ner'-i-tum,* a mountain of Ith'-a-ca.

νῆσος, ου, ἡ, Lat. *insula, an island.*

νηῦς, Hom. and Ion. for ναῦς, ἡ; Ion. and Ep. forms νηῦς, gen. νηός or νεός, dat. νηί, acc. νῆα or νέα, pl. νέες also νῆες, gen. νηῶν also νεῶν and ναῦφι(ν), dat. νηυσί, νήεσσι, and νέεσσι, also ναῦφι(ν), acc. νέας: Lat. *navis, a ship, ship of war.*

νίζω, f. νίψω, Lat. *lavare, to wash ; to wash off* or *wash* the hands or feet, *purify, cleanse, make clean,* Lat. *abluere :* mid. *to wash one's self.*

νικάω, f. ήσω, (νίκη,) Lat. *vincere, to conquer, excel, gain the mastery :* trans., Lat. *vincere, superare, to conquer ; to be superior to, surpass,* with gen.; with cognate acc., *to gain* or *win.*

νίκη, ης, ἡ, Lat. *victoria, victory.*

Νιόβη, ης, ἡ, *Ni'-o-be,* daughter of Tan'-ta-lus; for legend, see Classical Dictionary.

Νιρεύς, Ion. ῆος, δ, *Ni'-reus*, see Classical Dictionary.

Νίσα, ης, ἡ, *Ni'-sa*, a village in Bœ-o-'ti-a.

Νίσυρος, ου, ἡ, *Ni-sy'-rus*, an island.

νιφάς, άδος, ἡ, (νίφω,) snow, *a flake of snow*; in pl. *a storm of snow, snow.*

νιφόεις, εσσα, εν, (νίφα,) Lat. *niveus, snowy, covered with snow.*

νοέω, f. ήσω, aor. ἐνόησα, pf. νενόηκα, aor. pass. ἐνοήθην, (νόος,) *to see and know*; Lat. *intelligere, sentire, to perceive* B 371, *become aware of, recognize* Γ 396, *discern*; *to think, ponder*; *to devise, contrive*; *to intend, purpose*; *to think of.*

Νοήμων, ονος, δ, *No-e'-mon*; stric. *thoughtful.*

νόθος, η, ον, Lat. *non legitimus, illegitimate, spurious.*

νομεύς, Ep. gen. ῆος, δ, (νομός, (νέμω,)) Lat. *pastor, a shepherd*; *one who distributes, a distributer*, (νέμω).

Νομίων, ονος, δ, *No-mi-'on.*

νομός, οῦ, δ, (νέμω,) Lat. *pascuum, pasture*; *pasturage, food furnished by a pasture*, Lat. *pabulum*; ἐπέων πολὺς νομός, *wide the field of words.*

νόος, νόου or -οιο, δ, Lat. *mens, mind, understanding, power of thought, reason, consciousness*; *prudence*; *thought, design, intent, purpose, resolve, aim*; *counsel*; in gen. *the mind, heart, disposition, gist, sense.*

νοστέω, ήσω, (νόστος,) Lat. *redire, to return*; *to travel.*

νόστος, ου, δ, Lat. *reditus, a returning, a return*; *journey, travel.*

νόσφι(ν), adv., *apart, asunder, away*; prep. with gen. *far from, away from, except.*

νοσφίζω, ίσω, (νόσφι,) Lat. *segregare, to separate, remove*: mid. *to remove one's self* or *depart, stand aloof, go away*, Lat. *discedere*; *to abandon, leave, desert*, Lat. *relinquere.*

Νότος, ου, δ, Lat. *No'-tus, the South Wind.*

νοῦσος, ου, ἡ, Ion. for νόσος, Lat. *morbus, disease, sickness, malady,* of body or mind, also *suffering, distress.*

νύμφη, ης, ἡ, Lat. *nupta, a bride, a young married woman.*

Νύμφη, ης, ἡ, (stric. *a bride* or *young married woman*, Lat. *nupta*,) *Nymph, a goddess of lower rank.* These goddesses were known by different names, according to the localities or things over which they presided. Ναῖδες presided over *springs.* Νύμφαι ὀρεάδες presided over *mountains.* Νηρηΐδες presided over the *sea.* Νύμφαι ὑάδες were *rain-nymphs.* Νύμφαι πετραῖαι presided over *the rocks.*

νῦν, adv., often encl. νυ(ν) Γ 164, Lat. *nunc, now, just now*; also like Eng. *now, therefore, surely, indeed*; ἄγε νυν, *come now.*

νύξ, νυκτός, ἡ, Lat. *nox, night, nightfall*; *watch*; *sleep*; *nightfall*; *the West*; *death.*

νυός, οῦ, ἡ, Lat. *filii uxor, nurus, a daughter-in-law*; *a bride.*

Νυσήϊον, ου, τό, *Ny-sœ'-um*, a mountain in Thrace sacred to Bac'-chus.

νωμάω, f. ήσω, (νέμω,) Lat. distribuere, to portion out, distribute ; to swing, wield, handle, agitate, manage ; to hold, guide ; to meditate, consider, ponder, observe.

νῶροψ, οπος, ὁ, ἡ, Lat. splendidus, flashing.

νῶτον, ου, τό, Lat. tergum, the back ; B 159, surface.

Ξ.

ξανθός, ή, όν, Lat. flavus, yellow ; a pale golden color like that of ripe wheat ; chestnut, sorrel or yellowish red, Lat. fulvus.

Ξάνθος, ου, ὁ, Xan'-thus, a Tro'-jan ; also the name of two rivers ; see Classical Dictionary.

ξε(ι)νίζω, f. ίσω, (ξένος,) Lat. hospitio excipere, to entertain, receive as guest.

ξεῖνος, Ion. for ξένος, η, ον, compare Lat. adventor, hospes, a guest, any one with whom bonds of friendship and hospitality have been solemnly sealed, hence host as well as guest ; a stranger, and from this the word came to mean a hired soldier who entered a foreign service, see Xen'-o-phon's A-nab'-a-sis ; in Hom. usu. a guest.

ξεινοδόκος, ον, Ion. for ξενοδόχος, (ξένος, δέχομαι,) given or accustomed to entertaining guests, hospitable.

ξενεῖον, Ion. ξεινήιον, ου, τό, (ξεῖνος,) a present from a host to his guest on departing, entertainment or provision for a guest, hospitality ; a gift of friendship.

ξεστός, ή, όν, (ξέω,) shaved, scraped, made smooth.

ξέω, f. έσω ; Ep. forms are in -σσ- ; to scrape, scratch, rasp, scrape or plane to a polish ; to carve.

ξίφος, εος, τό, Lat. gladius, ensis, a sword, a large straight, two-edged sword.

ξύλοχος, ου, ἡ, (ξύλον, ἔχω,) a thicket or jungle ; a hiding-place for men or beasts, a lair.

ξύμ-, ξύν, see σύμ-, σύν.

ξυνέηκα, see συνίημι.

ξυνήιος, η, ον, (ξυνός), Lat. communis, common ; in neu. pl. as subst., τά ξυνήια, things held in common, common property.

ξυστόν, οῦ, τό, stric. neu. of adj. ξυστός, polished or scraped or worked down smooth, (ξύω,) the smooth wooden shaft of a spear, a spear or javelin ; compare Lat. hasta, hastile.

O.

ὁ, ἡ, τό ; the forms ὁ, ἡ, οἱ, αἱ, are procl. ; article *the*. Orig. a demon.
pron., and as such com. used by Hom. ; with subst. Lat. *ille, hic, that,
this*, A 20 *these ransoms* = *this ransom*, A 11 *that* = *the well-known, the,
this* or *that* (which is com. known) : standing alone, *he, she, it*, A 12 *he*,
A 29 *her ;* with relat. pron. refers back, as *he who*, etc. : ὁ μέν . . . ὁ δέ, *the
one . . . the other,* see Anabasis, Book I. chap. ι. sec. 7, τοὺς μὲν . . . τοὺς
δ', *some . . . others.* As article, *the ;* it may render the adj. a subst. in
sense, see Anabasis, Book I, chap. ιν. sec. 13, τὸ πολύ, *the greater part ;*
τό with infin. is equivalent to a neu. subst. ; before an adv. the two are
com. equivalent to an adj., but sometimes the adv. retains its adv.
sense streng. by the τό ; the neu. is used with a clause or sentence
treated as a subst. ; the neu. is used in cases like τὸ ἀγαθός, not to
agree with the *expressed word,* but to indicate something as *the idea* or
word good ; with gen. it agrees with a subst. suppressed. Not procl.
it is equivalent to ὅς, ἥ, ὅ, τὸ μέν A 234, *which indeed,* τῇ περ, see περ.
Certain cases are used as indefinite pron. τις, and like it are encl.

ὁαρίζω, f. ίσω, (ὅαρος,) *to hold free converse with* any one, *talk familiarly
with.*

ὀβελός, οῦ, ὁ, *a spit :* diminutive ὀβελίσκος, hence Eng. *obelisk.*

ὄβριμος, ον, *mighty ; heavy, large.*

ὀγδώκοντα, Lat. *octoginta,* indecl., *eighty.*

ὅγε, ἥγε, τόγε, (article as demon. pron., γε as streng. particle,) Lat. *is, ea,
id, he, she, it ;* often it has a force difficult to render.

ὀβριμοεργός, ον, (ὄβριμος, ἔργον,) *performing mighty deeds, of mighty* or *violent deeds, doing wrong acts.*

ὄγκος, ου, ὁ, Lat. *uncus, a curve* or *hook, the hook* or *barb on the point of a
barbed weapon.*

ὄγμος, οῦ, ὁ, (ἄγω,) *a straight* or *direct line, a straight road* or *track, a
straight path, a path, a straight row, a furrow* or *swath ;* see Lat.
sulcus.

'Ογχηστός, οῦ, ὁ, *On-ches'-tus,* a town of Bœ-o'-ti-a.

ὀδάξ, (o eu., δάκνω,) adv., Lat. *mordicus, with the teeth ;* ἕλον γαῖαν ὀδάξ,
to bite the dust.

ὅδε, ἥδε, τόδε, (article as demon. pron., encl. particle -δε to give greater
force) demon. pron., Lat. *hicce, this, this here ;* declined like article, Ep.
dat. pl. τοῖσδεσ(σι)ν ; more emphatic than οὗτος ; when οὗτος and ὅδε
are used in opposition, the former refers to what has gone before (see
ταῦτα Anabasis, Book I. chap. ιν. sec. 16) and the latter to what fol-

lows (see τάδε Anabasis, Book I. chap. iv. sec. 13); ὅδ' αὐτός, *this very here;* in adv. *sense,* but not adv., *here,* Ἀχιλλεὺς ἐγγὺς ὅδε: adv., τῆδε, *here, in this way:* τόδε, *for this reason,* with words of motion, *this way, hither.*

'Οδιος, ου, ὁ, *O-di'-us.*

ὁδός, οῦ, ἡ, Lat. *via,* a *way, road, pathway;* πρὸ ὁδοῦ, *farther along on the road;* a *journey, voyage, march,* Lat. *iter;* way, manner, method.

ὁδούς, ὁδόντος, ὁ, Lat. *dens,* a *tooth.*

ὀδύρομαι, f. ὀδυροῦμαι, aor. ὠδυράμην, Lat. *moerēre, lamentari,* to *lament, deplore, grieve for, mourn;* with gen., to *grieve because of;* with dat., B 290, to *mourn to:* intrans. to *grieve, lament, mourn.*

'Οδυσσεύς, έως, ὁ; Ep. gen. ῆος, *U-lys'-ses,* son of *La-er'-tes,* king of *Ith'-a-ca,* and hero of the *Od'-ys-sey.*

ὄζος, ου, ὁ, a *branch, bough;* a *twig* A 234, *shoot, scion, descendant;* ὕζος Ἄρηος, *child of Mars,* epith. of heroes.

ὅθεν, (ὅς,) adv., Lat. *unde, from whence* or *whom, whence; wherefore,* Lat. *quare, quamobrem.*

ὅθι, poet. for οὗ, (ὅς,) Lat. *ubi, where.*

ὅθομαι, to *heed, have a care for;* with gen. to *concern one's self about.*

ὀθόνη, ης, ἡ, Hom. uses pl. Ep. dat. ὀθόνῃσιν Γ 141, *fine linen;* a *web, sheet, fine linen cloth;* a *veil* or *garment of fine linen.*

ὅθριξ, ὅτριχος, ὁ, ἡ, (ὁμοῦ, θρίξ,) poet. for ὁμόθριξ, Lat. *similis capilli, having like hair.*

οἷ, Lat. *sibi,* dat. of 3 pers. pron. οὗ.

οἴγνυμι, Ep. impf. mid. 3 pl. ὠΐγνυντο; f. οἴξω; aor. ᾦξα; Ep. ὤϊξα; aor. pass. ᾤχθην: Lat. *patefacere, aperire,* to *open;* to *broach.*

οἶδα, see εἴδω.

οἰέτης, ες, for ὁμοέτης, (ὁμός, ἔτος,) Lat. *qui ejusdem aetatis est,* equal in point of years, of the same age.

ὀϊζυρός, ά, όν, (ὀϊζύς,) Lat. *miser, pitiable, miserable, wretched.*

ὀϊζύω, f. ύσω, to *wail, lament;* to be *afflicted, suffer;* as trans. to *suffer;* to *bewail.*

οἴκαδε, (οἶκος,) adv., Lat. *domum, homeward,* to *one's home,* either *country, house,* or *tent.*

οἰκεύς, έως, ὁ, (οἶκος,) Lat. *famulus, domesticus,* one *living in the family,* a *slave* or *servant,* a *domestic;* Ion. gen. οἰκῆος.

οἰκέω, f. οἰκήσω, aor. ᾤκησα, pf. ᾤκηκα, aor. pass. ᾠκήθην, (οἶκος,) Lat. *habitare,* to *inhabit, possess* and *dwell in,* to *occupy,* to *live in;* to *settle any one,* pass. to *be settled;* to *control, administer, manage.*

οἰκία, τά, pl. of οἰκίον, (οἶκος,) Lat. a *dwelling-place, abode; house;* a *lair; nest,* Lat. *nidus.*

οἴκοθι, and οἴκοι, (οἶκος,) adv., Lat. *domi,* at *home.*

οἰκόνδε, for οἴκαδε, (οἶκος,) Lat. adv., Lat. *domum, home, homeward*.

οἶκος, ου, ὁ, Lat. *domicilium, domus, a house, a place of abode; a tent; a room, hall, part of a house; a temple; household; a race, a house; household affairs; household substance* or *property*.

οἰκτείρω, f. τερῶ, aor. ᾤκτειρα, (οἶκτος,) Lat. *miserari, to commiserate, feel pity for, pity*.

οἶκτος, ου, ὁ, *pity*, both the *feeling* and *expression* of *pity;* compare Lat. *misericordia, commiseratio*.

οἰκτρός, ά, όν, (οἶκτος,) *to be pitied, pitiable;* compare Lat. *miserandus, miserabilis*.

'Οιλεύς, έως, ὁ, *O-i'-leus*.

οἰμάω, f. ήσω, (οἶμα,) *to fall* or *come suddenly and violently upon, swoop down upon*.

οἰμωγή, ῆς, ἡ, (οἰμώζω,) *a lamenting, a wailing*.

οἰμώζω, f. οἰμώξομαι, aor. ᾤμωξα, (οἴμοι,) Lat. *lamentari, plorare, to lament, wail*: trans. Lat. *deplorare, to bewail*.

Οἰνείδης, ου, ὁ, *son of Œ'-neus*.

Οἰνεύς, έως, or ῆος, ὁ, *Œ'-neus*, king of Cal'-y-don.

οἰνοβαρής, ές, (οἶνος, βαρύς,) Lat. *ebrius, vino gravis, heavy with wine, drunken*, A 225.

Οἰνόμαος, ου, ὁ, *Œ-nom'-a-us*, a Greek.

οἰνόπεδος, ον, (οἶνος, πέδον,) Lat. *vinum ferens, of wine-growing soil, wine-producing*.

Οἰνοπίδης, ου, ὁ, *son of Œ-no'-pi-on*.

οἶνος, ου, ὁ, Lat. *vinum, wine; the fermented juice of fruits* (water was mixed with the wine before drinking); *malt liquor*.

οἰοπόλος, ον, (οἶος, πέλομαι, *to be*,) Lat. *solitarius, lone; lonely, unfrequented*.

οἰνοχοέω, Ep. οἰνοχοεύω; Ep. impf. 3 sing. ἐῳνοχόει, A 598 οἰνοχόει; f. ήσω: (οἰνοχόος:) Lat. *vinum fundere, to pour out wine;* A 598, *was pouring out wine*.

οἰνοχόος, ον, (οἶνος, χέω,) *pouring out wine;* as subst. *wine-pourer*.

οἶνοψ, οἴνοπος, ὁ, (οἶνος, ὤψ,) *wine-colored, dark red*.

οἶος, οἴη, οἶον, Lat. *solus, alone, lone, lonely; unique, peculiar of its kind, alone of its kind, admirable,* Lat. *unicus;* with ἀπό, *alone from, separated from; alone* or *unaided, without aid, alone, single*.

οἶος, οἴη, οἶον, (ὅς,) Lat. *qualis, what sort of* B 820, *such as, as;* often used when the antecedent is indefinite or omitted, and is sometimes attracted into the case of its antecedent; the antecedent is often a clause; correlative of τοῖος Lat. *talis, such, such-like; such as to, capable of:* in adv. sense, οἶος *how,* οἶον δή *since then*.

ὅις and οἶς, gen. ὅιος and οἰός, ὁ, ἡ, acc. ὅιν, pl. ὅιες and contr. ὅις, dat.

7

ὄιεσ(σ)ι or ὄεσ(σ)ι, contr. acc. ὄις, Lat. *ovis*, *a sheep* Γ 198, both mas. and fem., sometimes there is added another word: supply the *digamma* and we have οϜις, which is the Lat. *ovis*.

ὄισατο, Ep. aor. mid. of ὄιω.

οἰσέμεν(αι), Ep. f. inf. of φέρω.

ὀιστεύω, f. εύσω, (ὀιστός, an arrow,) Lat. *sagittare*, *to shoot arrows, shoot.*

ὀιστός, οῦ, ὁ, (οἴσω,) Lat. *sagitta, an arrow.*

οἶτος, ου, ὁ, (οἴ,) *lot*; in bad sense, Lat. *infelix fatum, a sorrowful lot, calamity, misfortune, death, doom.*

Οἴτυλος, ου, ὁ, *Œt'-y-lus*, a town of La-co'-ni-a.

Οἰχαλιεύς, έως, ὁ, an *Œ-cha-'li-an.*

Οἰχαλίη, ης, ἡ, *Œ-cha'-li-a*, a city of Thes'-sa-ly.

Οἰχαλίηθεν, adv., from *Œ-cha-li-a.*

οἴχομαι, f. οἰχήσομαι: stric. pf. with signif. of pres., Ion. οἴχευμαι, *am gone; to have gone away, be gone, be absent* or *away,* Lat. *abesse; to have departed; to be lost, to vanish* Β 71, *slip away, escape;* Α 366 *to go, set out,* Lat. *proficisci; to depart, go away,* Lat. *abire; to fly, rush, haste, speed:* as trans. *to escape anything:* with cognate acc.

ὀίω or οἴω, Ep. mid. ὀίομαι; Ep. impf. 3 sing. ὠίετο; f. οἰήσομαι; aor. ὠισάμην, Ep. 3 sing. ὀίσατο; Ep. aor. pass. ὠίσθην: Lat. *opinari, suspicari, to think, believe, fear, suspect, hope, expect; to mean* or *intend* to do a thing, *purpose.*

οἰωνιστής, οῦ, ὁ, (οἰωνίζομαι,) *one who foretells by observing birds, an augur,* Β 858.

οἰωνοπόλος, ον, (οἰωνός, πολέω,) *observing the birds of omen, versed in the art of augury;* as subst. Lat. *augur, auspex, an augur, a seer.*

οἰωνός, οῦ, ὁ, (οἶος,) Lat. *ales, a bird of prey, a solitary bird,* hence *bird of omen,* as eagle, vulture, etc., from such birds omens were taken; *an omen.*

ὀκριόεις, εσσα, εν, (ὄκρις, *a rough point,*) *rough with projections, ragged.*

ὀκρυόεις, εσσα, εν, (= κρυόεις in sense, ὁ being prefixed for eu. effect,) *chilly, icy, cold;* metaph. *dread, chilling the heart, terrible, frightful, awful.*

ὀκτώ, indecl., Lat. *octo, eight.*

ὀλβιοδαίμων, ονος, ὁ, ἡ, (ὄλβιος, δαίμων,) *blessed by the deity, of blessed* or *happy lot.*

ὄλβιος, ον, (ὄλβος), compare Lat. *felix, fortunatus, beatus, happy, fortunate, prospered,* hence *wealthy;* also trans. *rich,* of things that make the possessor *rich.*

ὄλβος, ου, ὁ, *good fortune, happiness, riches, prosperity;* compare Lat. *divitiae, opes, gazae.*

ὄλεθρος, ου, ὁ, (ὄλλυμι,) *destruction, a destroying;* anything that causes destruction, *a scourge, a bane.*

ὀλέκω, iter. impf. ὀλέκεσκον, Lat. *perdere, to destroy, ruin, kill*; pass. *to die*; = ὄλλυμι.

ὀλιγοδρανέων, έουσα, έον or οῦν, (ὀλίγος, δραίνω,) *having ability to do little, able to do but little, not strong.*

ὀλίγος, η, ον, Lat. *paucus, exiguus, few, little, small*, opp. to μέγας and πολύς; *feeble, weak*; ὀλίγου, *of little, nearly* equivalent to ὀλίγου δεῖ, *lack only a little*, Lat *paene*: neu. as adv., ὀλίγον, *a little*, Lat. *paullum;* ἐν ὀλίγῳ, *finally, in short, in a little space, nearly;* with compar., *by a little.*

'Ολιζών, ῶνος, ἡ, *O-li'-zon*, a town of Mag-ne'-si-a.

ὀλλυ(μι)(ω), impf. ὤλλυν; f. ὀλέσ(σ)ω; aor. ὤλεσ(σ)α and ὄλεσ(σ)α; pf. ὀλώλεκα, 2 pf. ὄλωλα: Lat. *perdere, to lose,* also *to destroy, ruin, slay:* mid. Lat. *perire, to be destroyed, die, perish; to be ruined: see* ὀλέκω.

ὀλοιός, όν, ὀλουός, όν, poet. for ἀλοός, ή, όν, (ὄλλυμι,) Lat. *exitiosus, perniciosus, destructive, hurtful, deadly.*

ὀλοός, η, ον, (ὄλλυμι,) Lat. *exitiosus, perniciosus, destructive, ruinous, deadly, pernicious, hurtful,* Γ 365.

'Ολοοσσών, όνος, ἡ, *O-lo-os'-son*, a town in Thes'-sa-ly.

ὀλοόφρων, ονος, ὁ, ἡ, (ὀλοός, φρήν,) *evil in mind, meaning hurt; baleful, savage, stern.*

ὀλοφυδνός, ή, όν, (ὀλοφύρομαι,) Lat. *luctuosus, weeping, sorrowing,* also, *lamentable, pitiful.*

ὀλοφύρομαι, f. ροῦμαι, aor. ράμην, *to weep* or *lament, bewail; to pity* or *feel for others in trouble, show pity* or *sympathy;* with gen. or acc. *to have compassion on.*

'Ολύμπιος, ον, ('Ολυμπος,) *O-lym'-pi-an.*

'Ολυμπόνδε, adv., *to O-lym'-pus.*

"Ολυμπος, Ep. Οὔλυμπος, ου, ὁ, *O-lym'-pus,* a high mountain in Thes'-sa-ly, and home of the gods; see Classical Dictionary.

ὅμαδος, ου, ὁ, (ὁμός,) *the noise* or *tumult of a crowd* Β 396, *the noise of battle; a throng; strife.*

ὄμβρος, ου, ὁ, Lat. *imber, rain, a heavy fall of rain, a thunder-storm.*

ὁμηγερής, ες, (ὁμός, ἀγείρω,) Lat. *congregatus, assembled together.*

ὁμηλικίη, ης, ἡ, Ion. for ὁμηλικία, (ὁμῆλιξ,) Lat. *aetatis aequalitas, equality of age;* collective n., Γ 175, *society of equals in age, companions; a mate, comrade, companion.*

ὁμιλέω, f. ήσω, aor. ὡμίλησα, (ὅμιλος,) *to be in company with, associate with,* sometimes with παρά, μετά; with περί and acc. *to throng about; to meet,* either in friendly or hostile sense; *to live intimately with* or *be friends; to come into; to engage in.*

ὅμιλος, ου, ἡ, (ὁμου, ἴλη,) (what is the difference between Lat. *coetus, turba,* *turma*, and *multitudo?*) *a throng, assembled crowd, multitude, company, mass, host, army; tumult of battle.*

ὀμίχλη, ης, ἡ, Ion. for ὀμίχλη, Lat. *caligo, nebula, a fog, mist; steam; κο-νίης ὀμίχλη, cloud of dust.*

ὄμμα, ατος, τό, (ὦμμαι, pf. mid. of ὁράω,) Lat. *oculus, the eye; a sight, phantom, that which is seen, view.*

ὄμνυ(μι)(ω), impf. ὦμνυ(ο)ν; f. ὀμοῦμαι; aor. (ὤ)(ὄ)μοσ(σ)α Γ 279; pf. ὀμώ-μοκα; aor. pass. ὠμό(σ)θην: Lat. *jurare, to swear, affirm* or *declare by oath; to swear to anything;* with ὅρκον, *to swear an oath;* with inf., Α 76, *swear to me that you will assist, to swear by; invoke.*

ὁμοῖος, η, ον, (ὁμός,) Lat. *similis, aequalis, like, similar, resembling, equal,* Lat. *par; common; the same,* Lat. *idem; of the same condition in life.*

ὁμοιόω, f. ώσω, aor. ὡμοίωσα, aor. pass. ὡμοιώθην, (ὁμοῖος,) *to make like; to liken; to compare:* pass. Α 187, ὁμοιωθήμεναι ἄντην, *to compare himself face to face with me.*

ὁμοκλάω = ὁμοκλέω, iter. aor. ὁμοκλήσασκε, *to exclaim, shout* or *call out to,* either *to cheer* or *upbraid; to call out a command, shout to any one to do anything, to command in a loud voice.*

ὁμοῦ, (ὁμός,) adv., Lat. *una, together; at once, at the same time, together, alike, equally,* like ὁμῶς.

ὁμοφρονέω, (ὁμόφρων,) *to be of the same mind; live in harmony.*

ὁμόφρων, ονος, ὁ, ἡ, (ὁμός, φρήν,) Lat. *unanimus, unanimous.*

ὀμφαλός, οῦ, ὁ, *a navel; centre-point; the boss of a shield; the centre-knob of a yoke.*

ὀμφή, ῆς, ἡ, Lat. *divina vox, a divine voice; a warning voice; a prophetic voice; a report.*

ὁμῶς, (ὁμός,) adv., (what is the difference between Lat. *pariter, aeque, similiter?*) *together, together with, at once, also, alike,* very much like ὁμοῦ, Lat. *una; in equal parts, equally; equally as* or *with, just as, in like manner, like as,* Lat. *pariter ac.*

ὄναρ, indecl., τό, Lat. *somnium, a dream, that which is seen during sleep;* ὕπαρ is a *real appearance, seen when one is not asleep.*

ὄνειαρ, ὀνείατος, τό, (ὀνίνημι,) *anything that is useful* or *helpful, a help, an advantage; succor, aid; relief, refreshment; food.*

ὀνείδειος, ον, (ὄνειδος,) *disgraceful, shameful, injurious; reproachful, that incurs reproach:* also as subst.

ὀνειδίζω, f. ίσω, aor. ὠνείδισα, (ὄνειδος,) Lat. *exprobrare,* (what is the difference between *exprobrare* and *objicere?*) *to cast reproaches in one's teeth; to reproach, censure, blame.*

ὄνειδος, εος, τό, Lat. *probrum, a blame, a reproach* Α 291, *a disgrace; a report,* something like Lat. *fama,* (what is the difference between *fama* and *rumor?*)

ὀνειροπόλος, ον, (ὄνειρος, πολέω,) Lat. *ex somniis futura praedicens, foretelling future events from dreams;* as subst. Lat. *conjector* or *somniorum conjector, an interpreter of dreams.*

ὄνειρος, ου, ὁ, Lat. *somnium, a dream;* the God of Dreams, B 6; what is the difference between ὄνειρος and ὄναρ? a pl. ὀνείρατα is found.

ὄνησα, see foll.

ὀνίνημι, f. ὀνήσω, aor. ὤνησα, 2 aor. mid. ὠνήμην, aor. pass. ὠνήθην, Lat. *juvare, to help, profit, aid, benefit,* also, *to please, gratify, delight, cheer:* mid. *to profit by;* with ὃν θυμόν *to be profited in his mind, to receive aid; to take delight;* with gen., *to enjoy,* Lat. *frui* with the ablative.

ὄνομα, ατος, τό, Lat. *nomen, a name; reputation, fame,* Lat. *fama; name* in its general applications.

ὀνομάζω, (ὄνομα,) *to name; to nominate, mention; address* or *call by name:* mid. *to have named;* compare Lat. *nominare, appellare, designare.*

ὄνομαι, a μι-verb, with stem in ο, *to blame, censure; reject, scorn; find fault:* see Lat. *vituperare, reprehendere.*

ὀνομάκλυτός, όν, (ὄνομα, κλυτός,) *of great* or *renowned name.*

ὀξυβελής, ές, (ὀξύς, βέλος,) *sharp at the end* or *point.*

ὀξυόεις, εσσα, εν, (Hom. for ὀξύς,) *with a sharp point.*

ὀνομαίνω, f. ὀνομανῶ, aor. ὠνόμηνα, (ὄνομα,) Lat. *nominare, to call by name; to name,* Lat. *nuncupare; to name as, nominate, constitute, appoint; to pronounce, call over by name* B 488; (how do *nominare* and *nuncupare* differ?)

ὀξύς, εῖα or έα, ύ, Lat. *acutus, sharp, acute, pointed;* also, Lat. *acutus, clear, shrill, keen, sharp, piercing, quick; bitter, strong; quick, hasty, swift,* something like Lat. *acer:* adv. ὀξέως and ὀξύ.

ὄο, ὄου, ἔης, Ion. gen. of ὅς.

ὀπάζω, f. ὀπάσ(σ)ω, aor. (ὤ)(ὄ)πασ(σ)α, *to make to follow; to give to follow as a companion; to bestow upon, give, confer; to follow hard:* mid. *to take with one as associate, cause one's self to be accompanied.*

ὀπηδέω, (ὀπηδός,) Lat. *comitari, to accompany another, attend.*

ὀπίζομαι, (ὄπις,) Lat. *revereri, to reverence, revere, respect; to stand in dread of any one.*

ὄπιθε(ν), see foll.

ὄπισθε(ν), (ὄπις,) adv., Lat. *pone, a tergo, from behind; behind, after,* Lat. *pone; in future, hereafter,* Lat. *postea, in posterum; after, afterward,* Lat. *postea:* prep. with gen., *behind,* sometimes with the meaning *inferior to,* Lat. *pone* with acc.

ὄπ(π)η, adv., Lat. *qua, ubi, quo, where, by which way, whither, where? how? whither?*

ὀπίσσω, Ep. for ὀπίσω, (ὄπις,) adv., Lat. *retrorsum, retro, backwards;*

behind, Lat. *pone; afterward,* Lat. *postea; in the future, henceforth*
Γ 411, Lat. *in posterum; over again:* as prep. with gen., *behind, after,*
Lat. *pone* with acc. : πρόσσω καὶ ὀπίσσω, A 343, *the future and the past,*
indicating calculation and forethought.

ὅπλον, ου, τό, *a tool, an instrument; a weapon ;* in ships, *the ropes, rigging,
cordage,* etc., by which the vessels are managed ; in general, *any tools
or implements; a large shield* used by heavy-armed foot soldiers or *hop-
lites* or *heavy-armed;* in pl. *implements of warfare* whether *arms* or
armor.

ὁπλότερος, a, ον, sup. ὁπλότατος, of defective compar., (ὅπλον,) Lat. *junior,
minor natu, younger ; stronger, fresher, more capable of good service.*

'Οπόεις, όεντος, ἡ, *O'-pus,* a town of Lo'-cris.

ὀπός, see ὄψ.

ὁππότε, Ep. for ὁπότε, conj. adv., Lat. *quando, quum, when,* used with the
indic., subj., and opt. ; something is to be supplied before ὁππότε in
Γ 173 ; with subj. and opt. it may have a conditional force, *when =
whenever, in case that, if;* often used with κέν and ἄν, ὁππόταν =
ὁππότ' ἄν ; *whereas, since, because, for that.*

ὁπ(π)ότερος, a, ον, (πότερος,) Lat. *uter, which of the two; one or other of
the two,* Lat. *alteruter :* adv. ὁποτέρως and neu.

ὅππως, Ep. for ὅπως, Lat. *quomodo, in what way, how, after what fashion,
as;* with the sup. it has the same force as Lat. *quam:* final, Lat. *ut,
quo, that, so that, to the end that,* foll. by the subj. to express pres. or
f. purpose, by the opt. to express past purpose.

ὀπτάω, f. ήσω, Lat. *assare, to roast, broil ; to bake, burn,* Lat. *torrēre.*

ὄπωπα, 2 pf. of ὁράω.

ὀπώρη, Ion. for ὀπώρα, ας, ἡ, *the ripening time,* the time between the
rising of the Dog-star and Arc-tu'-rus, nearly the same as our *Dog-
days ; ripe fruits.*

ὀπωρινός, ή, όν, (ὀπώρα,) *of the ripening-time, of early autumn.*

ὁράω, Ep. ὁρόω ; f. ὄψομαι ; 2 aor. εἶδον ; pf. ἑώρακα ; 2 pf. ὄπωπα, οἶδα
with pres. sense ; plupf. ὀπώπειν ; aor. pass. ὤφθην : Lat. *vidēre, to see,
look,* also trans. *see, behold, perceive* (of the mind), *observe, be aware
of, discern, behold;* mid. *to gaze on with interest ;* ὁρᾶν φάος ἠελίοιο, *to
behold the light of the sun* or *day = to live.*

ὀρέγνυμι, par. form to ὀρέγω, f. ὀρέξω, pres. part. ὀρεγνύς A 351, Lat. *por-
rigere, to stretch forth* or *extend* anything, as the foot or the hands, etc. ;
to hand, give, offer: mid. *to stretch one's self ;* of horses, *to stretch themselves* or *go at full speed; to reach after* with the hands ; *to lunge* or
thrust out ; with ἰών, *to stretch one's self going* or *as he goes, stride
along;* with gen. *to grasp after, aim at,* also, *to long for, desire ;* with

acc. *to hit ;* that which is *aimed at* or *desired* is expressed by the gen. case, that which *has been reached* is expressed by the acc. case ; ὀρεκτῇσιν μελίῃσιν, *with outstretched spears.*

ὀρέοντο, Ep. 2 aor. 3 pl. of ὄρνυμι.

'Ορέσβιος, ου, ὁ, *O-res'-bi-us.*

ὀρεσκῷος, ον, Ep. for ὀρέσκοος, (ὄρος, κεῖμαι,) Lat. *in montibus degens, lying on the mountains, wild.*

ὀρέστερος, α, ον, (ὄρος,) Hom. for ὀρεινός, *of the mountains, mountainous.*

'Ορέστης, ου, ὁ, *O-res'-tes,* a Greek ; also, a son of Ag-a-mem'-non.

ὀρεστιάς, άδος, fem. adj., (ὄρος,) *of the mountains, mountain ;* used of mountain nymphs.

ὄρεσφι(ν), Ep. gen. and dat. of ὄρος, *a mountain.*

"Ορθη, ης, ἡ, *Or'-the,* a town of Thes'-sa-ly.

ὀρθόκραιρος, α, ον, (ὀρθος, κραῖρα,) *with horns projecting straight up.*

ὀρθός, ή, όν, (ὄρθαι,) *straight, direct ; straight up,* Lat. *arduus ; in a straight* and *direct line, straightforward ;* hence, *straightforward* or *upright* in a moral sense.

ὀρθόω, f. ὀρθώσω, aor. ὤρθωσα, (ὀρθός,) Lat. *arrigere, erigere, to erect, raise up, set up,* also, *to restore ; to regulate ; to lead aright, to set straight ; to extol :* pass. *to be raised up* or *set upright, stand ; to succeed, prosper ; to be upright* or *just* in character.

ὀρίνω, aor. ὤρινα, aor. pass. ὠρίνθην, (ὄρνυμι,) Lat. *concitare, agitare, to stir, awaken, raise, arouse, move, excite* Γ 395 ; *to scatter, frighten, stir up, confuse ; to move the mind.*

ὅρκιον, ον, τό, (ὅρκος,) *an oath, a solemn oath* accompanied by solemn rites ; *pledge* for fulfilment of an oath, something like Lat. *pignus :* in pl. and referring to the several things specified in a *treaty* as agreement, *articles of a treaty* or *a treaty ;* ὅρκια πιστὰ ταμόντες Γ 73, *after concluding friendship* and *a faithful treaty,* Lat. *foedus ferire ;* by metonymy, *victims* sacrificed to confirm a solemn oath.

ὅρκος, ου, ὁ, Lat. *jusjurandum, an oath ; that by which an oath is sworn, the witness* or the power or deity called upon as witness *of an oath.*

ὁρμαίνω, aor. ὤρμηνα, (ὁρμάω,) *to excite, move quickly* or *hurriedly,* something like Lat. *impetu ferre ; to ponder upon a thing* or *revolve it in the mind,* Lat. *animo volvere ; to ponder, meditate, consider, debate,* Lat. *cogitare ; to desire.*

ὁρμάω, f. ἡσω, aor. ὤρμησα, pf. ὤρμηκα, aor. pass. ὡρμήθην, (ὁρμή,) Lat. *impellere, concitare, excitare, to set moving, excite, urge, animate, rouse ; to move on* or *forward ; to rush* or *charge upon, attack,* Lat. *irruere ; to pursue :* intrans. *to set out ; rush on ;* with inf. *to desire eagerly* or *make an effort to do anything.*

'Ορμένιον, ου, τό, *Or-men'-i-um*, a town of Mag-ne'-si-a.

ὀρμή, ῆs, ἡ, (ὄρνυμι,) Lat. *impetus, an onset, an impulse, the first of an attack; violent impulse of the mind, zeal; the beginning.*

ὅρμημα, ατος, τό, (ὁρμάω,) *a strong desire;* the pl., in cases like B 590, is com. rendered *the struggles and groans on account of (the recovery of) Hel'-en.*

ὅρμος, ου, ὁ, Lat. *statio navalis, roadstead* or *anchorage,* A 435.

'Ορνειαί, ῶν, αἱ, *Or'-ne-ae,* a town of Ar'-go-lis.

ὄρνις, ιθος, acc. -ιθα or ὄρνιν, ὁ, ἡ, Lat. *avis, ales,* (what is the difference between *avis* and *ales?*) *a bird; a bird of prey,* hence *a bird of omen;* see οἰωνός.

ὄρνυμι, f. ὄρσω; aor. ὦρσα, iter. ὄρσασκε; 2 aor. ὤρορον, Ep. mid. 3 pl. ὀρέοντο; 2 pf. ὄρωρα, intrans.: Lat. *excitare, concitare, impellere, to stir up, move, excite, set on, impel; to arouse, instigate, encourage,* Lat. *instigare:* mid. and intrans. ὄρωρα, *to rouse* or *bestir one's self; to start up* Γ 349, *rise, arise,* Lat. *oriri; to be roused* or *excited.*

ὄρος, εος, τό, Ion. οὖρος, Lat. *mons, a mountain, hill.*

ὀρούω, f. σω, (ὄρνυμι,) Lat. *ruere, to dart, rush* or *hurry forward.*

ὀρυμαγδός, οῦ, ὁ, *any loud inarticulate sound* not made by human voices, *crash, roaring* as of water, *rattling, tumult of battle, noise of a crowd, clash of weapons,* etc.

ὀρφανικός, ή, όν, (ὀρφανός, hence Eng. *orphan,*) Lat. *orphanus, of an orphan, orphan, orphaned.*

ὅρχαμος, ου, ὁ, (ὄρχος,) *the first in rank, leader.*

ὀρχέομαι, (deriv. uncertain,) *to dance,* Lat. *saltare.*

ὀρχηστής, ου, or -στήρ, ῆρος, ὁ, (ὀρχέομαι,) Lat. *saltator, a dancer, one who dances.*

'Ορχομενός, οῦ, ὁ, *Or-chom'-e-nus,* name of two cities.

ὄρωρα, 2 pf. of ὄρνυμι.

ὅs, ἥ, ὅ; οὗ, ἧς, οὗ, Ep. ὅου, ἔης; dat. ᾧ, ᾗ, ᾧ; neu. acc. ὅ; Ep. dat. pl. ᾗς, ᾗσι. Sometimes used as a demon. pron. nearly equivalent to οὗτος and ὅδε, Lat. *hic, ille, this, that, he, she, it.* Relative pron. Lat. *qui, quae, quod, who, which, what, that;* the relative is often attracted into the case of its antecedent, and the antecedent is sometimes drawn into the relative clause, and even into the same case with the pron.; it is used to introduce a final cause like Lat. *qui* for *ut, who* == *that he might;* causal, *who* = *because he;* οὗ *when,* ἐξ and ἀφ' οὗ *since when,* ἐν ᾧ *while,* εἰς ὅ *till,* ᾗ *where,* Lat. *qua,* ᾗ with sup. == Lat. *quam,* ὅs καί *who even* or *also,* οἵ τ' ἄρα *and then (those) who,* ὅς γε *even, who at least,* see ὅs περ.

ὅs, ἥ, ὅν, poss. pron., Lat. *suus, his, her, its;* the Ep. forms ᾗφι and dat. pl. ᾗσι are found : used for σός, Lat. *tuus*, and for ἐμός, Lat. *meus*.

ὀσ(σ)άκι, (ὅ(σ)ος,) adv., Lat. *quoties, as often as.*

ὅσ(σ)ος, η, ον, Lat. *quantus, as much as, how much, as great as, how great, as long as, how long, as far as, how far;* simply *as:* τόσος . . . ὅσος, Lat. *tantus . . . quantus:* adv., Lat. *quantum, quantopere, as much as, as far as,* with compar. and sup., *by how much, by so far as, by as much as, so far as;* ὅσ(σ)ον τε, *about as far as.*

ὅς περ, ἥ περ, ὅ περ, Lat. *qui quidem, who* or *which indeed, which very;* see Anabasis, Book I. chap. IV. sec. 5, *which very thing.*

ὅσσα, ης, ἡ, (docs Lat. *rumor* or *fama* correspond to any of these definitions?) *rumor, report;* personified, *Fame, Rumor; a divine* or *warning voice; a voice.*

ὄσσε, τώ, Lat. *oculi, the (two) eyes,* neu. du., may take a pl. adj. or verb.

ὄσσομαι, (ὄσσα or ὄσσε,) Lat. *divinare, to see; to portend, presage, threaten, forebode; to picture to one's self, see in mind,* Lat. *in animo fingere.*

ὄσσος, Ep. for ὅσος.

ὅς τε and Ep. mas. ὅτε, ἥ τε, τό τε, Ep. for ὅς τε, ἥ τε, ὅ τε, only a stronger form of ὅς, *who* or *which in fact, who, which.*

ὀστέον, ου, τό, Lat. *os, a bone.*

ὅστις, ἥτις, ὅτι, gen. οὗτινος, ἧστινος, οὗτινος; Ep. forms, ὅτις, ὅττι, gen. ὅττεο, ὅτ(τ)ευ, ὅτεῳ, neu. nom. and acc. pl. ἄσσα, gen. ὅτεων, dat. ὀτέοισιν and ὀτέῃσιν, in nom. and acc. Hom. has also the usu. forms : Lat. *quicunque, quisquis, whosoever, whichsoever;* indirectly interrog.

ὅταν, for ὅτ' ἄν = Ep. ὅτε κεν ; see ὅτε.

ὅ τε or ὅτε, neu. of ὅστε, and Ep. mas.

ὅτε, Lat. *quum, quando, when;* may be correlative with any adv. of time ; *when, where, because, since, how;* εἰς ὅτε κεν *until, as long as,* πρίν γ' ὅτε *before (the time) when,* ὡς ὅτε *as when, just as,* ὅτε μή *save when* or *unless,* ὅτε δή ῥα *when truly indeed* or *as soon as,* ὅτε μεν . . . ὅτε δέ *at one time . . . at another, now . . . now,* ὅτε περ *when, just when, when indeed;* in the last example the encl. περ gives force to the adv., and is sometimes not rendered : as causal, Lat. *quandoquidem, since, whereas.*

ὅτι, Ep. ὅττι, Lat. *quod,* conj., *that;* orig. ὅ τι, neu. of ὅστις : ὅτι μή *except that, unless,* used after a neg. sentence ; μὴ ὅτι . . . ἀλλά, *not that* or *not only . . . but.*

ὅτι, Ep. ὅττι, causal particle, Lat. *quod, because, therefore;* with sup. to strengthen the force of the sup., like Lat. *quam, as . . . as possible.*

ὀτραλέως, (ὀτρηρός,) adv., Lat. *agiliter, quickly, promptly* Γ 260, *actively, nimbly; zealously,* Lat. *studiose.*

'Οτρεύς, έως, ὁ, O'-treus, a Phry'-gi-an prince.

ὀτρηρός, α, ον, (ὀτρύνω,) Lat. agilis, active, quick; busy, diligent, ready; zealous.

ὄτριχες, nom. pl. of ὄθριξ.

ὀτρύνω, iter. impf. ὀτρύνεσκον, Ep. f. ὀτρυνέω, aor. ὤτρυνα, to incite, stir up, encourage, arouse; to urge on, prompt; speed, hasten; (do Lat. incitare, instigare, impellere, maturare correspond exactly to these definitions?): mid. and pass. to make haste or bestir one's self.

οὐ, οὐκ, οὐκί, οὐχ, οὐχί, adv., Lat. non, not, used to express absolute negation, whereas μή expresses negation as imagined, assumed, willed, or sought for; οὐ may be used in independent or dependent clauses; οὐ is followed by acc. in solemn asseverations, no, by —; οὐ πάνυ, οὔτι, not by any means; οὐ πάμπαν, in no respect: interrog., οὐ is used in questions expecting an affirmative answer: see μή.

οὗ, Hom. ἕο, Lat. sui, 3 pers. pron. encl.; also reflexive pron., not encl.

οὖας, οὔατος, τό, Ep. and Ion. for οὖς, dat. pl. οὔασι, the ear, Lat. auris.

οὔασι(ν), Ep. dat. pl. of οὖς, which see.

οὖδας, δεος, τό, (ἕδος,) the ground, earth; surface of the ground on which we stand and walk.

οὐδέ, (οὐ, δέ,) Lat. neque, nec, nc . . . quidem, and not, yet not, but not, nor, nor yet, not even, and also not; οὐδέ . . . οὐδέ, not even . . . nor yet, nor . . . nor; οὐδὲ γὰρ οὐδέ, for by no means, or the neg. simply repeated for greater force, for not even, not even; μὲν οὐδέ, but not, but also not; οὐδὲ εἶς, not a soul, not a single one.

οὐδείς, οὐδεμία, οὐδέν, οὐδενός, οὐδεμιᾶς, οὐδενός, (οὐδέ, εἷς, μία, ἕν,) Lat. nullus, no one, none, no, lit. not one, and not one, not even one: neu. as adv., in no respect, by no means, in nothing.

οὐδέπω, Lat. necdum, and not yet, not yet, in Hom. separated by tmesis.

οὐδός, οῦ, ὁ, Ion. for ὀδός, (some older authorities say from ὀδός,) Lat. limen, a threshold.

οὐκ, see οὐ.

'Οὐκαλέγων, οντος ὁ, U-cal'-e-gon, a counsellor of Troy.

οὐκέτι, οὐκ-έτι, (οὐκ, ἔτι,) Lat. non amplius, adv. no longer, nor further, not any more.

οὐκί, see οὐ.

οὐλόμενος, η, ον, adj., orig. Ep. 2 aor. mid. part. of ὄλλυμι, something like Lat. perniciosus, deadly, destructive, direful; accursed, lost.

οὖλος, η, ον, Lat. perniciosus, destructive, fatal, baneful.

οὖλος, η, ον, (Ep. for ὅλος, Eng. whole), whole, entire; whole in the sense of incessant, constant, continuous; shaggy, thick, soft, woolly, curly.

οὐλόχυται, ῶν, αἱ, (οὐλαί, χέω,) coarsely-ground (parched) barley sprinkled

sprinkled coarse barley meal, A 449. It was com. salted and scattered over the altar and victim before the sacrifice ; οὐλοχύτας κατάρχεσθαι, *to begin the solemn rites by sprinkling on the coarse barley meal.*

Οὐλυμπόνδε, see Ὀλυμπόνδε.

Οὔλυμπος, see Ὄλυμπος.

οὖν, inferential, Lat. *ergo, igitur, itaque, therefore, then, accordingly, consequently, hence;* after any digression, οὖν serves to resume the thought, ὡς οὖν *when therefore* or *then,* ἐπεὶ οὖν *when then;* it serves also to append a circumstance to something that goes before, *yet, certainly, surely, truly;* οὖν renders a relative word less definite ; οὐκοῦν *therefore,* οὔκουν *not therefore.*

οὕνεκα = οὗ ἕνεκα, something like Lat. *propterea, therefore; because, that,* Lat. *quia;* lit., *on which account.*

οὐνομ-, Ion. for ὀνομ-.

οὔ ποθι, adv., Lat. *nusquam, nowhere.*

οὔ ποτε, adv., Lat. *nunquam, never.*

οὔ πω, adv., Lat. *nondum, not yet,* B 122.

Οὐρανίωνες, (οὐρανός,) Lat. *coelites,* as adj. ; *heavenly, of the heavens;* subst. *the gods.*

οὐρανόθεν, adv., Lat. *e coelo, from heaven.*

οὐρανόθι πρό Γ 3 = πρὸ οὐρανοῦ, *before the heavens* or *under the sky.*

οὐρανός, οῦ, ὁ, Lat. *coelum, heaven; the starry heavens, the sky, the firmament; seat* or *home of the gods.*

οὐρεύς, ῆος, ὁ, Ion. for ὀρεύς, Lat. *mulus, a mule.*

οὖρος, εος, τό, Ion. for ὄρος, Lat. *mons, a mountain.*

οὖρος, ου, ὁ, Lat. *secundus ventus, fair* or *prospering wind.*

οὐρός, οῦ, ὁ, (ὀρύσσω,) *a ship channel* leading to the camp.

οὖς, ὦτος, τό, see οὖας.

οὐτάζω, άσω, *to hit; to wound;* iter. οὐτήσασκε.

οὔτε, (οὔ, τε,) Lat. *neque, and not;* οὔτε . . . οὔτε, *neither . . . nor;* may answer to ὀδέ, οὐ, δέ, τε, καί.

οὔτι, adv., see οὔτις, *not at all, by no means,* B 833.

οὐτιδανός, adj., (οὔτις,) *worthless,* A 231, *useless.*

οὔτις, οὔτινος, (οὐ, τίς,) Lat. *nullus, no one, none;* neu. as adv., *by no means;* sometimes the parts are written separately, as οὔ μέ τι.

οὔτοι, (οὐ, τοί,) Lat. *non sane, assuredly not.*

οὗτος, αὕτη, τοῦτο, τούτου, ταύτης, τούτου, pl. οὗτοι, αὗται, ταῦτα, gen. τούτων in 3 genders, neu. acc. ταῦτα, Lat. *hic, this;* ἐκεῖνος refers to the more remote, οὗτος to the nearer, of two objects ; for οὗτος and ὅδε in opp. see ὅδε ; τοῦτο μέν . . . τοῦτο δέ, *partly . . . partly;* neu. pl. as adv., *on this account.*

οὕτως, οὕτω, Lat. *sic, thus, in this manner, so; simply, no more than; so*

Lat. *tam;* as opp. to ὧδε, it refers to what goes *before,* ὧδε refers to what follows.

όφείλω, f. όφειλήσω; aor. ὤφείλησα; 2 aor. ὤφελον, Ep. ὤφελλον; pf. ὤφείληκα: Lat. *debēre, to owe; be in debt; to be under obligation, ought.*

όφέλλω, Ep. for όφείλω, Ep. 2 aor. ὄφελον, Lat. *debēre, to owe, ought;* often with εἴθε or Ep. αἴθε, ὥς, μή.

όφέλλω, f. όφελῶ, aor. ὤφειλα, Lat. *augēre, to augment, increase, make more, enlarge; to make to thrive, further; to succor, aid.*

ὄφελος, ον, τό, (όφέλλω,) *aid, profit, advantage;* compare Lat. *utilitas, usus.*

όφθαλμός, οῦ, ὁ, (όφθῆναι,) Lat. *oculus, the eye.*

ὄφρα, conj., Lat. *ut, quo, in order that, that;* adv., Lat. *donec, quamdiu, dum, so long as; until,* Lat. *usquedum.*

όφρνόεις, εσσα, εν, (όφρύς,) stric. *indicating haughtiness by the elevation of the eyebrows, haughty, towering;* hence, *high, on the brow of a steep hill* or *rock, situated high up.*

όφρύς, ύος, ἡ, acc. pl. όφρύας or irreg. contd. -ῦς, Lat. *supercilium, the eyebrow, the brow,* also *the brow of a hill,* also *pride, gravity.*

ὄχα, (ἔχω,) Ep. adv., Lat. *eminenter, by far.*

όχεύς, Ion. gen. ῆος, ὁ, (ἔχω,) Lat. *retinaculum, any fastener or holder; the strap* passing under the chin *for fastening the helmet,* Γ 372, Lat. *lorum galeae; a bar, bolt, a clasp.*

όχέω, Ion. impf. όχέεσκον; f. ήσω; (ὄχος;) *to carry, convey, bear; to endure, suffer, sustain ; to hold.*

όχθέω, f. ήσω, aor. ὤχθησα, *to be vexed, be displeased,* Α 570, Lat. *graviter ferre, indignari.*

ὄχθη, ης, ἡ, Lat. *ripa, bank; shore,* Lat. *litus.*

ὄχος, εος, τό, (ἔχω,) *that which holds (and bears),* and so *a vehicle;* pl. *chariots,* Ep. dat. pl. ὄχεσφι.

ὄψ, όπός, dat. όπί, acc. ὄπα, Lat. *vox, voice; a word, speech, that which is spoken* (by the voice).

όψέ, adv., *after, afterwards, finally.*

ὄψεαι, see όράω.

όψίγονος, ον, (όψέ, γόνος,) Lat. *posthumus, late-born;* Γ 353, όψιγόνων άνθρώπων, *of men born in a later age* = *of posterity,* Lat. *posterorum.*

ὄψιμος, ον, (όψέ,) poet. for ὄψιος, Lat. *tardus, tardy, late.*

ὄψις, εως, ἡ, Ion. gen. ιος, (ὄψομαι, assumed f. of όράω,) *the power of vision, sight; that which appears to the sight, appearance, aspect;* compare Lat. *visus, adspectus, conspectus.*

όψιτέλεστος, ον, (όψέ, τελέω,) *accomplished* or *to be accomplished at a late period, late of fulfilment.*

Π.

πάγεν, 2 aor. Ep. 3 pl. of πήγνυμι, which see.

παγχρύσεος, ον, (πᾶς, χρυσός,) all of gold.

πάγχυ, Hom. for πάνυ, (πᾶς,) adv., Lat. omnino, altogether, entirely.

παιδνός, οῦ, ὁ, Lat. puer, a boy, child, lad : stric. adj., (παῖς).

παιδοφόνος, ον, (παῖς, φόνος,) child-murdering, child-killing.

παιηων, ονος, ὁ, a triumphal or festal song, pæan.

Παίονες, ων, οἱ, the Pæ-o´-ni-ans.

παῖς, παιδός, dat. παιδί, acc. παῖδα, gen. pl. παίδων, dat. παισί, Ep. παί-
δεσσι, ὁ or ἡ, Lat. puer, a child, either son or daughter ; ὁ, a son, boy,
youth ; ἡ, daughter, maiden, girl.

Παισός, οῦ, ἡ, Ap´-æ-sus, a town of Mys´-i-a.

παιφάσσω, to stare or rush wildly about, Lat. ruere.

παλαιός, ά, όν, (πάλαι,) see Lat. vetus, pristinus, antiquus ; old, ancient,
antiquated ; old, aged, venerable, Lat. senex.

παλαιγενής, ές, (πάλαι, γενέσθαι,) born long ago, aged.

παλάμη, ης, ἡ, Ep. gen. and dat. παλάμηφι(ν) Γ 338, Lat. palma, the palm
of the hand, hence the hand ; orig. a mechanical contrivance, hence a
device or contrivance ; violence.

παλάσσω, f. ξω, (πάλλω,) to spatter, stain, moisten, sprinkle, contaminate ;
root of Eng. plash ; to shake and draw lots.

παλίλλογος, ον, (πάλιν, λέγω,) Lat. recollectus, collected or brought together
again, counted again.

παλιμπλάζω, (πάλιν, πλάζω,) used in aor. pass. part. παλιμπλαγχθείς, Lat.
repulsus, repulsed ; driven back, Lat. retro repulsus.

πάλιν, adv., Lat. rursus, iterum, again, anew ; on the contrary, Lat. contra ; back, back again.

παλινάγρετος, ον (πάλιν, ἀγρέω,) revocable, that can be recalled.

παλίνορσος, ον, (πάλιν, ὄρνυμι,) darting back ; recurring, and so inveterate.

Παλλάς, άδος, ἡ, (πάλλω,) Lat. Pal´-las or Min-er´-va ; with Ἀθήνη or
Ἀθηναίη.

πάλλω ; f. παλῶ ; aor. ἔπηλα ; Ep. 2 aor. part. (ἀμ)πεπαλών, 2 aor. mid.
Ep. 3 sing. πάλτο ; pf. πέπαλμαι : Lat. vibrare, to shake till one leaps
out Γ 316, brandish, swing, hurl : mid. to cast lots among themselves,
draw lots ; to quiver through agitation : intrans. to tremble, quiver ; to
spring.

παλύνω, νῶ, (πάλη,) to strew upon, strew as with fine meal, etc. ; to sprinkle, moisten.

πάμπαν, (rep. of πᾶν,) adv., Lat. *omnino, altogether, entirely;* with neg. particles, *by no means, not at all, not by any means.*

πάμπρωτος, η, ον, (πᾶς, πρῶτος,) *first one of all, the first.*

παμφαίνω, (πᾶς, φαίνω,) *to shine clearly.*

παμφανόων, όωσα, gen. όωντος, Ep. part. from παμφαίνω, B 458 *all-shining, beaming.*

Παναχαιοί, ῶν, οἱ, (πάντες Ἀχαιοί,) Lat. *omnes A-chi'-vi, all the A-chai'-ans, host of the Greeks, united A-chai'-ans.*

παναίολος, ον, (πᾶς, αἰόλος,) *variegated, of changing hue all over.*

Πάνδαρος, ου, ὁ, *Pan'-da-rus,* commanded the Ze-le'-ans.

Πανέλληνες, ων, οἱ, (πάντες Ἕλληνες,) Lat. *omnes Grae'-ci, all the Greeks.*

πανάποτμος, ον, (πᾶς, ἄποτμος,) *all-unfortunate.*

παναφῆλιξ, ικος, adj., (πᾶς, ἀφῆλιξ (ἀπό, ἧλιξ,)) *entirely without companions of equal age.*

παναώριος, ον, (πᾶς, ἄωρος, (a priv., ὥρα,)) *all-immature, all-unseasonable.*

πανημέριος, a, ον, (πᾶς, ἡμέρα,) Lat. *per totum diem, all day long,* A 472.

Πάνθοος, ου, ὁ, *Pan'tho-us,* a counsellor of Troy.

παννύχιος, a, ον, (πᾶς, νύξ,) also πάννυχος, Lat. *pernox, totam noctem durans, lasting all night long, the whole night through* B 24; *all the remainder of the night.*

Πανοπεύς, έως, ὁ, *Pan'-o-pus,* father of E-pe'-us; a city of Pho'-cis.

πανσυδίη, Ion. for πανσυδία, (πᾶς, σύδην,) adv., stric. an old dat. from an obsol. nom., *with all haste, with the greatest speed.*

πάντη, and πάντῃ, (πᾶς,) adv., *on every side, in all directions; in every way; quite, altogether.*

παντοῖος, a, ον, (πᾶς,) *of all kinds, manifold, of every sort or kind.*

πάντοσε, (πᾶς,) adv., Lat. *undique, on every side; in all ways.*

παπταίνω, f. ανῶ, (πτήσσω,) *to look carefully and suspiciously around; to look or seek after; to search for.*

πάρ, or πάρα if foll. its case, Ep. for παρά; for πάρεισι, A 174, are *present;* for πάρεστι.

παρά, prep., Ep. πάρ, παραί: with gen. Lat. *a* or *ab* with ablative, *from, from beside;* of source, *from:* with dat. Lat. *juxta, apud,* with acc. *alongside of, by, beside, with; before,* Lat. *coram:* with acc. *to, towards; beside, along by, going along by, close to, by; unto; beside, except; against, contrary to; beyond,* παρὰ δύναμιν *beyond the strength; because of;* παρὰ τί, *on what account?* *by* or *according to* (as in the N. Testament), *compared with, as;* παρὰ πολύ, *by much; through:* in compo. παρά has the chief meanings found above; also, *amiss, wrong.*

παραβλήδην, (παραβάλλω, (παρά, βάλλω,)) adv., *thrown in sideways* or *at the side with evil intent ; deceitfully,* Δ 6.

παραβλώσκω, for parts see βλώσκω, (παρά, βλώσκω,) *to come* or *go beside any one to protect and aid.*

παραδέκομαι, Ion. for παραδέχομαι, which see.

παραδέχομαι, f. παραδέξομαι, (παρά, δέχομαι,) *to receive* or *obtain at the hands of another.*

παραιφάμενος, Ep. pres. mid. part. of παράφημι, which see.

παράκειμαι, (παρά, κεῖμαι,) impf. Hom. 3 sing. παρεκέσκετο, Lat. *adjacere, to lie near* or *next to, be close by.*

παρακοίτης, ου, ὁ, (παρά, ἀκοίτης,) *a bed-fellow, a husband.*

παράκοιτις, ιος, ἡ, (παρά, ἄκοιτις,) Lat. *uxor, a wife,* Γ 53.

παραλέγω, f. ἔξω, aor. παρελεξάμην, (παρά, λέγω,) *to lay near ;* mid. *to lie beside* or *near* Β 515, *lie with.*

παραπήγνυμι, f. ήξω, (παρά, πήγνυμι,) *to fix near.*

παρασχέμεν, Ep. 2 aor. inf. act. of παρέχω.

παράφημι, f. παραφήσω, (παρά, φημί,) *to exhort,* Lat. *hortari ;* Lat. *suadēre, to advise ; to win over ; to deceive ;* lit. *to speak to.*

παρδαλέη, ης, ἡ, *a panther* or *leopard skin.*

παρατρέχω, for parts see τρέχω, (παρά, τρέχω,) *to run past* or *along by, run up to* or *overtake.*

παρέζομαι, f. εδοῦμαι, (παρά, ἕζομαι,) Lat. *juxta sedēre, to sit near* Α 557, *take one's seat beside.*

παρειά, ᾶς, ἡ, (παρά,) Lat. *gena, the cheek.*

παραφθάνω, other parts from -φθα-, (παρά, φθάνω,) *to be before, anticipate ; to prevent ; to come up with* or *go by.*

πάρειμι, (παρά, εἰμί,) Lat. *adesse, praesentem esse, to be by* or *present at, be present, be at hand ;* with the dat. *to be near* or *in, be in one's power, belong to ; to be present* and *ready to assist,* (is Lat. *interesse* the equivalent of this ?) *to be at,* i. e. *to have arrived at :* impersonal, *to be possible, to be allowable* or *allowed.*

παρεῖπον, (παρά, εἶπον,) see εἶπον, Lat. *persuadēre, to advise, exhort, persuade ; to talk over, win over.*

παρεκέσκετο, impf. Hom. 3 sing. of παράκειμαι, which see.

παρέρχομαι, f. παρελεύσομαι, 2 aor. παρῆλθον, 2 pf. παρελήλυθα, (παρά, ἔρχομαι,) Lat. *praeterire, to pass by, go beside* or *beyond, vanish,* also *to pass over* without notice, *to escape notice, evade ; to surpass* or *pass by ; to pass on to* a place ; of time, *to elapse.*

παρέχω, for prin. parts see ἔχω, (παρά, ἔχω,) *to hold ready* or *beside, present, provide ; to offer, bestow, produce ; allow, grant, afford ; to bring* or *put forward ;* impersonal like Lat. *licet.*

παρήιον, ου, τό, Ion. for παρεῖον (a form which Hom. does not use), (some have suggested as deriv. παρά, ἠιών, but this does not seem probable,) *the cheek* or *jaw ; the cheek-piece.*

πάρημαι, (παρά, ἧμαι,) Lat. *adsidēre, to sit at* or *beside, sit near,* used with the dat. ; *to dwell among* or *with,* Lat. *versari apud.*

παρθενικός, κή, κόν, (παρθένος,) Lat. *virgineus, virginalis, maidenly, of* or *pertaining to maidens, virgin, maiden.*

Παρθένιος, ου, ὁ, (παρθένος,) *the Par-the'-ni-us,* a river of Paph-la-go'-ni-a ; lit. *of a maiden,* hence *pure.*

παρθένος, ου, ἡ, Lat. *virgo, a maiden, virgin.*

Πάρις, ιδος, and ιος, ὁ, *Par'-is,* son of Pri'-am, seducer of Hel'-en ; called by the Greeks Ἀλέξανδρος, which name is usu. found in the Il.

παρίστημι, see ἵστημι for prin. parts, also for trans. and intrans. tenses ; (παρά, ἵστημι,) trans. *to place beside* or *near, place before* or *offer ; suggest; to bring forward* or *place before, near* or *by,* in all the various applications ; mid. *to bring to* or *set by one's side, place near, persuade :* intrans. Lat. *adstare, to stand by* or *draw near,* also in the sense of *giving aid, to stand by and assist ; be close at hand, approach, to step up close to, to come over to the side of ; to submit ; to happen, present itself, occur.*

παρμέμβλωκε, Ep. pf. of παραβλώσκω, which see.

πάροιθε(ν), (πάρος,) prep. with gen., Lat. *ante, coram, pro, before, before the face, in one's presence ; before, previous to :* adv. *previously, formerly, heretofore,* Lat. *ante, antea.*

πάρος, adv., Lat. *ante, antea ; formerly, before ; previously, before, before that,* Lat. *antequam, priusquam ; too, rather;* of place, *before;* for πρίν πάρος . . . πρίν γε = πρίν . . . πρίν γε, *before that, rather* or *sooner . . . than,* Lat. *priusquam ;* prep. poet. for πρό.

Παρρασί(α)(η), ας, ἡ, *Par-rha'-si-a,* a town of Ar-ca'-di-a.

πᾶς, πᾶσα, πᾶν, παντός, πάσης, παντός, Hom. gen. pl. πασέων, πασάων, poet. dat. pl. πάντεσσι, Lat. *omnis, all ;* also something like ὅλος, Lat. *totus, whole, all, entire ; every,* Lat. *quisque ;* with ἅμα, *all together ;* with ὁμῶς, *all,* etc., *alike ;* with τίς, *each one ;* with εὖ, see εὖ ; δώδεκα πάντες, *twelve in all :* neu. as adv. *in all respects, utterly, wholly.*

πάσσασθαι, aor. Ep. inf. mid. of πατέομαι, which see.

πάσσω, parts formed from πασ-, Lat. *inspergere, to strew* or *sprinkle upon* anything.

πάσχω, f. πείσομαι ; 2 aor. ἔπαθον ; 2 pf. πέπονθα, Ep. 2 pl. πέποσθε Γ 99, Ep. part. πεπαθυῖα : Lat. *pati, to suffer, bear, endure ;* μή τι πάθω, *lest I suffer something* or *something happen to me ;* part. with interrog.

τί, *suffering what* or *what ails? why? wherefore?* with εὖ or κακῶς, *to suffer good* or *ill*.

πατέομαι, f. πάσομαι, aor. ἐπασάμην, pf. πέπασμαι, *to eat; taste; partake of, enjoy,* Lat. *frui.*

πατήρ, πατέρος, sync. πατρός, dat. pl. πατράσι, ὁ, Lat. *pater, father;* Zeus is called πατὴρ ἀνδρῶν τε θεῶν τε ; in pl. *ancestors,* Lat. *majores.*

πάτος, ου, ὁ, *a beaten* or *frequented path, a foot-path.*

πάτρ(α)(η), as, ης, ἡ, (πατήρ,) Lat. *patria, fatherland, home; a house, tribe,* Lat. *gens,* (why not *natio* too ?)

πατρίς, ίδος, ἡ, adj. (poet. fem. of foll.), Lat. *patria, of one's fathers, native.*

πάτριος, adj., *of one's fathers.*

Πάτροκλος, ου, ὁ, Hom. gen. Πατροκλῆος, acc. -κλῆα, and voc. -κλεις ; *Patro'-clus,* a friend of *A-chil'-les.*

πατρώϊος, α, ον, (πατήρ,) Lat. *paternus, paternal, from* or *pertaining to one's father, hereditary,* (what is the difference between *paternus* and *patrius ?*)

παῦρος, α, ον, *small; short; feeble;* pl. *few,* Lat. *pauci.*

παυσωλή, ῆς, ἡ, *rest, repose.*

παύω, f. παύσω, aor. ἔπαυσα, pf. πέπαυκα, aor. pass. ἐπαύ(σ)θην, deriv. meaning of Lat. *sedare, to check, restrain, suppress,* with part. *make to cease* or *leave off, stop, calm; abate; to keep back* or *stop from,* with gen. something like Lat. *reprimere; to put an end to:* mid. and pass. *to be made to stop, to desist, to cease, leave off, take rest from, cease* Γ 112, *rest.*

Παφλαγών, ονος, ὁ, *a Paph-la-go'-ni-an.*

παχύς, ῦια, ύ ; compar. πάσσων and παχίων, sup. πάχιστος ; Lat. *crassus, thick, large, coarse, stout, heavy; fat, stupid,* Lat. *pinguis; thick, clotted.*

πεδάω, (πέδη,) *to fetter; to bind, to ensnare, hamper.*

πέδιλον, ου, τό, pl. in Hom. *sandals, any foot-covering.*

πεδίον, ου, τό, (πέδον,) Lat. *campus, a plain, level ground, an open plain:* adv. πεδίονδε, *toward the plain.*

πεζός, ή, όν, (πέζα,) Lat. *pedester, on foot; on land;* in pl. *soldiers who fight on foot, infantry:* adv. πεζῇ, *on foot.*

πείθω, f. πείσω, Ep. πεπιθήσω, Hom. πιθήσω ; aor. ἔπεισα, Hom. part. πιθήσας ; 2 aor. ἔπιθον, Ep. πέπιθον ; pf. πέπεικα ; 2 pf. πέποιθα ; Ep. 2 plup. πεποίθεα, pl. ἐπέπιθμεν ; the Hom. forms πιθήσω (*I shall obey*) and πιθήσας (*trusting*) are intrans. : Lat. *persuadēre, to persuade, to influence any one, induce, prevail upon, win over; to move by persuasion, mollify, appease; to persuade to action, excite, impel, urge on:* mid. and pass. *to be persuaded, be prevailed upon, to yield to persuasion, yield;* hence *to obey, give obedience to,* Lat. *obedire ;* we have confidence in one who can *prevail upon* or *influence* us, hence *to confide* or *trust in,* Lat. *confidere ;* in a bad sense, *to prevail upon one to his hurt, mislead.*

πεινάω, inf. πεινῆν, Ep. πεινήμεναι, see Hadley and Allen's Grammar, 412 and D ; f. πεινήσω ; aor. ἐπείνησα : *to suffer hunger,* Lat. *fame premi ; to hunger for* or *crave, long for,* with gen.

πεῖραρ, ατος, τό, Hom. for πέρας, *the end, the extremity; the end* in the com. accepted sense of the word : see Lat. *finis, terminus.*

πειράω, f. πειρήσω or -μαι, aor. ἐπειρησάμην, pf. πεπείρημαι, aor. pass. ἐπειρήθην, Lat. *conari,* (are *tentare* and *experiri* Lat. equivalents ?) *to try, undertake, make trial, attempt, endeavor ;* with acc. *to attempt anything upon* some one ; with gen. *to make trial of* or *prove, put to proof, examine, prove, question.*

πειρητίζω, = foreg.

Πειρίθοος, ου, ὁ, *Pi-rith'-o-us,* son of Zeus and Di'-a.

Πείροος, ου, ὁ, *Pi'-ro-us,* a leader of the Thra'-ci-ans.

πείρω, f. περῶ, aor. ἔπειρα, pf. πέπαρμαι, 2 aor. pass. ἐπάρην, Lat. *transfigere, transfodere, to pierce entirely through, to pierce through, spit meat, transfix.*

Πελάγων, οντος, ὁ, *Pel'-a-gon.*

πελάζω, f. πελάσω, aor. (ἐ)πέλασ(σ)α, pf. πέπλημαι, aor. pass. ἐπ(ε)λά(σ)θην, Ep. 2 aor. pass. ἐπλήμην, (πέλας,) Lat. *appropinquare, to approach, come near :* trans. *to cause to approach, bring towards* or *near :* mid. and pass. *to be made to approach, come close to.*

Πελασγικός, ή, όν, *Pe-las'-gi-an.*

Πελασγός, οῦ, ὁ, *a Pe-las'-gi-an.*

πέλεκυς, εως, ὁ, Ep. dat. pl. πελέκεσσι, *a battle-axe, an axe,* (see Lat. *bipennis*).

Πελίας or ης, ου, ὁ, *Pe'-li-as,* uncle of Ja'-son.

Πελλήνη, ης, ἡ, *Pel-le'-ne,* a town of A-cha'-i-a.

Πέλοψ, οπος, ὁ, (πελός, ὄψ,) lit. *dark-faced, Pe'-lops,* from whom the name Pel'-o-pon-ne'-sus.

πέλεια, ας, ἡ, or ειάς, άδος, ἡ, (πελός,) *a wild dove* or *pigeon* of a bluish color.

πελεμίζω, f. ίξω, (deriv. uncertain, perhaps from πέλω,) *to shake anything, brandish :* pass. conveys also the idea of *to be shaken from a position* or *repulsed :* compare Lat. *quassare, movēre, commovēre.*

πέλω, dep. πέλομαι, iter. impf. πελεσκ-, sync. in 2 aor., 2 sing. ἔπλεο and ἔπλευ, *to be moving ; to come,* Lat. *venire ; to be* or *wont to be,* implying continuance, Β 480, Γ 3.

πέλωρ, τό, indecl., also πέλωρον, ον, B 321, Lat. *monstrum, a monster.*

πελώριος, adj., (πέλωρ,) Lat. *ingens, immanis, immense, huge, monstrous, enormous.*

πέμπω, f. πέμψω, aor. ἔπεμψα, 2 pf. πέπομφα, aor. pass. ἐπέμφθην, Lat. *mittere, to send ; to dismiss, send away,* Lat. *dimittere ; to send,* with something the sense of Lat. *trajicere, cast, send from one.*

πεμπώβολον, ου, τό, (πέμπε, ὀβολός,) *a five-pronged fork.*

πένθος, εος, τό, Lat. *luctus, sorrow, grief ; sadness, longing, a misfortune.*

πενθερός, οῦ, ὁ, *father-in-law.*

πένομαι, *to toil, work :* trans. *to toil at.*

πενταέτηρος, ον, poet. for πενταετής, (πέντε, ἔτος,) Lat. *quinquennis, five years old.*

πέντε, Lat. *quinque, five.*

πεντήκοντα, οἱ, αἱ, τά, Lat. *quinquaginta, fifty.*

πεπαρμένος, see πείρω.

πεπιθεῖν, Ep. 2 aor. inf. (ἐ)πέπιθμεν, plup. 1 pl. πεπιθήσω, Ep. f. of πείθω, which see.

πέπληγον, πεπληγώς, see πλήσσω.

πέπλος, ου, ὁ, *a cloth cover ; an outer garment* or *robe, a cloak,* Lat. *peplum ; a cover, curtain.*

πεπνυμένος, see πνέω.

πέποιθα, see πείθω.

πέπονθα, πέποσθε, see πάσχω.

πεποτήαται, see ποτάομαι.

πεπρωμένος, πέπρωται, see πόρω.

πέπων, ον, ονος, Lat. *maturus, mitis, ripe, mature, tender, mellow ; dear ; gentle, tender, weak,* Lat. *mollis ; faint-hearted, coward.*

πέρ, encl. particle, it emphasizes and adds force, is used with a variety of words, especially participles, *very* A 352, *much even, — at all, just ; besides, yet, however, as regards that* or *for that matter, at all events ;* καίπερ or καὶ . . . πέρ with a part. *though,* A 577 ; τῇ περ, *in which very ; as he* or *it is ;* πέρ is freq. separated from the word to which it belongs.

περάαν, Ep. for περᾶν, see περάω.

Περαιβοί, ῶν, οἱ, *Per-rhœ´-bi-ans,* a Thes-sa´-li-an tribe, about Do-do´-na.

πέπυσμαι, πεπύθοιτο, pf. and Ep. redupl. 2 aor. opt. of πυνθάνομαι.

πέρ(α)(η)ν, adv., Lat. *trans, ultra, beyond, across, opposite, over against.*

περάω, f. άσω, *to export and sell.*

περάω, Hom. 3 pl. περόωσι, inf. περᾶν, Ep. περάαν ; iter. impf. περάασκον ; f. περήσω, Ep. inf. περησέμεναι ; aor. ἐπέρησα ; pf. πεπέρακα : (πέρα :) *to pass through, pass across, to traverse, go over ; to penetrate,* Lat. *penetrare, permeare ;* with gen. *to exceed ; to extend.*

Πέργαμος, ου, ἡ, *Per'-ga-mos*, the name of the Tro'-jan citadel.

πέρθω; f. πέρσω; aor. ἔπερσα; 2 aor. ἔπαρθον, Ep. inf. παρθέειν; 2 pf. πέπορθα; Ep. 2 aor. pass. inf. πέρθαι: Lat. *vastare, to waste, ravage, pillage, destroy; to kill.*

περί, prep. with gen., dat., and acc. *about, around, round about, all about,* expressing the idea of being on *all sides* of anything, Lat. *circa, circum.* With the gen. *around,* Lat. *circa, circum; about, near,* Lat. *circa, propter,* with acc.; *for, in behalf of, about, concerning, as to, on account of,* Lat. *propter* with acc., *de* and *pro* with ablative; *over, above, surpassing, more than, beyond;* περὶ πολλοῦ, *of much importance.* With dat. Lat. *circa, circum, about* or *around,* indicating *close proximity; near; about, for, in behalf of, on account of,* Lat. *prae, de, pro.* With acc. *around, about, close by,* indicating *movement about,* etc., Lat. *circum, circa, propter; respecting, with regard to, about.* By anastrophe περί may become πέρι; see Grammar. περί or πέρι as adv. *near by, by, around: in a greater degree;* Lat. *magis, more; beyond measure, exceedingly, very.* In compo. its chief meanings are retained.

πέρι for πέρεστι.

περιβαίνω, for parts see βαίνω, (περί, βαίνω,) *to go about* or *around; to be or go around in order to defend, surround and protect,* Lat. *defendere.*

περιβάλλω, βαλῶ, for parts see βάλλω, (περί, βάλλω,) Lat. *circumjicere, to cast* or *throw around; to throw over, put on, invest another with; to throw the arms around, embrace, encompass, enclose,* Lat. *amplecti; to throw an accusation upon* (or *about*) *any one, attribute: to throw beyond, excel,* latter like Lat. *superare:* mid. *to surround one's self with, put on; to put around one's self for defence; to embrace; to obtain; to seek to acquire, aim at.*

περιδινέω, (περί, δινέω,) *to turn rapidly round:* περιδινηθήτην, aor. pass. 3 du.

περίδρομος, ον, (περιδραμεῖν, 2 aor. of περιτρέχω,) *running round about; circular, round; roaming about; capable of being run around, standing alone.*

περίειμι, (περί, εἰμί,) *to be round about; to be superior, excel, conquer, surpass, exceed,* Lat. *superior esse, superare; to remain over and above, survive; to exist.*

περιέχω, for prin. parts see ἔχω, (περί, ἔχω,) Lat. *complecti, circumdare, to be around, to surround; to surpass:* mid. *to surround* in the sense of *protect,* A 393.

περικαλλής, ές, (περί, κάλλος,) Lat. *perpulcher, very beautiful.*

περικλυτός, ή, όν, (περί, κλυτός,) *heard of on all sides; renowned,* Lat. *inclitus,* A 607.

περικτείνω, for parts see κτείνω, (περί, κτείνω,) *to kill near* or *around.*

περιλέπω, f. ψω, (περί, λέπω,) to strip off all round.

περιναιέτης, ου, ὁ, (περί, ναιετάω,) one of those who dwell around, a neighbor.

περισ(σ)είω, (περί, σείω,) to shake on all sides.

περιίστημι, f. περιστήσω, for parts see ἵστημι ; trans. in pres., f., and aor. ; intrans. in 2 aor., pf., and plup. : trans. Lat. circumdare, to place around : intrans. Lat. circumsistere, circumstare, to stand around, surround.

περίσχεο, Ep. for 2 aor. mid. imperat. of περιέχω.

περιτέλλομαι, (περί, τέλλω,) to go around, revolve, A 551 the revolving years.

περιτρέχω, see τρέχω for parts, (περί, τρέχω,) to run all round ; to go all through or over.

περιτροπέω, Ep. for περιτρέπω, (περί, τρέπω,) Lat. revertere, to turn around ; to go round in a circle ; B 295, returning or revolving year.

περιφραδέως, carefully.

περιχέω, Ep. περιχεύω, f. περιχέω ; aor. περιέχεα, Ep. περιχεῦα ; aor. pass. περιεχύθην : (περί, χέω :) Lat. circumfundere, to shed round about or over ; pass. to be shed or spread around.

Περκώσιος, α, ον, of Per-co'-te ; subst., a Per-co'-si-an.

Περκώτη, ης, ἡ, Per-co'-te, a town of Mys'-i-a.

πέσσω, f. πέψω, aor. ἔπεψα, pf. πέπεμμαι, aor. pass. ἐπέφθην, to make soft by boiling, also to ripen or mature, Lat. maturare ; to cook, prepare by fire, dress, Lat. coquere ; to digest food ; to keep down or under ; to brood over, nurse, cherish.

πέσων, 2 aor. πίπτω.

πέρνημι, like περάω, to transport for sale ; to sell.

πέταλον, ου, τό, a leaf.

πετάννυμι or πεταννύω, f. -τάσω ; certain Ep. parts are formed from -πτα-, Lat. pandere, to expand, spread out, open.

πετεηνός, ή, όν, Ion. of πετεινός, (πέτομαι,) Lat. volucer, winged, flying, B 459 ; fledged, winged ; in pl. as subst. flying creatures.

Πετεών, ῶνος, ἡ, Pe'-te-on, a village of Bœ-o'-ti-a.

Πετεώς, ῶ and ῶο B 552, Pe'-teus.

πέτομαι, f. π(ε)τήσομαι ; 2 aor. ἔπτην, ἐπτόμην, ἐπτάμην : to stretch out the wings for flight ; hence to fly, Lat. volare ; to run along.

πέτρη, ης, ἡ, Ion. of πέτρα, (compare Lat. saxum, rupes, scopuli,) a rock, crag, ledge, cliff.

πετρήεις, εσσα, εν, (πέτρα,) Lat. petrosus, rocky.

πέφανται, see φαίνω and φένω.

πέφνον, see φένω.

πέφρικα, pf. of φρίσσω, which see.

πεφυῖα, Ep. pf. fem. part. for πεφυκυῖα ; see φύω.

πῆ, interrog. particle, Lat. *qua? whither? where?* also *how?* Lat. *qua ratione.*

πη, encl., *in any way, somehow; somewhere, anywhere.*

πηγεσίμαλλος, ον, (πήγνυμι, μαλλός,) *having a thick fleece, thick-fleeced.*

πηγή, ῆς, ἡ, Lat. *fons, a spring, fountain;* πηγαί, *sources.*

πήγνυμι, f. πήξω, Ep. aor. πῆξα, 2 pf. πέπηγα, aor. pass. ἐπήχθην, 2 aor. pass. ἐπάγην, Lat. *pangere, to infix, plant firmly in, drive in, set, plant; to fix on; to fix; to make fast; to fasten* or *fix together, construct,* Lat. *compingere; to stiffen, make stiff* or *solid,* Lat. *congelare.*

Πήδαιος, or Πηδαῖος, ου, ὁ, *Pe-dæ'-us.*

πῆλαι, aor. inf. of πάλλω, which see.

Πηλείδης, Πηληιάδης, Ep. gen. εω and αο, ὁ, Πηλείων, ωνος, = Πηλείδης, *son of Pe'-leus,* i. e. *A-chil'-les,* A 1.

Πηλεύς, Ep. ῆος, ὁ, *Pe'-leus, son of Æ'-a-cus, father of A-chil'-les.*

Πηληιάδης, see Πηλείδης.

Πηλιάς, άδος, proper adj., fem., (Πήλιον,) *Pe'-li-an.*

Πήλιον, ου, τό, *Pe'-li-on, a mountain in Thes'-sa-ly.*

πῆμα, ατος, τό, (πάσχω,) *suffering, woe, misery, harm,* Γ 160.

πημαίνω, f. ανῶ, aor. ἐπήμηνα, *to cause any one suffering, harm, injure, distress;* intrans. *to do wrong,* Γ 299.

Πηνειός, οῦ, ὁ, *Pe-ne'-us, a river of Thes'-sa-ly.*

Πηνέλεως, ω, ὁ, *Pe-ne'-le-us, a Bœ-o'-tian leader.*

πηός, οῦ, ὁ, Lat. *affinis, a relation by marriage.*

Πηρείη for Πήρεια, ας, ἡ, *Pe-re'-a, a section of Thes-'sa-ly.*

πηρός, ά, όν, Lat. *mancus, maimed, injured* or *defective in limb* or *any part of the body;* applied also to organs of sense, B 599.

πίειρα, irreg. fem. of πίων, which see.

πιθέσθαι, 2 aor. mid. inf. of πείθω.

πίθος, ου, ὁ, *an earthen wine-jar.*

πικρός, adj., of arrows, missiles, etc., *sharp, piercing, keen:* of taste, *sharp, bitter,* Lat. *amarus:* of sound, *sharp, shrill:* in other applications, *sharp, cruel, severe, stern, bitter, harsh, hateful, hostile.*

πίλναμαι, (pass. of πιλνάω,) *to come near, approach.*

πίμπλημι, 3 pl. πιμπλᾶσι ; f. πλήσω ; aor. ἔπλησα ; Ep. 2 aor. ἐπλήμην ; pf. πέπλησμαι ; 2 pf. πέπληθα ; aor. pass. ἐπλήσθην : Lat. *implēre, to fill, satiate, satisfy:* with acc. and gen. or dat. *to fill full of* or *fill with: to fill* a position or office.

πίμπρημι, f. πρήσω, aor. ἔπρησα, *to set on fire; burn,* B 415.

πίναξ, ακος, ὁ, *a plank* or *board; a table* made of boards; *a tablet* for writing ; *a board* on which something has been painted, *a picture ; a trencher of wood, salver ; a tablet for index* or *for a list.*

πίνω, f. πίομαι, 2 aor. ἔπιον, Lat. *bibere, to drink.*

πίπτω, Ion. f. πεσέομαι; 2 aor. ἔπεσον ; pf. πέπτωκα, Hom. 2 pf. part. πεπτεώς : Lat. *cadere, to fall, fall down, fall in battle, subside ; fall over ; to fail, be defeated, fall short.*

πιστός, ή, όν, (πείθω,) Lat. *fidus, fidelis, faithful, trustworthy, to be trusted.*

πιστόω, (πιστός, πείθω,) *to take* or *obtain a pledge of fidelity, bind by a pledge :* mid. *to bind one another.*

Πιτθεύς, έως or ῆος, ὁ, *Pit-the'-us.*

πίτνας, part. of πίτνημι ; see πετάννυμι.

πίτνημι = πετάννυμι.

Πιτύεια, ας, ή, *Pit-y-e'-a,* a town of Mys'-i-a.

πιφαύσκω, found in pres. system, *to show, display ; to indicate* or *show in any way, make known, show, manifest, reveal.*

πίων, πῖον, gen. ονος, Lat. *pinguis, fat, in good condition ; fertile,* Lat. *fertilis ; rich, wealthy,* B 549, Lat. *opulens ;* compar. πιότερος, sup. πιότατος.

πλάζω, f. πλάγξω, aor. ἔπλαγξα, aor. pass. ἐπλάγχθην, Lat. *facere errare, to drive* or *turn one side, to cause to wander* or *go wrong ; to mislead, confuse :* mid. and pass. *to go astray, be driven about, wander.*

Πλάκος, ου, ή, *Pla'-cus,* a mountain in Mys'-i-a.

Πλάταια, ας, ή, *Pla-tœ'-a,* a town of Bœ-o'-t-ia.

πλατάνιστος, ου, ή, Lat. *platanus,* a *plane-tree.*

πλατύς, εῖα, Ion. -έα, ύ, gen. έος, είας, Lat. *latus, wide, spacious, broad : flat ;* with αἰπόλια αἰγῶν = adv., *wide-roaming.*

πλέας, B 129, acc. of πλέες.

πλέες, οἱ, Ep. for πλείονες, see πολύς.

πλεῖος, η, ον, Ion. for πλέος, α, ον, Lat. *plenus,* full ; with gen. *full of.*

πλεῖστος, η, ον, sup. of πολύς, Lat. *plurimus, very much, greatest, most :* neu. as adv. *most ; especially,* Lat. *maxime ; by far.*

πλείω, Ep. for πλέω, f. πλεύσομαι, aor. ἔπλευσα, pf. πέπλευκα, aor. pass. ἐπλεύσθην, Lat. *navigare, to navigate, to sail ;* πλεῖν ὑγρὰ κέλευθα, *to sail on the watery tracks.*

πλ(εί)(έ)ων, πλ(εί)(έ)ον, gen. ονος, compar. of πολύς, Lat. *plus, more ; greater :* Ep. and Hom. forms, nom. pl. πλέες, dat. πλεόνεσσι, acc. πλέας.

πλεκτός, ή, όν, (verbal adj. of πλέκω,) *twisted, braided, plaited.*

πλευρά, ᾶς, ή, *the side* or *flank, a rib.*

Πλευρών, ῶνος, ή, *Pleu'-ron,* a town in Æ-to'-li-a.

πλέων, ον, see πλείων.

πληγή, ῆς, ἡ, (πλήσσω,) Lat. *ictus, a blow; a wound from a blow*, Lat. *plaga*, (why not *vulnus?*) : the strict meaning is *a blow* or *wound* inflicted by a whip or stick, and not by a cutting instrument.

πλῆθος, εος, Ion. πληθύς, υος, τό, Lat. *multitudo, a crowd, large number; the greater number, mass, the populace, greater part, common people, majority* as opp. to the chiefs, Lat. *plebs*, hence *popular government, government by the people.*

πλήθω, (πλέος,) *to be full.*

Πληιάδες, Ion. for Πλειάδες, pl. of Πλειάς, άδος, ἡ, *the Plei'-a-des.*

πλῆξα, Ep. aor. of πλήσσω.

πλήξιππος, ον, (πλήσσω, ἵππος,) *striking* (= *driving*) *horses.*

πλησίος, α, ον, (πέλας,) Lat. *propinquus, vicinus, contiguous, close by, near, neighboring :* compar. -έστερος, sup. -έστατος.

πλήσσω ; f. πλήξω ; aor. ἔπληξα ; Ep. 2 aor. (ἐ)πέπληγον, Ep. inf. πεπληγέμεν ; 2 pf. πέπληγα, part. πεπληγώς, B 264 ; 2 aor. pass. ἐπλήγην Γ 31 : *to strike ; to strike and wound ; to strike dumb with amazement.*

πλοῦτος, ου, ὁ, Lat. *divitiae, abundance, wealth.*

πλυνός, οῦ, ὁ, *a tank* or *trough for washing clothes.*

πλύνω, f. νῶ, *to wash, cleanse by washing.*

πνείω, Hom. and Ep. for πνέω, f. πνεύσομαι, aor. ἔπνευσα, pf. πέπνυμαι, aor. pass. ἐπνεύσθην ; see ποιπνύω, Lat. *spirare, to breathe, live ; to blow*, Lat. *flare ; to emit an odor*, Lat. *odorem spirare ; to breathe with a quick and laboring breath, be out of breath, breathe short and hard*, Lat. *anhelare :* the poet. pf. pass. πέπνυμαι, part. πεπνυμένος Γ 203, is used as pres., *to have breath*, lit. *to have breathed, have a soul ;* hence *to be wise, prudent*, πεπνυμένος, Lat. *prudens.*

πνεύμων, ονος, ὁ, (πνέω,) Lat. *pulmo, lungs.*

πνοίη, Ep. for πνοή, ῆς, ἡ, (πνέω,) *a blast, wind, breath.*

Ποδαλείριος, ου, ὁ, *Pod-a-lir'-i-us*, surgeon of the Gre'-ci-an army.

ποδάρκης, ες, (πούς, ἀρκέω,) Lat. *pedibus valens, strong of the feet, swift of foot.*

Ποδάρκης, ους, ὁ, *Po-dar'-ces.*

ποδήνεμος, ον, (πούς, ἄνεμος,) *with feet like the wind, swift as the wind.*

ποδώκεια, ας, ἡ, (πούς, ὠκύς,) Lat. *pedum pernicitas, swiftness of foot.*

ποδώκης, ες, (πούς, ὠκύς,) Lat. *pedibus celer, swift of foot ; swift*, Lat. *velox.*

ποθέεσκε, Α 492, see ποθέω.

ποθέω, f. ήσω, (ποθή,) Lat. *desiderare, to desire earnestly, long for, yearn after*, also *to miss.*

ποθή, ῆς, ἡ, Lat. *desiderium, an earnest longing for, fond desire of :* with σή, *an earnest yearning for thee.*

ποθί, encl., indefinite adv., poet. = **πού**, Lat. *alicubi, somewhere, in any place ; somehow, perchance, possibly.*

ποιέω, f. ήσω, aor. ἐποίησα, Lat. *facere, to make, perform, create, produce, effect, do ; to cause to come about ; to make to become ; to beget ; to perform ; to render, think ; to make* or *represent in poetry, compose.*

ποιήεις, εσσα, εν, (ποίη,) something like Lat. *herbosus, graminosus, grassy, verdant.*

ποικίλλω, κιλῶ, (ποικίλος,) *to adorn with variegated work ; to work in embroidery ; to diversify* or *vary.*

ποικιλομήτης, ου, ό, (ποικίλος, μῆτις,) *having* many *plans, versatile.*

ποικίλος, η, ον, Lat. *varius, variegated, many-colored, mottled, spotted ; skilfully wrought, of cunning workmanship, elaborate, wrought, variegated work, embroidered in different colors,* Lat. *picturatus ; various in color ; carved, inlaid ; intricate, cunning, artful ; doubtful, capable of assuming various appearances.*

ποίμην, ενος, ό, Lat. *pastor, a shepherd, herdsman ; a keeper* or *watcher,* hence *a chief, leader.*

ποιμνήιος, η, ον, (ποίμνη,) *of the flock.*

ποινή, ῆς, ἡ, Lat. *poena, compensation* or *satisfaction for a deed of blood, expiation, penalty, ransom-money, vengeance, punishment ; reward, satisfaction.*

ποῖος, α, ον, Lat. *qualis, what ? of what kind ?* expresses indignant surprise.

ποιπνύω, f. ύσω, intens. from πνέω, see πνείω, *to puff from want of breath ; to make haste.*

πολέες, Ep. for πολλοί, see πολύς.

πολεμήιος, ον, Ion. for πολέμειος, (πόλεμος,) Lat. *bellicus, ad bellum pertinens, belonging to war ; martial, warlike.*

πολεμίζω, Hom. and poet. πτολεμίζω, f. ίσω, (πόλεμος,) intrans., Lat. *bellum gerere, to wage* or *carry on war ; to contend, dispute, wrangle :* trans., *to fight with* or *against, assault,* Lat. *impugnare.*

πολεμιστής, οῦ, ό, (πολεμίζω,) Ep. from πτολεμιστής, Lat. *bellator, one who fights, a warrior* or *soldier.*

πόλεμος, ου, ό, Hom. and Ep. πτόλεμος, Lat. *pugna, a battle, combat ;* also, *war,* Lat. *bellum.*

π(τ)όλεμόνδε, (π(τ)όλεμος, -δε,) *to the fight.*

πολιήτης, εω, ό, Ion. for πολίτης, which see.

πολιός, adj., Lat. *canus,* see also *albidus, hoary, whitish, gray.*

πόλις, εως, ἡ, Ep. and Hom. forms, πτόλις, gen. π(τ)όλιος, ηος ; dat. ηι, ι ; acc. ηα ; pl. ηες, ιες ; gen. ιων ; dat. ιεσσι, ισι ; acc. πόλιας, πόλις : Lat. *urbs, a city ; a state, commonwealth,* Lat. *civitas.*

8

πολίτης, ου, ὁ, (πόλις,) Lat. *municeps, civis, a citizen* or *inhabitant of a city, fellow-citizen.*

Πολίτης, ου, ὁ, *Po-li'-tes.*

πολλάκι(s), (πολύς,) adv., Lat. *saepe, frequenter, many times, frequently, often.*

πολλός, see πολύς.

πολυάιξ, άικος, ὁ, ἡ, (πολύς, ἀίσσω,) Lat. *impetuosus, violent; causing weariness by violent and impetuous movement.*

πολύαρνος, ον; the dat. πολύαρνι B 106 is not, stric. speaking, irreg., ἀρνός being gen. from obsol. nom. ; (πολύς, ἀρνός;) Lat. *multos agnos habens, having many lambs, rich in lambs* or *flocks.*

πολυβενθής, ές, (πολύς, βένθος,) Lat. *valde profundus, very deep.*

πουλυβότειρ(α)(η), (πολύς, βώσκω,) *many-supporting.*

πολυδαίδαλος, ον, (πολύς, δαίδαλος,) *much* or *cunningly wrought, wrought with elaborate art, skilful.*

πολύδακρυς, υ, ρυος, adj., (πολύς, δάκρυ,) Lat. *lacrimosus, of many tears, much-weeping, tearful,* also *causing many tears.*

πολυδάκρυτος, ον, (πολύς, δακρυτός verbal adj. of δακρύω,) *much mourned* or *wept :* also, *tearful.*

πολυδειράς, άδος, adj., (πολύς, δειρή,) *with many ridges* or *peaks, many-ridged.*

Πολυδεύκης, εως, ὁ, Lat. *Pol'-lux, Poly-deu'-ces,* brother of Cas'-tor ; see Classical Dictionary.

πολυδίψιος, ον, (πολύς, δίψα,) *very dry, arid.*

πολύδωρος, ον, (πολύς, δωρέω,) *of rich gifts, enriched by gifts.*

Πολύδωρος, ου, ὁ, *Pol'-y-do'-rus,* a son of Pri'-am ; see foreg.; see Classical Dictionary.

πολύζυγος, ον, (πολύς, ζυγόν,) Lat. *multa habens transtra, having many rowers' benches, many-benched* B 293.

Πολύιδος, ου, ὁ, *Pol-y-i'-dus.*

πολύκεστος, ον, (πολύς, κεστός,) *much-worked* or *embroidered, much-embroidered.*

πολυκλήις, ιδος, ὁ, ἡ, (πολύς, κλήις for κλείς,) *having many benches of rowers, many-benched.*

πολύκνημος, ον, (πολύς, κνημός,) *with many wooded hills ; having many shoulders of mountains,* hence *hilly, rough, mountainous.*

πολυκοιρανίη, Ion. for -ία, ἡ, (πολύς, κοιρανία,) *rule of many,* = *disorder* B 204.

πολυκτήμων, ον, (πολύς, κτάομαι,) *having many possessions* or *much wealth.*

πολυλήιος, ον, (πολύς, λήιον,) *of many cornfields, rich in corn.*

πολύμηλος, ον, (πολύς, μῆλον,) Lat. *multas habens oves, having many sheep, rich in sheep* or *flocks.*

Πολύμηλος, ου, ὁ, *Pol-y-me´-lus*, a Tro´-jan.

πολύμητις, ιος, ὁ, ἡ, (πολύς, μῆτις,) *of many devices, shrewd.*

πολυμήχανος, ον, (πολύς, μηχανή,) stric. *of many mechanical inventions;* Lat. *prudens, of many devices, inventive, full of plans,* B 173.

πολύμυθος, ον, (πολύς, μῦθος,) Lat. *verbosus, of many words, talking much, easy of speech ; much spoken of.*

Πολύξεινος, ου, ὁ, *Po-lyx´-e-nus*, leader of the E-pe´-i.

Πολυποίτης, ου, ὁ, *Pol-y-pœ´-tes*, a Thes-sa´-li-an.

πολύπτυχος, ον, (πολύς, πτύξ, πτύσσω,) *having many folds.*

πολύς, **πολλή**, **πολύ**, gen. πολλοῦ, πολλῆς, πολλοῦ, acc. πολύν, πολλήν, πολύ, no du.; Ep. and Ion. forms, πολλός, πολλή, πολλόν, and πουλύς, etc., gen. πολέος, pl. πολέες or -εῖς, gen. πολ(λ)έων, -έων, dat. πολέ-(ε)σ(σ)ι, acc. πολέας : compar. πλείων, πλέων, neu. πλέον or πλεῖν, sup. πλεῖστος : Lat. *multus, much, many, long, large ; profound, wide, far extended, broad,* Lat. *amplus;* πολὺν χρόνον, *for a long time ;* πολὺς ὕπνος, *deep sleep ;* τὰ πολλά, *the most :* neu. as adv. *much ; very particularly ; exceedingly, very,* Lat. *valde ; earnestly; often, repeatedly;* τὸ πολύ, *for the most part ;* with compar. to strengthen its force, *much, by far,* Lat. *multo,* πολὺ μᾶλλον, *much more ;* with sup. *much,* Lat. *longe.*

πολύσκαρθμος, ον, (πολύς, σκαίρω,) *much-springing, fleet, swift.*

πολυσπερής, ές, (πολύς, σπείρω,) Lat. *late disseminatus, much-spread; very numerous* B 804, *many.*

πολυστάφυλος, ον, (πολύς, σταφυλή,) Lat. *uvis abundans, rich in grapes.*

πολύστονος, ον, (πολύς, στένω,) *sighing much, much-groaning, mournful,* A 445.

πολυτρήρων, ωνος, ὁ, ἡ, (πολύς, τρήρων,) Lat. *columbis abundans, abounding in pigeons* or *doves.*

Πολύφημος, ου, ὁ, (πολύς, φήμη,) *Pol-y-phe´-mus.*

πολύφλοισβος, ον, (πολύς, φλοῖσβος,) Lat. *multo strepitu resonans, sonorus, loud-sounding.*

πομπή, ῆς, ἡ, (πέμπω,) the act of *sending, a dismissing ; an escort* to attend one that has been sent.

πονέομαι, subj. pl. πονεώμεθα ; f. ήσομαι ; aor. ἐπονησάμην ; pf. πεπόνημαι ; aor. pass. ἐπονήθην ; Hom. parts in (-)πονε(ε)(υ)-, (ἐ)πονει-: (πόνος :) Lat. *laborare, to labor hard ; to toil and greatly exert one's self in the conflict, labor, work hard, become faint and exhausted from exertion ;* of the mind, *to be anxious :* trans. *to work hard upon* or *be busy about :* in Hom. mostly dep. as above.

πόνος, ου, ὁ, (πένομαι,) Lat. *labor, hard work, fatigue, toil, labor ; a task ; a work ;* of the mind, *a hardship* B 291, *trouble, grief, distress, anxiety;* of body, *pain.*

ποντοπόρος, ον, (πόντος, πόρος,) Α 439, *going* or *sailing over the sea, seafaring.*

πόντος, ου, ὁ, Lat. *pontus, the deep, sea, high-sea,* (how do *pontus, mare, aequor, pelagus* differ ?)

ποποῖ, and **ὢ πόποι,** exclamation of astonishment, anger, or grief, *O ! O Gods ! shame !*

πόρος, ου, ὁ, (πείρω,) Lat. *vadum, a place where a passage is made, a ford ; a bridge, ferry ; way over, path, track ; the way* or *mode of accomplishing* or *doing anything.*

πορσαίνω or **πορσύνω,** Ep. f. έω, (πόρω,) *to proffer, furnish, provide, give ; to prepare* Γ 411, *attend to, make ready, arrange ; wait upon.*

πόρτις, ιος, ἡ, *a young cow.*

πορφύρεος, η, ον, (πορφύρα,) Lat. *purpureus, purple, dark red, reddish,* epith. of sea and blood ; *violet-colored, rosy.*

πόρω, 2 aor. ἔπορον, pf. πέπρωμαι, -ρωται, plup. -ρωτο, *to procure, bring about, contrive, be the cause of ; offer, bestow, commit to, give, furnish, present, grant ;* pf. pass. 3 sing. πέπρωται, *it has been ordered by fate ;* πεπρωμένος, *fated* Γ 309, *destined.*

Ποσειδάων, άωνος, ὁ, Hom. for **Ποσειδῶν,** ῶνος, Lat. *Nep-tu'-nus, Po-sci'-don,* god of the sea.

Ποσιδήιος, α, ον, poet. for **Ποσείδειος,** *sacred to Po-sci'-don* or *Nep'-tune.*

πόσις, ιος, ἡ, (πίνω,) Lat. *potio, potus, the act of drinking ; a drink,* Lat. *potus.*

πόσις, ιος, ὁ, Ep. dat. πόσεϊ, and acc. pl. πόσιας, Lat. *maritus, a husband ;* see ἀνήρ.

ποσσῆμαρ, (πόσος, ἦμαρ,) interrog. adv., *within* or *in how many days ?*

ποταμός, οῦ, ὁ, Lat. *flumen, a river.*

ποτάομαι, one of several poet. forms for πέτομαι, pf. Ep. 3 pl. πεποτήαται, Lat. *volare, to fly, flit about.*

πότε, Lat. *quando ? when ?*

ποτέ, encl. Lat. *aliquando, on a certain time, once, any time ; once, formerly,* Lat. *quondam.*

πότερος, α, ον, *which ?* used of two things or persons.

ποτί, see **πρός.**

ποτιδέγμενος, Dor. 2 aor. part. of προσδέχομαι, Β 137, Lat. *expectans, awaiting.*

πότμος, ου, ὁ, (πίπτω,) *one's portion* or *destiny, that which happens to one ; ill fate, death :* stric. *the lot that falls* from the shaken helmet.

πότνια, ας, ἡ, *madam, mistress, queen ;* as adj. *most honored, august, bearing rule,* Lat. *adoranda :* used only in addressing females, and is intended as a term of respect.

ποτόν, οῦ, τό, Lat. *potus, drink.*

ποῦ, (πός,) interrog. adv. Lat. *ubi? where? in what place.*

πού, encl. particle, *somewhere; doubtless; somehow; anywhere.*

πουλυβότειρ(α)(η), ἡ, Ion. for πολυβότειρα, (πολύς, βόσκω,) Lat. *alma, feeding many, much-nourishing, bountiful.*

Πουλυδάμας, αντος, ὁ, *Po-lyd'-a-mas,* a Tro'-jan.

πούς, ποδός, ὁ, gen. pl. ποδῶν, Ep. dat. ποσσί or πόδεσσι, Lat. *pes, a foot; the lowest part* or *foot, foundation,* Lat. *ima pars, radix;* in pl., of birds, *claws,* Lat. *ungulae,* of lower corners of a sail, *the sheets* or *ropes by which the sail is controlled.*

Πράκτιος, ου, ὁ, *Prac'-ti-us,* a river.

πραπίς, ίδος, ἡ, Ep. dat. pl. πραπίδεσσι, pl. *diaphragm, midriff;* like φρένες, *the heart, mind,* Lat. *praecordia;* the ancients thought that the mind was in the breast, hence the origin of many of our com. expressions.

πρεσβύτερος, α, ον, *older, more ancient; more venerable :* stric. compar. of πρέσβυς, *old.*

πρήθω, f. πρήσω, *to swell* or *puff out by blowing; to force* or *blow out, blow upon.*

πρηνής, ές, Lat. *pronus, prone, bent* or *bending forward* or *downwards, on the face, head first,* Lat. *praeceps.*

πρῆξις, ιος, ἡ, *an action, an act, a deed,* see Lat. *factum, actio :* Ep. for πρᾶξις, (πράσσω).

πρ(ή)(ά)σσω, f. πρήξω, aor. ἔπρηξα, 2 pf. πέπρηχα, aor. pass. ἐπράχθην, iter. impf. -σεσκον, *to go through a task and accomplish it,* hence *to accomplish, perform, effect, do, execute,* A 562, Lat. *agere; to complete,* Lat. *efficere; to transact; to follow a business; to be in a certain condition,* εὖ or κακῶς πρήσσειν, *to do* or *be well* or *ill;* οὕτω πράξας, *having fared so.*

Πριαμίδης, ου, ὁ, *son of Pri'-am.*

Πρίαμος, ου, ὁ, *Pri'-am,* king of Troy; why called Πρίαμος? see Classical Dictionary.

πρίν, conj. and adv., Lat. *prius, before, until, till, before that, ere, sooner,* also, *formerly, previously;* πρίν ἤ, Lat. *priusquam, before that, sooner than,* occurs twice in Hom.; Hom. uses πάρος for πρίν; πρότερον or πρόσθεν ... πρίν, πρίν or πάρος ... πρίν, *before ... than,* or the second word *than* is often better not rendered by any Eng. word; τὸ πρίν, *formerly.*

πρό, prep. *before, in front of;* with gen. Lat. *prae, pro,* with ablative, *ante* with acc. *before; in front of, in the presence of,* Lat. *coram* with ablative; *in front of* as a defender, *in defence of; in behalf of; because of;*

for, on account of, Lat. *prae; instead of; sooner;* πρὸ ὁδοῦ, *forward on the road, onward;* temporal, Lat. *ante, before,* opp. to μετά with acc., πρὸ χειρῶν, *at hand, in readiness:* adv. *before, forth, forward; sooner, before:* in compo., besides its gen. meaning as an adv., it has a streng. influence; *rather; defence;* in compo. with a verb, it does not lose the final vowel before an augment, see περί.

προβαίνω, f. προβήσομαι, contr. 2 aor. προὔβην, pf. προβέβηκα; Ep. pres. part. προβιβάς and προβιβῶν: (πρό, βαίνω :) *to step forward, make progress, advance,* something like Lat. *progredi; to go on:* of time, *to go on* or *wear away; to be past* or *gone: to go before* or *be superior to.* The f. προβήσω and aor. προέβησα have a trans. or causal sense, *to move forward, cause to advance, promote* or *aid.*

προβάλλω; f. βαλῶ; 2 aor. προύβαλον, iter. προυβάλεσκον; pf. προβέβληκα : (πρό, βάλλω :) Lat. *projicere, to throw forth* or *before, throw* or *put forward; to throw away; to bring forward* or *propose, pledge, hazard; to expose to; to present an argument* or *excuse:* mid. *to cast forth and throw before one's self,* A 458 ; *throw away; to put* or *hold before one's self; to put forward; to propose* or *represent to one's self; to excel,* lit. *to throw one's self beyond.*

προβέβουλα, see προβούλομαι.

προβλής, ῆτος, adj., (προβάλλω,) Lat. *projectus, thrown forward, projecting* B 396.

προβούλομαι, 2 pf. προβέβουλα, (πρό, βούλομαι,) Lat. *praeferre, to wish before* or *rather, prefer.*

προγενέστερος, compar. of προγενής, (πρό, γένος,) Lat. *major natu, senior, older.*

προγίγνομαι, for parts see γίγνομαι, (πρό, γίγνομαι,) *to be before; to exist before; to advance.*

προδοκή, ῆς, ἡ, (πρό, δέχομαι,) *a place for lurking* or *lying in ambush.*

προεῖδον, (πρό, εἶδον,) 2 aor., see ὁράω, *to see* or *look forward; to look forward* in the sense of *to provide.*

πρόειμι, inf. προιέναι, (πρό, εἶμι,) Lat. *procedere, to go forward, go forth, go before* or *in advance.*

προερέσσω, f. έσω, (πρό, ἐρέσσω,) *to row forward.*

προερύω, f. ύσω, Ep. aor. προέρυσσα A 435, (πρό, ἐρύω,) *to draw forward.*

προθέουσι, A 291, προθέω is regarded by some as an old form for προτίθημι, *to put forward, allow:* other leading scholars understand προθέουσιν, A 291, to be compd. of πρό and θέω *to run,* and render *press forward for utterance,* making οἱ a pron. in dat. case.

Προθοήνωρ, ορος, ὁ, *Proth-o-e'-nor,* a Bœ-o'-tian chief.

Πρόθοος, ου, ὁ, *Proth'-o-us,* a Mag-ne'-sian chief.

προθυμίη, ης, ἡ, Ion. for **προθυμία, (πρόθυμος,)** forward or ready will, zeal, a willing mind, readiness.

πρόθυρον, ου, τό, (πρό, θύρα,) a place before a door, vestibule, porch, entry.

προιάπτω, f. ψω, (πρό, ἰάπτω,) Lat. ante mittere, to send forward, send prematurely.

προΐημι, 3 sing. προΐει Β 752; f. προήσω; aor. προῆκα, Ep. προέηκα, Ep. 3 pl. πρόεσαν, Ep. inf. προέμεν: (πρό, ἵημι:) to send or throw forward, send forth, send as a messenger Γ 117; to dismiss; to let go, let drop; to discharge, hurl, or shoot a missile; to cast before, throw away; to give up Α 127; pours forth, Β 752; bestow: mid. to send from one's self, hence to dismiss, let go, give up, reject; to deliver or bestow over; to give lavishly, waste; to let go and be lost.

προὔχω, contr. of **προέχω,** for parts see ἔχω, (πρό, ἔχω,) to hold forward, hold before; to hold before in the sense of to defend; to put forth as a pretext; to hold before in preference or prefer: intrans. to be before or have the precedence, have the advantage; of place, to project out or forward; of honor or power, to be before or in position of power, be prominent; to surpass or be better than.

Προῖτος, ου, ὁ, Prœ´-tus.

προκαθίζω, f. ἴσω, (πρό, καθίζω (κατά, ἵζω),) Lat. ante, considēre, to sit down before; of birds, to alight.

προκαλέω, (πρό, καλέω,) Lat. evocare, provocare, to call forward or forth: mid., Lat. provocare, to challenge, lit. to call forth to one's self.

προκαλίζομαι, Lat. provocare, to challenge, = mid. of foreg.

προμαχίζω, f. σω, (πρόμαχος,) to fight in front, Γ 16.

πρόμαχος, ον, (πρό, μάχομαι,) fighting in the front: as subst. a champion.

πρόμος, ου, ὁ, (πρό,) Γ 44, the foremost one, principal person; champion.

προνοέω, (πρό, νοέω,) see Lat. providēre, to see beforehand; to see or look into beforehand, plan for a thing, take thought for beforehand.

προπάροιθε(ν), adv., Lat. ante, formerly, before; forward, Lat. prorsum; before, in front, Lat. coram: prep. with gen. before.

πρόπας, πρόπασα, πρόπαν, (πρό intens., πᾶς,) Lat. universus, totus. Α 600 πρόπαν ἦμαρ the whole day through, all together; as adv. entirely.

προπέμπω, f. ψω, (πρό, πέμπω,) Lat. praemittere, to send forward, before, or on, send forth Α 442; to dismiss, send away; to go before in order to conduct.

προπρηνής, ές, (πρό, πρηνής,) Lat. pronus, leaning forward or downwards, prone.

προπροκυλίνδομαι, (προπρό, κυλίνδομαι,) to keep rolling yet further on.

προρέω, (πρό, ῥέω,) to flow on forwards, flow towards.

πρός, in Hom. Dor. π(ρ)οτί, prep. with gen., dat., and acc. from, at, by:

with gen., Lat. *a* or *ab, from, from* or *on* in sense of position, *at the hand of, of ; on the side of ;* in swearing, *before, by, in the eyes of, in the presence of ; from before, from,* of origin and source ; *under* the command of ; *in front of, over against, looking towards ;* with pass. verb instead of ὑπό, *by ; on the part of, according to,* to denote what is appropriate or natural: with dat., Lat. *apud* with acc., *at, on, close by, near, in the presence of ;* besides, Lat. *praeter ; about* or *upon* as being occupied or busied *about* or *upon* anything : with acc. πρός indicates *tendency, direction, drift,* lit. *to the front of ;* Lat. *in, ad, to, towards, upon ; to = before ;* of relation or disposition, *towards, against, with, to, in answer to ; in reference to, with a view to, for,* also with this sense in questions, πρὸς τί, *for what ?* of time, *towards, about ; suitable to, according to ; in proportion* or *comparison to ; at ; by,* as a resort to ; πρός is never placed after its acc.: as adv. *besides, moreover, in addition to, also, over and above :* in compo. *to, towards ; in addition ;* gives idea of *remaining beside ;* in Hom. often separated from the verb with which it is compounded.

προσαμύνω, f. νῶ, (πρός, ἀμύνω,) *to come to aid* or *help one.*

προσανδάω, impf. προσηύδων, f. ήσω, (πρός, αὐδάω,) Lat. *alloqui,* (compare Lat. *alloqui, appellare, affari,*) *to address, accost, speak to.*

προσβαίνω, f. προσβήσομαι, 2 aor. προσέβην, pf. προσβέβηκα, (πρός, βαίνω,) Lat. *adire, to go to* or *towards, arrive at, approach,* also, *to come upon, attack ; to ascend,* Lat. *adscendere,* (compare Lat. *adscendere, scandere, escendere, conscendere, inscendere.*)

πρόσειμι, (πρός, εἶμι,) *to go* or *come to, approach.*

προσεῖπον, a 2 aor. with only a supplied pres., see Hadley and Allen's Grammar, 539,8 a : Lat. *alloqui, to accost, speak to, address.*

πρόσθε(ν), (πρό,) prep. with gen., Lat. *ante, before,* referring to both time and place : adv., of time, Lat. *antea, ante, formerly, aforetime, of old ;* of place, Lat. *ante, in* or *on the fore part ; forward.*

πρόσσω, see πρόσω.

πρόσφατος, ον, (deriv. uncertain, perhaps πρό, σφάζω,) *recently slain.*

πρόσφημι, (πρός, φημί,) προσέφην, Lat. *alloqui, to address, accost, speak to.*

προσφωνέω, f. ήσω, (πρός, φωνέω,) Lat. *alloqui, to call out to, accost ; to speak of* or *call by name,* Lat. *nominare,* (why not *nuncupare ?*); *to dedicate to any one,* Lat. *dedicare.*

πρόσω, poet. **πρόσσω,** (πρό,) adv. *further ; forward, to the fore part ; forward* in point of time, *in the future,* Lat. *in posterum.*

πρότερος, η, ον, compar. of πρό, sup. πρῶτος, Lat. *prior,* of time and place, *earlier, sooner, former, before, older,* in pl. also *men of former times,* Lat. *majores,* also neu. as adv. in much the same sense, Lat.

prius, priusquam : adv. **προτέρω** besides the neu. *further on, more forward.*

προτέρω, see foreg.

προτί, see **πρός.**

προτίθημι, f. *προθήσω,* aor. *προέθηκα,* 2 aor. *προέθην,* (*πρό, τίθημι,*) Lat. *proponere, to set* or *put before, offer, give,* also, *to set out to public view : to propose, put forward, set up ; to expose ; set forth ; to hold forth ; to prefer.*

προτιόσσομαι, (*προτί, ὄσσομαι,*) *to see beforehand ; to suspect ; to look upon.*

πρότονος, ου, ὁ, (*προτείνω,*) *a fore-stay reaching from the mast-head to the stern.*

προτρέπω, (*πρό, τρέπω,*) *to press* or *urge forward ; to force, incite.*

προφέρω, for prin. parts see **φέρω,** (*πρό, φέρω,*) *to bring forward* or *before, present, proffer ; to bring forth, produce,* Lat. *proferre ; to display ; to cast before, cast in* one's *teeth,* Γ 64, Lat. *exprobrare ; to assert.*

πρόφρων, ονος, ὁ, ἡ, (*πρό, φρήν,*) *with mind forward and ready to act ; willing, ready to act ; friendly, kindly,* Lat. *benevolus.*

προχέω, f. *προχεῶ,* aor. *προέχεα,* pf. *προκέχυκα,* aor. pass. *προεχύθην,* (*πρό, χέω,*) Lat. *profundere, to pour before* or *forth,* Β 465.

πρύμνη, ης, ἡ, Ion. and Hom. for **πρύμνα,** Lat. *puppis, the stern of a ship, the poop.*

πρυμνήσιος, α, ον, (*πρύμνη,*) *of* or *belonging to a ship's stern ;* neu. pl. as subst. *πρυμνήσια τά, stern-cables,* Α 436, (is Lat. *retinacula* the equivalent of this ?) ; ships were fastened by their sterns.

Πρύτανις, ιος, ὁ, *Pryt'-a-nis ;* stric. *a chief* or *head.*

πρώην, (*πρό,*) adv. *recently, lately,* Lat. *nuper ;* sometimes written *πρῴην.*

πρώϊζος, ον, *early ;* adv. *πρώϊζα, day before yesterday,* Β 303, *χθιζά τε καὶ πρώϊζ', yesterday and the day before.*

Πρωτεσίλαος, ου, ὁ, *Pro-tes'-i-la'-us,* a leader of the Thes-sa'-li-ans, first of the Greeks to set foot upon the Tro'-jan soil, and the first to fall.

πρώτιστος, adj., streng. Hom. sup. for *πρῶτος, by far the first, the very first* Β 702, *chiefest of all.*

πρωτόγονος, ον, (*πρῶτος, γόνος,*) *firstling, first-born.*

πρῶτος, η, ον, (sync. and contd. sup. of *πρό,*) Lat. *primus, first ; ἐν πρώτοις,* Lat. *in primis, among the first, especially ;* neu. as adv., Lat. *primum, above all, first, first of all, foremost.*

πτάμενος, 2 aor. part of **πέτομαι,** which see.

πτάτο, 2 aor. Ep. 3 sing. of **πέτομαι,** which see.

πτελέη, Ion. for **πτελέα,** ας, ἡ, *the elm.*

Πτελεόν, οῦ, τό, *Pte'-le-um,* name of two towns, one in E'-lis, the other in Thes'-sa-ly.

πτερόεις, εσσα, εν, (πτερόν,) Lat. *pennatus, feathered; winged,* Lat. *volatilis*
 A 201, ἔπεα πτερόεντα, *winged* or *swift words.*

πτέρνη, Ion. for πτέρνα, ης, ἡ, *the heel.*

πτέρυξ, υγος, ἡ, (πτερόν,) Lat. *ala, a pinion, wing,* (compare Lat. *ala,*
 penna, pinna, pluma); *the wing of a mountain; the wing of a garment,*
 the wing of a house, a rudder (or *wing*) *of a vessel.*

πτολεμίζω, poet. for πολεμίζω.

πτόλεμος, Ep. for πόλεμος.

πτολίεθρον, ου, τό, (πτόλις, Ep. of πόλις,) *a city;* A 164, *city of the*
 Tro'-jans.

πτολίπορθος and πτολιπόρθιος, ον, (πτόλις, πέρθω,) *destroying-cities,* B 278.

πτόλις, Ep. for πόλις.

πτυκτός, ή, όν, (πτύσσω,) *folded up, doubled over.*

πτύξ, πτυχός, ἡ (πτύσσω,) *a fold, a layer; a wrinkle, bend,* or *hollow,* hence
 a small valley, a dell.

πτώξ, ῶκος, adj., (πτώσσω,) Lat. *timidus, timid, easily frightened:* as
 subst. *a hare.*

πτώσσω, *to cringe, to cower through terror; to behave like a beggar, beg.*

Πυγμαῖοι, οἱ, (πυγμή,) *Pig'-mies,* a fabled race of dwarfs; lit. *a foot long,*
 or by deriv. *fistling.*

πυθέσθαι, 2 aor. of πυνθάνομαι.

Πυθώ, οῦς, dat. οῖ, ἡ, *Py'-tho,* old name for Del'-phi on Par-nas'-sus, where
 was the oracle of A-pol'-lo ; a still older form was Πυθών, ῶνος.

πύθω, *to cause* anything to *decompose* or *rot.*

πύκα, (πυκνός,) adv. *closely, firmly; carefully.*

πυκάζω, f. άσω, aor. ἐπύκασα, pf. πεπύκασμαι B 777, aor. pass. ἐπυκάσθην,
 (πύκα,) *to make dense, thick,* or *close; to cover closely,* B 777 ; *to wrap*
 up closely; to cover thick, overlay; to protect by covering, shelter; to
 overshadow; to shut up or *close.*

πυκινός, ή, όν, Ep. and Hom. leng. for πυκνός, (πύξ,) Lat. *densus, spissus,*
 close, firm, compact, close-packed, crowded, dense; thick; frequent,
 rapid, Lat. *creber, frequens;* of the mind, *close, collected, cautious,*
 prudent, sagacious, Lat. *prudent, callidus; well-made, strong, firmly-*
 put-together, compact; great: besides the adv. in -ῶς, the neu. is often
 used as adv., *firmly; closely; often; in excess, excessively; wisely.*

Πυλαιμένης, ους, ὁ, *Py-læm'-e-nes,* a Paph-la-go'-ni-an chief.

Πύλαιος, ου, ὁ, *Pyl'-æ-us,* from La-ris'-sa.

πύλη, ης, ἡ, Lat. *porta, a gate, entrance;* πύλαι, *the gates of a town,* a
 mountain pass *as entrance into* a country.

πυλαωρός, οῦ, ὁ, (πύλη, οὖρος,) as adj. and subst. *guarding the gate.*

Πυλήνη, ης, ἡ, *Py-le'-ne,* a town of Æ-to'-li-a.

Πύλιοι, ων, οἱ, the *Py'-li-ans*.

Πυλοιγενής, ές, (Πύλος, γενέσθαι,) *Py'-los born, born at Py'-los*.

Πύλος, ου, ὁ, or ἡ, *Py'-los*.

πύματος, η, ον, (πυθήν,) *last*.

πυνθάνομαι, πεύθομαι; f. πεύσομαι; 2 aor. ἐπυθόμην, Hom. opt. redupl.
3 sing. πεπύθοιτο; pf. πέπυσμαι, 2 sing. πέπυσ(σ)αι, -σται; plup. Ep.
3 sing. and du. (ἐ)πέπυστο, πεπύσθην: Lat. *sciscitari, to inquire, question; to learn by inquiry; to hear, find out, learn.*

πύξ, adv., *with the fist; in boxing*, Γ 237.

πῦρ, ρός, τό, Lat. *ignis, fire.*

πυράγρα, ας, ἡ, (πῦρ, ἄγρα,) *fire-tongs.*

Πυραίχμης, ου, ὁ, *Py-rœch'-mes*, a chief of the Pœ-o'-ni-ans.

Πύρασος, ου, ὁ, *Pyr'-a-sus*, a town of Thes'-sa-ly; also, the name of a Tro'-jan.

πύργος, ου, ὁ, Lat. *turris, a tower, turret; a tower of defence, bulwark, a single tower* or *castle; in pl. walls and towers; the turret* on *the highest part of a building; a close body of troops.*

πυρετός, οῦ, ὁ, (πῦρ,) stric. *the heat of fire; fever* or *heat of the feverish body.*

πυρή, ῆς, Ion. for πυρά, ᾶς, ἡ, *a place for a fire, a pile of wood for burning; a general pile*, Lat. *pyra, rogus;* by metonymy, *a sepulchre* or *grave; an altar* or *the fire on an altar.*

πυρκαϊή, ῆς, Ion. for πυρκαϊά, ἡ, (πῦρ, καίω,) stric. *a kindling of the fire; a place for kindling fire; a burning funeral pile.*

πω, encl. particle, *yet, hitherto;* rare. used alone and com. with neg., *not yet, in no wise.*

πωλέομαι, impf. iter. 3 sing. πωλέσκετο Α 490, f. πωλήσομαι, many parts are from the Ion. πωλευ-, Lat. *versari, to wander about* or *move up and down in a place; to frequent* a place, Lat. *ventitare, frequentare.*

πῶμα, ατος, τό, *a cover.*

πώποτε, (πω, ποτέ,) *ever yet, at any time;* is Lat. *unquam* the equivalent of this? οὐ πώποτε, *never yet.*

πῶς, interrog. adv., Lat. *quomodo? how? in what way? why?* πῶς γάρ, *for how is it possible?* πῶς ἄρα, *but how? how therefore?* πῶς ἄν with the opt. expresses a wish in the form of a question, also, *how could? how by any possible means?*

πώς, encl. adv., Lat. *aliquo modo, somehow, in some way, at all, in any way.*

πῶυ, εος, τό, Lat. *grex, a herd* or *flock*, of sheep; ὄιων μέγα πῶυ Γ 198: ὄιων is not always used.

P.

ῥα, ῥ', see ἄρα.

ῥαδαλός, see ῥοδανός. ?

ῥαιστήρ, ῆρος, ὁ, (ῥαίω,) a hammer.

ῥέα, ῥεῖα, Ep. adv. for ῥᾷ, Lat. facile, easily; lightly, carelessly.

ῥέεθρον, ου, τό, poet. uncontd. for ῥεῖθρον, (ῥέω,) a current, a stream; the channel or bed of a river, Lat. alveus.

ῥέζω, iter. impf. ῥέζεσκον, f. ῥέξω, aor. ἔ(ρ)ρεξα, to act; trans. to do any-thing, accomplish, Lat. facere; Α 444 to offer; with ἱερά to perform, Lat. sacra facere.

ῥέθος, εος, τό, a limb.

ῥεῖα, see ῥέα.

ῥέπω, to go gradually downwards, to sink lower and lower in the scale.

ῥέω, f. ῥεύσομαι, pf. ἐρρύηκα, 2 aor. pass. iu act. sense ἐρρύην, Lat. fluere, to flow; to drop off; to glide away; to flow freely or easily: trans. to cause to or let flow, pour.

ῥηγμί(ν)(ς), ῖνος, ὁ, (ῥήγνυμι,) the breaking, of the rising surge as it breaks over on the strand; surf, breakers; the beach or shore, that over which the sea breaks, Α 437.

ῥήγνυμι; impf. iter. 3 sing. ῥήγνυσκε; f. ῥήξω; aor. ἔρρηξα; Hom. pf. pass. ἔρρηκται; 2 pf. ἔρρωγα, has pass. signif. = intrans. use; 2 aor. pass. ἐρράγην: Lat. frangere, rumpere, (what is the difference between these Lat. words?) to break, break to pieces, shatter, rupture, fracture, burst asunder or through; to rend or tear; to unloose, let loose; to throw or dash down: intrans. to burst forth.

ῥῆγος, εος, τό, (deriv. uncertain,) a covering for bed or seat, a cushion.

ῥηΐδιος, ῥήΐδιος, Ion. for ῥαΐδιος, contd. ῥάδιος, η, ον, Lat. facilis, not diffi-cult, easy; light, without trouble; also, in this last sense, without trouble to one's self, thoughtless; pleasant in manners, easy of dis-position.

'Ρήνη, ης, ἡ, Rhe'-ne, a nymph.

ῥήσσω, Ion. for ῥήγνυμι, which see; also, Hom. to strike the ground with the feet, i. e. to dance.

ῥιγέω; f. ήσω; aor. ἐρρίγησα; 2 pf. ἔρριγα, as pres., subj. Ep. 3 sing. ἐρρίγῃσι: (ῥῖγος:) Lat. horrēre, to tremble with fear Γ 259, but stric. to tremble with the cold: inf. to fear or be afraid to.

ῥίγιον, adv., compar. neu. from ῥῖγος, colder; more terrific, more terribly, worse, more violently, Lat. magis horrendum.

ῥῖγος, εος, τό, Lat. frigus, cold.

ῥίμφα, adv., compare Lat. *statim, celeriter; readily, swiftly; easily; promptly.*

Ῥίπη, ης, ἡ, *Rhi'-pe,* a town of Ar-ca'-di-a.

ῥίπτω, iter. impf. ῥίπτασκον, f. ῥίψω, aor. ἔρριψα, 2 pf. ἔρριφα, aor. pass. ἐρρίφθην, 2 aor. pass. ἐρρίφην, Lat. *jacere, to hurl, throw; to throw forth,* Lat. *projicere; to cast down,* Lat. *dejicere;* with gen. *to throw at; to throw about,* Lat. *circumjicere; to cast out* or *away; to throw away; to scatter:* seemingly intrans. *to fall* or *cast one's self,* ἑαυτόν is understood.

ῥοδανός, ή, όν, *swaying backwards and forwards.*

Ῥόδιος, α, ον, (Ῥόδος,) *Rho'-di-an.*

ῥοδοδάκτυλος, ον, (ῥόδον, δάκτυλος,) *rosy-fingered,* epith. of Ἠώς, Α 477.

Ῥόδος, ου, ἡ, Lat. *Rho'-dus, Rhodes,* an island.

ῥοή, ῆς, ἡ, (ῥέω,) *a flowing, a current, stream, river.*

ῥύατο, 2 aor. Ep. 3 pl. of ῥύομαι, which see.

ῥύομαι, *to draw to one's self out of danger, rescue; to shield; to cover, hide; to draw back, hinder, check.*

ῥυστάζω, (ῥύω,) *to drag forcibly away, drag around; to do violence to.*

Ῥύτιον, ου, τό, *Rhyt'-i-um,* a town of Crete.

ῥωγαλέος, α, ον, (ῥώξ,) *split, rent, ragged,* Β 417.

ῥώομαι, an old Ep. word *to move with vigor, move rapidly; to move about with violence; to rush* or *dart.*

Σ.

σ', = σέ, = σοί, = σά.

Σαγγάριος, ου, ὁ, *San-ga'-ri-us,* the name of a river.

σακέσπαλος, ον, (σάκος, πάλλω,) *shield-brandishing.*

σάκος, εος, τό, *a shield,* it was made of wood or osier twigs plaited and covered with hides or leather.

Σαλαμίς, ῖνος, ἡ, *Sal'-a-mis,* the name of an island; a town of Cy'-prus.

Σαλμωνεύς, Ep. gen. νῆος, ὁ, *Sal-mo'-neus,* son of Æ'-o-lus.

Σάμος, ου, ἡ, *Sa'-mos,* the name of several Greek islands.

σάος, Lat. *salvus, sospes, unharmed, safe;* compar. σαώτερος.

σαόω, Hom. σώω and σώζω; impf. 3 sing. (ἐ)σάω, iter. σώεσκον; 2 sing. imperat. σά(ου)(ω); f. σώσω, Hom. σαώσω; aor. ἔσωσα, Hom. ἐσάωσα; pf. σέσωκα; aor. pass. ἐσώθην, Hom. ἐσαώθην; parts are formed from σο(α)-: Lat. *salvare, to save, preserve.*

Σαρπηδών, ονος, or οντος, *Sar-pe'-don,* son of Zeus and ally of the Tro'-jans.

σάφα, (σαφής,) poet. adv., Lat. *perspicue, clearly, manifestly, evidently.*

σάω, see σαόω.

σαώτερος, compar. of σάος.

σβέννυμι, f. σβέσω, 2 aor. ἔσβην, Lat. *extinguere, to extinguish, put out; to keep down, suppress, stifle.*

σεβάζομαι, (σέβας,) compare Lat. *venerēri, verēri, to stand in awe of, reverence.*

σέθεν, see σύ.

σεῖο, see σύ.

σείω, f. σείσω, aor. ἔσεισα, Lat. *quatere, vibrare, to shake, agitate, brandish, cause to quake; to move to and fro, to set in quick motion.*

Σέλαγος, ου, ὁ, *Sel'-a-gus.*

σελήνη, ης, ἡ, (σέλας,) Lat. *luna, the moon.*

Σεληπιάδης, ου, ὁ, *the son of Se-le'-pi-us, Eu'-e-nus.*

σέλινον, ου, τό, Lat. *apium, parsley,* B 776.

Σελλήεις, εντος, ὁ, *Sel-le'-is,* name of two rivers, one in E'-lis the other in Tro'-as.

σέο, see σύ.

σεῦ, see σύ.

σεύω; impf. mid. 3 pl. ἐσσεύοντο; aor. ἔσσευα, Ep. σεῦα; pf. ἔσσυμαι; aor. pass. ἐσ(σ)ύθην; 2 aor. mid. Ep. 3 sing. σύτο: Lat. *concitare, to put in violent motion; to drive, chase, pursue; drive away; to hunt; to hurl, cast, throw: to agitate, set on; to bring forth, cause to spring or come forth:* mid. and pass. *to be in rapid and violent motion, hasten, dart along; to strive for, be eager.*

σηκός, οῦ, ὁ, *an enclosure for sheep or goats, a fold, pen.*

σῆμα, ατος, τό, (is Lat. *signum* or *nota* the equivalent of this?) *a sign, mark; token; a spot; a banner, standard, battle-signal; a mark either as a letter or as a pictorial mark; a mound as the mark of a tomb, a tomb,* Lat. *tumulus; a sign from heaven; a distinctive mark, seal; a sign of the zodiac.*

σημαίνω; Ion. f. σημανέω, contr. σημανῶ; aor. ἐσήμ(η)(α)να; pf. σεσήμασμαι; aor. pass. ἐσημάνθην: (σῆμα:) Lat. *significare, to indicate or signify by a sign, to show; to intimate; to give a sign,* Lat. *signum dare; to give a signal,* hence *to rule; to affix a sign or mark,* Lat. *signare.*

σήπω; f. σήψω; aor. ἔσηψα; 2 pf. σέσηπα, B 135; 2 aor. pass. ἐσάπην, subj. Ep. 3 sing. σαπήῃ: Lat. *putrefacere, to corrupt, make putrid, to cause to fester:* pass., Lat. *putrescere, to become putrid or rotten, putrefy, ferment.*

Σήσαμος, οῦ, ὁ, *Ses'-a-mus,* a river of Paph-la-go'-ni-a.

Σηστός, οῦ, ἡ, ὁ, *Ses'-tos,* a town on the Hel'-les-pont.

Σθένελος, ου, ὁ, *Sthen'-e-lus,* see Classical Dictionary.

σθένος, εος, τό, Lat. vis, robur, strength, vigor, might, power, force.

σιγαλόεις, έσσα, εν, (σίαλος,) shining, worked smooth, splendid, rich in workmanship.

σιγή, ῆς, ἡ, (σίζω,) Lat. silentium, taciturnitas, silence; dat. σιγῇ as adv., Lat. tacite, in silence, secretly.

σιδήρεος, and Ep. σιδήρειος, η, ον, (σίδηρος,) Lat. ferreus, of or pertaining to iron or steel, iron; fig. iron.

σίδηρος, ου, ὁ, Lat. ferrum, iron; an iron weapon, anything made of iron, an iron tool.

Σικυών, ῶνος, ὁ, Sic'-y-on, a city on the gulf of Cor'-inth.

Σιμόεις, εντος, ὁ, Sim'-o-is, the name of a river.

Σιμοείσιος, οῦ, ὁ, Sim-o-is'-i-us, one of the Tro'-jans.

Σίντιες, οἱ, (σίνομαι,) Sin'-tians, inhabitants of the island Lem'-nos, lit. plunderers, pirates.

Σίπυλος, ου, ὁ, Sip'-y-lus.

Σίσυφος, ου, ὁ, Sis'-y-phus.

σῖτος, ου, ὁ, in sing., τά in pl., Lat. frumentum, grain, wheat, corn; also, that which is made from corn or wheat, and so food, Lat. cibus.

σιωπάω, Lat. silēre, to keep silent, keep still.

σιωπή, ῆς, ἡ, Lat. taciturnitas, stillness, silence, a being silent; dat. σιωπῇ as adv., in silence, silently, quietly, without noise, secretly, Lat. tacite, clam.

Σκαιαὶ πύλαι, the West Gate of Troy, see foll.

σκαιός, ά, όν, Lat. sinister, scaevus, left, relating to the left side, on the left side; left-handed, and so awkward: towards the west, western, lit. on the left of the οἰωνοσκόπος who faced to the north; unlucky, inauspicious.

σκαίρω, f. σκαρῶ, to leap, dance.

Σκαμάνδριος, α, ον, Sca-man'-dri-an; Σκαμάνδρος, ου, ὁ, the Sca-man'-der, the name of a river of Troy.

Σκάρφη, ης, ἡ, Scar'-phe, a town of Lo'-cris.

σκηπτοῦχος, ον, (σκῆπτ(ρ)ον, ἔχω,) Lat. sceptrifer, bearing a staff or sceptre, sceptre-bearing.

σκῆπτρον, ου, τό, (σκήπτω,) a staff; the staff or sceptre carried by kings as a symbol of power and dignity; a mace borne by a herald, priest, judge, etc.

σκιάω, Ep. σκιόω, used in pass. to be shaded, become dark; = σκιάζω, (σκιά).

σκίδναμαι, A 487, to be scattered, spread out, spread.

σκιόεις, εσσα, εν, (σκιά,) Lat. umbrosus, shaded, shadowy, shady.

σκόπελος, ου, ὁ, (σκοπός,) Lat. scopulus, a height, high peak, high rock, a look-out.

σκοπιή, ῆς, ἡ, (σκοπός,) a place for keeping watch, a look-out.

σκοπός, ὁ, ἡ, (σκέπτομαι,) Lat. observator, a watcher, watchman, B 792; a spy, scout, Lat. speculator; a messenger; one who watches over, hence a guardian or guide; the aim, object, mark, Lat. scopus; one who keeps watch, an inspector or overseer.

σκότος, ου, ὁ, darkness, esp. as applied to death, darkness of death.

σκύζομαι, to be enraged, Δ 23.

σκυδμαίνω, see σκύζομαι.

Σκῶλος, ου, ὁ, Sco'-lus, a town of Bœ-o'-ti-a.

σμαραγέω, f. ήσω, to resound, crash, roar, re-echo, B 210.

σμερδαλέος, η, ον, terrible, terrific, fearful: σμερδαλέον as adv., Lat. terribiliter, terribly.

Σμινθεύς, έως, ὁ, Smin'-theus, epith. of A-pol'-lo, for deriv. see Classical Dictionary.

σμῶδιξ, διγγος, ἡ, Lat. vibex, livor ab ictu, a weal or swelling from a blow.

Σόλυμοι, ων, οἱ, the Sol'-y-mi of Lyc'-i-a.

σόος, η, ον, safe, unhurt, sound, compare Lat. integer, incolumis, salvus.

σός, ἡ, όν, (σύ) Lat. tuus, thy, thine; gen. σοῦ.

Σπάρτη, ης, ἡ, Spar'-ta.

σπάρτον, ου, τό, a rope made from the σπάρτος; a rope or cable, B 132.

σπάω, the parts are formed from σπα-, to draw, draw forth, pull up.

σπεύδω, f. σπεύσω, aor. subj. σπεύσομεν, to urge or hurry any one on, spur on, hasten: seemingly intrans. to hurry (one's self) forward, hurry, make haste; to strive for.

σπινθήρ, ῆρος, ὁ, a spark.

σπλάγχνον, ου, τό, in pl., Lat. viscera, the entrails of a victim to be sacrificed, esp. the heart and liver which were eaten A 464; a feast after a sacrifice.

σπονδή, ῆς, ἡ, (σπένδω,) Lat. libatio, a libation made on occasion of making and concluding engagements, treaties, and covenants; in pl., a solemn covenant or treaty.

σπουδή, ῆς, ἡ, (σπεύδω,) Lat. ardor, eagerness; earnestness, close application, diligence, pains, Lat. industria; seriousness: zeal, Lat. studium: dat. sing. as adv. earnestly, promptly, hastily; with pains and trouble, hardly.

σταθμός, ου, ὁ, pl. τά, (ἵσταμαι,) Lat. stabulum, a place where men or animals stop or halt, a standing-place, stall, pen, stable, a hut, an abode, an inn, a station for travellers or strangers; a resting-place; a post; a weight for the balance; a day's march, about fifteen miles com., in which sense it is used in the A-nab'-a-sis.

στάσκε, Ion. for ἔστη, 2 aor. 3 sing. of ἵστημι, Γ 217.

στατός, ή, όν, (verbal adj. of ἵστημι,) made to stand; a bunch of grapes; standing.

σταφύλη, ης, ἡ, the *plummet of a level* from its resemblance to a bunch of grapes, *a level.*

στείρη, Ion. for **στεῖρα**, the *cutwater, the fore part of a ship's keel*, A 482.

στείχω, f. στείξω, Ep. aor. ἔστειξα, 2 aor. ἔστιχον, to *march, go forward, go.*

στέλλω; f. στελῶ, Ep. uncontr. στελλέω; aor. ἔστειλα; pf. ἔσταλκα; 2 pf. ἐστάλην: to *put in order, put in readiness, equip, fit out;* to *send, despatch on an expedition;* to *bring, take in, draw in.*

στέμμα, ατος, τό, (στέφω,) that which *crowns the head, a fillet, chaplet, wreath,* Lat. *vittae*, A 14.

στεναχίζω, f. ίσω, to *sigh, wail, moan;* to *bemoan, lament.*

στένω, to *groan, sigh;* to *lament.*

στέρνον, ου, τό, Lat. *pectus, the breast.*

στεῦμαι, Ep. and found only in forms στεῦται Γ 83, στεῦτο Β 597, and στεῦνται, pres. and impf., (ἴστημι,) to *appear, threaten, make a show, promise, engage:* lit. to *take a stand,* see deriv.

στεφάνη, ης, ἡ, (στέφω,) a *band for head, head-band;* a *helmet brim* (that part projecting over the forehead), and so a *helmet;* a *projecting cliff.*

στεφανόω, f. ώσω, (στέφανος,) to *surround, encircle, encompass.*

στέωμεν, see ἴστημι.

στῆθος, εος, τό, Lat. *pectus, the breast;* as with us at present the *breast* is spoken of to indicate the *feelings.*

στιβαρός, ά, ον, (στείβω,) *firm, trodden hard and compact; sturdy, strong, thick.*

στίλβω, f. ψω, Lat. *nitēre*, to *shine, gleam;* to *sparkle;* to *be brilliant, sparkling, glistening, resplendent*, Γ 392.

στίξ, στιχός, ἡ, (στείχω,) found only in gen. sing. and nom. and acc. pl., a *rank, order, row;* a *line.*

στιχάω, (στίχος,) to *place in regular order* or *rank:* mid. to *proceed in regular order;* impf. Ep. 3 pl. ἐστιχόωντο, Β 92.

στόμα, ατος, τό, Lat. *os, the mouth,* also, *the face;* in gen. *mouth; language, speech; the fore part of anything, front, point.*

στόμαχος, ου, ὁ, (στόμα,) Lat. *gula, guttur, the gullet, throat, the mouth* or *opening to the stomach:* hence Eng. *stomach.*

στοναχή, ῆς, ἡ, a *groaning, wailing.*

στονόεις, εσσα, εν, (στόνος,) *mournful, causing sorrow and groaning.*

στορέννυμι, f. στορέσω, parts are formed from στρω- and στορ-, to *spread; strew, scatter; spread down.*

Στρατίη, ης, ἡ, Strat-ti-a, a town of Ar-ca'-di-a.

στρατάω, (στρατός,) Lat. *castra ponere*, to *pitch camp;* impf. pass. Ep. 3 pl. ἐστρατόωντο Γ 187, were *encamped.*

στρατός, οῦ, ὁ, an *encamped army* A 229; *an army*, Lat. *exercitus; the soldiery* or *people of the army.*

στρέφω, f. ψω, aor. ἔστρεψα and iter. στρέψασκον, 2 pf. ἔστροφα, aor. pass. ἐστρέφθην, 2 aor. pass. ἐστράφην, to turn, wind, twist; to bend; to turn round; to turn back, torture, inflict pain: mid. and pass. to turn one's self or be turned, hence to turn.

Στρόφιος, ου, ὁ, Stro'phi-us.

στρουθός, οῦ, ὁ, ἡ, a small bird; a sparrow, Lat. passer, B 311; also, a bird; ὁ μέγας στρουθός, the large bird or ostrich, see A-nab'-a-sis, Book I. chap. v. sec. 2.

στυγερός, ά, όν, (στυγέω,) hated, odious, detested; hateful; malicious, terrible.

στυγέω, f. ήσω, aor. ἐστύγησα, ἔστυξα, 2 aor. ἔστυγον, Hom. drops ε in forming the last two parts, to hate, dread, loathe, detest; aor. to make one hated or hateful.

Στύμφηλος, ου, ὁ, Stym-pha'-lus, name of a town of Ar-ca'-di-a.

Στύξ, Στυγός, ἡ, (στυγέω,) the Styx, the name of a river of the lower world, see Classical Dictionary.

Στύρα. ων, τά, Sty'-ra, a town in Eu-bœ'-a.

στυφελίζω, f. ίξω, (στυφελός,) to beat or push away; thrust out roughly; to hustle, treat harshly, treat ill; to strike; to disperse, scatter.

σύ; gen. σοῦ, σοί, σέ, encl.; du. σφῶι or σφώ, gen. and dat. σφῶιν or σφῶν; pl. ὑμεῖς, gen. ὑμῶν, dat. ὑμῖν, acc. ὑμᾶς: Ep. forms, gen. σέθεν and σεῖο, σεῦ and σέο encl., dat. τοί, pl. ὕμμες, ὑμμείων, ὕμμι(ν), acc. ὕμμε, ὕμεας: Lat. tu, thou.

συγκαλέω, f. έσω, (σύν, καλέω,) Lat. convocare, to convoke, call together; mid. to call to one's self, invite, summon.

σύγχυσις, εως, ἡ, (συγχέω,) mixture; confusion, disorder.

συλάω, to strip, tear, or take off; take or carry away by force; hence to plunder, rob; to deprive of: compare Lat. detrahere, eripere, spoliare, depraedari.

συλεύω, f. εύσω, = foreg.

συμβάλλω, f. συμβαλῶ, 2 aor. συνέβαλον, pf. συμβέβληκα, aor. pass. συνεβλήθην; Hom. forms, ξυμβλη-, inf. ξυμβλήμεν(αι); to cast or dash together; to bring together, put together, collect, join, unite, Lat. conferre; to bring or cause to come together (in a hostile relation) for the fight, Γ 70, Lat. committere; to put (different circumstances) together and compare; hence to conclude, conjecture, infer.

Σύμη, ης, ἡ, Sy'-me, a small island north of Rhodes; Σύμηθεν, from Sy'-me.

συμμίσγω, Ep. and only form found in Hom. for συμμίγνυμι, f. συμμίξω, (σύν, μίσγω,) Lat. commiscēre, to mix together, join: intrans. to mingle, mix with, deal with; of a river, to mix with or flow into; aor. pass. 3 pl. -χθεν.

σύμπας, σύμπασα, σύμπαν, (σύν, πᾶς,) Lat. *universus, all together, the whole ;* Hom. ξυμ-.

συμφράδμων, ονος, ὁ, ἡ, *counselling with, giving counsel :* as subst. *counsellor,* B 372.

συμφράζομαι, f. άσομαι, (σύν, φράζομαι,) *to consult with, consider* or *deliberate together ; to deliberate* (*with one's self*) or *revolve in mind.*

σύν, or **ξύν,** prep. with dat., Lat. *cum* with abl., *with, along with, together with ; in connection with ; with the sanction of,* as *to fight with the sanction of,* see **μάχομαι ;** *supplied with ; by means* or *with the aid of:* as adv. *together* (*with*) ; *in addition, too, besides :* in compo., *with,* expressing the idea of *association ;* also, expresses *completion ; completely.*

συνάγω, (σύν, ἄγω,) for prin. parts see **ἄγω,** Lat. *conferre, to bring together, assemble, collect, gather together ; to bring together in union* or *unite ; to draw together into a narrow compass, narrow ; to bring together* (in a hostile sense) *for the fight.*

συναείρω, (σύν, ἀείρω,) *to join, put* or *yoke together.*

συνέχω, f. ἕξω, 2 aor. συνέσχον, (σύν, ἔχω,) intrans. Hom. 2 pf. συνόχωκα B 518, Lat. *continēre, to hold together ; to confine ; to constrain, hold in by force, check, hinder, oppress, distress,* Lat. *comprimere :* in gen., in pass. *to be oppressed* or *afflicted.*

συνδέω, f. ήσω, (σύν, δέω,) *to bind together ; to bind up.*

συνελαύνω, for parts see **ἐλαύνω,** (σύν, ἐλαύνω,) *to drive together, force* or *press together ; to bring violently together ;* also, *to bring together :* intrans. *to meet* or *come together in the fight.*

συνημοσύνη, ης, ἡ, *relationship, union ;* in pl. *compacts, unions* that have been formed.

συνθεσία, ας, ἡ, (συντίθημι,) *the act of putting together, the result of that act,* hence *an arrangement, agreement* or *compact* B 339 ; *a treaty.*

συνίημι, for prin. parts see **ἵημι ;** pres. 3 pl. συνιοῦσι, inf. συνιεῖν ; impf. 3 pl. ξυνίεσαν and ξύνιον ; ξυνέηκα, Ep. aor. for ξυνῆκα ; 2 aor. imperat. ξύνες : (σύν, ἵημι :) Lat. *committere, to bring* or *send together ; to bring together* in conflict, hence *cause to fight ; hear, learn ; to comprehend, perceive, understand :* mid. *to covenant, come to an agreement, make a contract.*

συνόχωκα, Hom. and Ep. 2 pf. of **συνέχω,** *to bend together,* B 218, intrans.

συνταράσσω, f. ξω, aor. -ετάραξα, aor. pass. -εταράχθην, (σύν, ταράσσω,) Lat. *conturbare, to confuse ; to confound ; to disturb ; to trouble, perplex.*

συντίθημι, for prin. parts see **τίθημι,** (σύν, τίθημι,) Lat. *componere, to put together, compose ; unite,* Lat. *conjungere :* mid. *to put together in one's own mind, perceive, heed, observe ; to put in order ; to agree on anything.*

σῦριγξ, -ιγγος, ἡ, a shepherd's reed or pipe; the case for a spear; hence Eng. syringe.

σφάζω, f. άξω, aor. ἔσφαξα, pf. ἔσφαγμαι, aor. pass. ἐσφάχθην Hom., 2 aor. pass. ἐσφάγην, Lat. jugulare, to cut the throat, butcher, slay for sacrifice.

σφεῖς, nom. pl. of 3 pers. pron., they: Ep. forms, gen. σφέων, σφείων; dat. σφι(ν), encl.; acc. σφέας, σφεῖας, σφέ.

σφι(ν), see foreg.

σφός, ἡ, όν, (σφέ, pl. from σφεῖς,) Lat. suus, his or her own.

σφί = σφίσι, Γ 300.

σφυρόν, οῦ, τό, the ankle.

σφωέ, τώ, τά, Ep. nom. and acc. du. of 3 pers. pron., they two, both; Ep. gen. and dat. σφωΐν.

σφῶι or σφώ, τώ, τά, Ep. nom. and acc. du. of 2 pers. pron., you two; also, gen. and dat. σφῶν, Ep. σφῶιν.

σφωίτερος, a, ον, poss. adj., (σφῶι,) of you both.

Σχεδίος, ου, ὁ, Sche'-di-us, the name of two men, one chief of the Pho'-ci-ans.

σχεδόν, (σχεῖν, see ἔχω,) adv., also prep. with gen. and dat. (compare Lat. cominus, paene, prope, fere, ferme,) near; hard by, close to; close upon; towards, to; nearly.

σχέθεν, see ἔχω.

σχέτλιος, adj., (σχεῖν,) holding out, enduring; hence much-enduring, hardy; hard, relentless, merciless, cruel, implacable, Lat. durus, cru-delis; miserable; wicked; rash, bold.

σχίζη, Ion. for σχίζα, ἡ, (σχίζω,) a piece of split wood.

σχοίατο, see ἔχω.

Σχοῖνος, ου, ἡ, (σχοῖνος, a rush,) Scho'-nus, name of a town and river of Bœ-o'-ti-a, so called because of the reeds that grow along the banks of the river.

σῶμα, τος, τό, the body, the dead body, carcass, Γ 23, Lat. cadaver, see δέμας; later meanings not here given.

σῶς, σῶν; compar. σαώτερος, from σάος: Lat. salvus, safe, sound, healthy, unhurt, entire; certain, sure, reliable.

T.

Ταλαιμένης, ους, ὁ, Ta-lœm'-e-nes, a Mæ-o'-ni-an prince.

Ταλαϊονίδης, ου, ὁ, for Ταλαΐδης, son of Tal'-a-us, B 566.

τάλαντον, ου, τό, a balance, scales, Lat. libra.

τάλαρος, ου, ὁ, *a basket*, esp. that of a wool-worker; *a basket* for gen. use; *an osier basket, cheese-basket*, Lat. *qualus*.

ταλασίφρων, ονος, adj., *stout-hearted, brave of heart*.

ταλαύρινος, ον, *having a tough ox-hide shield*.

Ταλθύβιος, ου, ὁ, *Tal-thyb'-i-us*, Ag-a-mem'-non's herald.

τἆλλα, τἄλλα, see ἄλλος.

ταμεσίχρως, οος, adj., (τάμνω (see τέμνω), χρώς,) *cutting* or *wounding the skin*.

ταμίη, ης, ἡ, *a housekeeper*, fem. of foll.; Lat. *dispensatrix*.

ταμίης, ου, ὁ, (τάμνω (see τέμνω),) *a steward*, mas. of foreg.; Lat. *dispensator*.

ταναηκής, ές, (ταναός, ἀκή,) *having a long point*.

τάμνω, Ion. for τέμνω, orig. τέμω, whence τέμει; f. τεμῶ; 2 aor. ἔτεμον, Ep. ἔταμον; pf. τέτμηκα; aor. pass. ἐτμήθην: Lat. *secare, to cut; to maim, wound; cut up; cut asunder; to slaughter, kill, sacrifice; to cut down* or *hew timber, lop off; to cut through, cut off* or *out; cut away; to cut* or *mark off* as an enclosure, *draw a line; to cut short* or *put an end to;* ὅρκια τέμνειν, *to ratify a treaty* or *oaths* with *sacrifices:* Eng. *atom*, (ἄτομος (a priv., τέμνω)); *anatomy*, (ἀνά, τέμνω).

τανύπεπλος, ον, (τανύω, πέπλος,) *with* or *wearing a long flowing robe*, Γ 228.

τανύω, for τείνω, f. ύσω, Ep. ύω; aor. (ἐ)τάνυσ(σ)α, pf. τετάνυσμαι; aor. pass. ἐτανύσθην: Lat. *tendere, to stretch out, extend, strain* or *stretch; to stretch out at full length* or *stretch to full capacity, draw tight:* mid. and pass. *to stretch for one's self; to stretch one's self to the course,* i. e. *run at full speed.*

τάπης, ητος, ὁ, Lat. *tapetum, tapes, a carpet, covering:* hence Eng. *tapestry*.

ταράσσω, f. ἀξω, aor. ἐτάραξα, pf. τετάραγμαι, 2 pf. τέτρηχα, and 2 plup. Ep. 3 sing. τετρήχει, intrans. *to be troubled, be in an uproar* or *confusion* Β 95, aor. pass. ἐταράχθην, Lat. *turbare, to disturb, stir up, throw into disorder, trouble* or *disquiet; alarm; vex.*

ταρβέω, f. ήσω, (τάρβος,) *to be terrified;* as trans. *to fear.*

Τάρνη, ης, ἡ, *Tar'-ne*, the name of a town.

ταρπήμεναι, see τέρπω.

Τάρφη, ης, ἡ, *Tar'-phe*, a town of Lo'-cris.

ταρφύς, adj., *dense, thick, crowded, close; frequent;* pl. -έες, -έα: neu. as adv.

ταῦρος, ου, ὁ, Lat. *taurus, a bull*.

τάφος, ου, ὁ, (θάπτω,) Lat. *sepultura, funus, a burial, funeral rites, interment; the grave, tomb:* Eng. *epitaph*, (ἐπί, τάφος).

τάχα, (ταχύς,) adv., (is *statim* the Lat. equivalent of this?), *swiftly, rapidly, quickly; speedily, soon.*

ταχύς, εῖα, ύ, Lat. *celer, swift, rapid, fleet; quick, prompt:* compar. ταχύτερος, ταχίων, irreg. θάσσων; sup. τάχιστος: adv., the neu. sing. ταχύ and compar. are used as adv. *quickly* and *more quickly;* neu. pl. sup. ὅτι τάχιστα, *as speedily as possible,* Lat. *quam celerrime.*

τέ, encl. particle, *and,* Lat. *que,* see καί; τε ... τε or τε ... καί, *both ... and,* the repetition καί ... καί does not appear in Ep.; in Ep. τέ is used very much in marking connection, and is thus often attached to rel. prons., particles, and advs., and cannot then be separately translated.

Τεγέη, ης, ἡ, *Te'-ge-a,* a city of Ar-ca'-di-a.

τείνω, Hom. τανύω, which see, f. τενῶ, aor. ἔτεινα, pf. τέτακα, plup. Ep. 3 sing. τέτατο, aor. pass. (ἐ)τάθην, the parts are formed from τ(εν-)(α-), Lat. *tendere, to stretch, draw out, strain; draw* or *bind tight; to stretch out at full length; to make longer, lengthen, prolong, extend:* intrans. *tend to; to pertain to; to aim at; to stretch; to stretch out over, stretch out.*

τείρεα, -έων or -ῶν, τά, Ep., Lat. *sidera, the stars, constellations;* pl. of τέρας, which see.

τείρω, *to wear away by rubbing, rub away; to tire out, weary, wear out, fatigue, distress, hard press:* hence Eng. *tire.*

τειχεσιπλήτης, ου, ὁ, (τεῖχος, πλήσσω,) *one who batters walls, a taker of cities.*

τειχιόεις, εσσα, εν, (τειχίον,) "*full of houses*" or *house walls,* "*well inhabited,*" see note on B 559.

τεῖχος, εος, τό, Lat. *murus, a wall; a fortification, a city-wall,* Lat. *moenia.*

τέκε, τεκέειν, see τίκτω.

τέκμωρ, Ep. for τέκμαρ, τό, *a limit, boundary, end, goal; the end, finishing, termination,* Ἰλίου τέκμωρ *the end* or *downfall of Troy; a fixed* or *sure sign, solemn assurance, solemn pledge,* A 526: stric. *a fixed and definite mark to indicate the end.*

τέκον, see τίκτω.

τέκνον, ου, τό, (τεκεῖν, 2 aor. of τίκτω,) *a child, a young animal; that which has been produced* or *born.*

τέκος, εος, τό, poet. for τέκνον, Ep. dat. pl. τέκεσσι or τεκέεσσι(ν), (τεκεῖν,) *a child;* see τέκνον.

τεκταίνομαι, (τέκτων,) *to construct* or *build with wood, work as a builder of wooden buildings; to plan, contrive.*

τέκτων, ονος, ὁ, *a carpenter, a wood-worker; a worker* in gen.; *a contriver.*

Τέκτων, ονος, ὁ, *Tec'-ton.*

Τελαμών, ῶνος, ὁ, (τελαμών,) *Tel'-a-mon.*

τελαμών, ῶνος, ὁ, *a strap for support, a sword-belt, shield-belt, a belt for the dagger ; a thong ; a bandage for wounds.*

Τελαμώνιος, ου, ὁ, *son of Tel'-a-mon.*

τέλειος, adj., (τέλος,) Lat. *perfectus,* stric. *finished, perfect, full, complete, whole ; mature, full-grown ; without blemish* or *fault ; accomplished, ended.*

τελείω, Ep. for **τελέω ;** f. -έσ(σ)ω, -έ(σ)ω or -ῶ ; aor. ἐτέλε(σ)σα ; pf. τετέλεκα ; aor. pass. ἐτελέσθην : Lat. *perficere, to terminate, complete, accomplish* A 388, *execute* or *perform, effect, finish ; bring to completion, fulfil ; to discharge a due* or *tax,* hence, *to pay a due.*

τελήεις, εσσα, εν, (τελέω,) Lat. *perfectus, complete, finished, perfect.*

τέλλω, f. τελῶ, aor. ἔτειλα, *to bring forth* or *cause to exist, to complete, perfect, accomplish* or *execute.*

τέλος, εος, τό, Ep. dat. pl. τελέεσσι, *that which has been achieved, the end, a fulfilment, accomplishment, issue, completion,* Lat. *exitus ; end, conclusion, sum ; a company of troops ; the end of life, death ; the end* (*of death*) *for death ; the* (*end of political ambition*) *magistracy.*

τέλσον, ου, τό, *that which marks a limit, a bound.*

τέμενος, εος, τό, (τέμνω,) *a piece of land marked off and set apart for any person* or *purpose ; a portion of land dedicated to a divinity,* Lat. *sacer ager.*

τέμνω, τέμω, see **τάμνω.**

Τένεδος, ου, ἡ, *Ten'-e-dus,* a small island off the coast of Tro'-as.

Τενθρηδών, ονος, ὁ, *Ten-thre'-don.*

τένων, οντος, ὁ, *a sinew,* esp. of the back of the neck, *tendon.*

τέο, Ion. for τοῦ = τίνος ; encl. **τεο, Ion.** for του = τινός, encl.

τέρας, τό ; Ep. forms in pl. τέραα and τείρεα, gen. τεράων, dat. τεράεσσι : *an unusual appearance, a sign* or *portent* from nature, *wonder ; an omen ; a monster,* Lat. *monstrum ;* see **τείρεα.**

τέρην, εινα, εν, gen. τέρενος, τερείνης, τέρενος, (τείρω,) *polished, made smooth by rubbing, rubbed* or *worn smooth ; soft, delicate.*

τέρμα, ατος, τό, Lat. *terminus, a terminus, a mark showing the end, a turning-post* or *stone ;* why not Lat. *finis* ?

τερπικέραυνος, ου, (τέρπω, κεραυνός,) *taking pleasure in thunder,* A 419.

τέρπω ; f. ψω ; aor. ἔτερψα ; aor. pass. ἐτ(έ)(ά)ρφθην, Ep. 3 pl. -θεν ; 2 aor. mid. ἐταρπόμην and τεταρπόμην ; 2 aor. pass. ἐτάρπην, Ep. inf. ταρπήμεναι and subj. τραπείομεν : *to fill, satiate,* hence *to satisfy ;* Lat. *delectare, to give enjoyment, refresh, please, delight :* mid. and pass. *to have enough, have enjoyment, be satisfied ; to enjoy* or *delight one's self, be merry.*

τεσσαράκοντα, (τέσσαρες,) indecl., Lat. *quadraginta, forty.*

τέσσαρες, τέσσαρα, Lat. *quatuor, four.*

τεταγών, όντος, ὁ, with gen. Α 591, *having taken hold of;* Ep. redupl. 2 aor. part.; not used in pres.

τέταται, pf. of τείνω.

τέτατο, plpf. pass. Ep. 3 sing. of τείνω, Γ 372.

τέταρτος, η, ον, Hom. τέτρατος, (τέσσαρες,) Lat. *quartus, fourth;* neu. as adv.

τέτηκα, see τήκω.

τέτλα-, ηως, see τλάω.

(ἐ)τέτμον, a defec. verb of 2 aor. system, *to come to, come upon, reach.*

τετραίνω, f. ανῶ, aor. (ἐ)τέτρηνα, *to pierce through.*

τετραπλῆ, adv., *fourfold.*

τετράφαλος, ον, (τετρα-, φάλος,) *with a four-ridged crest.*

τετραχθά, (τέσσαρες,) Γ 363, adv., *in four parts,* Lat. *quatuor modis.*

τετρήχει, υἶα, 2 plup. 3 sing. and part. of ταράσσω.

τετρίγει, see τρίζω.

τέττιξ, ιγος, ὁ, Lat. *cicada, a kind of grasshopper,* very com. in southern countries; it sits in trees or shrubs and makes a chirping noise with its wings.

τετύκοντο, see τεύχω.

Τεύθρας, αντος, ὁ, *Teu'-thras.*

τεῦ, τευ, encl., Ion. for τίνος, τινός.

Τευταμίδης, ου, ὁ, *son of Teu'-ta-mus.*

τεῦχος, εος, τό, (τεύχω,) Lat. *instrumentum, a utensil, any instrument of accomplishment, tool, a weapon, an implement; a book:* in pl. *arms, armor, warlike equipments, tackling accoutrements,* Lat. *arma.*

τεύχω, f. ξω, aor. ἔτευξα, 2 pf. τέτυχα, pf. mid. and pass. τέτυγμαι, pass. aor. ἐτύχθην; Ep. forms, 2 aor. act. and mid. τέτυκον, τετυκόμην, Α 467, pf. 3 pl. τετεύχαται, plpf. 3 pl. τετεύχατο, 2 pf. part. τετευχώς: Lat. *fabricari, to make* or *fabricate, build, form, construct, fit out, make ready, fashion* or *make out of a material, forge, weave; to create, form, cause, bring about, execute; prepare;* pass. Γ 101, *has been prepared* or *decreed;* pf. *has been made* or *caused to be,* hence *to be;* pf. part. may mean *well-constructed, well-wrought.*

τέχνη, ης, ἡ, Lat. *ars, cunning, skill, art; an art; a science, craft* or *trade, handiwork, work of art; a device* or *means* of doing or achieving, hence *a stratagem, cunning* in a bad sense.

τέως, or Ep. τείως, adv., *as long as; until; before; meanwhile, while.*

τήκω; f. τήξω; aor. ἔτηξα; pf. τέτηκα, intrans. with pres. signif., Γ 176 *to melt* or *waste away;* aor. pass. ἐτήχθην, rarely used; 2 aor. pass. ἐτάκην: Lat. *liquefacere, liquare, to cause to melt, liquefy, make liquid, melt:* mid. and pass. *to melt* or *waste away; to vanish.*

τῆλε, adv., *afar, far from.*

τηλεδαπός, η, ον, (τῆλε, δάπεδον,) *from a distant land, foreign; distant.*

τηλεθάων, (Hom. and poet. part. from θάλλω, *to bloom and be luxuriant,*) *blooming, luxuriant, verdant.*

Τηλέμαχος, ου, ὁ, (τῆλε, μάχομαι,) *Te-lem'-a-chus,* son of U-lys'-ses, lit. *fighting from afar;* see Classical Dictionary.

τηλίκος, η, ον, *of such an age.*

τηλόθε(ν), (τηλοῦ = τῆλε,) adv., Lat. *e longinquo, from afar, from a distance;* with gen.

τηλόθι, (τηλοῦ = τῆλε,) adv., Lat. *procul, afar;* with gen. *far away from.*

τηλόσε, adv., *far off, far distant.*

τηλύγετος, adj., (τῆλε, γίγνομαι,) *late* or *latest born,* hence *darling.*

Τήρεια, ας, ἡ, *Te-re'-a,* a mountain of Mys'-i-a.

τίεσκον, iter. impf. of τίω, which see.

τίη, Ion. for τί, interrog. *why? why then?*

τίθημι, τίθης or Ep. τίθησα, τίθησι or Hom. τιθεῖ; du. τίθετον; pl. τίθεμεν, τίθετε, τιθεῖσι (Hom.) or τιθέασι: impf. ἐτίθην, ης or εις, η or ει, 3 pl. (ἐ)τίθεσαν, iter. τίθεσκον: Ep. inf. τιθ(ή)(έ)μεν(αι): part. τιθείς: f. θήσω, εις, ει, etc.; Ep. inf. θησέμεν(αι): aor. ἔθηκα, (what other verbs have their aor. in κ?), du. ἔθετον, ἐθέτην: 2 aor. ἔθην: Ep. and Ion. sub. θ(εί)(έ)ω-, (η)ης, ῃ, pl. (ω)(ο)μεν: opt. θεί-, etc., 3 pl. ησαν or εν: Ep. inf. θέμεν(αι): pf. τέθεικα: the dif. parts are formed from (τι)θε-, and those that are not given here can be easily found in the Gram.: Lat. *ponere, to set, fix, put, deposit, place, lay; to set up; to put under arms; to place* or *lay down; to place* or *station; to make, render, cause, procure; to bring into a certain condition; to assign to a place; to believe, propose, consider, reckon; to fix, settle, appoint, determine; ordain, establish:* mid. *to place* or *lay up for one's self; to prepare for one's self* or *one's own benefit; to place* or *deposit for one's self.*

τίκτω; f. τέξω; 2 aor. ἔτεκον, τέκε B 714, inf. τεκέειν; pf. τέτοκα: Lat. *parere, gignere,* (what is the difference between these Lat. words?), *to bring forth, bring into the world,* also, *to engender, beget; to cause, bring about, occasion:* the root is τεκ, for sync. and change of τ and κ see Gram.

τίλλω, f. τιλῶ, aor. ἔτιλα, Lat. *vellere, to pull, pluck out, tear out:* mid. *to tear out one's own* or *from one's self, to tear the* (or *one's own) hair in token of sorrow.*

τιμάω, f. ήσω, aor. ἐτίμησα, pf. τετίμηκα, aor. ἐτιμήθην, (τιμή,) Lat. *honorare, to honor, esteem, value, respect, reverence, deem worthy of esteem; to estimate, value,* Lat. *aestimare.*

τιμή, ῆς, ἡ, Lat. *pretium quo res aliqua aestimatur, the price at which any-*

9

thing is estimated, the value of anything; hence honor, esteem, reverence, respect, Lat. honor; rank, situation of honor, dignity, distinction, Lat. dignitas; compensation, reward, and so punishment.

τιμήεις or ης, εσσα, εν, (τιμή,) compare Lat. honoratus, honorabilis, honored, esteemed; valued, prized highly.

τινάσσω, f. ξω, aor. ἐτίναξα, (τείνω,) Lat. quatere, to agitate, brandish, shake Γ 385; to shake off, upset, disquiet.

τίνυμαι, Hom. for mid. of foll., to punish, chastise.

τίνω, f. τίσω, aor. ἔτισα, pf. τέτικα, to pay, to pay back, repay, pay the worth or value, atone for, make return for, Lat. luere; Lat. dare poenas, to give satisfaction, pay the price of error or a penalty; to pay the price or claim, discharge an obligation: mid. to cause to be payed, exact payment, cause another to pay; to take satisfaction, take vengeance, punish, avenge one's self.

τίπ(o)τε, (τί, πότε,) adv., Lat. quidnam? cur? why pray? why? wherefore?

Τίρυνς, υνθος, ἡ, Tī'-ryns, an ancient town of Ar'-go-lis, one of the oldest Greek cities.

τίς, τί, gen. τίνος or τοῦ, dat. τίνι or τῷ, acc. τίνα, neu. τί, du. τίνε, τίνοιν, pl. τίνες, neu. τίνα, gen. τίνων, dat. τίσι, acc. τίνας, τίνα; the foll. forms are found in Hom., gen. τέο or τεῦ, gen. τέων, dat. τέῳ, τέοισι: interrog. pron., Lat. quis? who? which? what? τί δέ, but what? ἐς τί? how long? τί μοι? what happens to me? ἵνα τί, that what may happen? to what purpose? τὸ τί is used when the question refers to something going before; τί as adv., why? wherefore? how? τί τοῦτ' ἔλεξας, what is this that thou hast said? τί μήν? why or how in truth?

τὶς, τὶ, gen. τινός or τοῦ, dat. τινί or τῷ, acc. τινά, neu. τὶ, du. τινέ, τινοῖν, pl. τινές, neu. τινά, gen. τινῶν, dat. τισί, acc. τινάς, τινά; Ep. forms, gen. sing. τέο, τεῦ, dat. τεῳ, ἄσσα for τινά: indefinite pron., encl. used as subst. or adj., Lat. aliquis, quisquam, some, any, some one, any one; something, anything; it may express an indefiniteness, a kind of, a certain; like ἕκαστος, Β 355, Β 388 each one; sometimes collective in sense, but meaning individuals of the whole number, one here and there, certain ones, meaning men generally; a, an; some distinguished person, some great or well-known thing; some one of importance; with adj. to render it less definite, a sort of, somewhat, such a kind of, ἐγγύς τι pretty near, πᾶς τις, every one.

τιταίνω, aor. ἐτίτηνα, Lat. tendere, to stretch, strain; to extend, spread out or along, Lat. extendere; to draw along, Β 390, Lat. trahere: τιταίνω, as also τανύω, is Hom. for τείνω from root τα-, see τανύω.

Τίτανος, ου, ὁ, Tit'-a-nus, a mountain of Thes'-sa-ly.

Τιταρήσιος, ου, ὁ, *Tit-a-re'-si-us,* a river of Thes'-sa-ly.

τιτύσκομαι, *to prepare, make ready, get ready; to prepare* to throw or shoot, hence *aim,* with gen. *to aim at.*

τίω, iter. impf. τίεσκον, f. τίσω, aor. ἔτισα, pf. τέτιμαι, Lat. *aestimare, to rate at a price, value; to honor, esteem, prize,* Lat. *honorare.*

τλα-; f. τλήσομαι; Ep. aor. ἐτάλασ(σ)α; 2 aor. ἔτλην; pf. τέτληκα; 2 pf. of μι- forms, τέτλαμεν, opt. τετλαίην, imperat. τέτλαθι, inf. τετλάναι and Ep. τετλάμεν(αι), Ep. part. τετληώς: the pres. is not found, and the pf. has also the pres. sense; Lat. *tolerare, to bear, suffer, endure; to have fortitude, hold out; to dare, venture, hazard,* Lat. *audēre.*

τλήμων, ονος, adj., (τλα-,) *enduring, long-suffering, patient; persevering, daring.*

Τληπόλεμος, ου, ὁ, *Tle-pol'-e-mus,* son of Her'-cu-les and leader of the forces from Rhodes.

Τμῶλος, ου, ὁ, *Tmo'-lus,* a mountain range of Lyd'-i-a.

τό, adv. acc. *on this account, therefore.*

τοί, ταί, Hom. for οἱ, αἱ, and οἵ, αἵ.

τοι, Dor. and Hom. for σοι, dat. of σύ, Lat. *tibi.*

τοί, encl. streng. particle, *truly, verily, in truth, certainly, surely; therefore,* hence; τἄρα == τοι ἄρα, τἄν == τοι ἄν.

τοιγάρ, (τοι, γάρ,) *so then, therefore, on this account, accordingly; wherefore.*

τοῖος, η, ον, (τοῖο for τοῦ,) demon., Lat. *talis, hujusmodi, such-like, such;* Hom. com. uses τοῖος in relation to something before mentioned; it often corresponds to another word, as οἷος, etc.: with adjs. τοῖος has an adv. force streng. the meaning of the adj. *so much —, so very —:* neu. as adv., often with streng. force, *so very much,* etc.

τοιόσδε, -ήδε, -όνδε, (τοῖος, -δε,) a demon. somewhat stronger than the foreg., Lat. *talis, such,* B 120 *such and so great; such as the following,* see foll.

τοιοῦτος, τοιαύτη, τοιοῦτο, (τοῖος, οὗτος,) a strong demon., Lat. *talis, such, of such a kind; such as the preceding,* see foreg.

τοκεύς, έως, ὁ, (τεκεῖν, 2 aor. of τίκτω,) Lat. *genitor, one who begets* or *produces;* in Hom. Ion. pl. τοκῆες, Lat. *parentes, parents, ancestors.*

τολμάω, f. ήσω, (τόλμα,) *to have courage to undertake, to undertake; to bear, endure.*

τομή, ῆς, ἡ, (τέμνω,) *a cutting; a section; the part left after the cutting, the stump-end where the cut was made, the trunk* A 235.

τοῖχος, ου, ὁ, Lat. *paries, the wall* or *side of a house, house-wall; the side of a ship.*

τοπρίν == τὸ πρίν, see πρίν.

τοπρῶτον == τὸ πρῶτον, see πρῶτος.

τόξον, ου, τό, Lat. *arcus, a bow*, also *skill in archery*. The bow was a weapon little used in warfare by the Greeks, who practised fighting at close quarters, owing perhaps to their superior bravery; it consisted of several parts, the horn extremities (κορῶναι) to which the string (νευρ(ά)(ή)) was attached and the wooden middle piece (πῆχυς); hence the pl. τόξα is often used, like Lat. *castra*, for *one bow*, also for *bow and arrows*.

τοσσάκι, Ep. for τοσάκι, (τόσος,) Lat. *toties, so often, so frequently*.

τόσσος, Hom. for τόσος, η, ον, Lat. *tantus, so great, so much, so large; so wide, so long; so loud; so many:* τόσ(σ)ον as adv., *so, to such a degree, so much, so very, so strongly*, Lat. *tantum*.

τοσσόσδε, Hom. for τοσόσδε, -ήδε, -όνδε, (τόσος, -δε,) a stronger demon. than the foreg.; Lat. *tantus, so great, so much, so large; so wide, so long, so loud, so many:* neu. as adv., Lat. *tantum, to such a degree, so much, so very, so, so far, so strongly; only*.

τοσσοῦτος, Hom. for τοσοῦτος, αύτη, οῦτο, a demon. with force increased by being leng.; Lat. *tantus, so great, so much, so large, so wide:* neu. as adv., see foreg.

τότε, adv., Lat. *tunc, tum, then, at that time;* οἱ τότε, *the people of that time*.

τοὔνεκα, = τοῦ ἕνεκα, *for that reason, on this account, therefore, on account of that*.

τοὔνομα, = τὸ ὄνομα.

τόφρα, adv., *to that time, as long as, until, so long; meanwhile*.

τραπείομεν, Ep. 2 aor. pass. subj. of τρέπω, which see.

τράπεζα, ης, ἡ, *a table; a table for eating*, and so *a meal; any table or counter*, Lat. *mensa*.

τραπεζεύς, εως, adj., (τράπεζα,) *of the table, fed at the table*.

τραφέμεν, τράφεν, see τρέφω.

τρέπω, Hom. has also τρ(α)(ο)πέω, f. ψω, aor. ἔτρεψα, 2 aor. ἔτραπον, 2 pf. τέτρ(α)(ο)φα, aor. pass. ἐτρέφθην Hom. has ἐτράφθην; Ep. 2 aor. pass. subj. τραπείομεν: Lat. *vertere, to turn; to turn round, turn about; to turn one away; to turn back, turn to flight, rout*, Lat. *in fugam convertere*, (what is the difference between Lat. *vertere* and *convertere?*), *to turn to a purpose; to keep off, hinder; to divert:* mid. and pass. *to turn one's self, turn; to be turned* or *to change*.

τρέφω; f. θρέψω; aor. ἔθρεψα; Ep. 2 aor. ἔτραφον, inf. τραφέμεν, intrans. in Hom.; 2 pf. τέτροφα, intrans. in Hom.; aor. pass. ἐθρέφθην; 2 aor. pass. ἐτράφην: *to render more firm* or *compact, cause to grow and develop, make to increase by feeding, nourish, feed*, Lat. *nutrire; to rear, bring up, nurse, care for; to rear, tend; to keep, have:* pass. 2 aor. and 2 pf., *to increase, to thicken and develop, grow up*.

τρέω, to tremble from fear, fear; to flee because of fear: trans. to fear any-thing, stand in fear of.

τρήρων, ωνcs, (τρέω,) adj., of doves, trembling, fearful.

τρητός, ή, όν, (Ion. verbal adj. of τιτράω,) pierced, perforated.

Τρηχίς, ῖνος, ή, (τροχύς,) Tra'-chis, the name of a town.

Τρῆχος, ου, δ, Tre'-chus, the name of a Greek.

τρηχύς, Ion. for τραχύς, εῖα, ύ, Lat. asper, rough, uneven, rocky, ruggcd, jagged, also, rude, harsh, rough.

τρίζω, poet., f. ξω, 2 pf. τέτριγα with pres. signif., Ep. part. τετριγῶτες B 314, Lat. stridere, to make a shrill, stridulous sound or cry; to speak inarticulately; to squeak, hiss; to creak.

τριήκοντα, Hom. for τριάκοντα, (τρεῖς,) Lat. triginta, thirty.

τρι-, three —, thrice —.

Τρίκκη, ης, ή, Tric'-ca, a city of Thes'-sa-ly.

τρίπλαξ, ακος, (τρίς,) adj., Lat. triplex, triple.

τριπλῆ, adv., A 128, trebly, in threefold proportion.

τριπλόος, η, ον, (τρεῖς,) Lat. triplus, threefold.

τρίπολος, ον, (τρι-, πολέω,) thrice turned over with the plough, thrice ploughed.

τρίπος, poet. for τρίπους, (τρι-, πούς,) adj., having three feet; three-legged: as subst. a tripod, mas.

τρίς, (τρεῖς,) adv., Lat. ter, thrice.

τρίτατος, poet. and Hom. for τρίτος, Lat. tertius, the third A 252: the neu. with or without τό as adv., thirdly, in the third place, for the third time.

Τριτογένεια, as, ή, (Τριτωνίς, γίγνομαι,) born on the banks of lake Tri'-ton, Tri'-ton born, a name given to Min-er'-va.

τρίτον, τὸ τρίτον, adv., see τρίτατος.

τρίτος, η, ον, see τρίτατος.

τρίχα, (τρίς,) Hom. adv., Lat. in tres partes, trifariam, triple, in or into three parts; τρίχα νυκτὸς ἔην, it was at the third part of the night.

τρίχες, nom. pl. of θρίξ.

τριχθά, Hom. adv., see τρίχα, B 668.

Τροιζήν, ῆνος, ή, Træ'-zen, a town of Ar'-go-lis.

Τροίζηνος, ου, δ, Træ-ze'-ne.

Τροίη or Τροτη, ης, ή, Troy and its territory.

Τροίηθεν, adv. of direction, from Troy.

Τροίηδε, adv. of direction, to Troy.

τρόμος, ου, δ, (τρέμω,) Lat. tremor, a trembling from fear, fear.

τροχός, ου, δ, (τρέχω,) Lat. rota, a wheel; anything circular; a potter's wheel.

τρυγάω, f. ήσω, (τρύγη,) to gather the ripened fruit, to gather the vintage.

τρυφάλεια, as, ή, (τρύω, φάλος,) a helmet, a crested helmet.

Τρωαί, ῶν, αἱ, = **Τρωάδες**, *Tro'-jan women*, Γ 384.

Τρῳός, α, ον, (Τρώς,) *belonging to the Tro'-jans, Trojan.*

Τρώς, ωός, *Tros*, founder of Troy and the Tro'-jan race, see Classical Dictionary; pl. **Τρῶες**, dat. **Τρωσί**, Α 164, *Tro'-jans.*

τρωχάω, poet. for **τρέχω**, which see.

τυγχάνω; f. **τεύξομαι**; Ep. aor. **ἐτύχησα**; 2 aor. **ἔτυχον**, Ep. subj. **τύχωμι**; pf. **τετύχηκα**: *to hit a mark*, com. with gen., sometimes with the acc.; *to hit* in the sense of *to gain* or *obtain, reach, secure; to hit upon, chance to meet:* intrans., often with a part., *to happen*, see A-nab'-a-sis, Book I. chap. I. sec. 2, *to be by chance*, etc., *chance to be, happen so and so* (the part. being the prin. word); *to occur, befall, turn out.*

Τυδεύς, έως, ῆος, έος, ὁ, *Ty'-deus*, see Classical Dictionary.

τύμβος, ου, ὁ, *a tomb, a sepulchral mound over the urn containing the ashes of the dead*, Lat. *tumulus; a place where the body had been burned:* hence Eng. *tomb.*

τύπτω, f. **τύψω**, aor. **ἔτυψα**, 2 aor. **ἔτυπον**, pf. **τέτυμμαι**, aor. pass. **ἐτύφθην**, 2 aor. pass. **ἐτύπην**; parts are also formed from **τυπτε-**; Lat. *verberare, percutire, to strike; to strike so as to wound; to beat, smite.*

τυτθός, adj., *little, young:* neu. as adv., Α 354, *a little*, Lat. *paulum.*

τύφλος, η, ον, Lat. *caecus, blind.*

Τυφωεύς, Ep. gen. έος, ὁ, *Ty-pho'-eus*, a giant; see Classical Dictionary.

τυχήσας, aor. Ep. part. of **τυγχάνω**, which see.

τῷ, (stric. dat. of art.,) adv., Β 250 *for this reason, on this account, so, then, so then.*

τώς, adv., poet. for **ὥς** and **οὕτως**, Lat. *sic, thus, so, in this manner.*

Υ.

Ὑάμπολις, εως, ἡ, *Hy-am'-po-lis*, a town in Pho'-cis.

Ὑάδες, ων, αἱ, *the Hy'-a-des*, a constellation in the head of Tau'-rus. The deriv. is not certain, prob. **ὕω** as the rising of this constellation is at the beginning of the rainy season.

ὕβρις, Ep. gen. ιος, ἡ, *violence, insolence, haughtiness, arrogance, any haughty and outrageous abuse of power; riotousness; outrage; lewdness.*

ὑγρός, ά, όν, (ὕω,) Lat. *humidus, moist, wet; fluid, watery, liquid*, Lat. *liquidus; ἡ ὑγρή, ῆς, the sea;* alone or with **κέλευθα**, *the watery ways* or *the ocean;* neu. with article, *wetness, moisture; soft, pliant*, Lat. *mollis; nimble, agile.*

ὕδρος, ου, ὁ, like **ὕδρα**, ας, ἡ, (ὕδωρ,) Lat. *hydra, serpens aquatilis, a water-snake.*

ὕδωρ, ὕδατος, Ep. dat. ὕδει, τό, Lat. *aqua, water; rain:* stem. υδατ-, irreg. ω in nom.

υἱός, ου, ὁ; besides the reg. declension, it is also inflected irreg., from stems υἱυ-, υἱ-, gen. υἱέος, υἱος, dat. υἱέι, υἱεῖ, υἱι, acc. υἱέα, υἱα, du. υἱέε, υἱε, and υἱέοιν, pl. υἱέες, υἱεῖς, υἱες, gen. υἱέων or υἱῶν, dat. υἱέσι(ν), υἱάσι, acc. υἱέας, υἱεῖς, υἱας: Lat. *filius, a son;* υἱες Ἀχαιῶν = *A-cha'-ians.*

υἱωνός, οῦ, ὁ, (υἱός,) Lat. *nepos, filii filius, a grandchild, the son of a son.*

ὑλακτέω, (ὑλάω,) *to bark, yelp,* of dogs.

ὕλη, ης, ἡ, Lat. *silva, a wood, woodland, forest, timber, trees, felled timber, wood for fuel,* also, *material* or *stuff out of which anything is made, raw material, matter,* also, Lat. *materia; shrubs, brambles, underbrush, copse;* material for building was of wood, hence the deriv. meaning *raw material* of any kind.

Ὕλη, ης, ἡ, *Hy'-le,* a town in Bœ-o'-ti-a.

ὑλήεις, εσσα, εν, (ὕλη,) *wooded, covered with wood.*

ὑμέναιος, ου, ὁ, (Ὑμήν,) Lat. *hymenaeus, a nuptial song.*

ὕμμες, Ep. for ὑμεῖς, see σύ.

ὑπαείδω, ὑπὸ ... ἀειδ-, contr. **ὑπᾴδω,** (ὑπό, ᾄδω or ἀείδω,) *to sing (after or) an accompaniment.*

ὑπαί, poet. for ὑπό, which see.

ὕπαιθα, (ὑπαί,) adv., *from under, under at one side:* prep. with gen.

ὑπαΐσσω, f. ξω, (ὑπό, ἀίσσω,) with acc. *to start up under;* with gen. *to shoot* or *start suddenly out from under,* B 310.

ὑπακούω, 2 pf. ὑπακήκοα, (ὑπό, ἀκούω,) *to lend an ear, listen, to listen by stealth; to listen and reply,* hence *to reply; to listen and obey.*

ὑπάλυξις, εως, ἡ, (ὑπαλύσκω,) *an escaping, a slipping away.*

ὕπατος, άτη, ον, contr. for ὑπέρτατος, (ὑπέρ,) *the highest,* hence *the greatest.*

ὑπείκω, f. ὑπείξω, aor. ὑπεῖξα, in Hom. often uncontr. ὑποει-, Lat. *cedere, to give place, yield, retire; to give way, give up, submit:* trans. *to flee* or *elude;* often with dat. of pers. and gen. of thing.

ὑπείρ, ὑπειρ-, Ep. for ὑπέρ, which see.

Ὑπείρων, ονος, ὁ, *Hy-pi'-ron,* a Tro'-jan.

ὑπέ(κ)(ξ), (ὑπό, ἐκ,) adv., *out from under.*

ὑπεκφεύγω, (ὑπό, ἐκ, φεύγω,) *to escape secretly.*

ὑπένερθε(ν), (ὑπό, ἔνερθε,) adv., Lat. *infra, subter, under, below, beneath, in the abode of the dead;* with gen.

ὑπέρ, Ep. ὑπείρ, but parox. when foll. its subst., prep. with gen. and acc., Lat. *super, over, above:* with gen. *over, above, across, beyond; for, in behalf of, for the good of, by reason of,* Lat. *pro; for the sake of, instead of; of, concerning,* Lat. *de:* with acc. *over, beyond, exceeding; beyond* *measure; over against, in opposition to:* in compo. *over, beyond; in behalf of; exceedingly.*

ὑπεράλλομαι, f. ὑπεραλοῦμαι, aor. ὑπερηλάμην, (ὑπέρ, ἅλλομαι,) *to jump or spring over.*

ὑπερβασία, or ίη, ης, ἡ, (ὑπερβαίνω,) Lat. *transgressio, a going beyond or too far, a transgression; an injustice, violence.*

'Υπέρεια, as, ἡ, *Hyp-e-re'-a,* see Classical Dictionary.

ὑπερέχω, for prin. parts see ἔχω, Ep. forms in ὑπειρ-, *to hold over; to hold over and protect; to be over, be situated or stand above, overlook, rise above* Γ 210 ; *to excel, surpass; to get over or across.*

ὑπερηνορέων, οντος, (ὑπέρ, ἠνορέη,) adj., *being beyond manliness, overbearing, oppressive.*

'Υπερησίη, ης, ἡ, *Hyp-e-re'-si-a,* a town of A-cha'-i-a.

ὑπέρθε(ν), (ὑπέρ,) Lat. *desuper, from above; above.*

ὑπέρθυμος, ον, (ὑπέρ, θυμός,) *high-hearted, magnanimous, high-spirited,* Β 746 ; in bad sense, *over-spirited.*

ὑπερκύδας, αντος, adj., (ὑπέρ, κῦδος,) *very renowned, most glorious.*

ὑπερμενής, ές, (ὑπέρ, μένος,) *over strong, powerful, exceedingly strong, mighty;* in bad sense, *violent, overbearing.*

ὑπέρμορον, (ὑπέρ, μόρος,) adv., = ὑπέρ μόρον, Β 155, *contrary to destiny.*

ὑπεροπλία, as, ἡ, (ὑπέροπλος,) dat. pl. Α 205, *presumption, arrogance, defiance; proud courage.*

(ὑπέρ)(ὑπείρ)οχος, ον, (ὑπερέχω,) *elevated, eminent, superior.*

ὑπερπέτομαι, for parts see πέτομαι, (ὑπέρ, πέτομαι,) *to fly over or beyond.*

ὑπερφίαλος, ον, (ὑπέρ, φιάλη,) *beyond measure; overbearing,* Γ 106 ; *arrogant, insolent:* adv. *exceedingly; haughtily, insolently.*

ὑπερῴη, ης, ἡ, *the palate or upper part of the mouth.*

ὑπερώιον, uncontr. for ὑπερῷον, ου, τό, neu. of ὑπερῷος, ά, όν, *the upper apartment of the house, upper chamber.*

ὑπέστην, see ὑφίστημι.

ὑπημύω, Ep. pf. ὑπεμνήμυκε, *to stoop down, bow down.*

ὑπισχνέομαι, Ion. ὑπίσχομαι; f. ὑπισχήσομαι; 2 aor. ὑπεσχόμην; pf. ὑπέσχημαι: (ὑπό, ἴσχω (see ἔχω):) *to undertake anything,* lit. *to hold one's self under or be responsible for any undertaking,* hence *to promise,* Lat. *promittere.*

ὑπίσχομαι, see foreg.

ὕπνος, ου, ὁ, Lat. *somnus, sopor* (what is the difference between these two Lat. words?), *sleep, slumber:* personified, *the god Sleep.*

ὑπό, Hom. and poet. ὑπαί, prep. with gen., dat., and acc., *under,* Lat. *sub,* when foll. its subst. it is parox.: with gen., *of agent, by,* lit. *under,* Lat. *a* or *ab; in consequence of, by reason of; under, under-*

neath; out from under: with dat. under, of place; under, with the idea because of, by; under one, subject to, subordinate to, dependent upon: with acc., of motion, to a position under, in under, towards, into; without motion, under, under protection of; of time, near, about: as adv. beneath, down, underneath, under; secretly, gradually: in compo. under, secretly, slightly, step by step; toward and under; together with; a little, some, somewhat.

ὑποβλήδην, (ὑποβάλλω,) adv., throwing-in into another's conversation interrupting.

ὑποδείδω, f. δείσω, aor. ὑπέδεισα, Ep. aor. ὑπέδδεισα, Ep. 2 pf. ὑποδείδια; poet. pf. ὑπαιδείδοικα, 2 plup. Ep. 3 pl. ὑποδείδισαν, (ὑπό, δείδω,) (are Lat. subtimēre, subverēri the equivalents of this word?), to fear somewhat, have some fear, trans. to be somewhat in apprehension about, shrink from (anything) with some suspicion.

ὑποδέχομαι, f. δέξομαι, aor. εδεξάμην, pf. δέδεγμαι, aor. pass. εδέχθην, Ion. parts from -δεκ-, (ὑπό, δέχομαι,) to receive under one's protection, receive hospitably, hence receive; to take upon one's self, undertake, promise; to endure, suffer.

ὑποδέω, ήσω, (ὑπό, δέω,) to bind or fasten under: mid. to bind under one's feet, hence, to put on one's shoes; ὑποδεδεμένος, having put on shoes or having one's shoes on.

ὑπόδρα, (ὑποδρακεῖν,) poet. adv., angrily, askance, menacingly; A 148, ὑπόδρα ἰδών, looking askance or menacingly.

ὑποείκω, see ὑπείκω.

Ὑποθῆβαι, ῶν, αἱ, Hyp-o-the'-bœ, a town of Bœ-o'-ti-a.

ὑποθωρήσσω, f. ήξω, (ὑπό, θωρήσσω,) to arm quietly or secretly.

ὑποκρίνομαι, (ὑπό, κρίνομαι,) to answer; to explain or interpret, make response.

ὑπολαμβάνω, f. λήψομαι, 2 aor. ὑπέλαβον, Hom. ελλαβ- Γ 34, 2 pf. ὑπείληφα, pf. pass. ὑπείλημμαι, (ὑπό, λαμβάνω,) Lat. suscipere, to take under or underneath, seize under or below, to take anything up by getting under it and supporting it, to take up, catch up; to take up the word and answer, answer back, ἔφη ὑπολαβών answering he said; to take by surprise; to take up an opinion, to understand, conceive; to take by stealth or underhandedly, get the advantage of; to surmise.

ὑπολίζων, ον, ονος, (ὑπό, ὀλίζων (Hom. compar.),) something less.

ὑπολύω, f. λύσω, aor. ὑπέλυσα, pf. ὑπολέλυκα, (ὑπό, λύω,) A 401, to loosen from under; to loosen gradually or little by little; with γυῖα, to loosen or make the limbs relax under one; to unyoke, to free from any restraint; to secretly set at liberty; to deal a death-blow or cause the body to relax in death, slay.

ὑποπεπτηῶτες, see ὑποπτήσσω.

ὑποπλάκιος, α, ον, (ὑπό, πλάξ,) on the plain.

ὑποπτήσσω, f. ήξω, Ep. 2 pf. part. ὑποπεπτηώς, ῶτες, (ὑπό, πτήσσω,) to cower down timidly; to be humble, modest; to fear.

ὑπόρνυμι, aor. ὑπῶρσα, 2 aor. mid. Ep. 3 sing. ὑπῶρτο, 2 pf. ὑπῶρορα, (ὑπό, ὄρνυμι,) to rouse up gently or little by little; to rouse from under.

ὑποστεναχίζω, f. ίσω, (ὑπό, στεναχίζω,) to groan beneath, groan a little.

ὑποστρέφω, f. ψω, (ὑπό, στρέφω,) to turn about: intrans. to turn about, turn one's self about; to flee; to turn and go back.

ὑποσχέσθαι, 2 aor. mid. inf. of ὑπισχνέομαι.

ὑπόσχεσις, εως, ἡ, (ὑπισχνέομαι,) Lat. promissio, the act of promising, a promise.

ὑποτανύω, Hom. for ὑποτείνω, (ὑπό, τείνω,) to stretch under; to extend or hold out towards; to offer or hold out expectations, hence to promise: mid. to offer or submit.

ὑποτρομέω, (ὑπό, τρομέω,) to tremble a little; to tremble under.

ὑπότροπος, ον, (ὑποτρέπω(ὑπό, τρέπω),) returning, liable to turn back.

ὑποφεύγω, (ὑπό, φεύγω,) to flee under or secretly, escape.

ὑποχάζομαι, (ὑπό, χάζομαι,) Hom. 2 aor. -κεκαδόμην, to shrink or give way gradually or a little.

ὑποχωρέω, (ὑπό, χωρέω,) to draw back a little, retire; to recede, give way.

ὑπόψιος, ον, (ὑπόψομαι,) Lat. suspectus, seen or viewed from below or with suspicion, suspected; with gen. ὑπόψιον ἄλλων Γ 42, suspected of or by the rest.

ὕπτιος, α, ον, (ὑπό,) Lat. supinus, resupinus, laid on the back, on the back, bent backwards, supine; steep.

Ὑρία, or ίη, ας, ἡ, Hyr'-i-a, a town of Bœ-o'-ti-a.

Ὑρμίνη, ης, ἡ, Hyr-mī'-ne, a town in northern E'-lis.

Ὑρτακίδης, ου, ὁ, son of Hyr'-ta-cus, i. e. A'-si-us.

ὑσμίνη, ης, ἡ, irreg. dat. sing., B 863, ὑσμίνι as if from nom. ὑσμίν, a battle, conflict.

ὑσμίνηνδε, adv., into the battle, see foreg.

ὑσμῖνι, irreg. dat. of ὑσμίνη.

ὕστατος, η, ον, Lat. postremus, the last, most remote; the extreme; the lowest: neu. as adv. finally, at the last: a sup., for compar. see foll.

ὕστερος, α, ον, Lat. posterior, coming after, later, after, succeeding, following, the latter; too late; with gen. after or later than, too late for; standing or coming after in the sense of inferior to: ἐς ὕστερον, following, next, afterwards; with γένει, later in point of birth or younger, Lat. natu minor: neu. as adv. after that, hereafter: a compar., for sup. see foreg.: there is no posit. in use.

ὑφαίνω, poet. **ὑφάω**, and Ep. 3 pl. ὑφόωσι; iter. impf. ὑφαίνεσκον; f. ὑφανῶ; aor. ὕφηνα; pf. ὕφασμαι; aor. pass. ὑφάνθην: Lat. *texere, to weave*, also *to fabricate, make; to plan, devise; to spin.*

(ὑφ)(ὑπ)αιρέω; B 154, ὑπὸ δ' ᾕρεον, impf.; for prin. parts see **αἱρέω**: (ὑπό, αἱρέω :) *to seize beneath* or *secretly; to take out from under, to draw quietly away*, Lat. *subtrahere:* mid. also, *to take by stealth, pilfer* or *purloin.*

(ὑφ)(ὑπ)ίημι, for prin. parts see **ἵημι**, (ὑπό, ἵημι,) Lat. *submittere, to send under, let go under, put under*, also, *to send privily:* intrans. *to let down, yield, give up, relax, cease, submit:* pass. *to submit.*

ὑφίστημι, for prin. parts see **ἵστημι**, (ὑπό, ἵστημι,) as in *ἵστημι*, so in its compds., the causal or trans. tenses are pres., impf., f., aor., and the intrans. tenses are 2 aor., pf., f.pf.; causal or trans., Lat. *substituere, to place, lay*, or *set under; to place* or *set secretly; to suggest; to set before:* intrans. *to stand* or *be under; to be under* or *out of sight, to be hidden: to be under an obligation*, hence *to promise, engage, undertake; to yield* or *submit to; to withstand* (or *stand well under*) *an attack*, Lat. *subsistere; to stand and wait an attack.*

ὑψηλός, ή, όν, (ὕψος,) Lat. *altus, high, lofty*, metap. *high-toned, proud.*

Ὑψήνωρ, ορος, ὁ, *Hyp-se'-nor.*

ὑψιβρεμέτης, ου, ὁ, (ὕψι, βρέμω,) Lat. *altisonans, thundering-on-high, high-thundering, loud-roaring.*

ὑψίζυγος, ον, (ὕψι, ζυγόν,) *high on the cross-beam* or *rowers' bench; seated* or *throned on high.*

ὑψιπετήεις, εσσα, εν, -πέτης, (ὕψι, πέτομαι,) *high-flying, soaring aloft.*

ὑψιπύλος, ον, (ὕψι, πύλη,) *having high gates, high-gated.*

ὑψόροφος, ον, (ὕψι, ὀροφή,) *having a high roof, high-roofed.*

ὑψόσε, (ὕψος,) adv., Lat. *alte, on high, above, aloft.*

ὑψοῦ, (ὕψος,) adv., Lat. *alte, above, aloft, on high,* A 486.

Φ.

φά(α)νθεν, A 200, aor. pass. Ep. 3 pl. of **φαίνω**.

φαεινός, ή, όν, (φάος,) (is Lat. *splendidus* the equivalent of this word ?), *brilliant, beaming, resplendent, shining, gleaming, radiant; fine, splendid.*

φαεσίμβροτος, ον, (φάος, βροτός,) *bringing the light to mortals.*

φαίδιμος, adj., (φαίνω,) *shining brightly; glorious; splendid.*

φαινέσκετο, iter. impf. of **φαίνω**, which see.

φαινομένηφι(ν), Ep. dat. of mid. part. of **φαίνω**, which see.

Φαῖνοψ, οπος, ὁ, *Phœ'-nops.*

φαίνω; f. φανῶ; aor. ἔφηνα; pf. πέφαγκα; 2 pf. πέφηνα, intrans.; aor. pass. ἐφάνθην; 2 aor. pass. ἐφάνην; Ep. and Hom. forms, iter. impf. φαινέσκετο, iter. 2 aor. φάνεσκε intrans., aor. pass. 3 sing. φαάνθη and pl. φάανθεν, 2 aor. pass. inf. φανήμεναι: (φάω:) *to bring to light, show, make known; to disclose, expose to view, display, produce, exhibit:* intrans. and pass. *to be seen* or *shine, to give light* or *evidence by which anything is made to appear,* hence *to appear* or *come forth to light* or *view, be visible; to seem.*

Φαῖστος, οῦ, *Phœs'-tus,* the name of a man, and also of a town in the south of Crete.

φάλαγξ, αγγος, ἡ, *a line of battle, column; the rank of an army:* other and later meanings not given.

φάλος, ου, ὁ, Lat. *conus galeae,* a *ridge* or *ornament on a helmet fitted with a socket to receive the plume.*

φάος, Ep. **φόως**, gen. φάεος, dat. φάεϊ, pl. φάεα, τό, (φάω,) Lat. *lux, light* as spread around us, *daylight,* φόωσδε *to the daylight;* in gen. *light,* hence *happiness, joy, deliverance, victory, safety.*

φαρέτρη, Ion. for **φαρέτρα**, ας, ἡ, (φέρω,) Lat. *pharetra, a quiver.*

Φᾶρις, ιος, ἡ, *Pha'-ris,* a town of La-co'-ni-a.

φάρμακον, ου, τό, Lat. *pharmacum, medicamentum, medicamen, a medicine, a remedy, a drug, an antidote;* also, in a bad sense, *a poison,* Lat. *pharmacum; a dye-stuff, a coloring matter:* hence φαρμακεύς, Eng. *pharmaceutist.*

φᾶρος, εος, τό, *a large cloth; a sail; a wide loose cloak* or *outer garment,* (does Lat. *palla* correspond to this meaning?); *a veil.*

φάσγανον, ου, τό, (σφάζω,) *a cutting instrument; a sword, a knife,* see Lat. *ensis, gladius.*

φάσθαι, inf. mid. of φημί.

φάτις, Ion. gen. ιος, ἡ, (φημί,) *a saying; rumor, report,* Lat. *rumor, fama,* (how do these Lat. words differ?); *reputation, name.*

φάτνη, ης, ἡ, *a manger, crib.*

Φείδιππος, ου, ὁ, *Phid-ip'-pus,* see Classical Dictionary.

φειδωλός, ή, όν, (φειδώ,) *sparing, saving, parsimonious.*

φεν-, φα-, Ep. 2 aor. ἔπεφνον and πέφνον, pf. πέφαμαι, f. pf. πεφήσομαι, *to kill;* obsol. in pres., only these tenses being formed from the root φεν- (φα-).

Φένεος, ου, ὁ, and ἡ, *Phe'-ne-us,* a town of Ar-ca'-di-a.

Φεραί, ῶν, αἱ, *Phe'-ræ,* a town of Thes'-sa-ly.

Φέρεκλος, ου, ὁ, *Pher'-e-clus,* the name of the man who built the ship in which Hel'-en was carried off.

φέριστος, η, ον, = φέρτατος, which see.

φέρτατος, η, ον, (φέρω,) best, bravest, strongest, most excellent: sup. to compar. φέρτερος, α, ον.

φέρω, f. οἴσω, irreg. aor. ἤνεγκα, 2 aor. ἤνεγκον, 2 pf. ἐνήνοχα, aor. pass. ἠνέχθην : Ep. forms, subj. 3 sing. φέρῃσι, imperat. 2 pl. φέρτε, irreg. aor. ἔνεικα, inf. ἐνεῖκαι and ἐνεικέμεν, aor. imperat. οἶσε, inf. οἰσέμεν(αι); Ion. forms, iter. impf. φέρεσκον, irreg. aor. ἤνεικα, 2 aor. ἤνεικον seldom used by Hom., aor. pass. ἠνείχθην : Lat. *ferre, to carry, convey, bear, carry along; to bring, give; to bear, produce, bring forth; to carry around, scatter; to carry off or away either as booty or something won, win, accomplish; to carry away or receive pay or due; to carry about news, to report or speak much of; to vote for; to bear with the sense of endure or suffer; to lead, conduct; to extend:* mid. *to carry away, take or receive for one's self, bring for one's own use; where one wins or gets for one's self:* pass. *to be borne or swept along; to run, hasten; to be impelled or rush.*

φεύγω; iter. impf. φεύγεσκον; f. φεύξομαι; 2 aor. ἔφυγον; 2 pf. πέφευγα, Ep. part. πεφυζότες: Lat. *fugere, to flee; to fear, hesitate or flinch; to escape or avoid anything; to flee one's country, go into exile,* Lat. *exulare,* see ὑπό; *to escape.*

φή = ὡς, *just as, as, like.*

Φηγεύς, εως, ὁ, *Phe'-geus,* a Tro'-jan.

φηγός, οῦ, ἡ, *an oak* having an eatable nut.

φημί, (parts are formed from φάσκω = φημί,) φής or φῇς, φησί, du. φατόν, pl. φαμέν, φατέ, φασί; sub. φῶ; opt. φαίην; imperat. φάθι or φαθί; inf. φάναι; part. φάς; impf. ἔφην, ἔφης, com. ἔφησθα, ἔφη, du. ἔφατον, ἐφάτην, pl. ἔφαμεν, ἔφατε, ἔφασαν; f. φήσω; aor. ἔφησα; verbal φατός and φατέος; Ep. forms, impf. φῆν, etc., ἔφα(σα)ν; subj. 3 sing. φήῃ; opt. φαῖμεν; the pres. indicat. mid. is not used, and mid. forms are rare in Att. but com. in other dialects; Hom. has impf. ἐφάμην, etc., imperat. φάο, φάσθω, inf. φάσθαι, part. φάμενος; other mid. forms, pf. pass. πέφασμαι, imperat. 3 sing. πεφάσθω: encl. in pres. indicat. except the 2 pers. sing., (do Lat. *aio, inquit,* and *fari* correspond to this word?): *to say, relate, tell; declare, announce, make known; to speak one's views, to announce as one's opinion,* hence *to suppose.*

φήρ, φηρός, ὁ, Lat. *ferus, a wild beast;* Φῆρες, the Cen'-taurs: Æol. for θήρ.

Φηραί, Φηρή, ῆς, ἡ, *Phe'-ræ;* see Classical Dictionary.

Φηρητριάδης, ου, ὁ, *son* (grandson) *of Phe'-res, Ad-me'-tus,* Β 763.

Φθειρῶν ὄρος, (φθείρ,) the name of a pine-covered mountain near Mi-le'-tus.

Φθίη, ης, ἡ, *Phthi'-a*, a district of Thes'-sa-ly, the home of Pe'-leus and A-chil'-les; Hom. speaks of a *town* by that name, the residence of A-chil'-les; adv. **Φθίηνδε**, *to Phthi'-a*.

φθινύθω, both trans. (*to consume*) and intrans. (*to waste away*), see foll.

φθί(ν)ω, poet. pres. **φθινύθω**; f. φθίσω; aor. ἔφθισα; 2 aor. ἔφθιον; Ep. 2 aor. mid. (also plup.) ἐφθίμην, 3 sing. ἔφθιτο, Ep. 3 pl. (ἐ)φθίατο, Ep. subj. φθίο-, Ep. 3 sing. subj. φθίεται, Ep. opt. φθίμην, and 3 sing. φθῖτο, Ep. inf. φθίσθαι, Ep. part. φθίμενος; aor. pass. ἐφθίθην, Ep. 3 pl. ἔφθιθεν: intrans. in all tenses except f. and aor., *to sink, fall away, pine away, decline, become less and less, decay; to perish, die, come to an end:* trans. in f. and aor., *to consume* or *cause to decay* or *become less, to waste, destroy*.

φθισήνωρ, ορος, ἡ, ὁ, (φθίνω, ἀνήρ,) *destructive to man, deadly*.

-φι or **-φιν**, Ep. termination of dat. and gen., sing. and pl.

φθογγή, ῆς, ἡ, (φθέγγομαι,) *a tone, the voice, an effort of the voice*.

φιλέω, Ep. inf. φιλήμεναι; iter. impf. φιλέεσκε, Γ 388; f. ήσω, Ep. inf. φιλησέμεν; aor. ἐφίλησα; pf. πεφίληκα; aor. pass. ἐφιλήθην, Ep. 3 pl. ἐφίληθεν B 668; aor. Ep. mid. ἐφιλάμην, 3 sing. ἐφίλατο, imperat. φίλαι: (φίλος:) Lat. *diligere*, (why not *amare?*) *to love; to treat with regard, treat kindly, receive kindly, befriend, hold dear, welcome, treat hospitably; to embrace, kiss; to love to do anything,* hence *be wont* or *accustomed*.

φιλοκτέανος, ον, (φίλος, κτέανον,) *loving possessions, grasping*, A 122.

Φιλοκτήτης, ου, ὁ, *Phil-oc-te'-tes*, a Thes-sa'-li-an chief.

φιλομειδής, poet. **φιλομμειδής**, ές, (φίλος, μειδάω,) Lat. *risus amans, laughter-loving, cheerful, gay*.

φίλος, η, ον, as poss. pron., like Lat. *meus, tuus, suus, my, thy, his* or *hers;* Lat. *amicus, carus, loved, dear;* and so *loving, friendly;* φίλα φρονεῖν, *to be friendly inclined.* Orig. φίλος was, or was used as, a poss. pron., Lat. *suus, his.* Hom.'s frequent use of φίλος with the parts of the body gives proof that its primary meaning was that of a poss. pron., and that the acquired meaning *dear* comes naturally from the idea of possession.

φιλότης, ητος, ἡ, (φίλος,) *friendship; love; hospitality*, Γ 354; *sexual love; friendship* or *treaty*, Γ 73; see ὅρκιον.

φλοιός, οῦ, ὁ, (φλέω,) *the bark of a tree, the soft inner bark*.

φοβέω, f. ήσω, aor. pass. Ep. 3 pl. -βηθεν (φόβος,) Lat. *terrēre* (why not *absterrēre?*), *to terrify, strike with dismay; to put to flight by fright*, Lat. *fugare;* mid. and pass. *to be put to flight, to flee*.

Φόβος, ου, ὁ, *Pho'-bos*, son of A'-res.

Φοῖβος, ου, ὁ, (φάος,) *Phœ'-bus, the Pure* and *Bright One*, epith. of A-pol'-lo.

φοῖνιξ, ικος, ὁ, Lat. *purpura*, *purple*, *a color*; *the palm-tree, the fruit of the palm* or *the date*: as adj., *purple, dark red*; of horses, *bay*.

φοιτάω, Ion. -έω, (φοῖτος,) *to wander about, roam at large, to go up and down, go hurriedly around, go to and fro*; *to go about in a state of frenzy, rave, wander in mind*.

φολκός, οῦ, ὁ, *bow-legged*.

φόνος, ου, ὁ, (φένω,) Lat. *caedes, bloodshed, murder, slaughter*; *gore, shed blood*, Lat. *cruor*; *the body of a murdered victim*.

φοξός, ή, όν, *tapering, conical*, B 219.

φορεύς, Ion. gen. ῆος, ὁ, (φορέω,) *one who carries, a porter, carrier*.

φορέω, Ep. inf. φορ(ῆ)(ήμε)ναι, B 107; iter. impf. φορέεσκον, B 770; f. ήσω; aor. ἐφόρησα: (φέρω :) (is Lat. *gestare* freq., and does it correspond to this word?), *to convey, carry forward* or *about, bear on the person habitually*, hence *to wear, display, possess*.

φορῆναι, φορήμεναι, see foreg.

Φόρκυς, υνος, υος, ὁ, *Phor'-cys*; see Classical Dictionary.

φορμίζω, f. ίσω, φόρμιγξ,) *to play the lyre*.

φόρμιγξ, ιγγος, ἡ, a kind of *harp* or *lyre* used by the Greeks in Hom.'s time, having seven strings, and used to accompany singing. This is the instrument used by A-pol'-lo; it was carried on the shoulder, hence deriv. φέρω.

φόως, φόωσδε, see φάος.

φράζω; iter. impf. φραζεσκ-; f. φράσω; aor. (ἔ)φράσ(σ)α; Ep. and Hom. 2 aor. (ἐ)πέφραδον, inf. πεφραδέ(ειν)(μεν); pf. πέφρακα; aor. pass. ἐφράσθην: *to point out, explain, declare, pronounce*; *to advise* or *counsel*; *to order, bid, dictate, direct, command, decree*: mid. and pass. *to consider with one's self, revolve in the mind, reflect, consider* A 83, *make clear to one's self*; *to plan, meditate and form a resolution, design, purpose, plan, machinate*; *to notice, know, comprehend*: see λέγω.

φρήν, φρενός, ἡ, often in pl., Lat. *praecordia, diaphragm*; *the diaphragm and heart, breast*: the ancients regarded the breast or heart as the seat of the *mind, emotional feelings, reason, will, soul*, etc., hence also, *the heart, understanding, reason, seat of the will, passions, and feelings, mind, soul*, Lat. *praecordia*; in pl. *life, seat of the vital powers of life*.

φρήτρη, ης, ἡ, *a clan*.

φρίσσω, f. ίξω, *to be rough* or *bristling, to have the surface rough* or *bristling*; *to shudder with cold*, as cold causes the hair to stand up on the limbs, and from this *to shudder with fear, shudder at*.

φρονέω, f. ήσω, (φρήν,) *to think, be conscious*; *to be alive*; *to have understanding*; *to hope* Γ 98; *to be minded so and so, intend, design*; *to consider, deliberate, plan, meditate*, A 542; *to mind, attend to,* think of, take care of, take precaution against; A 542 to have secret designs.

Φρυγία, or ίη, ή, Phryg'-i-a ; see Classical Dictionary.

Φρύξ, Φρυγός, ὁ, a Phryg'-i-an.

φυή, ῆς, ἡ, (φύω,) form, shape, growth in body; beauty, a noble growth, · a fine form; by their deriv. δέμας denotes the build or something built (δέμω), and φυή, the form as the result of growth, A 115 ; one's nature, disposition, character, natural ability, mental development, talents, native powers, (is Lat. natura the equivalent in this case ?); the prime of manhood.

Φυλάκη, ης ,ἡ, Phyl'-a-ce, a town of Phthi-o'-tis, on the slope of Mount O'-thrys ; stric. a guard or watch, watch-tower, (φυλακή,) prob. so named from its position.

Φυλακίδης, ου, ὁ, son of Phyl'-a-cus, Iph'-i-clus.

φύλακος, ου, ὁ, poet. for φύλαξ, ακος, (φυλάσσω,) Lat. custos, a guard, guardian, keeper, watcher.

φυλάσσω, f. άξω, aor. ἐφύλαξα, 2 pf. πεφύλαχα, aor. pass. ἐφυλάχθην, Lat. vigilare, to watch, be on the watch, lie in wait, be on guard : trans. Lat. conservare, custodire, to defend, guard, preserve, to keep watch or guard over, maintain ; to be on the watch or look out for : mid. to watch over one's self, to be on one's guard, watch for one's self, take heed, be cautious.

Φυλείδης, ου, ὁ, son of Phy'-leus, Me'-ges.

Φυλεύς, έως, ὁ, Phy'-leus, son of Au'-ge-as.

φύλλον, ου, τό, Lat. folium, frons, a leaf ; a flower.

φῦλον, ου, τό, (φύω,) a race ; a nation, people ; a kind ; a family, a tribe ; in pl. a troop, host, band, swarm, of one kind.

φύλοπις, ιδος, ἡ, (φῦλον, ὄψ,) the voice or noise of the multitude, hence the noise of conflict ; the conflict.

φῦσα, as, ἡ, a pair of bellows ; a blast of wind.

φυσάω, to blow, to breathe.

φυσίζοος, ον, (φύω, ζωή,) Lat. vitam producens, life-producing Γ 243, life-giving, creating.

φυταλι(ά)(ή), ᾶς, ἡ, an orchard, vineyard ; a plantation.

φυτεύω, (φυτόν,) to plant young trees, plants, or vegetables, hence to bring about, produce.

φύω, f. φύσω, aor. ἔφυσα, 2 aor. ἔφυν, pf. πέφυκα ; Ep. forms, 2 aor. 3 pl. ἔφυν, 2 pf. 3 pl. πεφύασι, 2 pf. part. πεφυώς : trans. or causal in pres., f., and aor., intrans. in 2 aor. and pf., Lat. gignere, parere, producere, generare ; compare these with each other and with the definitions given below ; trans. to bring forth, produce, to cause to exist ; to put forth ; to *generate, engender, beget; to get, acquire, gain, secure:* intrans. *to come forth, spring up; to grow.*

Φωκεύς, *έως, ὁ,* (Φωκίς,) the name of *a Pho'-ci-an.*

φωνέω, (φωνή,) *to utter* or *produce a distinct sound; to speak, call out, speak clearly, raise the voice; to pronounce; to sound;* trans. *to call to, accost, call* or *name.*

φωνή, *ῆς, ἡ,* Lat. *sonus, vox, a tone, sound of the voice* as produced by the natural organs of sound ; *a voice; a cry,* as *the cry of a herald; speech, language,* Lat. *lingua: the voice* or *cry of a beast* or *bird;* also, *a distinct sound not of the voice.*

φώς, *φωτός, ὁ,* poet. for *ἀνήρ,* which see.

X.

χάζω ; Ep. parts, redup. f. *κεκαδήσω,* 2 aor. *κέκαδον;* poet. *to make to yield* or *give way;* with gen. *to deprive of:* mid. *to draw off, yield, give way.*

χαίνω, f. *χανοῦμαι,* 2 aor. *ἔχανον, to yawn, open, gape; to open wide.*

χαίρω; f. *χαιρήσω;* aor. *ἐχαίρησα;* pf. *κεχάρηκα;* 2 aor. pass. *ἐχάρην*: Ep. forms, iter. impf. *χαίρεσκον,* f. *κεχαρήσω,* aor. mid. (ἐ)χηράμην, 2 aor. mid. *κεχαρόμην,* pf. part. *κεχαρηώς, κεχαρ-*: Lat. *gaudēre, to rejoice, be pleased* or *joyful;* with dat. and acc., *to rejoice at* or *with;* with part. *to rejoice in doing anything; χαίρω σου τὸν μῦθον ἀκοῦσαι I delight in hearing (having heard) thy voice;* imperat. *χαῖρε* a salutation at meeting, Lat. *salve, hail,* at parting, Lat. *vale, adieu, farewell, χαιρέτω let him be gone, ἴθι χαίρων go rejoicing* or *joyfully.*

χαίτη, *ης, ἡ,* Lat. *coma, the long flowing hair of the head; mane of a horse,* Lat. *juba.*

χαλεπαίνω, f. *ανῶ,* aor. *ἐχαλέπηνα,* (χαλεπός,) Lat. *saevire, to be vexed towards, treat harshly, persecute, assail;* intrans. *to be angry, to be indignant, storm, deal roughly.*

χαλεπός, *ή, όν, serious, grievous, hard; difficult,* Lat. *difficile; dangerous, injurious, rough, rocky; hostile, troublesome, harsh, cruel, difficult, dangerous, furious, morose, discontented, angry, severe.*

χάλκε(ι)ος, adj., Ion. *χαλκήιος, η, ον,* also fem. *χαλκέη,* (χαλκός,) Lat. *aereus, aeneus, brazen, of brass, bronze,* or *copper;* of the voice, *loud.*

χαλκεύς, *εως, ὁ,* (χαλκεύω,) *a copper* or *bronze worker;* in gen. *a smith, a worker of iron, gold, silver,* etc.

χαλκήρης, *ες,* (χαλκός, ἀραρεῖν (see ἀραρίσκω),) *fitted with brass* or *copper; armed* or *pointed with brass* or *copper.*

Χαλκίς, ίδος, ἡ, *Chal'-cis*, a town of Eu-bœ'-a ; also the name of a town in Æ-to'-li-a.

χαλκοβατής, *ές*, (χαλκός, βαίνω,) *going* = *standing* or *resting on a brazen base*, A 426.

χαλκογλώχιν, *ινος*, adj., (χαλκός, γλωχίν,) *having a brazen point, bronze-pointed.*

χαλκοκορυστής, *οῦ*, adj., (χαλκός, κορύσσω,) *with brazen helmet* or *armor.*

χαλκός, *οῦ, ὁ*, Lat. *aes, copper, bronze;* poet. *a weapon, axe, knife, shield, breastplate, sword, spear, money,* because these were made of bronze, a metal suitable for making cutting instruments ; *any instrument made of copper; metal* in gen., because copper was the first metal worked.

χαλκοχίτων, *ωνος, ὁ, ἡ*, (χαλκός, χιτών,) *wearing a brazen garment* or *coat of mail, brazen-clad.*

Χαλκωδοντιάδης, *ου, ὁ, son of Chal'-co-don, El-phe'-nor.*

χαμάδις, (χαμαί,) adv., poet. for foll.

χαμᾶζε, (χαμαί,) adv., Lat. *humi, on the ground ; to the ground,* Lat. *in terram.*

χαμαί, adv., see foreg.

χανδάνω, f. χείσομαι, Ep. 2 aor. χάδον, 2 pf. κέχανδα, *to contain; to include.*

χαράδρ(α)(η), *ας, ἡ*, (χαράσσω,) *a deep rut* or *gully, the track* or *bed of a mountain stream which the torrent has cut for itself,* also *the mountain stream* or *torrent itself.*

χάρη, 2 aor. pass. Ep. 3 sing. of **χαίρω**.

χαρίεις, *ιεσσα, ιεν*, (χάρις,) *graceful, beautiful, charming, pretty, winning, lovely,* compare Lat. *formosus, pulcher, venustus; elegant, well-bred, polite,* Lat. *elegans; witty.*

χάρις, *ιτος, ἡ*, acc. χάριν and χάριτα, *grace, joy, favor, gracefulness, attractiveness, charm.*

χάρμα, *ατος, τό*, (χαίρω,) *a pleasure, joy; (a source of) delight,* Γ 51; does Lat. *gaudium* apply in this case !

χάρμη, *ης, ἡ, the pleasure that one takes in the conflict and his eagerness for it ; conflict, battle.*

Χάροπος, *ου, ὁ*, (χαρά, ὤψ,) *Char'-o-pus,* king of Sy'-me ; lit. *bright-eyed.*

χατέω, see foll.

χατίζω, f. ίσω, *to earnestly desire ; to want, be in need of,* with gen. of thing, B 225.

χει(ά)(ή), *ῆς, ἡ, a hole, a snake's den.*

χεῖλος, *εος, τό*, pl. χειλε-, dat. χείλεσ(σ)ι, *the tip, margin, border, rim.*

χειμάρροος, *ου*, (χεῖμα, ῥέω,) *a winter torrent ; a torrent caused by the melting of snow and ice on a mountain.*

χειμέριος, α, ον, (χεῖμα,) wintry, like winter, of winter, Γ 222; tempestuous.

χειμών, ῶνος, ὁ, (χεῖμα,) Lat. bruma in poet. sense, winter Γ 4; wintry or stormy weather, the cold of winter, a storm, tempest, Lat. hiems, see tempestas.

χείρ, χειρός, du. χεροῖν, gen. and dat. pl. χειρῶν, χερσί; Ep. χερ-, dat. pl. χείρεσ(σ)ι; ἡ, Lat. manus, the hand; the entire hand and arm (does manus apply in this case?); the hand (or skill) of an artist, execution, handwriting, touch, etc., Lat. manus; handiwork; a band of men, Lat. manus; ἐκ χειρός, off hand, near, close; εἰς χεῖρας ἐλθεῖν, to come to an engagement; see ἀπό and πρό; Greek χείρ, Lat. manus, Eng. hand seem to have nearly the same uses and applications.

Χείρων, ωνος, ὁ, (χειρουργός, Eng. chirurgeon,) Chei'-ron, one of the Centaurs; see Classical Dictionary.

χέρειον, neu. of χερείων.

χερειότερος, α, ον, Ep. for foll.

χερείων, ὁ, ἡ, neu. -ειον, Hom. and poet. for χείρων, compar. of κακός; defect. forms, dat. χέρηι, acc. χέρηα, pl. χέρηες, neu. χέρηα and χέρεια: Lat. pejor, worse, inferior.

χερμάδιος, ον, (χέρ for χείρ,) a large stone of the size to fit the hand and fit for throwing.

χερνίπτομαι, f. ψομαι, (χείρ, νίπτομαι,) to wash the hands with lustral water.

χέω, f. χεῶ, aor. ἔχεα, pf. κέχυκα and κέχυμαι, plup. 3 sing. κέχυτο, aor. pass. ἐχύθην; Ep. forms, χείω, f. χεύω, aor. ἔχευα, subj. χεύομεν, aor. mid. ἐχευάμην, other Ep. forms in χ(ε)υ-, 2 aor. ἐχύμην: Lat. fundere, to pour; to pour out, to shed, to pour down; to pour around, hence to scatter, let fall around, strew; to pour or spread, let flow, shed around; to cause to flow, melt, make liquid; to shed, throw, or put around; to shoot out; to throw up, heap: mid. to pour; to make or pour a libation; to pour for one's own benefit; to throw the arms around: pass. to be poured out or around; to flow; to melt; to be spread out.

χήν, χηνός, ὁ, ἡ, (χαίνω,) Lat. anser, a gander, goose.

χήμεῖς = καὶ ἡμεῖς.

χῆρος, η, ον, Lat. viduus, bereaved, widowed B 289, often with gen.

χηρόω, f. ώσω, Lat. viduare, to bereave, to reduce to the state of widowhood, make desolate; to deprive of; often with gen.

χηρωστής, οῦ, ὁ, a legal heir that is not a child.

χῆτος, εος, τό, want, indigence, destitution, want of.

χθιζός, ή, όν, (χθές,) Lat. hesternus, yesterday A 424, yesterday's; neus. are used as advs.: see πρώιζος.

χθών, χθονός, ἡ, Lat. *humus*, (what is the difference between Lat. *humus, terra, tellus, solum?*), *the ground, earth, soil, land; region, country.*

χίμαιρα, as, ἡ, *a female goat;* hence Eng. *chimera.*

Χίμαιρα, as, ἡ, *the Chi-mœ'-ra,* a fabulous monster; see Classical Dictionary.

χιτών, ῶνος, ὁ, Lat. *tunica, a garment worn next to the body, an undergarment, a shirt, body-jacket;* it was *a woollen shirt* worn by both sexes next to the body, com. without sleeves, and gen. short; *a coat of mail, cuirass; a coat, a covering, skin,* Γ 57.

χιών, ονος, ἡ, *snow, snow that has already fallen.*

χλαῖν(α)(η), ης, ἡ, Lat. *laena,* (why not *palla?*), *a woollen blanket* or *cloak* worn loose over the χιτών and fastened by a clasp on the shoulder.

χόανος, ου, ὁ, (χέω,) *a hollow place (in the hearth of a forge) for melting metals, a melting pit* or *pot.*

χολάς, άδος, ἡ, (χολή,) *the bowels, intestines.*

χόλος, ου, ὁ, Lat. *bilis, bile,* also, *wrath, anger.*

χολόω, f. ωσω, *to rouse one's bile; to provoke,* A 78, see notes, *make angry, enrage, exasperate, embitter:* mid. and pass. *to have one's anger kindled, be angry,* A 9 *enraged.*

χορός, οῦ, ὁ, *a dance, a circle* or *ring dance,* Γ 393, 394; *a dance accompanied with singing, choral dance,* hence *a choir* or *chorus,* Lat. *chorus, a dancing-place.*

χόρτος, ου, ὁ, *an enclosed place, enclosure; a feeding-place; a court-yard;* Lat. *hortus, chors, cohors.*

χραισμέω, not used in pres. system as early as Hom.; f. χραισμήσω and Ep. inf. χραισμησέμεν, aor. (ἐ)χραίσμησα, 2 aor. (ἐ)χραῖσμον A 242; (χρήσιμος, χράομαι,) Lat. *defendere, to defend; to be useful to, assist, aid, succor, help.*

χραύω, f. σω, Æol. for χράω, *to touch the surface, touch lightly; to graze, scratch, wound slightly.*

χράω, *to lay violent hands upon, fall upon, assail, assault; to handle roughly; to attempt, be anxious.*

χρειώ, Ep. for foll.

χρεώ, όος, ἡ, (χρέος,) *want, pressing need, necessity; longing;* with gen., acc., and inf.

χρή, ῆς, ἡ, *need, want, necessity; use, profit.*

χρίω, f. ίσω, *to touch a body lightly, graze; to anoint; to rub over with a substance, smear, to color:* mid. *to touch one's self; to smear* or *anoint one's self:* verbal χριστός, hence Eng. *Christ.*

Χρομίος, ου, ὁ, *Chro'-mi-us,* the name of several warriors mentioned in the Iliad.

Χρόμις, ιος, ὁ, *Chro'-mis,* chief of the Mys'-i-ans.

χρόνος, ου, ὁ, Lat. *dies,* (why not *tempus?*), *time; a long time; an age, a definite period, a season, a measure of time,* Lat. *tempestas;* B 299 *a time* or *a little while;* χρόνῳ, *in course of time,* see ἐν; see πολύς, ἀεί, ἀνά, ἐπί, ἐς.

χρυσάορος, ον, (χρυσός, ἄορ,) *with golden (hilted) sword.*

χρύσεος, adj., Ep. **χρύσειος,** (χρυσός,) Lat. *aureus, made of gold, golden,* A 15, 374; *gilded* or *adorned with gold;* applied also to the gods and what they wear or possess; *golden-colored, golden-yellow, of golden hue, golden; precious, excellent; valuable.*

Χρύση, ης, ἡ, *Chry'-sa,* the name of a city, A 37.

Χρυσηίς, ίδος, ἡ, *daughter of Chry'-ses, As-tyn'-o-me.*

χρυσήνιος, ον, (χρυσός, ἡνία,) *with* or *having golden reins.*

Χρύσης, ου, ὁ, *Chry'-ses,* priest of A-pol'-lo at Chry'-sa.

χρυσόθρονος, ον, (χρυσός, θρόνος,) *having a golden seat* or *throne, golden-throned.*

χρυσός, οῦ, ὁ, Lat. *aurum, gold.*

χρώς, ωτός or οός, ὁ, *the surface, the skin; the appearance of the surface, color, complexion; the body,* but in this sense it applies particularly to the body as represented by its *surface.*

χύμενος, (ἔ)χυτο, see χέω.

χυτός, ή, όν, (verb adj. of χέω, which see,) *poured out; shed; melted; piled up, heaped.*

χωλεύω, f. εύσω, (χωλός,) *to go lame, be lame, limp.*

χωλός, ή, όν, Lat. *claudus, lame, limping; defective, unequal; injured.*

χώομαι, *to be perturbed; to be displeased, angry, enraged;* with gen. *to be angry because of,* A 429; *to be in great agitation.*

χωρέω, f. ήσω, (χῶρος,) *to make room, leave a space,* hence *to make room, retire, give place, yield, withdraw.*

χώρη, ης, ἡ, Ion. for -ρα, = χῶρος, which see.

χῶρος, ου, ὁ, *space, room, a spot* or *place; a region, land,* or *country,* Lat. *regio.*

χωσάμενος, Γ 414, aor. part. of χώομαι.

Ψ.

ψάμαθος, ου, ἡ, (ψάμμος, ψάω,) *sand; the sands upon the shore, the sea sands* A 486, *sandy shore.*

ψεδνός, ή, όν, (ψέω,) *worn off, scanty* B 219.

ψεύδομαι, f. ψεύσομαι, *to lie, speak an untruth, speak falsely; to lie about* *any one, calumniate ; to cheat, deceive; to violate a solemn engagement ; to be false.*

ψεῦδος, εος, τό, (ψεύδω,) Lat. *mendacium, falsitas, an untruth, lie,* B 349.

ψυχή, ῆς, ἡ, (ψύχω,) Lat. *anima, breath of life, breath, life ; also, the soul, that which exists after death,* Lat. *animus ; a soul, a departed spirit ; the spirit* as opp. to the body ; *the mind, reason, seat of the mental faculties, disposition,* Lat. *mens.*

ψυχρός, ά, όν, Lat. *frigidus, cold, cool ; cold, unimpassioned, hard-hearted ; cold, vain, useless.*

Ω.

ὦ, sign of address.

ὦ, interj., *O ! oh !*

ὧδε, adv. from ὅδε, *so, thus, in this wise ; so exceedingly ; as follows, in the following manner ; here, hither ;* see οὕτως.

ὠθέω ; iter. impf. ὤθεσκε ; f. ὠθήσω, ὤσω ; aor. ἔωσα, Ep. ὦσα, iter. ὤσασκε ; pf. ἔωκα ; aor. ἐώσθην : Lat. *pellere, to move* or *push out of the way, force back ; to force, drive, push, shove ;* metaph. *to hurry on.*

ὦκα, (ὠκύς,) adv., *quickly, rapidly, fast,* A 447.

Ὠκαλέ(α)(η), ας, ἡ, *O-ca'-le-a,* a village of Bœ-o'-ti-a.

Ὠκεανός, οῦ, ὁ, *O-ce'-a-nus, a water god ;* in the time of Hom. this name was applied to a river that was supposed to surround the whole earth ; see Classical Atlas for the world as it was thought to be in time of Hom., hence Eng. *ocean.* See *O-ce'-a-nus* in Classical Dictionary.

ὠκύμορος, ον, (ὠκύς, μόρος,) *quickly-dying, short-lived ; causing a quick* or *speedy death.*

ὠκύπορος, ον, (ὠκύς, πόρος,) *fast-going, fast-travelling.*

ὠκύπους, ουν, gen. οδος, (ὠκύς, πούς,) *swift of foot.*

ὠκύροος, ον, (ὠκύς, ῥέω,) *fast-flowing.*

ὠκύς, ὠκεῖα, ὠκύ, gen. ὠκέος, ὠκείας, ὠκέος ; Ep. fem. ὠκέα, acc. pl. ὠκέας, ὠκε-, ὠκει(α)-: Lat. *celer, rapid, swift, quick, fleet ; at once, prompt ;* Hom. sup. ὤκιστος.

Ὠλενίη, B 617 *the O-len'-i-an rock,* the summit of Mount Scol'-lis separates E'-lis from A-cha'-ia.

Ὤλενος, ου, ἡ, *Ol'-e-nus,* a town of Æ-to'-li-a.

ὠμηστής, οῦ, adj., (ὠμός, ἐσθίω,) *feeding on raw flesh,* hence *savage, ferocious.*

ὠμοθετέω, also, ὠμοθετέομαι, (ὠμός, τίθημι,) *to place the raw pieces of flesh which have been cut from the victim upon the thigh-bones which have been wrapped in the fat;* it is then placed upon the altar as an oblation.

ὠμός, ή, όν, Lat. *crudus, raw, not cooked ; unripe, premature.*

ὦμος, ου, ὁ, Lat. *humerus, the shoulder and part of the arm.* What is the difference between Lat. *armus* and *humerus?*

ᾤμωξα, see οἰμώζω.

ὤνησα, see ὀνίνημι.

ὥρη, Ion. for ὥρα, ας, ἡ, Lat. *hora* (hence Eng. *hour*), *time, season, a definite and fixed period; a time of day, an hour; a season of the year; the spring-time* or *season of blooming,* B 468 or *in their season* (see below); *a period in human life, the spring-time of life, manhood; spring-time, summer; the right* or *suitable time, the time for anything:* personified, *the Hours,* goddesses of the seasons; they caused the production of flowers and fruits and gave beauty to them; see *Ho'-rae* in Classical Dictionary.

'Ωρίων, ωνος, ὁ, *O-ri'-on,* for the fable of his love, etc., see Classical Dictionary; the name of a constellation.

ὤρορε, redupl. 2 aor.; see ὄρνυμι.

ὦρσα, see ὄρνυμι.

ὡς, adv., Lat. *ut, as,* procl. but accented when foll. its word or standing at the end of a sentence; *as, just as, as soon as; as,* in the sense of *for; as,* in the sense of *because of, inasmuch as, seeing that;* used with preps.; used as prep. *to; how,* Lat. *quam;* ὡς αἰεί, *how ever;* streng. sup. like ὅτι, Lat. *quam.*

ὡς, conj., in indirect speech, Lat. *quod, that;* final, *in order that, so that,* Lat. *ut;* = ὅτε, *when; as, since.*

ὧς, adv., Lat. *sic, thus, so; so then;* μηδ' ὧς or οὐδ' ὧς, *not even thus.*

ὦσα, see ὠθέω.

ὡσεί or ὡς εἰ, adv., Lat. *quasi, as if; like, just as; about.*

ὥσπερ or ὥς περ, adv., Lat. *quemadmodum, veluti,* Α 211, *as, even as, just as, the same as, as if; as soon as.*

ὥστε, (ὥς τε,) adv., = ὥσπερ, *as, just as:* conj. *so that; that, so as.*

ὠτειλή, ῆς, ἡ, *a wound.*

ὤφελλον, see ὀφείλω.

ὦχρος, ου, ὁ, Lat. *pallor, whiteness, paleness; paleness from fear,* Γ 35.

ὤψ, ὠπός, ἡ, (ὄψομαι, see ὁράω,) (compare Lat. *os, facies, vultus, oculi*), *the eye, the look, face, aspect, countenance.*

ADDENDUM.

Ζέλεια, ας, ἡ, *Ze-le'-a,* a town near Mount I'-da.

www.ingramcontent.com/pod-product-compliance
Lightning Source LLC
Chambersburg PA
CBHW020121070726
47497CB00021B/2095